THE EAGLE IN THE DOVECOTE

A HISTORICAL NOVEL OF ANCIENT ROME

LAURA DOWERS

ISBN: 978-1-912968-22-0 (PAPERBACK)

ISBN: 978-1-912968-23-7 (MOBI)

ISBN: 978-1-912968-24-4 (EPUB)

ALSO BY LAURA DOWERS

THE TUDOR COURT

The Queen's Favourite

The Queen's Rebel

The Queen's Spymaster

The Queen's Rival: A Short Story

The Queen's Poet: A Short Story (*Exclusive to subscribers*)

The Tudor Court: Books I—III (Boxset Edition)

Master Wolsey

THE RISE OF ROME

The Last King of Rome (Book I)

STANDALONE NOVELS

When the Siren Sings

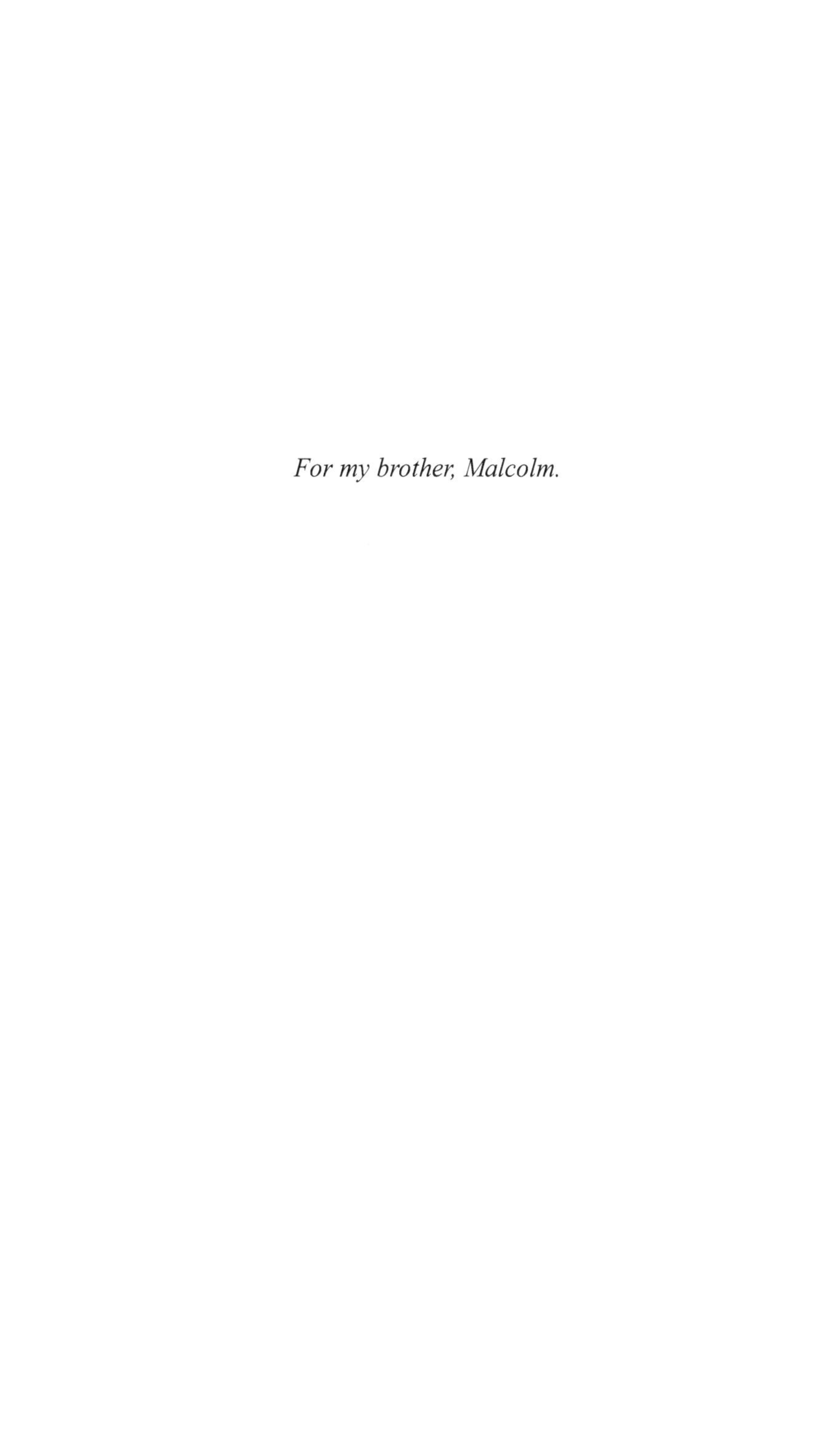

For my brother, Malcolm.

DRAMATIS PERSONAE

THE ROMANS

Caius Marcius 'Coriolanus' – patrician, soldier
Volumnia – mother to Caius
Caecilius Marcius – father to Caius
Virgilia Marcius (née Paetina) – wife to Caius
Vibinius Sidonius – grandfather to Caius
Aemilia Sidonius (née Perperna) – grandmother to Caius
Kaeso Sidonius – uncle to Caius
Menenius Agrippa – patrician, soldier, senator
Gabinia Agrippa – wife to Menenius
Publius Valerius – patrician and senator
Valeria Valerius – friend to Volumnia
Lucius Tarquinius – deposed king of Rome
Lolly Tarquinius – wife to Lucius
Titus Tarquinius – son of Lucius and Lolly
Lucius Iunius Brutus – nephew to Lucius Tarquinius
Collatinus – patrician

Mettius Trebonius – patrician, statesman
Cordia Apellina – friend of Virgilia
Aulus Postumius – commander
Lucius & Marcus Aquilii – patricians, nephews of Collatinus
Titus & tiberius Brutus – patricians, sons of Brutus
Manius & Marcellus Vitellii – patrician, nephews to Brutus
Cominius – patrician, soldier, friend to Caius
Pamphilus – patrician and soldier
Cipius – friend of Titus Tarquin
Sicinius Vitellus – plebeian, tribune
Junius Brutus – plebeian, tribune
Appius Claudius – consul
Titus Lartius – commander
Publics servility - senator
Decius Buccio - senator

THE VOLSCI

Tullus Aufidius – soldier
Gallio Aufidius – father to Tullus
Salonia Aufidius – mother to Tullus
Junia Aufidius – wife to Tullus
Atilia – friend to Salonia
Canus Elerius – elder
Virius – soldier

OTHERS

Galerius – Greek tutor
Trupo – slave
Rufius – arms master
Fadius – slave to Caius

Cispia – slave to Volumnia

Timon – slave

Vopiscus Cantius – a Tarquinii

"Cut me to pieces, Volsces; men and lads,
Stain all your edges on me. Boy! false hound!
If you have writ your annals true, 'tis there,
That, like an eagle in a dove-cote, I
Flutter'd your Volscians in Corioli:
Alone I did it. Boy!"

— William Shakespeare, *Coriolanus*, Act V, Scene VI.

PART I

534 BC - 513 BC

1

Aemilia Perperna flopped down on the dusty steps of the basilica, lifted her hair away from the nape of her neck and gave a deep sigh. It was on days like this, when the heat made her hot before she even rose from bed and the dust of the city's streets settled at the back of her throat, that Aemilia wished her father had let her marry earlier in the year. She might have been at the coast now, her skin being cooled by a sea breeze instead of sweating here in Rome.

Her bored eyes wandered over the forum. There were so many people still in Rome, despite the heat, and the number surprised her. Of course, the people before her were mostly plebeians and foreigners, people who, unlike Rome's patricians, didn't have seaside villas and country farms to which they could retreat, but even so, she thought, surely they had somewhere they could go to get away from the heat? She watched them for a few minutes longer, until her head started to throb and she closed her eyes, leaning her head back onto the step behind.

As she sat there, her head pounding and her dress growing damp, Aemilia wondered why she had not listened to her mother and stayed at home. Her mother had warned her the heat was too great, that she was sure to get one of her headaches, but Aemilia had been insistent – she wanted to buy the ivory hair combs she had seen and she was going to the forum. Her mother had tutted in annoyance and turned away, muttering to herself that children never listened to good sense, and Aemilia had clicked her fingers at the slave who was to accompany her and left the domus.

But even as she walked along the Via Sacra towards the forum, Aemilia had pondered on why she had been so insistent. It was true she wanted the ivory hair combs dearly, for they would set her dark brown hair off well, but she could have asked the trader to come to the domus or sent her slave to buy them. There really had been no need for her to go. As it was, she had sent the slave off to buy the combs while she waited in the shade. But she had awoken that morning with a desire — no, it was stronger than that, it had been a need — to go to the forum. It was a strange feeling; she had never felt so before.

After ten minutes or so, Aemilia opened her eyes, wincing as the light hit them, and looked for her slave in the crowd. It took her a few moments, but she found him, haggling with the ivory trader. She had told the slave to knock the trader down to two aes, and it looked like the trader wasn't budging. Aemilia knew he would eventually; the trader wouldn't want to miss out on a sale.

She let her gaze drift over the forum. Her eyes settled first on the beggar who always sat by the shrine of Janus, naked save for a filthy loincloth, his long straggly beard hanging between his legs. He would pray to the gods for you for a bowl of food. Turning her head to the left, she saw the scribes hunched over their small crooked tables, ready to write up court documents and wills for illiterate customers, their fingertips permanently stained with ink.

A shout drew Aemilia's attention towards the centre of the forum where she recognised the butcher who provided her household arguing with another man. The butcher was shiny with sweat, his forearms streaked with the blood of his freshly killed meat, and Aemilia's lip curled in distaste, knowing from experience he would smell as bad as he looked.

The butcher abruptly quietened as his gaze shifted from his interlocutor to a point over his shoulder. Curious, Aemilia craned her neck to see what he was looking at. She watched as a channel formed in the crowd. People were moving aside, stepping back into one another to make way for a figure wearing a heavy woollen cloak, the hood up.

Aemilia frowned. Why would anyone wear a cloak on such a blistering hot day? She looked the figure up and down, noticing its slightness, and concluded a woman was beneath the wool. The channel closed up behind this perplexing creature as the people, grown bored with staring, resumed their business. Only Aemilia continued to give the stranger her full attention.

The stranger made her way to one of the many braziers that burned in the forum, fire being essential, even in such heat, for so many of the trades performed there, and pushed back her hood. Aemilia had been expecting a hag, a creature grown eccentric with age, but the woman now revealed could only have been ten or fifteen years older than herself. Jet-black hair hung loosely about the round face and rat-tail tendrils stuck to cheeks that seemed unnaturally pale. A scrawny arm emerged from the cloak and delved into the bag hanging over her left shoulder. When it withdrew a moment later, the bony fingers were clasped around three scrolls of parchment.

Aemilia pushed herself up, grazing the skin of her elbows in her haste to see what the woman did next. Even from a distance, she could see the scrolls were of high quality. The wooden finials were expertly carved and there was even a hint of gilding, for they sparkled when the sunlight caught them. Each of the parchments was tied with a red silken cord.

She watched, intrigued, as the woman held the scrolls over the brazier. The parchments blackened quickly, then the fire caught hold, and they were dropped into the iron basket. The woman pulled her hood back up over her head and returned the way she had come, the crowd parting and closing behind her once again.

Aemilia got to her feet and hurried to the brazier, hoping she would not be too late to save the scrolls. She reached the brazier and gave a cry of dismay. The parchment on two of the scrolls had already burned down to ashes and the flames were licking at the wooden cores. She looked desperately for the third scroll and saw that it had fallen down inside the basket where the fire was nothing but a red glow. She thrust her hand into the basket, wincing at the heat that singed the hairs on her forearm, and grabbed the scroll. The silk cord was still intact. Her fingers fumbled with excitement as she untied the knot. Holding her breath, she unrolled the parchment carefully.

She groaned in frustration. The text written on the parchment was not Latin. She couldn't read a word.

Aemilia hurried through her domus, heading for the small room beside the kitchen that served as a bedroom for her brother's tutor, Galerius. She flung the wooden door open, its jagged, rotting bottom shuddering against the uneven stone floor.

Galerius was sitting on a low stool by the wall, his feet in a large bowl of water scented with rose petals. His ankles were mottled and swollen, and thick yellow toenails peeped above the surface of the water.

She grimaced at the sight. 'Must you?'

'It is the only comfort I can get, domina,' Galerius said, making a feeble attempt to stand.

'Stay,' Aemilia ordered, 'and read this if you can.' She handed him the scroll.

Galerius took it, his eyebrows rising as he examined the elaborate finials, obviously impressed. He unfurled the parchment, angling it towards the light that came in from the small window above him.

'You can read it, then?' Aemilia asked, seeing his lips move to form silent words.

Galerius nodded. 'It is written in Greek. I learnt Greek many years ago, in my youth.' He ran his fingers over the finials. 'This is very fine, domina. I have only seen such scrolls in the hands of priests. Where did you get it?'

'A woman put it and two more into a brazier in the forum.'

Galerius lowered the scroll and looked up at her with a frown. 'Why would anyone destroy such a beautiful thing?' he mused. 'What of the other two?'

'They were burning by the time I got to the brazier. That one had fallen down the side and hadn't been touched by the flames.'

'Most fortunate,' he breathed. 'This is a treasure, domina.'

'Stop fondling it and tell me what it says.'

But Galerius looked up at her again. 'You said a woman was burning these scrolls?'

Aemilia nodded, wondering why the old man was looking so excited.

'What woman?' he asked. 'What did she look like?'

'She was quite young, dark-haired, pale skin. She was... strange.'

'Strange?'

Aemilia reconsidered. 'Well, peculiar, I suppose. She was wearing a cloak. In this heat. And the people made way for her as she walked through the forum. I've never seen them do that for anyone, not even the king.'

'I wonder...'. Galerius tapped the scroll thoughtfully, a vertical frown line deepening between his brows.

Aemilia was growing impatient with his ramblings. 'What do you wonder, old man?'

'No, I…'. He shook his head vigorously and waved his hands at her. 'It is nothing, I am sure.'

'What is nothing?'

'I should not say—'

'If you don't, Galerius, I will have you whipped. Speak.'

'There is a rumour,' he said carefully, his voice trembling a little at her threat, 'that the Sibyl has come to Rome.'

Aemilia's eyes widened. She had heard of the Sibyl, the prophetess of Apollo, who lived in a cave at Cumae and was said to have led Aeneas to the entrance to the Underworld. The Sibyl was a creature of the gods, no ordinary woman. 'What have you heard?'

'That she has come to see the king. To warn him.'

'Of what?'

'That is not known,' Galerius shook his head sadly. He tapped the scroll again. 'But I wonder if this, and the others she burned, were something to do with him.'

'But if they were meant for the king, why did she still have them? Why did she burn them? Why—'

'Oh,' Galerius put his hands up to his ears, 'so many questions, domina. I do not have the answers you seek.'

Aemilia snorted in annoyance. 'But you can read that,' she pointed at the scroll. 'Tell me what is written there.'

Galerius lay the parchment out over his bony knees and traced his finger along the lines of text. 'This scroll appears to contain lines of prophecy.'

'Well, of course, it does. The Sibyl is a prophetess,' she said testily. 'What else would it contain?'

'Domina,' Galerius sighed and put his head on one side, 'you insisted I tell you—'

'Yes, yes.' Aemilia sank to her knees, her face level with the scroll. 'What does it prophesy, Galerius?' she asked more kindly.

Galerius put his right forefinger to the beginning of one line of text. 'This says a child of the winged serpent will be born who will bring great woe to Rome. The child will be loved by Mars and loathed by the people in equal measure.' He looked up at Aemilia.

The dreadful expression upon the old man's face made her stomach lurch. 'What does it mean?' Aemilia asked, not sure she wanted to hear the answer.

'Oh, domina,' Galerius whispered, 'I fear for you.'

'Fear for me!' Aemilia said, her voice shaking a little. 'Why should you fear for me?'

He pointed a crabbed finger at the parchment. 'The gods spoke through the Sibyl and she wrote these words with her own sacred hands. The gods told her to come to Rome and deliver this prophecy. Maybe it was meant for the king, but maybe…'. His voice trailed off.

'You mean maybe it was meant for me?' Aemilia laughed

but there was no humour in it, only fear. 'That's ridiculous. Why would she have a prophecy for me? And how would she know I would be there in the forum? I only decided to go this morn—' She turned away, her words catching in her throat as she remembered her insistence on going to the forum. Had that desire been put in her heart by the gods?

'You feel it, don't you?' Galerius cried. 'I see it in your eyes.'

'I don't… no, I'm not sure…'.

'We cannot know how the gods work, domina, but I do know the gods like to play games with us. I believe you were meant to witness the Sibyl burning the scrolls and that the gods meant for you to save this one.'

'But what does it mean?' Aemilia cried helplessly.

'The winged serpent,' Galerius said, stabbing the parchment with his forefinger. 'You have seen such a creature, domina. Think.'

Aemilia shook her head and looked down at the ground. She scrunched up her eyes and searched her mind. An image began to form: small, white on black. Yes, that was it!

'Vibinius's ring,' she cried, holding up her right hand and wiggling her little finger to show where her future husband wore his seal ring. 'His intaglio is a winged serpent.'

Galerius nodded. 'Now you understand.' He reached out and took hold of her hand. 'This prophecy is a warning, domina, that you must not marry Vibinius Sidonius.'

Aemilia snatched her hand away and got awkwardly to her feet. 'Not marry Vibinius?' Her voice was strong now, outraged. 'Of course I will marry him, you old fool.'

'But the prophecy—'

'Mere words,' she said, flicking her fingers at the parchment.

'No, it is your destiny,' Galerius insisted, his feet moving in agitation, splashing water over the side of the bowl. 'Take it to a priest. Have him interpret it if you will not believe me.'

'Are you mad? A priest would tell the king. And if these scrolls were meant for him, there's no saying what he would do if he knew I had one.' She shuddered at the thought of the king's anger.

'Then believe me, domina. If you marry into the house of the winged serpent, a child will come who will bring great harm to Rome.'

Aemilia snatched the scroll from Galerius's lap and briskly rolled it up. 'I want to marry Vibinius and I will. I cannot worry about what may be. After all, who is to say the prophecy means a child of mine? Vibinius has a sister, it may mean her, or it may mean my granddaughter or great-granddaughter, and I will be dead by then. I will not sacrifice my happiness because of a few silly lines of Greek.' Aemilia looked down her long nose at the old man. 'You will not speak of this to anyone, Galerius, do you understand?'

'But—'

'To anyone. I will have you whipped if I so much as hear a whisper about this.'

Galerius folded his hands in his lap and nodded. 'Not a word will escape my lips, domina.'

Aemilia turned and left him alone in the little room. Clutching the scroll to her breast, she hurried to her cubiculum and pulled out the chest she kept beneath her bed. Lifting the heavy lid, she pushed the contents to one side, placing the scroll at the bottom and replacing the other items on top.

Galerius had talked nonsense, she told herself as she shoved the chest back into its hiding place. What did he know of gods and prophecies? Perhaps the woman had not been the Sibyl at all, just a strange, mad creature who wore heavy cloaks in summer and had a liking for burning scrolls. To think that a prophecy written by a servant of the gods was intended for her was ridiculous, as ridiculous as she bringing forth a child who would be an enemy of Rome. After all, who was she? She was a nothing, a nobody.

Aemilia heard her mother calling for her and headed for the door. As she put her hand on the latch, she halted and cast a long look back at the chest beneath her bed. Would it be better to burn the scroll, she wondered, to finish the Sibyl's job? She bit her lip. Part of her wanted to burn it, to destroy it physically in the hope she could rid it from her mind. But Galerius had been right about one thing: the Sibyl was the instrument of the gods. If the gods had meant her to have the scroll, to destroy it would be to risk their anger.

Her mother called again, and Aemilia shouted back that she was coming. She nodded to herself, decision made, and stepped out into the corridor, closing the door behind her. The scroll would stay at the bottom of the chest, her guilty little secret.

2

Twelve Years Later

Caecilius Marcius clambered to his feet, smiling ruefully, pretending not to mind he was being laughed at. He had caught his foot in a rabbit hole and fallen flat on his face, and now he was a source of amusement for his new companions. His ankle was swelling, and his palms and knees were dirty with mud and grass stains. Perfect!

A hand thrust his fallen torch at him. He took it and looked into the grinning face of Prince Titus. 'Thank you,' Caecilius said, taking the torch.

'Hurt?' Titus asked.

Caecilius shook his head. 'Only my pride.'

'Come on, then,' and Titus waved the party forward.

Caecilius put his left foot down gingerly, feeling pain in his injured ankle. He grimaced. He would have to bear the pain. He would look a complete fool if he backed out now and returned to the camp.

Whose wonderful idea had it been to go on a raid? he wondered as he limped after the party. True, the diplomatic mission to Gabii had been extremely dull and their return journey to Rome uneventful, there being nothing to do for days now but drink and rut with the whores who followed them, but to mount a senseless raid on a nearby village! Why? Not that Caecilius had anything against a little action. He had never been on a raid, but where was the profit in it? To attack villagers who would have nothing worth stealing and no women worth humping was worse than pointless. It was stupid. There would almost certainly be consequences for both King Lucius and Rome, so why had Prince Titus agreed?

More to the point, he asked himself, *why did you agree?* He already knew the answer, though it gave him no pleasure to acknowledge it, and his wife's words before they parted came back to him, telling him he was a fool and an embarrassment to be so obvious a social climber, wanting to get close to the prince. But there would be advantages to being in the prince's inner circle of friends, he had told her with assurance. Who knew what could come of such a friendship?

Caecilius hurried to catch up. 'Won't they see us coming?' he asked Cipius, gesturing at the flaming torches half of the party held.

Cipius, one of the prince's closest friends, shrugged. 'Doesn't matter if they do. They're shepherds and farmers. Won't know one end of a spear from the other.'

'But we won't have the element of surprise.'

Cipius laughed. 'Trust me, Marcius, we've done this before. They'll be too busy screaming and running away to be any danger to us.'

'How many times?'

'What?'

'How many raids have you been on?'

'I don't know. Six or seven.'

'With the prince?'

'Sometimes.'

'Does the king know?' Caecilius gave an embarrassed half smile as Cipius looked at him sideways. 'Just wondering.'

'You scared, Marcius?'

'No, only—'

'The king knows. Doesn't care. He used to go on raids himself. So, there's no need to worry your pretty head you'll end up in trouble.' He ruffled Caecilius's hair roughly, laughing.

Caecilius jerked his head away, cursing himself for not holding his tongue. Now, Cipius would tell the prince what he had said, the prince would think him a coward and not worth bothering with, and that would be the end of any friendship, over before it had even begun. There was nothing else for it, he decided. He would have to prove himself worthy on this raid. He would show no mercy and laugh at his victims' cries. In short, he would be the loudest, the fiercest, the most ruthless bastard of them all.

Salonia Aufidius clenched her jaw and grunted as another spasm of pain wrenched its way through her lower body. As the pain receded a little and she could breathe again, she clutched a small stone figurine of Lucina to her breast and begged the goddess for help.

Her friend, Atilia, heard her words. She grinned, showing the gaps in her teeth. 'Hurts, doesn't it? I told you it would.'

Salonia grunted and moved onto all fours, panting. 'How much longer?' she demanded, as she pressed her knees into the hardened earth floor of her hut.

'Hard to say, this being your first. Another hour, perhaps.

Now, don't go on like that,' Atilia said as Salonia started to whimper. 'There's nothing to be done. Babes comes when they're ready.'

'I didn't know it would be like this. I should never have married.'

'You'll forget the pain and there will be more babes. There always are.'

'Oh no, there won't. I won't let Gallio touch me ever again.'

Atilia didn't bother to reply. Over the years, she had acted as midwife to many women and been witness to the pain, the curses and the prayers, and always there came the vow the woman would not lie with her man again, as if she had any choice in the matter. But Atilia also knew how this part of motherhood felt, knew the anger that welled up at being put through such agony, and knew she had said the same words herself as some kind of solace. She busied herself in the small hut, making sure she had all that was needed for when the child came: a bowl of water, cloths for cleaning and a knife for cutting the afterbirth. Yes, all was ready, just as it should be.

'What's that?' Salonia asked, hearing shouts from outside the hut, but before Atilia could answer, the door burst open and Salonia's husband rushed in.

'We must leave,' Gallio declared, pushing Atilia out of his way and moving to a chest by the wall. Wrenching the chest open, the lid banging against the mud wall, he rummaged inside and drew out his sword. He held it up to examine the blade, his heavy square face shadowy and strained in the light of the single oil lamp that burned. He looked down at Salonia crouched on the ground. 'We must move her,' he said to Atilia.

'She can't be moved, you fool,' Atilia cried. 'The baby's coming.'

Gallio put his hand under Salonia's armpit and tried to pull her up onto her feet.

'Leave me alone,' Salonia screamed and pulled out of his grasp.

But Gallio grabbed her again. 'The Romans are attacking. The lookouts have seen their torches on the other hill.' He heaved his wife to her feet, taking her weight as she fell against him. He bent as if to lift her into his arms, then thought better of it. 'You'll have to walk. If I carry you, I won't be able to fight. Atilia,' he called, turning towards the door where the old woman stood, peering out into the darkness, 'help me get her to the trees. You can hide in the wood.'

Frightened, Atilia made no further argument but moved to Salonia's other side and took hold. She and Gallio half lifted, half dragged Salonia out of the hut. They ran as fast as they could towards the trees. When they were only halfway across the field, they heard the shouts of the Roman raiders. Gallio and Atilia looked back over their shoulders to see the flames of the torches against the black night closing fast on their village.

'Hurry,' Atilia cried.

They reached the treeline and hurried into the wood, not stopping until they had gone in at least twenty feet. Gallio let go his hold of Salonia and she collapsed on the ground. Atilia bent over her, but her attention was on Gallio, who had taken a few steps back towards the edge of the wood.

'You can't leave us,' Atilia said, careful to keep her voice low.

'They're burning the grain store,' Gallio said.

'We can replace the grain. She can't replace you as easily.'

Salonia gave out a long, low snarl of pain and Gallio returned to kneel beside her. 'You must be quiet, my love,' he said in her ear. 'If they hear you—'

'I can't… it's coming,' Salonia protested, her fingers digging into the ground as she tried not to scream.

'Here, put this in her mouth.' Atilia handed Gallio a short stick she had found on the ground. 'Bite down on it, Salonia.'

Salonia did as she was told, closing her eyes as she panted. Gallio positioned himself behind a tree a few feet away, taking care to stay out of sight, watching as the straw roofs of the village huts went up in flames.

Trying to block out the terrible noises coming from the village, and trying not to think about her husband, whether he was dead or alive, Atilia tended to her friend, murmuring comforting words she had no faith in herself. Out here in the cool night air, the shock of the attack, the strain of their escape, Atilia thought it unlikely the baby would live. A large part of her hoped the child would die inside Salonia. A newborn babe would cry and alert the Romans to their presence here in the wood. And then the Romans would come with their dripping red swords and butcher them all. Gallio would do his best to defend them, Atilia knew, and maybe he would even kill one or two, but there were always more. Oh yes, there were always more Romans. *Hear me, Lucina,* she closed her eyes and prayed silently, *let the babe die in Salonia's womb. Or if that is not your wish, I beg you, let it not come yet.*

But the goddess either wasn't listening or didn't care about Atilia's fears. Salonia suddenly moved onto all fours and began pushing out her baby with all her strength, her teeth biting through the bark of the stick, her eyes squeezed shut and leaking tears.

Fighting back tears of her own, Atilia positioned herself

behind Salonia. Salonia bent low, her face touching the ground, and growled into the earth as her baby slithered from her body into Atilia's waiting hands. The afterbirth followed, plopping onto the ground with a squelch. The baby squirmed, opened its mouth and cried loudly.

The noise brought Gallio running. 'Quiet it.'

'Give me your sword,' Atilia whispered and held out her hand.

Gallio hesitated, unsure of what Atilia meant to do, but when she snapped her fingers at him, he handed it over. With relief, he watched as she cut the umbilical cord.

He didn't need to ask for his sword's return. Atilia thrust the hilt towards him as soon as she was done. Then she stuck her finger in the child's bawling mouth. The baby sucked on it and Atilia lifted it towards her chest to muffle any further sounds, careless of the blood and mucus that soiled her clothes.

Gallio returned to his lookout tree, returning a few minutes later. 'They're going,' he said, staring at Salonia who had fallen over onto her back. Her legs were bent and spread. She was crying.

Atilia jerked her head towards the village. 'Is anything left?'

'I don't know.' Gallio knelt beside Salonia. 'We'll go back when you've recovered a little. I am so sorry you had to do this, my love.'

'It's not your fault,' Salonia said, wiping her cheeks. 'Is the child well?'

Gallio looked to Atilia for the answer. She nodded. 'Well enough.'

Salonia sniffed. 'Why did they attack us?'

'Because that's what Romans do,' Gallio snarled.

'Is it safe to go back now?' Atilia asked.

Gallio went to see. The flaming roofs illuminated the village and Gallio saw men moving about, some trying to put out the fires, others tending to bodies lying on the ground. 'It's safe. Come.'

They made a halting journey back to their village, Salonia whimpering with every step. Gallio and Atilia were both impatient to reach the village, but they forced themselves to walk at her pace. When they reached the first few huts at the edge of the village, Atilia thrust the baby into Salonia's arms and hurried away to find her husband.

Gallio and Salonia went to their hut. Compared to their neighbours, they seemed to have been fortunate. Their roof was untouched, but the hut had been ransacked, their few pieces of furniture broken into pieces, smaller items scattered over the floor. Salonia looked around her invaded home, fresh hot tears falling freely. She held her child close against her body and bent her head to its cheek. It was warm against hers. 'Our home, Gallio.'

'At least we are alive, Salonia,' Gallio said, taking her gently in his arms so as not to crush the child between them. 'We can repair the village. But if those bastards had found you, they would have put a spear through your belly, and I wouldn't have either of you.'

'Oh, don't,' Salonia pleaded. She looked up sharply as wails rent the air. 'Ye gods, that's Atilia.'

'Stay here,' Gallio said and hurried out. Salonia pressed fierce kisses to her child's head, her eyes fixed on the doorway. When Gallio returned, his face was grim. 'Her husband's dead.'

'I should go to her.'

'No,' Gallio said firmly, 'you've been through enough. I'll see she's looked after.' And before she could argue, he was gone.

Salonia eased herself to the floor, wincing at the pain between her legs, and realised neither she nor Gallio knew whether they had a son or a daughter. She pulled aside the shawl Atilia had wrapped the child in. They had a son, she saw, as he started to cry. She pulled her dress away from her breast and guided her nipple to the little mouth. He started to suckle.

'Tullus,' she said aloud, trying the name to see how it sounded. 'Tullus Aufidius. The gods favoured you and brought you safe to us.' She closed her eyes and raised her face to the roof. 'And now I call on Nemesis to make you strong so that when you are old enough to wield a sword and spear, you will destroy the Romans for all the Volsci people. Oh Nemesis, hear me.'

She opened her eyes to see a goose flapping noisily past the open hut door. Salonia grinned. The goddess had heard her.

3

517 BC

Aemilia scanned the kitchen table and performed a quick calculation. Nine dishes in all: bread and cheese, pork, asparagus, figs, grapes, plums, olive oil and honey… oh dear, would there be enough? She had only planned for one guest at their dinner. Now, Caecilius had sent one of his slaves to tell her he was bringing Menenius Agrippa with him, and Menenius Agrippa was known to be a big eater. Aemilia had ordered two more jugs of wine for the table, the best their farm could offer, just in case.

She wished she could stop the butterflies fluttering in her stomach. They weren't caused by the prospect of the dinner party; she had given plenty of those over the years. It was the prospect of the Sidonius family taking an irrevocable step towards a destiny of which she didn't want to be a part.

It wasn't the first time she had felt this way. The first time had been on her wedding day, when Vibinius's intaglio ring had kept flashing in her eyes, and the memory of the Sibyl's scroll in the chest beneath her bed had refused to stay buried.

But no god had struck her down as the wedding ceremony progressed, and she had allowed herself to relax.

Then she had become pregnant, and the butterflies had returned. All throughout her first pregnancy, she had stroked her swollen belly and wondered if inside her was the child who was to bring calamity upon Rome. But then her baby was born, and in her contentment, the prophecy was dismissed. For her son was surely the least likeliest creature to be a danger to Rome. He was not perfect, for he had a harelip and a club foot, and time would prove him to be simple. Vibinius suggested exposing the child, but Aemilia had screamed at him and he had held out his hands, taken aback by her fury. Aemilia had named her son Kaeso and rejoiced in the knowledge that such a baby would never be beloved of Mars, or of any other god, for that matter.

Her second pregnancy had been a trial. The baby had drained her of all energy, and her labour was long and painful. When it was finally over, she was an exhausted lump, ripped and sagging, and never likely to bear another child. She was thankful. She didn't want another. Unlike Kaeso, this child, a daughter, had been perfect: no disfigurement, and as time passed, no evidence of mental backwardness. And yet, somehow, Aemilia felt not a fraction of the love for her daughter that she felt for her son. Her daughter was a cold creature, undemonstrative, aloof, showing no particular affection for her parents and none whatsoever for her brother. The prophecy reared its head in her memory once again. If she was to be the mother of this fated child, then Aemilia thought there was no greater candidate than her daughter Volumnia.

But then, Aemilia had reasoned, being a girl, Volumnia was unlikely to ever be in a position to do harm. She would have no say in how Rome was ruled, she would not be able to fight in Rome's wars… what else was there? And so, she had relaxed once more, content in her belief that the prophecy could not have meant the fruit of her womb at all. No doubt it referred to a much later generation of the family Sidonius, at a time when she would be dead and not in a position to care any longer. Whoever it referred to, it was not her, she was sure.

At least, she was sure until Vibinius announced he had arranged a husband for their daughter. She should have considered this, Aemilia told herself angrily. Kaeso would not marry, of that she had no doubt. No family would want their daughter marrying such as he lest it pollute their bloodline, but of course, Volumnia would wed and then there would be children. What if a child of Volumnia's was the enemy of which the prophecy spoke? Perhaps, she thought, it would be best if Volumnia did not marry, just in case. And so Aemilia had tried to dissuade Vibinius from the idea of their daughter marrying, but he was adamant. It was a good match, he told her, and had invited the husband-to-be to dinner to meet Volumnia and so that the details of the wedding could be settled.

Aemilia had met Caecilius only once before and had not liked him. She couldn't put her finger on why she had taken a dislike to him; there was just something in his way of talking, his obvious contempt for her husband's tendency towards boastful pomposity that vexed her. But, she considered ruefully, Caecilius was probably just the type of man Volumnia would like. They would suit one another.

If there was anything good to be got out of this marriage, it was knowing that Volumnia would soon be leaving the family domus. Aemilia's love for her daughter was borne of duty rather than nature, and she could not pretend she wouldn't enjoy the peacefulness of a domus without Volumnia in it. She and Kaeso would be allowed to live without continual criticism, for one thing, and that was not to be sniffed at. As it was, Aemilia had had to order a slave to take Kaeso out of the domus for the evening because Volumnia had said she didn't want her brother embarrassing her before Caecilius. *Yes,* she thought, a smile creeping onto her face, *Volumnia's absence would be something to be grateful for.*

———

'You're dragging your feet.'

Caecilius moved out of the way of an oncoming handcart laden with sacks and sighed. 'Stop nagging, will you?'

His friend, Menenius Agrippa, frowned. 'Why such a bad mood, Cae? You should be happy.'

'Why should I be?' Caecilius said.

'Why? You're going to be married again,' Menenius said. 'No more lonely nights in your domus, someone to look after all your needs. And,' he poked Caecilius in the arm, 'a chance to be a father.'

'And that's the only reason I'm doing this.'

'Oh, surely not!'

'Will you stop being so bloody cheery? It's very irritating.'

Menenius chuckled, amused by his friend's bad temper. He could guess why Caecilius was so irritable. Caecilius had been with the prince the night before and, no doubt, Titus had been ribbing him about his bride, saying he would be nagged to death before too long. There was some truth in that, Menenius acknowledged, thinking of his own wife, Gabinia, but not all wives were shrews, and it was possible that this Volumnia Sidonius was young enough to be moulded into the perfect wife. She was young enough to be fertile, certainly, and that was all that seemed to matter to Caecilius.

Menenius understood. Caecilius's first wife had died in childbirth and the child itself had not lived past an hour. With their deaths had died Caecilius's chance of continuing his bloodline. The Marcius men had always been obsessed with their bloodline, for there was no denying it was an impressive one; Caecilius could trace his ancestors back to a king of Rome, Ancus Marcius. Caecilius had been a widower for a few years now, and he obviously felt time passing him by and so had sought out a bride. Why he had chosen the daughter of Vibinius Sidonius, though, Menenius had no idea. Menenius knew little about the Sidonius family. He had met Vibinius and thought him to be a decent man if something of a bore; his wife, Aemilia, he had met but once and she had not made much of an impression upon him. The daughter, Volumnia, he had not met at all, though he had seen her at various dinners and thought her to be quite pretty.

'I suggest you put a smile on your face,' he said, pointing to a door a few feet away whose posts boasted the emblem of a winged serpent. 'We're here.'

Caecilius fiddled with his toga, checking it hung properly over his left shoulder. 'Thank you for agreeing to come tonight.'

'I always say yes to a free dinner,' Menenius grinned. 'Though why you want me here, I don't know.'

'I can't stand old Vibinius all on my own, that's why. If he starts talking about the price of salt, interrupt him, I beg you.'

'I will,' Menenius promised. 'Now, let's go in. I want to meet your bride.'

Volumnia Sidonius was certainly unlike other women of her age, Menenius thought as he accepted another cup of wine from their hostess. She seemed prettier to him than he had originally thought, not a beauty, it was true, but there was spirit in her eyes and a pleasing curve to her lips that made him envy Caecilius his nights. But he felt there was more to Volumnia than a quite pretty girl of a good patrician family. During the dinner, he had discerned an intelligence and determination in her that was quite out of the ordinary for a girl. He had expected her to be silent during the dinner, only speaking when spoken to, but Volumnia had been loquacious. Vibinius had indeed started talking about the price of salt, and Menenius, following a glance from Caecilius, had been about to steer the conversation onto other matters when Volumnia performed that task for him by asking about his experience of war. Volumnia quite astonished him with her enquiry, for few young girls wanted to hear of warfare, and he must have shown his surprise because Vibinius had tried to quiet his daughter. But Volumnia would not be put off by her father and persisted until Menenius had been forced to provide an answer. He told her of the battles he had fought in, adding loyally that Caecilius had fought bravely in some too, and she had listened with a fervour that was both gratifying and unsettling. She urged him to talk more of the killing, wanting to know what it felt like to pierce an enemy's flesh with a sword or spear, and to know how quickly the life passed from a man once struck. She was disappointed when he told her he did not know, for in battle he struck and moved swiftly on to the next enemy, not waiting to see if the men he pierced died there and then or later.

'I wish I had been born a man,' Volumnia said when he had finished.

'I, for one, am glad you were not,' Caecilius said, his

expression saying clearly he didn't know if he should take her declaration seriously.

Volumnia waved her hand dismissively. 'You would have found another girl to wed.'

'Volumnia, really,' Aemilia said, widening her eyes at her daughter, an instruction to behave. 'Caecilius would be heart-broken not to marry you, wouldn't you, Caecilius?'

'What? Oh, yes, heartbroken,' Caecilius nodded, thumping his chest and belching.

'Why do you wish you had been born a man?' Menenius asked Volumnia, genuinely curious.

'Because men are able to do so much. You can fight, you can debate, you can go where you please, do what you please. You don't have to spend day after day endlessly spinning wool.'

'Volumnia finds wool spinning exceedingly tiresome,' Aemilia explained apologetically.

'And so would they if they had to do it,' Volumnia retorted, gesturing at Caecilius and Menenius. 'Tell me, Mother, how can a woman find glory in her life?'

'A woman is not supposed to desire glory, Volumnia,' Aemilia said. 'A woman finds contentment in her family and the deeds of her husband and sons.'

'As you have done, Mother?' Volumnia demanded haughtily. 'Tell me, what have you to be content about? A son who is an embarrassment and should have been exposed at birth and a daughter who wishes she had been born a man?'

'I won't have you talking like this in front of guests, Volumnia,' Aemilia said, and Menenius saw the pain in her eyes, the muscles tightening in her jaw. Volumnia's words had greatly upset her. Indeed, their hostess seemed on the verge of tears.

'It's getting late,' Menenius said, thinking it would be a

kindness to leave before Aemilia and her daughter quarrelled further. 'My wife will wonder what has become of me.'

'It's not so very late,' Vibinius protested.

'No, Menenius is right,' Caecilius said, getting to his feet a little too enthusiastically. 'We must go. Lady,' he turned to Aemilia, 'thank you for a delicious dinner.'

'You're very welcome, Caecilius,' Aemilia said, forcing a smile.

Vibinius and Aemilia showed their guests to the door. Vibinius took hold of Caecilius's hand and held on to it, intent on saying a few words to his soon-to-be son-in-law before he went.

'I fear you are upset by your daughter's words, lady,' Menenius said quietly to Aemilia.

'She hates my son, my Kaeso,' Aemilia said, turning her back on Volumnia as though unable to bear looking at her. 'I don't know why she does. He is such a lovely boy.'

'Perhaps she speaks so out of nerves,' Menenius suggested, though doubting it was true. 'She is to be a wife in only a few days and I'm sure that may be a source of great anxiety to a girl.'

Aemilia looked at him coolly. 'My dear Menenius, I've never known Volumnia to be nervous about anything. I promise you, she meant every word she said tonight. I imagine that when you set out for here, you did not expect to be interrogated about battles and the men you have killed. I am sorry if Volumnia brought back memories you would rather have forgotten. But she is so bloodthirsty, so unnatural a woman.' She glanced at Caecilius, who was trying to extricate himself from her husband. 'I wouldn't blame Caecilius if he changed his mind about marrying her after tonight. And maybe that would be for the best...'. Her voice trailed off as she stared at him.

'Lady?' Menenius prompted.

'What?' Aemilia looked at him, as if suddenly remembering he was there. 'Oh, nothing. I'm a little tired and my mind wanders. Thank you for coming tonight, Menenius. I have enjoyed your company, and I am glad Caecilius has such a friend. Once he marries my daughter, he's going to need all the good company he can get.'

Gallio ran the whetstone down the blade of his sword, bringing it up and repeating the action to sharpen the metal. He had performed this sharpening so many times that the blade was becoming thin. He supposed he would have to get another one made by the blacksmith soon, but he had a strong attachment to this sword and would be reluctant to see it thrown into the melting pot. This sword had been his weapon in many a battle and had protected him well, but that was not why it was special to him. It was this sword that had cut the cord of his son on that dreadful night five years before, and Gallio had come to believe it was a lucky sword. He, his wife and his son might have died that night as many of his neighbours and friends had died, and his sword had become a talisman, a symbol of his family's endurance against their enemies. He would take no pleasure in giving it up.

He looked up and smiled. The son he had been thinking of was standing a few feet away, watching him work. 'Come here, Tullus,' he said, gesturing him over. The small boy stepped nearer, his eyes fixed on the sword. Gallio knew the weapon fascinated his son. 'Would you like to hold it?'

Tullus nodded and held out his arms. Gallio laid the sword across them, saw them dip a little at the weight, and sat back. His son stared at the gleaming metal with its leather-wrapped hilt.

'Now, hold it as it should be held,' Gallio said, taking hold of the blade and turning the hilt to his son.

Tullus stretched out his right arm and his little fingers curled around the hilt. Gallio let go. The sword pitched towards the ground, knocking the little boy off balance.

'Heavy, isn't it?' Gallio grinned. 'Try lifting it up.'

Tullus brought his left hand to join his right on the hilt. Pursing his mouth, he took a deep breath, his small chest heaving, and raised the sword, bringing the tip to his father's chin.

'Do you like it?' Gallio asked, feeling the point tickle his beard.

'Can I have it?' Tullus said in answer.

'In time. You are a little young for such a weapon.'

'I'm five,' Tullus protested as if it was a great age.

'How old were you when you learnt to fight, Gallio?' Salonia asked from the doorway, a woven basket full of linen on her hip. 'No older than Tullus, I seem to remember you telling me.'

Gallio took the sword from Tullus and sheathed it. 'My father wanted me to learn early.'

'So you could defend yourself and those you loved, no?' Salonia raised an eyebrow. 'Why deny Tullus the same lessons?'

'You want our son to fight?' he asked angrily. 'To be hurt?'

'I want him to be able to defend himself,' Salonia said, her jaw tightening. 'It's a dangerous world we live in, husband. It is best he is prepared for it.'

'I grow weary of war, Salonia.'

'Then you grow weary of living,' she snapped. 'There

will always be war, Gallio. If not war with the Romans, then it will be war with the Greeks or the Etruscans or the Gauls.'

'Have you been in a war, Father?' Tullus asked, sitting down at his father's feet and crossing his legs.

'Not for some years,' Gallio replied. 'Not since we came to live here in Antium. The last was some eleven years since when we fought the tyrant.'

'Say his name, Gallio,' Salonia cried. 'Or are you afraid to?'

'I am not afraid.'

'Then say it. Say the tyrant Lucius Tarquin, King of Rome.'

'What's a tyrant?' Tullus asked, his mouth struggling to form the unfamiliar word.

'A tyrant is a man who mistreats his people,' Gallio said, 'who grinds them down by taking everything they have of any worth for his own. He's a man who forces his people to fight wars so he can grow richer on the spoils of victory. Such a man is King Lucius, my son.'

'Is he our enemy, Father?'

'The greatest enemy,' Salonia said, setting down her basket and running her hand through her son's dark hair. 'You will fight him one day when you are older. Your father will teach you how. Won't you, Gallio?'

Her stare was a challenge. Gallio returned it, holding her gaze for a long moment, trying to see behind her eyes and know her mind. How different she was from the woman he had married. The night of Tullus's birth had changed her. She had been soft before then, a woman who always sought to calm, not to enrage. That woman was gone, frightened away by a birth in the dark of a wood while her home was destroyed and her friends slaughtered by laughing Romans.

Gallio wished his son would not have to fight, that he

could live out his life in peace and amity with the Romans and the Etruscans and all the other tribes that inhabited Italy. But that was a fantasy. Salonia was right; they did not live in such times. There would always be fighting, there would always be wars to be won, and Tullus would have a greater chance of a good and long life if he knew how to protect himself and those he loved. Gallio looked at Tullus, his young face eager and open, wanting to hear the answer to his mother's question.

'Yes, I will teach you, Tullus,' Gallio said. 'I will teach you to be a great warrior.' He considered a moment, then reached down and picked up his sheathed sword. 'This is yours now. You must learn to use it and—'

'I will kill the tyrant Tarquin with it,' Tullus cried happily.

Gallio looked at Salonia, whose face had softened and bore an adoring smile. 'Do that, my son, and you will have pleased your mother greatly.'

Aemilia had risen early, wanting to pick the flowers that would decorate the domus herself. It would be a pleasant hour, she had reasoned, in an otherwise exhausting day, to walk the garden paths and smell the flowers, to choose the prettiest ones and arrange them beautifully.

Once done, she had gone into the kitchen and ensured the slaves were working hard on the wedding feast. A quite ridiculous expense, in her opinion, but Vibinius had insisted the Sidonius family would put on a good show. And so, there were dishes of beef, dormouse and peacock, and all of the family's wine had been brought up in amphorae from the farm. Aemilia thought ruefully that she, Vibinius and Kaeso would have to eat frugally for quite a few months after this wedding.

Telling herself the expense was worth it, Aemilia had left the kitchen and retired to her cubiculum to dress. She had taken great care with her dress and makeup, but as she put the hand mirror down, waving her slave away, Aemilia wondered why she bothered. She did not like what she had seen in the hammered metal: a face older than her years, furrows etched deep into her cheeks, eyes framed by crisscross lines. It was only fifteen years since she had been a bride and yet, here she was, on her daughter's wedding day, looking like an old woman.

Aemilia left her cubiculum and headed along the corridor to her daughter's room. She pushed the door open. 'You're up,' she said in some surprise, closing it behind her. When she had looked in earlier, Volumnia had still been fast asleep. She moved to the dressing table where Volumnia sat and inspected her daughter's hair. Volumnia's dark brown hair had been smoothed and separated into six long locks, the ends tied with ribbons.

'Does my hair meet with your approval?' Volumnia asked with a wry smile.

'It does,' Aemilia said, taking a seat on the bed. 'I'm pleased you are sticking with tradition and having your hair dressed appropriately. From your manner and words at dinner the other night, I thought you were doing your best to scare Caecilius off by being so very unconventional.'

'Would that not have pleased you?' Volumnia asked with a raised eyebrow. 'Do you know, Mother, I believe you don't want me to marry Caecilius.'

Aemilia opened her mouth to protest but shut it again, dropping her gaze to her hands fidgeting in her lap.

'You don't deny it,' Volumnia said.

'I'm not going to bother denying such nonsense,' Aemilia muttered.

'Is it nonsense? Father told me you kept asking him to reconsider.'

'Your father had no business telling you that.'

'You think I am not good enough for Caecilius.'

'It is not that, not that at all,' Aemilia retorted irritably.

'Then what is it?'

She didn't want to speak of her worry, didn't want to let the prophecy intrude into a day that should have been happy. Aemilia decided to lie to her daughter. 'I just did not think we would see you marry so soon.'

Volumnia gave her the most doubting of looks. She turned back to her dressing table and held up the mirror. As she checked her hair, she said, 'You are only too glad to be rid of me, Mother, don't pretend. There, all done.'

Her hair finished, Volumnia stood and shrugged off her woollen dressing gown. She raised her arms above her head so the slave could dress her in the simple white tunic she would wear for the wedding ceremony. Aemilia watched as the slave tied a belt around Volumnia's waist, then made the knot of Hercules that Caecilius would have to undo before he consummated their marriage. Volumnia slipped her feet into the new slippers Aemilia had dyed with saffron and straightened as the slave floated a flame-coloured veil over her head. A wreath of verbena and sweet marjoram was put on her head to keep the veil in place.

'I'm ready,' Volumnia said with a gentle toss of her head that set the wreath wobbling. 'Let's get this over with.'

Aemilia followed her daughter out of the cubiculum. 'You know Caecilius isn't here and that he's sent a letter of intent to marry you? I do think he could have made the effort to turn up in person. I know him sending a letter makes it legal, but really.'

'Don't fuss, Mother, it doesn't matter,' Volumnia said, her long stride causing her mother to take two steps for her one. 'I shall see him later.'

Aemilia thought she detected the first note of anxiety in her daughter's last words and guessed Volumnia was not looking forward to her wedding night. Should she have told her what to expect? Aemilia wondered as they entered the atrium where the wedding guests were already assembled. She shrugged the thought away. Volumnia probably knew what was expected of her and would have been scornful of accepting her mother's advice. After all, she had never asked for advice from her mother before.

Vibinius had returned from the temple where he had witnessed a priest perform the auspices to confirm it was a propitious day for his daughter to be married and was waiting in the atrium. He was very happy; this was a successful day for him, the joining of his family name with one of Rome's most illustrious patricians, and Aemilia saw that his cheeks and nose were already very red from the wine he was passing freely among the guests.

Volumnia barely granted their guests a smile and took herself off to stand by the altar. Eager to make up for her daughter's rudeness, Aemilia stepped forward to greet Menenius and his wife, Gabinia.

'Aemilia, how lovely you look,' Menenius said, taking her hand and covering it with his own.

Aemilia could almost believe him, but the memory of her mirror was still fresh in her mind and she knew the image had not lied. She smiled and thanked him for the compliment.

The squealing of a piglet diverted their attention. The ceremony was beginning. A hush fell over the guests as the priest laid the piglet down on the altar and slit its throat. Volumnia stepped back hastily to avoid the blood splattering her dress. Aemilia grimaced as the blood dripped off the table onto the stone floor, hoping the slaves would be able to stop it staining and cursing herself for not instructing them to strew the floor with straw. She felt Menenius's hand on the small of her back.

'A very special day this,' he murmured close to her ear.

'Yes,' she agreed. 'We're all very happy.'

'Indeed. Who knows what great Romans shall be born from the union of two such families.'

A shiver ran down Aemilia's spine at his words. Menenius had spoken the substance of her thoughts, but without the sense of foreboding the Sibyl's prophecy engendered in her. Was she seeing omens in everything these days? She supposed it was only natural for Menenius to speculate about the children Caecilius and Volumnia would have; that was the purpose of marriage, after all. Or had the gods put those words in his mouth, a reminder their ultimate purpose was still unknown?

Without the bridegroom present, the wedding ceremony came swiftly to an end and Aemilia's concerns were of no further matter. The deed was done, the seed sown, for Caecilius would have Volumnia in his bed, and if the gods desired it, she would conceive his child tonight.

Would that child, Aemilia wondered as she raised a cup of wine to her lips to toast the couple, be the enemy of Rome the Sibyl's scroll had prophesied?

Volumnia watched Caecilius as he closed the door of his cubiculum. *My cubiculum now,* she reminded herself, glancing around the room, noticing that it was not all that different to her own back at home. She smiled to herself. She would have to learn a whole new language now: her and her husband's cubiculum, her and her husband's home. It sounded strange in her head. How strange would it sound when she said those words aloud?

'Why are you smiling?' Caecilius asked, setting down the oil lamp on a table.

'I was just thinking how much my life has changed, and in only one day.'

'For the better, I hope you realise,' Caecilius said, sitting down on the bed and untying his sandals.

'Could you not have come yourself to marry me this morning? Would it have been so very tiresome?'

'I had to be elsewhere,' he said, standing and shrugging off his toga, letting the heavy woollen cloth pool at his feet. He pulled his tunic over his head.

'Where did you have to be?' she asked. 'Why?'

Caecilius moved towards her and began to untie her belt. 'Prince Titus wanted to see me. You wouldn't have me refuse the prince, would you?'

'Did he know it was your wedding day?'

'It wouldn't have mattered if he had known. Titus doesn't think a prince should have to wait on anyone's pleasure.' Knot untied, Caecilius tossed the belt aside.

'Will he do anything for you?'

'Such as?'

'Oh, I don't know. Contracts for new olive oil exports, reduced tariffs on grain imports?'

Caecilius stared at her, his brow furrowing. 'What goes on in that brain of yours that you talk of imports and exports and tariffs?'

'I am not my brother, Caecilius,' Volumnia snapped, her

heart starting to beat faster as he opened the clasps on her shoulder and her dress fell away from her body. 'I am not a woman who only concerns herself with spinning wool and keeping the slaves in line.'

'Yes, you said so before we married, but that was then. Your parents allowed you such liberties. But you're my wife now and I will not be so lenient. Wool spinning and keeping the slaves in line is your duty, Volumnia. You will not concern yourself with my business affairs.'

The rebuke stung, but she knew now was not the time to argue. 'Must we do this tonight?' she said with a sigh. 'I am very tired.'

'Get on the bed,' he said in answer.

Resignedly, Volumnia moved to the bed and slid her subligaculum over her hips to fall to the floor. She lay down on the bed and spread her legs in readiness. Caecilius climbed on top of her, his chest hair tickling her nipples. It felt strange having his weight upon her, his breath hot and moist on her neck. She held her breath as he pushed into her. It hurt, and she turned her head away from his, biting her bottom lip to stifle her cry. Caecilius was not gentle, but she had neither expected nor wanted him to be. She closed her eyes while he grunted and thrust until he gave a moan and held himself still. A moment later, he rolled off her, and she reached for the blanket and wiped herself. Caecilius laughed lazily.

'What's funny?' she asked sharply.

'I was just thinking of Menenius and how he envies me this.' He turned on his side to face her. 'He wants you, you know. I've seen it in his face.'

'And you don't mind?'

'Why should I mind? You belong to me.'

'But I might encourage him?'

Caecilius teased a strand of her hair away from her forehead. ‘Might you?’ he said, a smile playing upon his lips. ‘Yes, I suppose you might. But you would risk a great deal if you did. I would kill you, my dear, if you ever betrayed me.’

‘You would?’

‘Yes, I would.’

She held his gaze for a long moment, determining if he meant what he said. He did, she realised. ‘You will never have cause to mistrust me,’ she said and gestured at their bodies. ‘I don’t like this and will certainly not seek it out. In fact, I hope you won’t be bothering me too often in this way.’

Caecilius turned over onto his back and closed his eyes. ‘All I want from you are sons, Volumnia. Give me those and I will take my pleasure from our slaves.’

Satisfied, Volumnia pulled the sheet up to her chin. It had been a long day and she fell asleep soon after Caecilius began snoring in her ear.

4

Kaeso ran into the kitchen where Aemilia was keeping an eye on the new slave as he prepared the afternoon meal. Only the previous month the household had been laid low with food poisoning, the result, Aemilia had no doubt, of a kitchen slave who did not wash his hands after visiting the latrine, and she wasn't taking any chances. The slaves would keep themselves clean or they would be sold on.

'Mother,' Kaeso said, panting, 'Volumnia is here.'

Aemilia turned with an exclamation of annoyance. 'We're not expecting her today, are we?'

Kaeso shrugged and moved to the table. He dipped a finger into the garum sauce and brought it to his lips.

'Don't do that, dear,' Aemilia said absently. She cast another look at the slave. 'Remember what I've said,' she told him and took hold of Kaeso's hand. He allowed himself to be pulled along behind her to the triclinium where Volumnia waited. 'Volumnia,' Aemilia greeted her daughter with a forced delight. 'You didn't send word you would be calling today.'

'Do I need to?' Volumnia's voice was sharp and Aemilia saw her give a look of irritation at Kaeso.

'No, of course you don't,' Aemilia said. 'We enjoy seeing you, don't we, Kaeso?'

Kaeso nodded, and the vigorous movement caused a line of spittle to leak from the corner of his mouth. It dropped onto his chest and soiled his clothing.

'Ugh,' Volumnia cried. 'Must he do that?'

Aemilia snatched up the hem of her dress and wiped his mouth. 'He can't help it, as well you know.' A lump formed in her throat as Kaeso looked from her to Volumnia, not understanding how he had offended his sister. 'Kaeso, why don't you go and play with the dogs?'

Kaeso liked this idea and hurried clumsily away.

'I wish you would not be so unkind to your brother.'

'Oh, don't start,' Volumnia said, settling herself onto one of the couches. She pointed to a small cage hanging from the ceiling. In it, a sparrow sat on a crossbar. 'That's new, isn't it?'

'Yes, it had fallen out of its nest. Your father thought I would like to look after it.'

'Oh, really, isn't Kaeso pet enough?' Volumnia laughed at her own joke and looked around. 'Is Father not here?'

'No, he had business in the forum.' Aemilia sat down and frowned. 'Is something wrong, Volumnia?'

Volumnia started. 'Why do you ask that?'

'You seem a little... I don't know, fed up.'

'Oh...,' Volumnia shrugged, 'it's nothing.'

'Is it Caecilius?' Aemilia pressed. 'Is he not treating you well?'

'It's not Caecilius, Mother. For one thing, I hardly see him. He's always with the prince.'

'And you are well?' Aemilia nodded at Volumnia's belly. It bulged a little.

'Yes, I'm fine. Well, if you can call being fat fine.'

'There's nothing of you yet. And I rather liked being pregnant,' Aemilia said, smiling at the memory of her first pregnancy. Not, she thought with a glance at Volumnia, her second.

'You would,' Volumnia snorted. She looked sideways at her mother. 'I have it again, you know. That feeling you are displeased at my situation.'

'What do you mean, Volumnia?'

'You're not pleased I'm going to have a baby.'

'I've never said so.'

'You haven't had to say so, it's obvious. But it's strange. I thought you would be pleased.'

'I am pleased,' Aemilia protested feebly.

'You're nothing of the sort. Will you tell me why?'

Aemilia considered a moment, tugging on her earlobe painfully. 'There is something I've never told you, Volumnia,' she said at last. 'Something I've never told anyone.'

Volumnia sat up straight, intrigued. 'What?'

'Just before I married your father, a prophecy came into my hands, never mind how. My brother's tutor, Galerius, read it and told me he thought the prophecy was to do with the family, that is, your father's family.'

'How exciting.'

'It wasn't exciting. It was frightening. Galerius said I shouldn't marry your father because the prophecy said a child of the winged serpent would bring woe to Rome, the winged serpent being the Sidonius family emblem. But I was determined to marry. The prophecy didn't specify which generation of the family the child would be born to. I thought —

hoped — it meant another woman, not me.' She sighed. 'When I became pregnant with Kaeso, I was worried, but then he was born and it was obvious he would never hurt anyone. Then I had you.' She looked meaningfully at Volumnia.

'You think I am the child the prophecy meant?' Volumnia asked, her eyes wide and incredulous.

'No, you were a girl, you could harm no one. But,' Aemilia pointed at Volumnia's belly, 'the child in your womb might.'

Volumnia rubbed her hand over her swollen belly. Her expression hardened. 'That's ridiculous. I would never have a child that would harm Rome. And besides,' she said as a thought occurred, 'my child will be a Marcius, not a Sidonius.'

'But with Sidonius blood.'

Volumnia tutted. 'Do you still have this prophecy?'

'Yes, I still have it, but it is written in Greek, you would not be able to read it.'

'Where did it come from?'

'From the Sibyl at Cumae. She came to Rome to see King Lucius, so the rumours went. I saw her put three scrolls into one of the forum's braziers. I saved one of them from the flames.'

'Let me have the scroll. I will find someone to translate it properly.'

Aemilia shook her head. 'No, I don't think that's a good idea.'

'Mother!'

'No. I've told you more than I should. I sometimes think it would be better if the gods left us alone to get on with our lives. Volumnia, forget everything I've said, please.' She looked earnestly at Volumnia. 'You will, won't you?'

Volumnia's eyes narrowed at her mother. Then her

expression brightened, and she leant back on the couch with a protracted sigh. 'Yes, if you wish it,' she said. 'I expect it is all nonsense, anyway. Not worth thinking about.'

Does she really mean that? Aemilia wondered as Kaeso came lumbering in, carrying one of the dogs in his arms. Laughing, he tried to put it in his sister's lap. As Aemilia gently pulled Kaeso away from her scowling daughter, she thought it was so unlike Volumnia to capitulate so quickly to her wishes that she doubted if her daughter thought the prophecy nonsense at all.

She was being reckless, she knew. To leave Rome with only a slave for protection, a young woman of not yet seventeen, was reckless. But she had to find out more about the prophecy her mother had spoken of. If it truly was about her, then she had to know what was in store for her and her child.

Volumnia had prepared well. She had chosen the largest slave in their household to accompany her, ordered him to be silent about his mission, and told him to furnish himself with one of his master's swords and enough food to feed them both on the journey, there and back. She had waited until Caecilius was away from home, off on one of his month-long jaunts with Prince Titus. She knew he would have stopped her had he known what she intended, not out of any concern for her, but for the child she carried.

It was early, still dark, when Volumnia and the slave set out for Ostia, the coastal port that would provide her with a boat to sail to Cumae. She had dressed in her dullest clothing, an unattractive brown dress that would not show off her true patrician status. This dress she had covered with a cloak taken from one of her other slaves, a threadbare thing that smelt of grease and sweat and failed entirely to keep her warm.

It was thrilling to be embarking on an adventure. And adventure it was, for it was no small matter to travel to Cumae, where the Sibyl was to be found. It was dangerous enough for a woman to travel alone — a slave could not be considered company — but for a Roman woman to travel alone past enemy territory was potentially fatal.

Volumnia and the slave reached Ostia by the late afternoon, not having stopped at all on the way from Rome. She ordered the slave to find a boatman willing to take them along the coast and waited while a price was negotiated. When the slave reported back, Volumnia winced. The sum demanded was high and would reduce her allowance significantly, but it could not be helped. The price paid, half up front, the other half promised on the return, Volumnia climbed into the boat and settled herself beneath the wooden shelter at the stern. Very weary, she fell asleep to the soothing sound of the water.

Volumnia had never been on the sea before and she discovered she didn't care for it. It was not only the constant rise and fall of the boat that she disliked; it was also the company she was forced to keep. She kept to the stern, crouched down beneath the shelter, trying to ignore the lascivious looks and vulgar comments they made regarding her. Some of the comments she didn't understand, for the men were foreigners and didn't speak Latin, but she understood their gestures well enough. She was heartily glad when, almost two days later, the boatman pointed to the cliff face and said, 'Cumae.'

The boat moored at the jetty that projected out from the beach. There were a few hovels on the shore, their timbers turned grey by the salt breeze. Their occupants exhibited mild curiosity about the boat but did not leave their shelters.

Volumnia supposed they received so many visitors wanting to see the Sybil that one more was not of great interest, though no doubt they would have their hands out when she passed. Well, they could forget that. She had already made too much of a dent in her allowance.

'You have to climb,' the boatman told her when he saw her frowning at the cliff-side. He pointed to an almost vertical ladder attached with ropes to the side of the cliff.

'Up that?' she cried.

The boatman grinned. 'It's the only way up there.'

'Domina, are you certain you—?' the slave began.

Volumnia shushed him, knowing he had no concern for her safety but for his own. If she had an accident in his care, he would do better to run away than return to Rome; Caecilius would have him killed for his negligence. The thought of climbing the ladder was not pleasant, but she had not come all this way to be cowardly now. She reminded the boatman he was to wait for her, ordered the slave to stay by the boat, and made her way to the bottom of the ladder.

She grabbed the rungs and tugged. The ladder seemed secure enough. Volumnia put her right foot on the bottom rung and began to climb. She made the mistake, about twenty feet up, of looking down and giddiness struck her, making her tighten her grip on the struts so that her knuckles whitened and press her body towards the cliff. She waited until the dizziness passed, then telling herself not to be such a coward, lifted her foot to the next rung. She managed to reach the top and clambered onto the clifftop, aware that if the boatman and slave were watching, they would probably be laughing at her undignified crawl.

Volumnia got to her feet carefully, thanking the gods she was on firm ground again. She felt the earth slide beneath her sandals and realised she stood on shale. Small shards and pebbles crept over her soles and bit into the soft undersides of her feet as she began her descent. She could see where she needed to go. There was an opening cut into the cliff halfway down, triangular, edged with cut stones. She made for it, slipping every now and then, having to clutch at plants and tufts of grass to stop herself sliding further.

She reached the entrance to the cave and gave a startled cry as a creature loomed out at her from the cave's entrance. It was ragged thing, half naked, a pelt covering its lower region. The rest of its body — she could not truly describe it as a man — was covered in crusted mud, and the stench coming off it was foul. Volumnia covered her nose and mouth with her hand. The thing made a strangled noise. She shook her head, uncomprehending, provoking another sound and another.

'I don't understand,' she shouted at it.

The thing opened its mouth and Volumnia saw its tongue was missing. She looked around, hoping someone would appear to help her, but there was no one. The thing grabbed her wrist and she tried to pull away. It held on tight and opened its other hand to show the palm. Relieved to finally understand, she delved into the purse on her belt and put an aes into its hand. Its fingers closed over the bronze bar and released her. She rubbed the place where its fingers had been, the skin tender, red and dirtied.

The entrance clear, she hesitated for a moment, nerves stilling her feet. Then she set her shoulders and stepped inside.

Her heart was banging in her chest; she could feel it thudding up through her throat, making the blood rush in her ears. It had been warm and bright on the cliff, but here the air was cool and damp; it felt almost thick and weighed her down. She had thought only the entrance had been managed by man, but as she walked, she saw the passage too had been worked by human hands. Like the entrance, the passage was triangular, carved with axes and chisels, and faced with stones to give a smooth finish.

Her way forward was slow, each step deliberate, considered. Her nose wrinkled the further she went, for her nostrils were filled with a sickly sweet odour. It was dark too, for oil lamps burned only at irregular intervals. Her eyes gradually adjusted to the dark, and she spied the end of the passage, a widening out into darkness. The smell of smoke entered her nostrils, and it was almost as if she was being pulled forward. Her pace quickened, and she had a sudden uneasy feeling that her will was no longer her own.

She emerged into a large chamber. Its walls had been left as nature carved them, no hand of man had worked its talent here. Oil lamps, stuck up on high stone ledges, threw dark shadows. The smell of decay was strong and, looking around, she saw that the cave was filthy with debris. Upon the floor were dried leaves and twigs, scraps of cloth, and, she saw with alarm, bones. She looked harder, her mind trying to work out whether they were animal or human, but she had no knowledge or ability to distinguish between the two and forced her gaze away. She moved in further, taking care where she stepped. A large stone chair was set against the furthest side of the cave. Lichen, moss and tree roots grew on and around it so that it had almost become part of the cave itself.

And someone was sitting in it!

Volumnia cried out in surprise and sank to her knees, head bowed, feeling the floor litter dig into her flesh.

There came no response or answer, and Volumnia raised her head. The figure hadn't moved. It remained shrouded in darkness, only one weak oil lamp burning above it illuminated it at all. Confused, Volumnia scrambled to her feet and edged closer. She peered up and jumped backwards. It was a desiccated body that sat in the chair, skin so shrunken over the skull that it had torn in places to show the white bone beneath. And now she remembered what she had heard of the Sibyl, how the current prophetess always shared her cave with the carcass of her dead predecessor, the corpse being left to dry and shrivel. Only a dead body, she told herself. No doubt other visitors would be scared away by such a frightful sight, but not she.

Her breathing slowed. She stepped away from the chair and looked around again. There was another doorway to the side of the chair, and she headed for it. Here was a much smaller chamber, and the stench was even greater. It was not only the stench of decay, but that of a warm and unclean body. Volumnia instinctively knew she was not alone. A small fire burned in the centre, creating a ceiling of swirling smoke.

There was a rustle and cracking of twigs, and a figure lurched out of the darkness. She, for it was a she, stared at Volumnia, then moved to crouch beside the fire. Was this the Sibyl, Volumnia wondered, this woman with her matted hair, her face and body smeared with mud and who knew what else? The woman began muttering to herself in a language Volumnia could not understand.

'Are you the Sibyl?' Volumnia asked, and she heard the tremble in her voice.

The woman stopped her muttering and looked up, a long hard stare that chilled Volumnia to the bone. Then the woman laughed. It was light and high, almost musical. It seemed odd coming from such a foul creature. The Sibyl, for so she must be, spoke.

'So, she comes with fear in her heart,

But will she stay to learn of her part?
The prophecy made, will it grieve or please?
The future known, yet the way unseen.'

'I would know,' Volumnia began, but the woman's body jerked violently at the interruption and she fell silent.

'Volumnia, Aemilia's fair daughter,
Your future is set, surrounded by slaughter.
But not your hands that cause others to bleed,
Though your heart harbours that lust that all
soldiers need.'

'Do you mean Caecilius?' Volumnia asked excitedly. 'Will I make my husband kill?'

'A wife cannot such a man make,
For he has been fashioned for his ancestors'
sake.
Yet a mother has power to create what she
will,
And mould a son, her ambition to fulfil.'

Volumnia's hands clasped her belly. 'Yes, yes, I am pregnant. A son, you say?'

'But glory may not last, and misery may
ensue.
A price worth paying, will she think that too?
Act to change her fate, or walk the path so
spoken?
Her blood lust unchanging, though hearts be
broken?'

'Will he be glorious?' Volumnia breathed rapturously, her eyes closing as she conjured up an image of her son being applauded by all Rome.

> 'The she-wolf barks, but she must also bite.
> Room in her heart for one, put others out of
> sight.
> Babes will come and babes will go,
> None to rob son of adoration and foe.'

The Sibyl sank back on her haunches and stared at Volumnia.

'What does all that mean?' Volumnia pleaded, desperately trying to remember everything the Sibyl had said.

The Sibyl moved onto all fours, arched her back and hissed. Volumnia stumbled backwards, her body pressing against the damp cave wall as the woman shuffled around the fire, her back towards Volumnia. The audience was over.

Volumnia ran out of the chamber, through the next and down the long passageway, eager to breathe fresh air again. The sunlight dazzled her, and she fell as she burst out of the cave's entrance. Her heart was pounding again and her breath was coming fast. She hurried back up the cliff, eager to be away, to get on the boat and sail back to Rome. Her descent down the ladder was hasty and several times she slipped, but still she did not stop, not until her feet touched down onto the shore. Remembering she was now observed, she willed herself to calm down, and made as dignified a walk back to the jetty as she was able.

'Find out what you wanted?' the boatman asked as he wound a length of rope around his hand and elbow.

Volumnia could tell from his expression that he was expecting her to voice her fear, to admit she had made a mistake, that she was only a woman, not brave enough for such an encounter. But she was not going to let him have his enjoyment. She stepped over the gunwale and said, 'I did. Cast off at once. I want to get home.'

Denied his amusement, the boatman sulkily obeyed. Her slave offered Volumnia a cup of wine. She snatched it from his hand and drank eagerly, holding the cup out for a refill. As the wine streamed down her throat and warmed her chest, she began to relax. Her hand strayed over her belly. Inside her was a son, she told herself, a son who would be great if she made him so and make her proud. The journey to this dreadful place and the encounter with the Sibyl, terrifying though it had been, had certainly been worth it.

Seven months later

Volumnia clutched her pendant of the goddess Lucina and screamed. Ye gods, but she had not expected pain like this and she had been cursing ever since her labour pains had begun, cursing Caecilius for doing this to her, cursing the midwife who kept poking around her privates and muttering imprecations and instructions to do this and that, to push and to breathe, as if she was not already doing all she could to expel the babe from her body.

Remember what this child will mean for you, she kept telling herself every time a stab of pain ran through her. This babe would be the son the Sibyl had told her of, the son that would bring glory to the Marcius name.

'Breathe,' Aemilia called as she came into the room with a bowl of water.

'I am breathing,' Volumnia snarled, gripping the pommels of the birthing chair so hard her knuckles turned white.

'Will it be soon?' Aemilia asked the midwife.

The midwife nodded. 'Not long now, domina.'

'There, you hear that, Volumnia, it won't be long.'

Volumnia screamed. 'Please, make it stop.'

Aemilia grimaced at her daughter's pain, almost feeling it herself. She wiped Volumnia's dripping forehead with a cloth, drawing her hand back quickly as Volumnia wrenched her face away. Realising there was no comforting her daughter, she moved to the table where she had set down the bowl of water and busied herself with making all neat.

The midwife had spoken true: the baby came within the half hour, a half hour during which Volumnia screamed and howled and hit out at her attendants for their part in the tortuous affair. When the baby slithered into the world, the midwife tutted and Volumnia, seeing and hearing the tut, demanded to know why.

'He's small,' the midwife said.

Volumnia shook her head. How could her child be small when he had caused her so much pain? 'He can't be. Bring him to me.'

The midwife thrust the baby under Volumnia's nose, annoyed at being called a liar. Volumnia looked him over. The midwife had not lied. Her baby was a scrawny thing. But how could he be? How could this small creature be great? Looking at him, she wondered whether he would even survive the day.

'He hasn't cried,' Aemilia said to the midwife.

The midwife turned the baby upside down and slapped its buttocks. The child coughed and spluttered and then gave out a hearty wail.

Volumnia, to her surprise and to her mother's, burst into

tears. 'He cries loudly,' she declared through her tears. 'He will grow, won't he, Mother?'

Aemilia looked down at the child being cleaned with honey and salt. 'I am sure of it, daughter,' she said with a conviction she did not feel. She moved to the table and joined the midwife in staring at the afterbirth that had been slipped into a bowl. 'Will he live?' she asked quietly.

The midwife took a moment to consider, her thin finger poking at the slippery mass. 'He'll live,' she said with a nod. 'In fact, he'll grow big with the right upbringing, I reckon.'

'Lucina be praised,' Aemilia breathed, turning to look over her shoulder at Volumnia who had been helped to the bed by the slave and had collapsed against the pillow. Her eyes were closed. *She will be asleep in a moment*, Aemilia thought, turning back to see the midwife putting the baby into a straw basket.

The door opened and Caecilius appeared. He looked towards the bed, then at Aemilia. 'Is it over?'

'You have a son, Caecilius.'

Caecilius strode to the basket and looked in. 'What's that?' he said, pointing at the baby.

Aemilia looked into the basket too, worried by her son-in-law's sharp question. Caecilius was pointing at the baby's left thigh. There was a deep red mark on the skin. 'It's a birth-mark,' she said with a relieved laugh, pulling the blanket over the baby. 'That's all it is.'

'A birthmark?' Caecilius frowned. 'Not a deformity?'

Aemilia knew what he was referring to and snapped, 'Of course not. It is no more a deformity than a mole or a freckle.'

Caecilius appeared unconvinced. 'He seems small.'

'Oh Caecilius, you are determined to find fault with your

son. He is perfect. Now, please, leave. Let your wife sleep in peace.'

Caecilius looked across the room to Volumnia, who had indeed fallen asleep. 'When will she be able to conceive again?'

'You must let her recover, Caecilius,' Aemilia said testily. Was that all he could say? He hadn't even asked how Volumnia was.

'How long?' he persisted.

Aemilia plucked a figure from the air. 'Six months.'

'That's too long. If this child is not strong, he may die. I need another.'

'I have told you, the child is perfectly healthy. Volumnia needs time to recover. Babies that follow too soon after one another often die in the womb.' But she could tell Caecilius wasn't listening to her. His square chin was thrust out, his brow furrowed.

'She is not to suckle the child,' he said. 'To do so would prevent her conceiving, I know that. Can I entrust you with finding a suitable wet nurse for the child?'

'Volumnia wanted to feed him herself,' Aemilia said. 'She told me so.'

'Will you find a wet nurse?'

Caecilius's expression was fierce and Aemilia was not equal to it. 'I will,' she said with a feeble shrug and looked away to her daughter. What would Volumnia say when she told her?

Caecilius nodded, turned on his heel and left the room. The door banged after him.

Volumnia started awake. 'What was that?'

Aemilia hurried to the bedside. 'That was your husband.'

'Caecilius was here? Did he see him?' Her neck was

craning to look into the basket, but it was too far away and she sank back into the pillow.

'He looked for a moment.'

'Was he pleased? What did he say?'

'Nothing,' Aemilia forced a smile. 'Just that he was a little on the small side. And that he had a mark on his thigh.'

Volumnia started. 'I didn't notice a mark.'

'No, nor did I at first. But it is there.'

'Bring him to me, Mother. I want to see.'

Aemilia considered telling Volumnia that she should let her son sleep, but she had never before won an argument with her daughter and suspected she would not now. She moved to the basket and lifted the small bundle into her arms. The baby screwed up his red face and wriggled but did not wake. Aemilia passed him to Volumnia and watched as an expression Aemilia had never seen on her daughter's face appeared, one of tenderness, of love. Volumnia was smiling as she settled back against the pillow and cradled her son.

Volumnia parted the cloth over the baby's legs. The birthmark was plain to see, a streak of dark red, a cross-like blotch at one end. 'It looks like a sword,' Volumnia said, her breath catching. 'See, Mother?'

Aemilia looked. It did indeed look like a sword. 'Is that good, do you think?'

'Of course it is good. It is the mark of Mars.' The baby woke and started to cry. 'Why does he cry, Mother? Have I done something wrong?'

Aemilia smiled and shook her head. 'He's hungry.'

'Oh,' Volumnia said, and moved to pull down her dress from her shoulder.

'No, Volumnia, I pro—', Aemilia began, then broke off.

'What?' Volumnia glared up at her.

'Caecilius said you were not to breastfeed,' she said apologetically. 'He has asked me to find a wet nurse.'

Volumnia's expression darkened. 'I'm not having a stranger feed my son. He will have no milk but mine.'

'Caecilius was very insistent, my dear.'

Volumnia pulled down her dress and guided her nipple to her son's mouth. He sucked on it greedily. 'I am not frightened of Caecilius, even if you are, Mother. He will not come between me and my son. Hire your wet nurse if you feel you must obey him, but do not expect me to use her.'

'Then be discreet in your feeding, daughter, I beg you,' Aemilia said. 'Let Caecilius believe the wet nurse feeds him. It will be for the best. Although he will wonder if you do not conceive again soon.'

'Let him wonder. Do not worry yourself about me, Mother,' Volumnia said, keeping her eyes on her son. 'Caecilius is so rarely here, I doubt I will have to be discreet about anything.'

5

513 BC

Caecilius waved away the last of his clients and the slave showed them out of the tablinum. Straightening his tunic, Caecilius made his way to the yard, eager to see his son start his first lesson in arms training. Volumnia had been nagging him for months to hire an arms trainer for Caius, but Caecilius had put it off, worried the boy simply wasn't up to it. Caius was four years old and still small for his age. His legs were spindly, his back not at all straight. Caecilius found it difficult to believe Caius would be a great soldier one day, as Volumnia insisted he would be.

Caius was already in the yard when Caecilius arrived. That was something; the boy was keen, if nothing else. Caecilius stepped out into the sunlight, taking pleasure in the warmth upon his face after all morning spent indoors. He turned his head and his pleasure faded. 'Volumnia, what are you doing here?'

Volumnia looked up at him from her seat against the wall, shielding her eyes from the sun. 'Why shouldn't I be here?'

'It is too hot, and this can be too much noise and activity for someone in your condition.'

Volumnia smoothed her hand over her rounded belly. 'What nonsense you talk.'

'I won't have my unborn child put at risk. You have lost two babes since Caius was born. Your womb is obviously delicate.' He knew she hated for any part of her to be called so and used the word deliberately. 'And besides, you'll distract Caius, you always do. Go inside.'

He had used his harshest, no-nonsense tone and Volumnia, he saw with satisfaction, conceded defeat. She did huff, it was true, but said nothing, striding past him into the domus.

'Caius,' Caecilius called and pointed his son to the middle of the yard, 'stand there.'

Caius hurried to obey.

Caecilius took a sword from the arms master who stood nearby and held it before Caius. Caius stared at it reverently. 'What is this, Caius?'

'A gladius, Father,' Caius answered promptly.

'And what is it for?'

'Fighting.'

'No,' Caecilius said, and he saw his son's face darken, annoyed at himself for giving the wrong answer. 'It's for killing.' He began to circle his son. 'Fighting is something you play at, Caius. If you have a sword in your hand, you have to be ready to use it to take another man's life. Do you understand?'

Caius nodded.

Caecilius held out his hand, and the master swapped the gladius for a wooden sword. Caecilius held it up before Caius. 'This is a rudius. It is made of wood. You will practice with this until you are ready to use a real sword. I trust that will not be too long, Caius. You will work hard every day with this sword and you will excel. Do you understand?'

'Yes, Father.' Caius turned his head towards the domus. 'Will Mother watch me train?'

Caecilius followed his son's gaze. He saw Volumnia's face peering out of a small window, her eyes fixed on them. He pursed his lips in annoyance. 'Your mother has no place in your training. You will attend only to me and to Rufius.' Caecilius pointed at the arms master. 'Do you understand?' Caecilius waited for his son's reply. It seemed to take a great effort for Caius to draw himself away from his mother's gaze.

'Yes, Father,' Caius said eventually, looking up at Caecilius with big dark eyes.

Caecilius grunted, not entirely satisfied. 'Then let us begin.'

FOUR MONTHS LATER

Volumnia had been staring at the ceiling for the last hour, listening to the rain beating against the leather flap that covered the cubiculum window. Caecilius, lying beside her, had been snoring for most of that time.

Her back aching, she turned over onto her side. It occurred to her she hadn't been able to lie on her side for months without discomfort. Not now. Now, her belly was empty and soft, and she could not help but think what a waste her latest pregnancy had been. Nine months of bodily inconvenience, all those aches and pains, and then the cruel punishment of childbirth to have... what, at the end of it all? A child she was ashamed to own as hers.

And she was to blame for the child being the way it was,

Caecilius had made that very clear. When he had returned home a few hours after the birth, he had looked into the baby's woven basket and jerked away, disgusted by the sight that met his eyes.

'It looks like your brother,' he said accusingly, for the baby had a harelip, just like Kaeso.

Volumnia had cursed her blood. Her blood was responsible for the hideous deformity in her son, just as her mother's blood had been responsible for Kaeso. She thanked the gods Caius had been perfect. His face was beautiful, without blemish or deformity, and he had the promise of being handsome when a man. True, Caius had been small when he was born, but he was making up for that now. Just a few months of arms training had wrought such a change in her son.

It was no good, Volumnia decided, she couldn't sleep and Caecilius's snores were getting on her nerves. She got out of bed, taking care not to disturb Caecilius, and padded softly out of the cubiculum.

The stone floor was deliciously cold beneath her feet as she made her way to where Caius and the baby slept. She opened the door, wincing as it creaked, and peered in. The slave that slept there was asleep, curled up on the floor in the corner of the room like a dog. Volumnia moved to Caius's bed first, smiling at him frowning in his sleep, before moving to the basket. The baby was asleep too, a wheezing sound coming from the nose. It really was an ugly little thing. She felt no love for the baby, only revulsion. Having not engaged a wet nurse, out of a determination to defy Caecilius, she had been forced to feed it herself. She had hated having it at her breast. It had struggled to suck and when it finally did, had dribbled all over itself and her, white milk and spittle running down her breasts and belly. The midwife had warned her it would need special care if she were to keep it.

Volumnia had no desire to take care of a deformed child. It would be a kindness to get rid of it, she decided; if it lived, it would only suffer the ridicule of others. She had seen it with Kaeso, how her friends had pointed and laughed, until Aemilia had kept him out of the way so their taunts would not upset him. And she had no intention of having to look after a child well into his adulthood as her mother was having to do with her brother. Volumnia took one last look at the baby and nodded to herself, decision made. She returned to her cubiculum and climbed into bed.

'What have you been doing?' Caecilius mumbled sleepily.

'Looking at the baby.'

'What for?'

'To be sure.'

'Of what?'

'That we should expose it.'

Caecilius turned over to look at her. 'You think so?'

'You don't want it, do you?' she snapped.

'No,' he admitted, 'it's not a child I can be proud of.'

'I feel the same,' she said, tucking the sheet around her. 'It is best if it is got rid of.'

Caecilius yawned. 'I'll tell one of the slaves to do it in the morning then.'

'No, I'll see to it. It would be just like one of them to take pity on it and hand it over to a peasant to raise, and I'm not having that.'

'As you please.'

Volumnia was glad Caecilius had agreed so easily; she had half expected an argument. If he was in such an obliging mood, she would venture to voice the thought she had had in her mind ever since the baby had been born and she had seen its deformity. 'Caecilius, I think we should see this as an omen. I have lost two babies, and this one is deformed. Who knows what kind of monster would come next? I feel the gods do not mean us to have another perfect child.'

'You mean—'

'I think it best if we do not try to have any more children.'

Caecilius considered her for a long moment, his expression showing plainly he understood what Volumnia meant. 'Very well. I suppose we have Caius and he is growing strong, far more so than he promised when born. He will have to do.'

'Oh Caecilius, Caius more than does,' Volumnia rebuked him heatedly. 'He is the best of boys. You'll see how strong he will be.'

'So you keep saying.' He turned his back to her, and Volumnia soon heard him snoring.

That had been easy enough, Volumnia thought happily. To be rid of the baby she had never wanted and an assurance from her husband that he would trouble her no more in the marital bed. Excellent. From now on, she would be able to devote herself entirely to Caius.

The rain of the previous night had made the ground wet but had succeeded in dampening down the dust. It was cooler too, a welcome relief from the muggy days of the past few weeks. The baby had been crying loudly and awoken Volumnia as the sun was rising. The noise aggravating her sorely, she rose and dressed, determined to have the child out of the domus. Not stopping to eat, she pulled her shawl up over her head and nodded to Trupo, the slave who was to accompany her on the journey, to fetch the baby.

He brought it from the nursery in its woven basket. It was

still crying, for though the nursery slave had attempted to feed it with goat's milk while Volumnia was dressing, she had had little success and the baby was hungry. Volumnia told her it didn't matter that the child was hungry as it would be dead soon enough.

The child continued to cry all the way out of Rome, making Volumnia's head ache and shortening her temper. After almost an hour, she and Trupo reached a spot she thought would do, and they moved off the road, into the country where grass, flowers and tall weeds grew.

'Set it down,' Volumnia instructed, and Trupo put the basket at her feet. She bent and peeled back the linen cloth that covered the baby. As she did so, an earthy smell filled her nostrils; the baby had soiled itself. She made a noise of disgust and altered her intention. She had thought to lift the child out, but had nothing to wipe her hands on. So, she tipped the basket on its side and gave a shove; the child rolled out onto the earth. Crying with gulping breaths now, the child kicked its filthy legs as it tried to right itself.

Volumnia stood and pointed Trupo to the basket. He picked it up, tucking the dirty linen inside. He looked down at the writhing baby.

'Stop that,' Volumnia said as she saw his chin begin to wobble and Trupo turned aside. She took one last look at her child. There was no denying this was difficult. A woman could not abandon her child without feeling some remorse, but it really was for the best. The child would suffer for its deformity. She and Caecilius would suffer. And more importantly, Caius would suffer. If she kept the child, it would need all her attention. What part of her then would be left for Caius? No, it was better this way.

She turned back towards the road and heard Trupo following. Her steps were hurried; she felt grit and stones bite into her soles, but didn't slow her pace. She wanted to get home and barked at Trupo to hurry up, for he was dragging his feet. He was probably hoping she would change her mind.

A foolish hope. Already, her thoughts had turned to Caius. He was probably waking up this very moment and the nursery slave would soon be giving him his breakfast. If she hurried, she might be in time to join him.

As she and Trupo began walking back towards the city, Volumnia heard a low growl. She half-turned her head and thought she saw the swish of a grey tail through the weeds out of the corner of her eye. A moment later, her child's cry was abruptly cut off.

Volumnia arrived back at the domus too late to breakfast with Caius; the bread and oil were already being cleared away. The clatter of the dishes was loud and her head was pounding, so she ordered the slave to leave the dishes where they were, handed the girl her shawl and told her to fetch a bowl of water so she could wash her hands. She sat down at the table.

Caecilius entered and stood staring at her, his hands on his hips. 'Is it done?'

'It's done,' she said. She rubbed her temples.

'Are you… well?'

His question annoyed her, for such solicitude was not in his nature, and she had no need of his concern now. 'I have a headache. The long walk, I expect.'

'You haven't eaten either.'

'I'm not hungry.' The slave entered at that moment with the bowl of water and Volumnia submerged her dusty hands into it. It felt good to wash the dirt off and she pressed her wet fingers to her eyes, leaving them there for a long moment. 'Where's Caius?'

'Where he should be, at his training. And where you should not,' Caecilius called as Volumnia rose from the table and headed for the yard.

Black spots danced before her eyes as she emerged into the yard. She raised her hand to her forehead to shield her eyes against the sun and waited for the spots to disappear.

Caius was in the middle of the yard with Rufius, his arm outstretched as he tried to jab the point of his wooden sword into Rufius's stomach. He had not yet seen her, and Volumnia took the opportunity to study her son. Caius was coming along well. He was still small, but his spindly legs were gaining muscle and his chest no longer had a puny aspect. It was a joy to know Caius enjoyed his training. He would train all day if he could, but Caecilius had given orders to Rufius that Caius was not to be allowed to over-exert himself, worried that to do so would cause damage to his developing body.

Caius suddenly caught sight of Volumnia. His face broke into a grin, and he ran over to her. He playfully pushed the tip of the sword into the sagging flesh of her belly. 'The baby wasn't in my room this morning,' he said.

'The baby's gone, Caius. It won't disturb you again.' Volumnia moved to the table by the wall where a jug of wine and cups were set out. She poured herself a cup and downed all the liquid, sinking onto the stool in the shade.

Caius followed her. 'Where's it gone?' he asked, swinging the sword.

'I took it into the country and left it there. To die,' she added when she saw him frown.

'How will it die?'

Volumnia thought of the wolf she was sure she had seen and the cut-off cry of her child. 'A wolf will kill it.'

'Did you take it there because of what was wrong with it?' He pointed to his upper lip.

'Yes.'

Caius frowned. 'Uncle Kaeso has the same thing, doesn't he?'

'Yes, he does.'

'So, why isn't Uncle Kaeso dead too?'

'Because your grandmother wasn't brave enough to get rid of him.'

'But you were brave enough,' Caius grinned.

'Yes,' she smiled back, flattered Caius thought her brave, 'I was.' She had been brave. Not every woman could do what she had done. She had hardened her heart and done what was necessary for the wellbeing of her family. What was that if not bravery? 'You see, if I had kept the baby, Caius, it would have taken a great deal of care. I would have had no time for you.'

'Then I'm glad it's gone,' Caius burst out, thrusting the sword tip against the wall and twisting it. Stone dust trickled to the ground. 'I like it best when it's just you and me.'

'And your father?' Volumnia asked with a smile.

Caius pushed the sword into the stone further. His bottom lip jutted out. 'No. Just you and me.'

PART II

510 BC - 509 BC

6

'I don't know how you manage to run through so many slaves,' Aemilia complained as she and Volumnia fought their way through the streets to the forum. 'I only have to buy a new one once a year.'

'That's because you're happy to do most of the housework yourself. I don't have time for all that. I have other matters to deal with.' Volumnia pressed her hands to the flank of a donkey and pushed to get it to move. The donkey expressed its displeasure loudly and refused to budge. Volumnia tutted and moved around it.

'What other matters?' Aemilia scoffed, following after her.

'Attending to Caius, of course. He takes up all my time.'

Aemilia stepped over a pile of dung. 'I really don't think you should make him your only concern, Volumnia. You should think of your husband too.'

'Caecilius doesn't need me to think of him, Mother.'

'So you say, but have you considered that it is your lack of attention that makes him spend so much time with the prince?'

'Caecilius has always spent time with the prince because he likes him. It has nothing to do with me. Besides, he says the friendship is good for the family.'

'I'm sure that's true, but I still think you should not give Caius all your love and leave none for your husband.'

Volumnia gritted her teeth. She so wanted to tell her mother what she knew about Caius, about the future glory the Sibyl had prophesied. But Aemilia had spent years worrying about the Sibyl's scroll and Volumnia would never hear the end of it if she told her mother how she had travelled to Cumae alone while pregnant to visit the Sibyl herself. She would forever be reminded of the danger she had put herself in, with Aemilia rolling her eyes and covering her open mouth, and what the Sibyl had said would be received with horror too. Volumnia could just imagine the scene, and it was one she could well do without.

'Caius needs me,' was all she said in a tone that put an end to their conversation.

They reached the forum and pushed their way through to where the slaves were sold. *Mother is right about one thing*, Volumnia thought, *I do seem to run through slaves quickly*. Some she sold on because she found them lazy or insolent, but the slave she had come to market to replace had died of an infected foot, the appendage having turned green and giving off a vile smell.

Volumnia had made a mental list of the qualities she wanted in a slave this time: it was to be young, female, docile and with good teeth. But such slaves were very expensive, and she hoped she would be able to haggle a reasonable price with the slave trader if she found a slave that matched her specifications.

The slaves were being paraded on the wooden platform. Most of them were male, Volumnia saw with dismay, and her hopes sank. She told the slave trader, holding her hand over her mouth and nose because he stank of garlic and onions, about the type of slave she was after, and he disappeared into a leather-covered cart at the back of the platform. A moment later, he reappeared, pulling a young girl behind him.

'This is what you want, lady,' he declared, pushing the girl forward. He lifted her dirty tunic to show off her muscular thighs and Volumnia nodded satisfaction, then asked to see her teeth. The trader stuck his fingers in the girl's mouth and pushed her jaws open.

'Well, what d'you think?' the slave trader asked when Volumnia had thoroughly examined the girl.

Volumnia was about to reply when there was a sudden hubbub in the forum, a shouting and calling, a shifting of bodies and craning necks. Aemilia, being the taller, stood on tiptoe to get a better view.

'What is going on?' Volumnia asked crossly.

Aemilia shook her head. 'I'm not sure. There's a body being carried on a bier, but I don't think it's a funeral, the body isn't shrouded. It's a woman, though, I can see. Her dress is stained. I think it's blood.'

The purchase of the slave forgotten for the moment, and annoyed at receiving this information second-hand, Volumnia forced her way through the crowd in the direction everyone was staring. The slave trader began protesting at Aemilia about having his time wasted, but she waved him away and followed after her daughter.

A heavily laden cart prevented the women from moving any further. Undeterred, Volumnia climbed onto it and pulled Aemilia up behind her. They had a good view from this position, far better than if they had stayed on the ground. Volumnia narrowed her eyes to see better. Her mother had been right; it wasn't a funeral, despite the body. The body had been borne into the forum by slaves but there were two men by the bier, patricians judging by their clothing, and one of them pointed for the slaves to lay the body on the ground before the rostra.

Volumnia frowned. 'Isn't that Collatinus?'

'Is it?' Aemilia asked eagerly, recognising the name. 'Who's that with him?'

'I think it's Lucius Iunius Brutus, the king's nephew. Caecilius says he's the idiot of the Tarquin family. The princes are always playing jokes on him.'

'Poor man,' Aemilia tutted.

'Oh, listen to you,' Volumnia said scornfully. 'If the man is an idiot, then he won't feel any hurt, will he?'

But Aemilia wasn't listening. 'Oh, Volumnia,' she gasped, putting her hand to her mouth. 'I think that's Lucretia.'

'Who?'

'You know her. Lucretia, Collatinus's wife. You met her at Menenius Agrippa's a few months ago when he had that party.'

'Oh, yes, I remember her. She told me she rises at four every morning to do her spinning and asked if I wanted to join her. As if I would want to do that.'

'Oh, hush, Volumnia. I wonder what happened to her? Perhaps she was attacked. Some villains trying to rob her, I expect.'

They fell silent as Brutus patted the air, asking for silence. The crowd obeyed and Brutus, in a voice cracked with emotion, began to speak. He told a terrible story, of how his friend's wife, Lucretia, had been violated by Prince Sextus, the youngest of the king's sons, and how, unable to bear the shame, she had killed herself before his and her husband's very eyes. Women in the crowd began to cry and men murmured grimly.

Volumnia shook her head. 'The stupid bitch.'

'Volumnia!' Aemilia cried.

'Well, she was. It wasn't her fault she was raped, was it? Why kill yourself for something someone else has done?'

'She was ashamed.'

'The shame was the prince's. What Lucretia should have done is told her husband to revenge her by killing him. Not that Collatinus could get away with killing the prince, of course, the king would see to that. But that's what I would have told him if he had been my husband. Collatinus would have kept his honour that way.'

'Oh, do be quiet,' Aemilia snapped. 'I can't hear what Brutus is saying.'

Brutus, for all his reputed idiocy, commanded the attention of the entire forum. The story of Lucretia's rape was only the prelude to his main point, which was that Rome had no need to endure the rule of the Tarquins any longer. Rome, he said, did not need a king, especially a king such as Lucius Tarquinius, who ground his own subjects under his heel, bled them dry of their hard-earned money and then took advantage of their sons and daughters, husbands and wives. Brutus was calling for nothing less than a revolution, and Aemilia and Volumnia listened open-mouthed. Was this really happening? their eyes asked silently as they looked at one another.

The mood of the crowd quickly changed from grief to anger. Brutus had moved the crowd to his purpose; there were shouts of agreement, cries of outrage, and both Aemilia and Volumnia suddenly felt exposed and very vulnerable on the cart.

'We must get away from here,' Aemilia whispered in her daughter's ear and clambered down from the cart.

Volumnia climbed down too. The crowd was all bustle,

but somehow, they reached the edge of the forum and hurried into the almost deserted Via Sacra.

'We cannot really be in any danger, can we, Mother?' Volumnia asked, hurrying to keep up with Aemilia. 'We are not Tarquins.'

'You don't know the mob,' Aemilia said grimly. 'We are patricians and that will be a good enough reason for them to attack us. Hurry, Volumnia. We'll go to your domus, it's nearer.'

They reached the Marcius domus and Aemilia banged on the door. The slave waiting behind it opened it at once.

'Put the bar down,' Aemilia instructed him as soon as they were inside, and he slid the heavy wooden bar into place. 'Make sure all the doors are barred.' The man looked to Volumnia for permission, received it in a curt nod, and scurried off to obey.

'What's the matter, Mother?' a high-pitched voice asked. Caius had come into the atrium and was looking at his mother and grandmother with shrewd, dark eyes.

Volumnia went to Caius and took him into her arms. 'There is trouble in the forum, Caius. Your grandmother and I had to rush home.'

Caius pulled away and looked at her severely. 'Did someone threaten you?'

'No, my love,' she assured him, tucking his hair behind his ears.

'But they might have done,' Aemilia said, sinking onto a stool and fanning herself. It had been quite a dash from the forum, and she was hot and sweaty. 'It makes you wish Caecilius was not away from home so much, doesn't it, Volumnia? After all, if he were here, he would be able to defend us. As it is...'. She let the sentence hang, her meaning was clear.

'Father is away at war, Grandmother. Besides, you don't need Father,' Caius told her with conviction. He looked up at Volumnia. 'I'll protect you.'

He meant it too; Volumnia saw the determination in the young, black eyes. His jaw was set, his fists clenched, and she had no doubt he would have rushed out into the streets with his wooden sword and attack anyone who dared to touch his mother. Impulsively, she kissed him. 'I know you will, Caius, but I'm sure we are safe in here.' She glanced at Aemilia, who was still looking worried. 'We mustn't fret, Mother. This whole silly affair will blow over, you'll see. The king will hear what Brutus said and will have him executed for daring to speak so, and then everything will carry on as before. Now, Caius, my love, let us show your grandmother how clever you've become with your sword.'

I must be getting old, Caecilius thought ruefully as he looked out across the camp and cursed the Rutuli for this latest war. He seemed to like being on campaign less and less these days. Time was when he would have given anything to leave Rome to fight in a battle. Now, he woke up each morning missing his domus, the delicious food and fine wine, the slaves who knew his likes and dislikes without having to be told and, to his surprise, he found he was missing Volumnia and Caius. Yes, he was definitely getting old.

He walked up and down the lines of ranked men, feigning interest in the state of their weapons and armour and trying to ignore their discontent. Time was when the men kept their complaints between themselves, the officers only hearing of them third hand, but lately, the men had become bold and made their complaints directly to him. The complaints were always the same: they were tired of soldiering, tired of being away from their homes, tired of seeing their farms run into the ground because they were not there to see them managed properly. The men had Caecilius's sympathy. He had seen his own estate and farm diminish because of these seemingly endless campaigns of the king. King Lucius always seemed to be at war with someone and Caecilius was beginning to wonder if there wasn't a better way for Rome to be. He finished his inspection quickly and headed for his tent.

His friend Pamphilus caught up with him. 'All done?'

'For today,' Caecilius said, screwing up his face as smoke from the campfires got into his eyes and stung them. He rubbed his knuckles into the sockets. 'Any idea how much longer we'll be here?'

'None at all,' Pamphilus shook his head. 'Bloody waste of time, don't you think?'

Caecilius shushed him. 'Not before the men.'

'Oh, nonsense, Cae. They're all saying the same thing.'

'And if your words get back to the king?' Caecilius raised his eyebrows at Pamphilus. 'Do you want to explain to King Lucius why you are discontented?'

'Oh, very well,' Pamphilus said sulkily, fully aware of how ruthless King Lucius could be to those who displeased him. He glanced over Caecilius's shoulder and frowned. 'What's this now?'

Caecilius turned and saw one of the men he had dispatched the day before to Rome with letters for the Senate ride into the camp, his horse sweating and straining. The man looked agitated. Caecilius and Pamphilus hurried over to him.

'What news?' Caecilius asked peremptorily.

The man dismounted and saluted Caecilius. 'There is trouble at Rome, sir,' he said, struggling to catch his breath.

'What trouble?' Caecilius demanded.

'Lucius Iunius Brutus has addressed the people from the rostra. He brought the body of Collatinus's wife into the forum and laid it out for everyone to see. He said she had killed herself because she had been raped by Prince Sextus and couldn't bear the shame.' The man dropped his gaze. 'That's what he said, sir.'

Caecilius met Pamphilus's eye. They both knew Prince Sextus had often taken women without their consent, but he had mostly confined himself to low-born women and so no one had minded. But if he had raped the wife of Collatinus, a patrician, then that was a different matter.

'What else did Brutus say?' Caecilius asked.

The man looked uncomfortable as he replied. 'He said the king should be deposed, sir. He was trying to rouse the people.'

'By all the gods in Hades,' Pamphilus breathed. 'The nerve of the man.'

'Sir, I must tell the king what has happened,' the man said, pointing at Lucius's tent.

'I'll come with you,' Pamphilus said, taking a step towards the tent. He halted. 'Cae, are you coming?'

'Not just yet,' Caecilius said quickly. He gestured at his men, who had gathered to listen to the soldier's news. 'I will settle the men first. Stop any rumours from spreading.'

Pamphilus nodded, and he and the soldier hurried away. Caecilius addressed the men, told them there was nothing to worry about and to get about their business. Many of them gave him mutinous looks, but they turned away and returned to their duties. He watched them go, his brain working.

Caecilius didn't know Brutus well, but he had always suspected Brutus was not quite the idiot he played. He had seen the shrewd, calculating look in Brutus's eyes when Titus had used him as the butt of their jokes, had seen the resentment swallowed down. Titus had also admitted to him one night when he had had too much to drink that the king had ordered the killing of Brutus's brother many years earlier, and in Caecilius's opinion, that was not the sort of thing that could be forgotten or forgiven. He knew he would never do so. If he were Brutus, he would have sought out every opportunity to avenge himself on the king.

And now, it seemed Brutus had seized his chance. But was the rape of a patrician's wife by the youngest son of the king enough to make the people rise up? Caecilius thought it might be. He felt sure the people were ready to rise up at the slightest provocation if the grumbling of his men was anything to go by. Lucius was not loved. He was feared. Worse, he was hated, he and all his family. If King Lucius really was in danger, where did that leave Caecilius Marcius, a loyal supporter of the king and close friend of Prince Titus?

Knowing he should present himself to the king, that any delay on his part would look like disloyalty, Caecilius made his way to Lucius's tent. He heard raised voices before he had even given the password to the guards and been allowed to enter.

The soldier was standing before the king. He looked terrified, and Caecilius could not blame him. Lucius was not against killing him for being merely the bearer of such ill news. Caecilius saw Lolly, the king's wife, who was sitting in a chair at the side of the tent, narrow her eyes as he entered. He knew Lolly didn't like him. The feeling was mutual.

'I need more information,' Lucius said, starting to pace up and down the tent and forcing Pamphilus to step hurriedly out of his way. 'How serious is this? Is it just that idiot Brutus making a nuisance of himself or what?'

'I don't know, my king,' the soldier said, ducking his

head, bracing himself for the blow he thought would follow. He looked up, surprised, when it didn't come.

Caecilius stepped forward, determined to grab this opportunity. 'I can find out, my king. I'll go to Rome and make enquiries.'

'Why you?' Lolly asked sharply.

'Why not me, lady?' Caecilius asked as innocently as he could. 'Am I not as good as any that might be sent?' He returned his gaze to Lucius. 'Of course, my king, if you would rather I stayed here, then here I will stay. But I feel I could do you good service in Rome.'

Lucius stared at him for a long moment, gnawing on his bottom lip. He looked across to Lolly and shrugged. 'I see no reason why Caecilius should not go.'

Lolly gave Caecilius a long, examining look, then shrugged agreement.

'Caecilius,' Lucius said, 'you go to Rome and you find out what exactly is happening. Discover what that fool Brutus is up to. Come back as soon as you know, is that clear? I won't have you lingering in Rome while we kick our heels here.'

'Of course, my king,' Caecilius bowed his head. 'I shall leave at once.'

He turned, catching sight of Lolly's scowling expression as he strode out of the tent.

7

The leather tent flap snapped open and Lolly stormed in. ‘Really, the manners of your men are deplorable.’

‘They’re soldiers, my dear,’ Lucius said, not looking up from his stool at the tent’s small table. ‘What do you expect?’

‘I expect them to show respect for their queen.’ Lolly looked over his shoulder at the letter he was reading. ‘News?’

Lucius grimaced. ‘It’s confirmed. The gates of Rome have been barred, and no one is allowed in or out without a permit from the Senate.’

‘Did Caecilius send that?’

‘No. It came from a merchant who got out just before the gates were closed. He was told he would not be allowed to re-enter without permission. He asked who he should apply to for permission and, listen to this, Lolly, he was told only Lucius Iunius Brutus could give permission.’ Lucius screwed up the papyrus and threw it across the tent. ‘Curse that man. To think he has turned Rome against me.’

‘I told you to be careful of the Brutus family,’ Lolly said, bending to pick up the papyrus and smoothing it out. ‘You did have the brother killed, after all.’

'But Brutus knew nothing of that.'

'I wouldn't be so sure. There was always a look about him I didn't like. Sly, I thought. There was more going on in that woolly head of his than we thought.'

'He's an idiot.'

'Not such an idiot if he has been able to convince others to rise against us.' Lolly read a few lines of the letter, then tutted. 'So, Caecilius has neither returned nor written, despite your orders.'

'He may not have found anything out yet,' Lucius said. 'This merchant came away from Rome two days ago. Caecilius may have been too late to get in the gates. He may have nothing to report.'

'Why are you defending that man? If he has nothing, then he should have reported so. If he could not get into Rome, why has he not come back? I tell you, Lucius, he is up to something.'

'He is one of Titus's closest friends,' Lucius protested, but there was a note of doubt in his voice. 'Titus trusts him implicitly.'

'That is because our dear Titus has a trusting nature. He cannot see when his goodness is being abused. You mark my words, we will not see Caecilius again. He will have seized his chance and sided with Brutus. I've said to Titus before that Caecilius had ingratiated himself for his own ends.'

Lucius frowned. 'No, you are wrong, my love. I'm sure Caecilius Marcius is working for us.'

'Doing what, may I ask? If he did get into Rome, is he rallying our supporters? Is he rousing his clients to fight for you?'

'Yes, I expect so.'

'Oh, you're a fool, Lucius,' Lolly said, slapping him hard on the shoulder. 'You never used to be so trusting. It's your age, I expect. Mark my words, Caecilius is rather too clever to support you without working out whether it is the best thing for him. He is biding his time, seeing what will happen.' She slumped down onto the bed and groaned. 'We are going to have to fight for Rome. I can feel it.'

'If we must,' Lucius nodded sadly.

'Must! Don't you want to?' Lolly cried. 'For the love of Jove, Lucius, we have been refused admission to the city our family helped create and our sons have been threatened with disinheritance. The throne belongs to our eldest son when you die, not this rabble who think they can take it from us on a whim just because some stupid girl kills herself.'

Lucius turned to her, his jaw tightening in irritation. 'Lolly, have you had your eyes open when you've walked outside this tent? Have you seen how few men I have? Half of my army has deserted and the other half are thinking of doing so.'

'I'm glad they've gone if they are so cowardly,' Lolly declared. 'We don't need them.'

'Do we not? How are we to fight without them?'

'We have friends, Lucius. Not in Rome, perhaps, but elsewhere. The Tarquinii, for instance. They will aid us.'

'Why should the Tarquinii come to our aid?'

Lolly shook her head. 'Really, Lucius, where would you be without me? I love you desperately, but you are so simple sometimes. The Tarquinii will help us because they know what they get with the Tarquins. What kind of trade will the rabble do with them, do you think? What of our treaties with them? Will they all be suddenly rendered worthless? You mark my words, Lucius, the Tarquinii would much rather we ruled in Rome than the mob.'

'You're right,' Lucius nodded, cheered by her words. 'We will go to the Tarquinii and tell them they must help us.'

'We will ask for their help,' Lolly corrected. 'I know it goes against your nature, my love, but you will need to be a little humble. And then, hopefully, if the gods allow, we can live in a civilised manner, in a proper domus once more rather than in this filthy, stinking camp. I swear if I have to squat in a field once more to relieve myself, I am going to kill someone.'

'I'm surprised the king and queen let you leave the camp,' Menenius said as he handed Caecilius a cup of wine.

Menenius had been fast asleep when Caecilius banged on his domus door. His wife had used her foot to push him out of bed and see what all the noise was about, and Menenius had been ready to shout abuse at whoever had disturbed him. That thought had departed as soon as the slave opened the door and Caecilius stepped inside.

'The queen didn't want to,' Caecilius said, downing the wine in one gulp and holding the cup out to be refilled. 'You should have seen the look she gave me.'

Menenius took the jug off his slave and told him he could go. He poured more wine for Caecilius. 'Aye, she's a suspicious one.'

'They've closed the city gates, you know. I arrived just in time. I would have had to return to the camp if I hadn't been able to get in.'

'And if you had, the king wouldn't have liked to hear you had no news,' Menenius chuckled. 'Probably have you executed.'

'That's not funny, Menenius.'

'It's just a joke.'

'I'm not in a joking mood. By Hades, can't you see the

position I'm in? That we're all in? If Brutus has his way, the monarchy is dead.'

'I do see that, Cae.'

'So, where does that leave us?' Caecilius cried, slumping onto the couch.

'I don't understand you. Who are 'us'?'

'Those who are known to be friends with the Tarquins. What if Brutus takes it into his head to lump me and all the patrician families like mine in with the Tarquins and banish us all?'

'He won't do that,' Menenius said.

'You don't know he won't.'

'No,' Menenius admitted, 'but there aren't all that many patricians who are close friends of the Tarquins.'

'Only fools like me. That's what you mean, isn't it?'

'You're determined to find fault with me, Cae,' Menenius said stiffly, growing annoyed with his friend. 'You know you deliberately allied yourself with Prince Titus because you thought it would be advantageous. It's not my fault that doesn't seem such a wise choice now, so don't rail at me.'

Caecilius stared into his cup, chastened. 'So, what do I do now?'

'I'm surprised you've even got to think twice about this, Cae. You don't agree with Brutus, you don't want to get rid of the Tarquins, so why didn't you stay in the camp with the king?'

'Because it would have meant that I had chosen a side. But I'm tired of war, Menenius, and that is all the king seems to want to do. He's not as good at it as he used to be, it's costing more and more, and the army has grown resentful. The men have been growing ever more vocal about how their lives are being ruined by the king's wars and I think there is a very real chance that the king will lose against Brutus if he has the people with him.'

'There's Titus,' Menenius pointed out.

'Yes, there's Titus,' Caecilius agreed, 'but if Lucius is kicked off his throne, then Titus will have nothing. And if he has nothing, then I can expect nothing from him.'

'I thought he was your friend.'

'He is, but I have to think of my future, and I have to think of Volumnia and Caius.'

'Well, it's about time. You've never seemed to consider them before.'

'If you're going to abuse me, I shall leave,' Caecilius said, getting to his feet.

'Oh, sit down, you fool,' Menenius waved him back to the couch.

Caecilius sat. 'I need to be on the winning side, Menenius. Tell me honestly. Brutus has the people with him. Does he have the Senate too?'

'Yes, I think he does,' Menenius said. 'The Tarquins have never been popular, Cae. The patricians have suffered just as much as the people under their rule. This is a great chance to be rid of them.'

'Are you with Brutus, then?'

Menenius hesitated a moment before answering. 'Yes, I suppose I am.' He moved to sit beside Caecilius, who was rubbing his forehead as if he had a pain. 'It's difficult for you, I know. What does Volumnia say you should do?'

Caecilius sighed. 'I haven't been home yet.'

'Oh, Cae,' Menenius said reproachfully, 'you should have gone home before coming here.'

'Volumnia will tell me I should have stayed with the king.'

'Is she so keen on the Tarquins, then?'

'She's keen on the proper order of things. Volumnia sees things very clearly, Menenius. The king is the ruler of Rome; therefore, he must always be the ruler of Rome. It doesn't matter what he does, he is the king. It wouldn't matter what I wanted or what was best for me. Always what is best for Rome.' He laughed bitterly. 'Except when it comes to Caius. Caius first, Rome second, me…', he threw up his hands, 'nowhere.'

'She is an excellent mother,' Menenius said, wondering if Caecilius's assessment of Volumnia's inclination was entirely accurate. He knew Volumnia was a royalist — her attitude towards the plebs made that a necessity — but she was also a pragmatist. She wouldn't want to see her family ruined by association with the Tarquins, if not for Caecilius's sake, then for the sake of Caius's future. Menenius knew she would do nothing to endanger her son's safety and fortune.

'Is there any food in this domus of yours, Menenius?' Caecilius asked.

Menenius grinned and went to the kitchen where he ordered bread, figs and pork to be taken to his guest in the triclinium. This done, he went to his tablinum and wrote a letter to Volumnia, telling her Caecilius was with him. He thought it right Volumnia should know of her husband's whereabouts and give her time to think about what he should do when he returned home.

'This is more like it,' Lolly said softly to Lucius as they entered the domus of their Tarquinii host. She was treading on tiles instead of dirt, and the walls were solid stone rather than cloth that bent and billowed with every breath of wind. The furniture was excellent too, quite on a level with that she had enjoyed in Rome in her own domus. Lucius pressed his lips to her temple, a quick, chaste kiss that told her he understood and shared her feelings.

Their host held his arms wide in greeting and drew them deeper inside his home, pointing out proudly his latest acquisitions: a vase from Greece, a gold bowl made by a celebrated Etruscan artisan. Lucius and Lolly expressed their appreciation of his finery, while Titus, following close behind, smiled and nodded, less pleased than his parents at leaving the camp and the remnants of the royal army while his birthright was being threatened.

The party, consisting of a select few of Tarquinii's most notable citizens, settled on the dining couches and the conversation immediately turned towards the treacherous behaviour of the Tarquins' subjects. Lolly, skilful on such occasions, led the talk, and in short time, managed to steer the conversation onto how the Tarquinii could help their guests.

'It seems I must take my throne back by force,' Lucius said with an air of regret. 'And yet, I don't see how I can do that. My army is greatly depleted. My soldiers, encouraged by what has been happening in Rome, have deserted. Those left are my finest men, of course, and would take on the whole of Rome single-handedly if I asked them, but I don't want to do that. Victory, I feel, must be assured before we stir ourselves.'

He looked at Lolly for confirmation he had done well, that he had spoken his lines correctly, that he had been suitably humble. The slightest nod confirmed Lolly was pleased with his performance.

'What moves are afoot inside Rome?' one of the Tarquinii asked. 'To return you to the throne, I mean?'

Lolly glanced at Titus, who, taking his cue, said, 'It is the mob who have turned on us. The patricians are wholeheartedly behind us, but regrettably, the mob hold sway. But we have reliable information that the houses of Vitellii, the Aquilii and many more are eagerly awaiting to hear our plans.' It was a lie. Titus had heard from none of his friends in Rome. He hoped this was because it had proved impossible to send any letters and not because they had gone over to the rebels.

The Tarquinii exchanged glances among themselves. Then their host asked their guests if they would kindly retire to another room so they could discuss the matter in private. Lucius was about to protest that he would have an answer at once when Lolly's hand on his forearm prevented him. He, Lolly and Titus were shown to another room and the door closed upon them.

'What do you think?' Titus asked quietly.

'I think they have already decided to help us,' Lolly said, patting his arm. 'They just have to make a show of coming to a decision.'

'That bastard Brutus,' Titus spat. 'I should have seen this coming after our trip to Delphi. The Oracle predicted this.'

'What are you talking about?' Lucius asked irritably. It had been a strain having to be so courteous, so amenable to the Tarquinii, and his temper, notoriously short, was close to breaking.

'You remember, don't you, Mother?' Titus asked. 'I told you what happened when we went to Delphi to see the Oracle.'

'Yes, something about a kiss,' Lolly said.

'That's right. The Oracle said the first of us to kiss his mother would be king. My brother and I assumed she meant you, Mother, that's why we both hurried to kiss you on our return, but we were wrong. That I didn't see it at the time makes me hate myself. Brutus fell on his face when we left the temple, deliberately, I know it now, and he kissed the ground. Well, don't you see, Father?' he said when Lucius's frown grew deeper. 'By our mother, the Oracle meant the earth, she meant Gaia. Brutus understood that right from the start and planned to rouse the people from that moment on.'

Lucius strode over to Titus and cuffed him about the head. 'You fool. You mean to say you suspected Brutus would do this months ago and didn't tell me?'

'Not then, Father,' Titus protested, rubbing his stinging ear. 'I have only realised his intentions these past few days.'

But Lucius was not appeased. 'Had I known then what you have just told me, I would have had Brutus killed the moment he returned to Rome and we wouldn't be in this wretched state now.'

'I'm sorry, Father.'

'It is done, Lucius,' Lolly said, pulling him away from Titus, worried he would hit their son again. She didn't want to see Titus and Lucius fighting but she was also conscious of the poor impression it would make on their Tarquinii hosts were they to witness such animosity between father and son. 'When we have won Rome back, you can have your revenge on Brutus.'

'Oh, I will,' Lucius assured her. 'I will have his head cut off and his whole family disembowelled on Mars Field.'

'Yes, my love,' Lolly said soothingly. 'But let us win Rome back before you console yourself with such plans.' She turned as the door opened.

Their Tarquinii host stood in the doorway, a benevolent smile upon his face. 'We have decided to help you,' he said.

8

Collatinus paced up and down outside the Senate house, hands clasped behind his back, head down, staring at his feet. The Senate had received a message from the Tarquinii that they were sending envoys to treat with Rome on King Lucius's behalf. This had been expected; it was supposed by none of the senators that the king would accept exile without a fight, but Collatinus felt that to accept the envoys at all would be a prelude to a negotiated return, and that was something he couldn't accept. He could not bend his knee once more to the family that had been the cause of his wife's suicide.

No, he was decided. If, as he feared, the Senate agreed to give Lucius back the throne, then Collatinus would leave Rome. The way he saw it, with Lucretia gone, he had nothing much to stay for anyway, not with Brutus acting the way he was.

Collatinus couldn't help but feel a little resentful towards Brutus. He had expected his friend to back him and tell the Senate that they would not even give the Tarquins' envoys an audience. Brutus had the Senate in the palm of his hand. No one, least of all Collatinus, would have thought it possible a month ago — the renowned idiot leading the Senate house — but all the senators listened to Brutus. And yet, Brutus had said they would receive the envoys but that their arrival should be kept from the people, lest there be civil unrest at the news.

'Why shouldn't there be civil unrest?' Collatinus had cried. 'Let the people know what the Senate is up to.'

But Brutus had smiled condescendingly at him and told him not to be such a bloody fool, they didn't want unnecessary bloodshed. Collatinus had looked around at the senators, hoping that at least some of them would be on his side, but not one of them spoke up for him, not even Mettius Trebonius, who he knew hated the Tarquins almost as much as he.

The Senate meeting broke up, Brutus saying that only he, Collatinus and Mettius would receive the envoys. Collatinus had followed the departing senators out of the Senate house and paced up and down outside, waiting for the envoys to arrive. He wished he had the courage to defy Brutus and shout out to all the people in the forum that the tyrant was sending his lackeys to the Senate, but he did not. *What was the point?* he told himself.

He waited, looking enviously on the people in the forum going about their daily business. How he wished he could forget the death of his wife as easily as they seemed to have done. They didn't care about the tragedy that had befallen him; they were just glad it had resulted in the expulsion of the tyrant king and his family from Rome. They didn't have to go home to an empty domus, slide into an empty bed and know that he would never see his beloved wife Lucretia again until he too passed into the Underworld. Why had she taken it upon herself to end her life? There had been no need. She would have borne no taint as far as he was concerned. No matter what Prince Sextus had done to her, to him she would have been as pure as the day he married her.

Collatinus shook his head to rid himself of the memory of his dead wife. It wasn't manly for a man to dwell on his grief. His eyes narrowed, focusing on two men heading towards him. They seemed intent on their path and Collatinus drew in a deep breath as he recognised the determined step of those on official business. These were the king's men, no doubt. He turned and hurried into the Senate chamber.

'They're coming,' he told Brutus who sat on the chamber's stone chair that had once belonged to the king of Rome. There had been talk of removing it from the Senate house, but it was extremely heavy and would have been difficult to lift. So, it had been left in situ and Brutus, ever since addressing the people from the rostra on that tragic day of Lucretia's death, had made good use of it.

'How many?' Brutus asked.

'Two.'

'We should execute them,' Mettius sniffed, coming up behind the chair and leaning casually over its back.

'They are not Tarquins, they are envoys from Tarquinii and we have no grievance against them,' Brutus said patiently. 'We agreed to give them safe passage. We must not appear unreasonable.'

'You astonish me, Brutus, you really do,' Mettius said. 'You have no reason to love the Tarquins, perhaps less reason than any of us, and yet you would listen to these people who come speaking on the Tarquins' behalf.'

'The Roman people expelled the Tarquins because of their tyranny. We would be no better than they if we execute these envoys because they represent the Tarquins.' Brutus waved Mettius aside as two figures appeared in the doorway. 'Quiet now.'

'We come from King Tarquin,' the elder of the two men announced and Collatinus heard the tremble in his voice.

Brutus gestured them to step forward. 'Say what you have come to say.'

'King Lucius Tarquinius sends his greetings—'

'What is Lucius Tarquinius king of?' Mettius interrupted. 'He has no kingdom.'

The envoy looked bewildered and glanced at his companion for help in making an answer but the companion shook his head, nonplussed.

'Enough,' Brutus said, scowling at Mettius. To the man, he said, 'Speak on.'

Relieved, the man continued. 'The king asks that his goods and property be restored to his family. They are privately owned goods and property and do not belong to Rome.'

'No, but they were got by the sweat of decent Romans,' Mettius retorted angrily.

Brutus put out his hand and grabbed Mettius's wrist to quiet him. 'And how is the Tarquins' property to be transferred to them?' he said to the envoy. 'I will not allow them to return to Rome.'

Collatinus's eyebrow rose at Brutus's use of the personal pronoun and involuntarily met Mettius's angry eye. Mettius's eyebrows also rose.

'The properties can be sold,' the man suggested.

'I suppose they can,' Brutus said, 'if a buyer can be found.'

'The properties are highly desirable. I am sure finding a buyer will be relatively easy. Perhaps you…', the envoy gestured at Brutus.

Brutus's top lip curled. 'I have not the taste for luxury my uncle has.'

The envoy, realising he had blundered, shuffled his feet.

'I suppose the Tarquinii have welcomed the Tarquins,' Mettius said mockingly.

'We have,' the man said with a touch of defiance. '*We* remember our friends.'

'You can have him as your king then,' Mettius laughed, 'seeing as how you love him so much.'

The man's lips tightened. He turned back to Brutus. 'May we have your decision as to our very reasonable request?'

'We will discuss it and give you our answer tomorrow,' Brutus said.

'Oh, send these minions packing, Brutus,' Mettius said, waving his hand at them. 'Lucius Tarquin has forfeited any goods he had. They are ours now. Why should we give them back?'

'We will discuss it,' Brutus repeated, silencing Mettius with a stare. 'Leave us,' he said to the envoys, 'and we will send word to you tomorrow. Where will you be?'

'We have your assurance we will not be harmed if we stay in Rome?' the man asked.

'I have given you safe conduct,' Brutus said. 'You will not be harmed.'

The man nodded and said they would stay at an inn in the southwest corner of the Forum Boarium. He made to bow to Brutus in farewell but then thought better of it, perhaps remembering that Brutus was not a king but a man, as he was. He plucked the sleeve of his companion and the pair of them turned and left the Senate house.

'Why should we not keep the goods?' Mettius demanded impatiently when they had gone.

'Because we are not thieves,' Brutus replied, smoothing down the folds of his toga.

'You have far too many scruples, Brutus. What do you think, Collatinus?'

Collatinus looked at Brutus from beneath lowered lids. He agreed with Mettius; he felt entitled to the Tarquin goods and properties, but he didn't feel up to an argument he knew he would not win. 'Brutus knows what he is doing. We must appear better than those we have deposed.'

Mettius grunted unhappily. 'I tell you, I know the Tarquins. You give them what they ask for, and they'll be back, asking for more. They're never satisfied.'

'They will have what is theirs and nothing more,' Brutus insisted.

Mettius moved to stand in front of Brutus. 'Why are you so keen to give the Tarquins the means by which they can thrive?'

'What would you have me do?'

'Beggar them, that's what I would have you do. Make them starve, if you can. It's what they deserve.'

'They will not starve,' Brutus said, gesturing for him to stand aside. 'They are being entertained by the Tarquinii.'

'Exactly. And if we give them back their fortune, and they wave it under the noses of the Tarquinii, what do you think the Tarquinii will do, eh? They'll think there's more gold to be had in Rome if Tarquin gets his throne back.'

'What do you mean, Mettius?' Collatinus asked.

'I mean, Collatinus, that the Tarquinii will help Tarquin raise an army to reclaim his throne with all that gold we're giving him.'

'Brutus,' Collatinus pleaded, 'if Mettius is right—'

'It is right they have what is theirs,' Brutus roared, slamming his hands down on the arms of the chair.

Mettius grimaced and stepped away. 'Very well. I know your opinions,' he nodded at both Brutus and Collatinus. 'I'll discuss this with the rest of the Senate and let you know ours. You shouldn't be surprised if we're not so eager as you to make the Tarquins rich again.' He strode out of the Senate house.

'We should listen to him, Brutus,' Collatinus urged.

'We must stick to our principles, ' Brutus insisted, 'else we will be just as corrupt and tyrannous as the Tarquins. And I will have no one able to say that about me.'

About you? Collatinus thought as Brutus walked out of the Senate house. *When in Hades did the death of my wife make this all about you?*

Caecilius stared down at the letter before him, wishing it had not come. He didn't have an answer for it, and the Tarquinii envoys who had passed the letter on and instructed him to keep it secret, were expecting him to give them one.

He looked up as he heard footsteps outside his tablinum and hastily covered the letter with some other papers. Too late.

'What are you hiding, Father?' Caius was hanging off the door frame, his head at an angle, his eyes flicking between Caecilius and the piles of papyrus on the desk.

'Nothing,' Caecilius said nonchalantly, checking the letter was covered. 'What are you doing there?'

Caius's answer was a shrug. 'You hid something.'

'No, I didn't. You shouldn't contradict me, Caius.'

He wasn't believed, Caecilius could see that. His son's eyes continued to wander between him and the desk. Suddenly, Caius disappeared from the doorway. Caecilius heard his swift footsteps and knew he was running off to tell Volumnia what he had seen. He sighed. There would be no hiding this letter now. *Might as well sit here and wait*, he decided.

It was only a matter of minutes before Volumnia arrived, Caius at her heels. 'Caius said you are hiding something.' She pointed at the pile. 'There.'

'You should teach him not to be such a little sneak,' Caecilius said, casting a hard stare at his son who stared unashamedly back.

'What have you hidden?' Volumnia asked, ignoring him.

Caecilius sighed and slid the letter out from between the other papers. 'It's a letter, if you must know.'

'From whom?'

'From Prince Titus.'

'How did he manage to get a letter to you?'

'Via envoys the Tarquinii have sent to negotiate with the Senate.'

Volumnia's eyes narrowed. 'Does the Senate know the prince has written to you?'

'Of course not,' he snapped, 'don't be a fool.'

She made a face at the insult. 'What does he want?'

'He's appealing to me to rally support in the city. Me and some of his other friends, the Vitelliis, the Aquilii...'. He passed the letter to her. 'Read for yourself.'

Volumnia quickly scanned the lines, her mouth forming the words she found in the letter. 'The king intends to re-enter the city under cover of darkness and wants to have an army ready to destroy the Senate,' she read. 'Oh, by all the gods, is he mad?'

'I don't think it's mad,' Caecilius said. 'Dangerous, but not mad.'

'You're not thinking of going along with this, are you?'

'Why shouldn't I? Titus is my friend. I owe him.'

'Now, who's being the fool?' Volumnia said, sitting down on a stool by the desk.

'Titus would have given me much once he was king.'

'Exactly. Would have,' Volumnia scoffed. 'He's unlikely to ever be king now.'

'You've given up very easily, my dear. I never thought you would be for a republic.'

'I'm realistic. Brutus has the whole of Rome with him. The king won't be able to fight the Senate and the people.'

'The king has the Tarquinii with him. The other tribes may be with him too, for all we know.'

'Really?' Volumnia narrowed her eyes. 'Maybe we should ask Menenius's opinion on this,' she said thoughtfully, re-reading the letter.

Caecilius snatched it back. 'I forbid you to tell Menenius about this letter. In fact, I forbid you to tell anyone.'

'But Menenius is our friend—'

'He's for the republic. He's glad the Tarquins are gone.'

'Even so, what are you scared of? Menenius wouldn't betray you.'

Caecilius didn't answer, not having the same faith in his old friend as his wife had.

'Caecilius, I insist you do not answer that letter,' Volumnia said, rapping the table to get his attention.

'Very well, and what do I do about this one?' Caecilius slid out another letter from the pile. 'This letter came not half an hour ago from Lucius Aquilii. He's hosting a dinner tonight for those he calls 'friends of the king'. I expect he wants to discuss raising an army. But whatever he wants, he wants me to stand with him and his brother.' He passed it to Volumnia. She barely glanced at it, and threw it back on the table.

'What will happen if you ignore it?'

Caecilius shrugged. 'The Aquilii may come round here to find out why I am silent.'

'We can't have that,' Volumnia said. 'Write back saying you are ill and cannot come.'

'Lie low, you mean, until it's obvious which is the winning side?'

'It never pays to be hasty,' Volumnia said impatiently. 'Do stop all this hand-wringing, Caecilius. Your priority must be to protect yourself and your family. So, do as I say. Send a reply to Lucius Aquilii declining his invitation because you are ill in bed and cannot rise.'

Caecilius couldn't deny there was sense in Volumnia's words and he was past arguing. In fact, he realised it was a relief to be told what to do. He reached for a sheet of papyrus. As he wrote, he jerked his head at Caius. 'Tell him not to breathe a word of this, Volumnia, to anyone.'

'He's no telltale.'

Caecilius laughed. 'He told on me to you, didn't he? He can't keep his mouth shut. But if he speaks about this, we could all be dead, so make it clear to your son that he's to say nothing of the letters.'

She wanted to argue with him, Caecilius could see that, but she evidently divined the wisdom in his words for Volumnia pulled Caius onto her lap and held up a warning finger.

'You are not to speak of this to anyone, do you understand?' she said.

Caius looked from her to his father and back to Volumnia. 'No one, Mother?'

'No one at all. Not to the slaves, not to your friends—'

'What about Uncle Menenius?'

Volumnia glanced at Caecilius. 'Especially not to Uncle Menenius,' she said. 'Promise me.'

'I promise, Mother,' Caius said.

'There,' Caecilius said, throwing down his stylus. He rolled up the papyrus and sealed it. 'It's done.' He held it out to Volumnia. 'Would you like to send it to Lucius Aquilii, my dear?'

Volumnia took it, her mouth pursing in irritation at his manner. 'There's no need to be so sour, Caecilius. It's for the best.'

'It might be for the best but it's not very honourable.'

'No, but it is pragmatic, Caecilius. Of course, I would prefer it if the monarchy were still ruling in Rome, but we must face the truth. I just hope the Senate will keep the plebs under control. And who knows, perhaps we will prosper under a republic.'

'And what of honour? Am I to live without it from now on?'

Volumnia sighed. 'You have your honour still,' she said, putting her hand on his briefly. 'And we must consider what is best for Caius,' she said, kissing her son's black hair.

Caecilius slumped back in his chair. 'Of course,' he said, 'we must all do what is best for Caius.'

House of the Aquilii

Vindicius bent low, offering the tray to the last of his master's visitors to arrive. That made four men who had come to the house in secret, not including his master's brother, Marcus. The women in the house had been told to keep to their rooms. Something was going on.

Vindicius wished he could have been among the household slaves who had been instructed to keep to their duties at the rear of the domus. His master, Lucius, had already flung a cushion at his head for spilling some of wine. The gods knew what else his master would do in such a mood and Vindicius would rather be out of the way.

Marcellus Vitellii and his brother, Manius, had been the first to arrive, and Vindicius knew they both took great delight in tormenting slaves, kicking them when they bent over to send them sprawling, smashing their faces into the cold stone of the floor, or making them undress and parade before their friends, both male and female, pointing out where they were lacking in manhood. Vindicius hated the Vitellii brothers and braced himself for their taunts. But they didn't seem interested in tormenting slaves this night. They were strangely quiet and yet excited, their fists clenching and unclenching as they rested them on their knees, their eyes flicking continually between each other and the door. Their agitation increased further when Titus and Tiberius Brutus arrived. Vindicius served the wine and then retreated to the corner of the room, standing ramrod straight against the wall.

'Is this all of us?' Manius Vitellii asked, looking around the small company.

'Who else were you expecting?' Lucius Aquilii asked.

'I don't know,' Manius threw up his hands. 'Canus Pilatus, Vopiscus Bestia, Caecilius Marcius.'

'Canus and Vopiscus didn't reply to my letters,' Lucius said. 'I'm not surprised, they've always been cowards. Caecilius Marcius sent word he is ill in bed and cannot come.'

'If you can believe that,' his brother, Marcus, sniffed.

'You don't?' Titus Brutus asked in a surprised tone.

'I saw him yesterday,' Marcus shrugged. 'He looked well enough to me.'

'The coward's too scared to join us,' Tiberius Brutus shook his head.

'We don't know that,' Lucius said.

'It's better this way,' Marcellus Vitellii said decisively. 'The fewer who know of this, the more certain the success and the greater the glory for us. It will show King Lucius who his true friends are.'

'*If* he comes back,' Lucius said.

'*When* he comes back,' Marcus insisted. 'We will be successful, brother. The alternative is abominable.'

Titus got to his feet. 'We're decided then. So, how do we go about restoring the king to his throne?'

'We form our own army. We can get more than two hundred men between us,' Marcus gestured between himself and Lucius. 'How many can you each get?' he asked the others.

Marcellus and Manius Vitellii spoke quietly together and came up with a figure of roughly one hundred and fifty. Titus and Tiberius Brutus surprised them all by claiming they could raise near three hundred men.

'All because of your name?' Manius asked scornfully.

'It is a worthy name,' Junius said, his chin rising a little higher.

'It is also the name of the man who started this all, the man everyone thought to be an idiot,' Manius pointed out. 'You must have known he was not.'

Tiberius's jaw tightened. 'Do not speak of our father so, Manius Vitellii.'

Marcellus put a restraining hand on his brother's arm and glared at him. Manius reluctantly quietened. 'You claim you can get three hundred men,' Marcellus said to Tiberius. 'Are they your men or your father's? Because if they are your father's, then I'm sorry to say it but you're hoping for the moon.'

'They will fight for us once they understand the rightness of our cause,' Titus Brutus insisted before his brother could answer. 'Our father is mistaken in his expulsion of the king. He bears an old grudge against the Tarquins. It's personal and men won't follow personal grievances.'

'Oh, won't they?' Manius laughed bitterly. 'How very sure you are.'

'Enough, Manius,' Marcellus barked. 'Tiberius and Titus will bring as many men as they can muster and so, we will have our army. Moving on, we need to work out a strategy. Who will be our allies?'

'The Tarquins have been given shelter by the Tarquinii, who have promised aid,' Titus said. 'They want King Lucius back on the throne because they have too many trade agreements that may suffer otherwise. They will be our chief allies. And the Tarquinii army will be formidable.'

Marcus nodded. 'We can attack the Senate on two fronts. The Tarquinii from outside Rome, us from within it.'

Tiberius held out his hand. 'Wait a moment, Marcus. You speak of attack. I thought our army was just to be a threat to the Senate. We wouldn't actually use it.'

'Why gather an army you don't intend to use?' Marcus asked.

'To be a show of force,' Tiberius said vehemently. 'I am not so ready as you to shed the blood of my fellow Romans.'

'And how do you imagine we can overturn the Senate without a fight?' Marcus retorted.

'We reason,' Tiberius said. 'We show them they're wrong. We use the army as a threat, nothing more.'

Marcus glanced up at Lucius; an understanding passed between them.

'Very well, Tiberius,' Lucius said, 'we won't use the army against the Senate, only against the people if they stand in our way.'

Tiberius nodded. 'Good, that's good. I would not be with you, nor would my brother, if harm came to my father or our friends.'

'Only plebeian blood need be spilt,' Marcus assured him with a grin. 'Come, let us drink to our success.'

The conspirators drank a toast to the king, then the four visitors tied on their cloaks and pulled up their hoods, ducking out of the front door and hurrying quickly away into the dark of the Roman streets.

'The rebels should be executed,' Marcus said, slumping back down onto the couch when the door had closed. 'Brutus, Collatinus, Mettius, all of them, even the Senate.'

'And they will be, brother,' Lucius promised. 'We just need to keep Tiberius and Titus quiet and compliant for the time being. They'll be in too far to back out by the time they realise what we truly intend.'

'Suits me.' Marcus burped. 'Their father is the reason we're in this mess, all because he values the body of a dead whore more than he values his country. A man like that doesn't deserve to live.'

'Nor to spread his dangerous ideas,' Lucius agreed. 'Can you imagine what would happen to Rome if we allowed Brutus and his fellow rebels to get away with this? The people will think they can rise up any time they have a grievance. We would be forever putting down revolts. We need to deal with the plebs now and ensure they never feel strong enough to rise against us again.'

'And Caecilius Marcius,' Marcus said, his words beginning to slur. He had drunk a great deal of wine that evening.

'What's that?' Lucius asked, confused by the mention of Marcius.

'Caecilius Marcius should be executed too. Ill, my arse. If you ask me, that wolfish wife of his told him to stay at home, to stay out of trouble. And any man who heeds his wife before his friends is no man at all and deserves death.'

Lucius considered his brother's words for a long moment. 'Very well,' he said at last. 'It will be death for Caecilius Marcius too.'

Vindicius was still standing by the wall, forgotten and unnoticed.

Publius Valerius threw down his stylus and massaged his fingers, grimacing as his knuckle bones cracked. He had been working for hours, since before the sun was up, and his hands were cramping. There was so much more work of late, ever since the Tarquins had been expelled from Rome. There were letters from the other Latin states, enquiring whether their usual trades were going to suffer, relatives and acquaintances simply wanting to hear the latest news, all in addition to the usual run of correspondence he had to deal with. Publius had never been so busy.

'Dominus.' Timon, his slave, had entered his tablinum and was standing before the desk.

'Yes,' Publius answered testily. 'What is it?'

'There is a person to see you.'

'I'm not seeing anyone until my accustomed hour, Timon, you know that. Don't bother me now.'

'This is not a client, dominus,' Timon persisted. He bent over the desk and said conspiratorially, 'It's a slave.'

Publius peered up at Timon. 'Why should I see a slave? Am I in the habit of giving audiences to slaves?'

'You'll want to see this one, unless I'm no judge.'

'Oh, very well,' Publius said with a sigh, 'show this slave in.' He wiped his fingers on his pen cloth idly, wondering what this slave wanted. It wasn't like Timon to be so mysterious.

Timon re-entered, waving at the figure behind him to hurry up and enter. 'This is the slave, dominus.'

'Your name, slave?' Publius asked.

Vindicius gave it in an inaudible whisper, his head down.

Timon tutted and pulled the thin leather thong around Vindicius's neck closer to his face. He read the circle of metal at its end. 'Slave to Lucius Aquilii, dominus.'

'The Aquilii? What business have you with me?' Publius asked surprised, for he had no dealings with either of the Aquilii brothers.

'I come to tell you of a plot against the Senate,' Vindicius said.

Publius got to his feet, his stool scraping noisily against the stone floor. 'A plot. Do you mean your master?'

Vindicius nodded. 'There was a meeting at my master's house last night. They met to discuss how they would return the king to Rome.'

'Who met?'

'My master and his brother, the brothers of the house of Vitellii and the brothers of the house of Brutus. There were supposed to be others, but those were the only ones who came.'

'The sons of Lucius Iunius Brutus?' Publius was aghast.

Vindicius nodded.

'I don't believe it,' Publius declared. 'The sons act against their father?' He looked at Timon, who shook his head and shrugged. Publius's eyes narrowed at Vindicius. 'Why are you telling me this? Why are you betraying your master? Are you a lying slave trying to get your master into trouble?'

Vindicius took a step back, only to step back into Timon's unyielding body. 'No, no. I'm not lying. The meeting took place, as I said.'

'I don't approve of slaves telling tales,' Publius said. 'I should tell your master and insist he have you whipped.'

'Please,' Vindicius begged, falling to his knees, 'I'm telling the truth. I don't want there to be bloodshed.'

Publius fell down onto his stool at his words. 'Bloodshed? Who spoke of bloodshed?'

'My master and his brother.'

Publius gestured for Vindicius to rise and speak on.

Vindicius swallowed nervously as he got to his feet. 'The Brutus brothers refused to support the king if it meant attacking the Senate. They said they wouldn't act against their father if his life was threatened. So, my master said he wouldn't be. Only—'

'Only what?' Publius snapped.

'Only he said he hadn't meant it when they had gone. He told his brother that whoever opposed them would be executed.'

'By Janus,' Timon breathed.

Publius stared, open-mouthed. 'Why would they do this?'

'Prince Titus wrote to them, asking for their support,' Vindicius said.

'What!' Publius spluttered. 'And you leave this news to the last?'

'I didn't think that was important,' Vindicius protested.

'Not important? May the gods save me from the imbecility of slaves. Listen here, you dog. The king, the same king who has been exiled, has written to patricians within this city, inciting them to take up arms in support of him, and you think that unimportant?'

'That's slaves for you,' Timon said, shaking his head at Vindicius.

'So,' Publius said, taking a deep breath, 'there are letters from the Tarquins? At your master's house?'

'I suppose so.'

'Is there anything else you have neglected to tell me?'

Vindicius thought for a moment. 'No, that's everything.'

'Timon,' Publius said, 'gather what men you can muster immediately. Have them arm themselves and have them ready in the atrium.'

'I will, dominus,' Timon said excitedly. 'What are we going to do?'

'Do? Do?' Publius cried. 'We're going to arrest the Aquilii, of course.'

Volumnia rose at the sound of the front door opening and closing. She would never have admitted it, but she had been on edge ever since Caecilius had sent his reply to the Aquilii, declining their dinner invitation on the grounds of ill health. Would it be believed, she wondered? And if the brothers didn't believe Caecilius was ill but merely shamming, what damage could they do him?

'Oh, it's you,' she cried with relief when Menenius moved into view.

'Well, I've had better welcomes,' he said, a little affronted.

'Forgive me, Menenius,' Volumnia said, waving him forward. 'I am truly glad to see you. Is something wrong? You look quite flustered.'

Menenius took a seat. 'I've just come from the Senate.' He shook his head. 'Such goings-ons, Volumnia.'

'What, what?' she said urgently, sitting beside him. *Oh, Jove have mercy on me and my family and bring no bad news*, she silently prayed.

'There's no need to fear,' he said, taking her hand. 'You are safe.'

She snatched her hand away. 'I don't know what you mean.'

Menenius smiled understandingly. 'I don't know,' he said carefully, 'but I suspect Caecilius received a letter from the Aquilii.' He raised his eyebrows at Volumnia, asking for a confirmation.

She considered for a long moment, wondering whether to admit it, but then gave a tight nod.

'It was fortunate he was too ill to attend,' Menenius said.

'He *was* ill,' Volumnia protested.

'Of course he was, and a very wise illness it was too. Your doing, I daresay.'

She ignored the implied compliment. 'What is it, Menenius? What has happened?'

Menenius told her of how he had been in the Senate when Publius Valerius had burst in with an armed guard surrounding the Aquilii brothers and of how he had uncovered a plot to restore the Tarquins to Rome. Publius had added that he had sent another armed guard to arrest the Vitelliis and the sons of Brutus. This last statement had been greeted with gasps and heads had turned towards the father, Brutus himself, who had said nothing, simply stared as if in shock at Publius.

'The sons of Brutus were part of this plot?' Volumnia whispered, hardly able to believe it.

Menenius nodded. 'We all thought it must be a mistake,

but no, they were plotting to bring the king back, against their own father. I never thought to see such a day.' He took a deep breath. 'Volumnia, all the brothers are friends of Prince Titus. As is Caecilius.'

'Was his name mentioned?' she asked, half fearing the answer.

'No, but he must be careful. The letters—'

'I told him to burn them,' she said quickly.

'Good, that was the right thing to do. I am sure you have nothing to worry about as long as Caecilius doesn't do anything stupid in the name of honour.'

'I won't let him,' she said vehemently.

'No, I imagine you won't,' he nodded, smiling. 'I know this must be difficult for you. But I believe it is Rome's destiny to be a republic. There have been signs in the heavens that it is so, the priests have confirmed it. There is no going back. A king will never again rule here.'

Volumnia gave a little bitter laugh. 'I had hoped… but no, you are right. We cannot defy the will of the gods.' She breathed deeply and smiled. 'So, we are all to be republicans now. How things do change.'

'I think it is a change for the better, Volumnia. We may even find that we prosper as a republic.'

'Well then,' she smiled at him, 'We must welcome this new Rome.' She raised her hand. 'All hail the republic.'

9

Brutus settled himself further into the stone chair, pulling the wolf pelt over his legs. He kept his eyes down, not wanting to look at his fellow senators. He could imagine what they thinking, what they were whispering to one another: Brutus doesn't even know what's going on in his own family, so how can we entrust the governance of Rome to him? Turns out he is the idiot we always believed him to be. Perhaps we would be better off with the Tarquins, after all.

Were they right? he asked himself, casting sideways glances from beneath lowered lids at the men who gathered in small groups in the Senate house. *Have I been fooling myself?*

When he had watched Lucretia plunge a knife into her heart, he had been shocked and appalled, of course, but there had been a small part of him that had sensed an opportunity. Even as Collatinus cradled his dying wife in his arms and pleaded with Brutus for help, Brutus has been thinking, *Prince Sextus did this terrible thing. The people will not stand for it.*

Yes, he had thought the death of Lucretia was a chance the gods were giving him to take his revenge on the whole

Tarquin clan. Was he to be blamed for that? His beloved brother had been murdered on the king's orders, he had witnessed his mother snubbed by the queen on public occasions, and he had been continually mocked by the princes for being an idiot, the part his mother had begged him to play so she would not lose another son to King Lucius's paranoia. So, yes, he had seen in Lucretia's suicide a chance for revenge, may any blame him who will. And this is how he was rewarded, turned upon by members of his own family.

It had caused him physical pain to learn that his own sons had conspired to bring the Tarquins back. Publius Valerius had ordered their arrest and his armed guard had brought them to the Senate house to be denounced. There they now stood, Titus and Tiberius, huddled with the other traitors, snivelling into their togas. *They should weep,* he thought savagely*, and they will weep more before I have done with them.* Even in their sorrow, they were an embarrassment. The Vitellii and Aquilii brothers did not weep. They stood proud and defiant before the senators, not a tear bedecking their cheeks. Brutus could almost admire them. They had had the courage to begin this conspiracy and had no less now it had been exposed. He could not say the same of his sons.

He heard footsteps drawing near and turned his head. Out of the corner of his eye, he saw Mettius coming towards him, no doubt dying to gloat.

'You were right,' Brutus said, wanting to say it before Mettius did.

Mettius frowned. 'About what?'

Aye, feign ignorance, twist the knife. 'About the Tarquins. They cannot be trusted.'

'I'm glad you see it now, though I wish it could be under different circumstances, for your sake.'

'Do not say so,' Brutus snapped. 'I have need of neither

your sympathy nor your pity. I am at fault. I didn't see the treachery within my own family.'

Collatinus, standing by his side, tutted. 'Titus and Tiberius have always been easily led. The others would have convinced them it was the right thing to do to bring the king back to Rome.'

'There's no need to make excuses for them. They are traitors and deserve no understanding.'

Collatinus held up his hands in capitulation and backed away from Brutus, sliding a glance towards Mettius who met it with equal wariness.

'What is to be done with the prisoners?' Mettius asked Brutus.

'They must be tried and punished.'

'The trial will be a mere formality, of course,' Mettius said. 'We know they are guilty. We have the evidence,' he held up the letter from the prince Publius had given him, 'and they have not denied it. But what is to be the punishment?'

Brutus raised his chin as he stared past Mettius into nothingness. 'They will be executed.'

'You can't mean that, Brutus,' Collatinus said, shocked. He turned despairingly to Mettius. 'Talk to him.'

'Collatinus is right, Brutus,' Mettius said. 'We can't ask you to execute your own children.'

'They're not my children,' Brutus said. 'I disown them. They are traitors and must be punished. To allow them to live would be the act of a tyrant, showing mercy to some and not to others.'

'The people will understand, Brutus,' Collatinus pleaded.

Brutus shook his head. 'You place too much faith in the people, Collatinus.' He stood and turned to Collatinus, his gaze unflinching. 'Execution must be for all of them. No exceptions.'

Brutus had not said another word. He had taken himself off to one side of the Senate house with the air of someone who wanted to be alone. Collatinus and Mettius had watched him, neither speaking but both wondering what in Hades had happened to Brutus to turn him into such a monster.

They had turned to the other senators and ushered them out of the Senate house, signalling to the guards to do the same with their prisoners. As they emerged into the daylight, the people in the forum stopped what they were doing and drew towards the Senate steps. As they saw the armed guard and the prisoners they surrounded, they began to turn to one another and wonder what was happening. Their voices swelled and Collatinus saw the looks of confusion on their faces. *They have a right to be confused,* he thought grimly. *Here stand the sons of three of Rome's noblest families, under guard and shackled.* He saw the people glance from Titus and Tiberius to their father, who had come out of the Senate house and lingered at the back of the senators, and back again, shaking their heads at one another and shrugging their shoulders.

Mettius, having put himself forward as spokesman, moved to stand on the rostra. 'People of Rome, hear me. These men,' he gestured at the prisoners, 'are accused of the most heinous of crimes. Treason.' He paused as the crowd gasped. He half-turned to the prisoners and held out his arm, his index finger extended. 'Lucius and Marcus Aquilii, Marcellus and Manius Vitellii, and,' he paused and glanced at Brutus, 'Titus and Tiberius Brutus.' The crowd gasped again and a few shouts were heard. 'These men have been accused of conspiring to restore the tyrant to his throne. We have evidence of their treachery. Letters from the tyrant's eldest son writing on his father's behalf, and an eyewitness account of their meeting to discuss how Tarquin's restoration was to be accomplished.'

'Who?' Marcus Aquilii shouted, struggling to break through the armed guards. 'Bring your witness. Let us see him.'

Out of the corner of his eye, Collatinus saw Brutus nod to the guard standing beside him. The guard disappeared inside the Senate house and reappeared a moment later, his hand gripped around the upper arm of Vindicius. Vindicius blinked in the glare of the sunlight, shuffled his feet and needed to be prodded by the guard to move forward.

'This is our witness,' Mettius declared.

'You treacherous bastard,' Lucius Aquilii roared, recognising his slave.

'No,' Brutus bellowed, stepping forward and displacing Mettius on the platform, 'a true Roman. This is Vindicius, a slave in the house of the Aquilii. He heard every word uttered by these traitors and hurried to do his duty by Rome and tell of their treachery. It is because of him that their despicable plot has been uncovered. It is to Vindicius we owe our continued liberty.' Brutus grabbed Vindicius and dragged him forward, thrusting him before the people. Vindicius looked terrified but the crowd began to cheer. A bewildered smile spread upon his face.

Collatinus looked back at the prisoners. The Aquilii were both spitting and shouting venom at the slave, no doubt just as furious with themselves for not considering he might be a threat to their security. *That's the way with slaves,* Collatinus thought, *you grow so used to their constant presence, you barely notice when they are in the room. It's easy to forget they have eyes, ears and mouths.* He made a mental note never to speak anything he did not want repeated before a slave of his again. The Vitellii were also looking angry, though so far they had remained silent. Only the sons of Brutus showed any fear.

The trial began. Mettius charged the prisoners with treason and demanded their response. The Aquilii brothers didn't hesitate. They were not guilty of treason, they declared hotly. It was the Senate and the people of Rome who were the guilty ones, guilty of mistreating their king. The Vitellii gave the same pleas, but not the same retorts. The sons of Brutus declared they were not guilty of treason, that they had been misled and deceived by the others. They had not wanted bloodshed, they said through their tears, they had specifically said the senators were not to be harmed. Mettius queried Vindicius on this, and the slave confirmed the truth of their words. They relaxed visibly at his affirmation, no doubt believing he had made them safe, though they had to endure the fury of their co-conspirators, who swore and spat at them.

Mettius turned to the senators. 'How do you find the prisoners?'

The senators did not hesitate. 'Guilty,' came the collective cry, and the crowd cheered.

Collatinus moved to Brutus, who stood rigid, his eyes on a distant spot above the crowd. Leaning in close, he whispered, 'Do not insist on death, Brutus.'

'The senators have found them guilty,' Brutus said, not looking at Collatinus.

'But you are our leader. If you say there must be a different punishment, they will listen to you.'

'I have said what the punishment must be.'

'These are your sons, Brutus,' Collatinus cried desperately. 'How can you put them to death?'

Brutus slowly turned his head towards Collatinus, his eyes hard and narrowing. 'The prisoners have been found guilty,' he shouted to the crowd who immediately quietened. 'The punishment for such a crime against the Roman people is death. But this man,' he pointed at Collatinus, 'would have me ignore the law and not have these traitors executed. He would have me show pity because two of the guilty are of my blood. He would have us exile these creatures as we have exiled their master. To do so would be madness.'

Brutus paused and Collatinus took advantage of his silence to appeal to the crowd. 'We cannot ask a man to kill his sons.' Even as he spoke, he wondered why he risked Brutus's wrath to save the sons his old friend wanted to kill. Murmurs came from the people, and Collatinus sensed that some, if not many, agreed with him.

But Brutus found his voice again. 'They are not my sons,' he declared. 'They are maggots eating away at the purity of my family. See,' he pointed at a party of three women immediately below the rostra, their heads covered, their faces buried in their hands, 'see there my wife, my daughters. See how they weep, all because of these wretches who were once my sons but are no more.'

'Save them for your wife, man,' Collatinus pleaded.

Brutus rounded on him and Collatinus saw nothing but madness in his eyes. 'Traitor,' Brutus screamed. 'My people, this man cannot be trusted. Let him know that if he continues to defend the allies of Lucius Tarquin, he too will be found guilty of treason.'

Collatinus stared open-mouthed at Brutus, realising he meant what he said. He closed his mouth and stepped away. He would protest no more but no more would he be party to this madness. If this was the new Rome, Collatinus decided, Brutus could keep it. He would go to his domus, pack all his belongings he could carry and leave. There was a whole world beyond Rome's walls. He would seek a new home and a new life elsewhere.

Ever since the trial of the conspirators, Volumnia had deemed it prudent to prolong the fiction of Caecilius's illness and for them both to stay shut up in the domus, but the enforced isolation was getting on her nerves. She knew Caecilius loathed himself for his lies and he had turned that loathing towards Volumnia. When she refused to rise to his taunts that she was a coward as much as he, he turned to wine for comfort, and had been drinking steadily so that he was now barely conscious. Volumnia preferred him this way — at least he was quiet — and told Caius to stay out of their cubiculum to where Caecilius had retreated.

But she needed to know what was happening in the city. She didn't trust her slaves to find out or bring her accurate news, so she decided she would make the journey to the forum herself and hear the praeco, Rome's herald. She dressed so as not to draw attention to herself and slipped out the front door, pulling her shawl up over her head.

'Volumnia, is that you?'

She halted, her heart in her mouth. She was hardly six steps from her domus. Were they being watched that she should be accosted so early in her journey?

'Volumnia?'

A hand touched her elbow and she jumped, turning her head slowly. 'Oh, Menenius, it's you,' she said, her entire body relaxing.

'Well, who did you think it was?' he laughed. 'I was just on my way to see you and Caecilius.'

'My husband is drunk,' she said with a curl of her lip. 'You won't get anything sensible out of him.'

'Oh, I shan't bother then. But where are you going?'

'To the forum.'

'No, I don't think you should, my dear.'

'Why not?' Volumnia asked, a trifle fearfully.

Menenius shuffled his feet. 'Why don't we go back to the domus?'

'I'm going to the forum, Menenius,' she said, forcefully.

'You will not want to, I assure you.' He sighed as she stared at him, refusing to budge. 'The conspirators are to be executed today. That is why I was coming to visit you. I didn't have the stomach to witness the executions.'

'I want to see it,' Volumnia said, a trickle of ice running down her spine. What if they confessed all before they died? If her family was to be named, she wanted to know it. 'I shall go, Menenius, you will not stop me.'

'If you insist, then I shall go with you,' Menenius said, clearly annoyed by her stubbornness. 'Caecilius would never forgive me if I left you to go alone. Shall we?' He extended his arm for her to take.

Volumnia stared at it for a moment, annoyed at his insistence on escorting her as if she was a child, but she didn't want to waste time arguing and so curled her arm around his. They began to walk, neither saying a word to one another.

They reached the forum. It was crammed full of people and she had to elbow her way through towards the Senate house outside which the executions were to take place. Menenius followed her reluctantly through the crowd, cursing and groaning at intervals whenever someone stepped upon his toes or elbowed him in the ribs.

Volumnia spotted her mother in the crowd, standing almost

a head above everyone else, for Aemilia was a tall woman. She changed direction towards her mother, telling Menenius to follow. She grimaced when she saw her brother Kaeso was also there. 'Mother,' she said, 'have you come to see the executions?'

'No, I have not,' Aemilia said scornfully, nodding a greeting at Menenius. 'Your brother and I were shopping and then the executions were announced. I would like to leave but there is hardly room to breathe and I don't want to have to fight my way out of here. Besides,' she lowered her voice, 'Kaeso is excited and wants to see them.' Kaeso was clinging to Aemilia's arm, grinning stupidly. 'Menenius,' Aemilia frowned, 'shouldn't you be up there with the other senators?'

'I excused myself, lady,' he said, looking towards the grouped senators behind the steps. Brutus was there, standing a little apart, his face grim. 'Like you, I didn't relish the spectacle. I can take you all home if you wish. Perhaps it would be better.'

'Menenius, will you be quiet?' Volumnia snapped. 'I want to see the executions and I'm not going home.'

Aemilia gave Menenius an exasperated look, but just then, the prisoners were brought onto the steps, and all faces turned in their direction. Volumnia looked upon the prisoners and a shiver ran through her body as she realised it could just as easily be Caecilius standing up there, his wrists and ankles shackled, surrounded by armed guards. Thank the gods she had had the sense to warn him against going to the Aquilii that night.

The prisoners were stripped of their clothing so they stood naked for all to see. Then the armed guards tied each man to a cart that had been brought forward for the purpose, their bodies bent forward, their backsides in the air. Six of the guards were furnished with rope whips, their several cords knotted at intervals. On Brutus's command, the guards struck, again and again. The prisoners cried out, at first with each strike, then continually as the pain did not recede before the next blow but throbbed and stung, their backs nothing but red, raw flesh, their blood trickling over their flanks and down their legs to speckle the Senate house stones. Onlookers standing in the front row of the crowd were daubed with their blood as the whips flew.

It was mesmerising to watch, to see the blood flow, to hear the men's cries. It was only when the whips stilled that Volumnia heard the sound of the crowd in her ears and realised that not everyone was cheering. Aemilia had her head down, her hand over her eyes. Kaeso had lost his expression of excitement; his face now bore an expression of shock and confusion. Volumnia caught Menenius's eye.

'You should go home,' he said, his voice shaking. 'Caecilius would not want you to see this. I was wrong to let you come.'

She gave a snort of disgust. 'You are not my husband, Menenius, to tell me what I can and cannot do. And why should I not see this?'

'It is not fit for a lady's eyes,' Menenius persisted, his hands on her shoulders as if he could force her bodily from the forum. 'Such brutality.'

'But this is justice, isn't it? Those men have been denounced as traitors.'

Menenius shook his head and released her. 'I don't know how Brutus could stand by and watch his sons be punished in this way.'

'I understand him,' Volumnia said, her eyes seeking out Brutus. He hadn't moved. He had his arms folded over his chest and his eyes were fixed on his sons. She couldn't tell from such a distance but he didn't look as if he had yet shed a tear. 'He's a true man, mindful of his honour. His sons disgraced his family and he cannot allow that to go unpunished. I would do the same.'

'You would?' Menenius asked, horrified.

'If I were a man and had the power,' Volumnia nodded. 'Of course, Caius would never do anything to disgrace his family so I will never be placed in such a situation, but I would do it if I had to.'

Menenius stared at her for a long moment, then shook his head. 'You would not, Volumnia. I do not believe you.' He leaned in close. 'And besides, I thought you were in favour of the monarchy. I thought you would have applauded the conspirators' efforts to bring Tarquin back, not revel in their failure.'

'Perhaps I have been wrong,' Volumnia shrugged carelessly, returning her gaze to the prisoners. 'I don't believe the king would ever have had the strength of character to execute his sons, and the gods know, they have disappointed him often. Quiet now.'

The prisoners were being released from the carts. The Brutus and Vitellii brothers stumbled as the guards tried to make them form a line before the crowd, but Marcus and Lucius Aquilii walked almost proudly to their appointed spots. All six were forced onto their knees. The guards drew their swords and moved to stand behind them.

Mettius Trebonius gave the word and the guards plunged their swords downward. The men cried out, their bodies writhing as the swords continued their path through their spines, severing the vertebrae. The guards pulled their swords out and the men collapsed, dead.

Volumnia breathed a sigh of relief. The men had died without naming her husband as their co-conspirator.

The sound of women screaming broke the silence that had

fallen. Volumnia stood on tiptoe to try to see who had screamed. 'Who is that?' she asked Menenius.

'That will be Brutus's wife and daughters, I expect,' Menenius said.

'There's Brutus now,' Aemilia said, pointing towards the platform.

Brutus was moving forward, stepping over the bodies to reach the front of the platform. He held up his arms. 'For his services to Rome, the slave Vindicius is to be given his freedom.' Brutus waved Vindicius forward, and the slave came forward tentatively, trying not to look at the bodies. Brutus pressed a small leather bag into his hand and some of the crowd cheered.

'What did he do?' Volumnia asked Menenius.

'He was Lucius Aquilii's slave. He overheard the whole plot and told Publius Valerius.' Menenius's lips curled in distaste. 'That a slave should be rewarded for informing on his master. It goes against all we hold dear.'

'I agree,' Volumnia nodded. 'If any slave of mine opened his mouth to tell of what went on in our family, I wouldn't just have him whipped, I can tell you.'

They watched as the bodies of the conspirators were gathered and hauled onto the cart, the guards slipping and sliding in the blood they left behind.

'It's over now, Volumnia, you've seen all there is to see,' Menenius said, taking hold of her elbow. 'Lady Aemilia, would you like to come with us?'

'Yes, we would,' Aemilia said earnestly. 'Thank you, Menenius.'

The crowd began to disperse and movement became easier. Aemilia grabbed Kaeso's wrist and pulled him along behind her. She was visibly shaken by what they had all witnessed, Volumnia knew, but then her mother had always been weak.

As they walked back to the domus, Volumnia's mind was on Brutus and how brave he had been. It took a special kind of person to sacrifice their children for the good of Rome. Brutus must truly believe in the idea of a republic. And if as strong a man as Brutus believed a republic was for the good of all Romans, then maybe it was time for Volumnia to become a true republican too.

10

Lucius bit down on the plum, feeling the juice spill over his lips and run down his chin. Before it could spill onto his toga, Lolly had pressed a linen cloth to his chin and wiped the juice away. He smiled at her and she smiled back.

Life had certainly improved since arriving in Tarquinii. For one thing, Lolly had stopped complaining about the hardships of living in tents. One of Tarquinii's more sycophantic citizens had vacated his domus and offered it to the Tarquins, theirs for as long as they chose to remain in the city. It was not as spacious or as luxurious as their own royal domus in Rome had been, but it was a more than acceptable substitute for their tent.

And there was entertainment to be enjoyed too, something that had been sorely lacking in the Roman camps. Tonight, he and Lolly were enjoying a troupe of dancers at another citizen's domus, an exuberant finale to the fine dinner they had consumed. The dancers were excellent, Lucius thought as he swallowed the plum, probably Etruscan, like his ancestors, for everyone knew all the best performers were Etruscan. Except the Romans, he thought ruefully. They wouldn't know good dancers if they kicked them in the face, just as they hadn't appreciated him as their king. The dance came to an end, and he clapped vigorously in appreciation but his thoughts were still on his former Roman subjects. *I'll show them,* he told himself. *If they thought I was ruthless before, then as soon as I'm back in Rome, I'll show them how vengeful I can be.*

'Weren't they good, Lucius?' Lolly said, leaning up against him. 'We should hire them when we get back to Rome.'

Lucius nodded an assent and looking up, caught sight of Titus threading his way through the audience, making for them. 'Where has he been?'

'He said the envoys from Rome were returning tonight and he wanted to meet them.' Lolly beamed up at her son as he approached. 'Titus, such a shame you've missed the dancers.'

'Yes, I'm sure, Mother,' Titus said distractedly, crouching down before them.

'What's the matter?' Lucius asked, noticing his son's grim expression.

'The envoys have returned, Father.' He shook his head. 'It isn't good news.'

'Wait,' Lolly said, putting her hand on Titus's shoulder as he opened his mouth to continue. She stood and addressed their host sitting a few feet away. 'Thank you, it's been a wonderful evening. But we must go to our beds now. I'm very tired.' Gesturing to Lucius to rise, Lolly made their farewells, and all three strode out of the domus. As they entered the cool night air, and the torch boys roused themselves to escort them home, Titus tried to speak again, but again Lolly shushed him. It wasn't until they were back in their loaned domus that she allowed him to deliver his bad news.

'The envoys were lucky to get out of Rome alive,' Titus said. 'They met with the Senate and asked for our goods and property back. The Senate were considering it, they said, though the envoys said there was no true enthusiasm to make restoration. My letter was delivered to the Aquilii and they acted on it. They had the support of the Vitellii and, you'll like this part, Father, Brutus's own sons, Tiberius and Titus.' He smiled, but then the grin dropped off his face. 'But it was all for nothing. They were betrayed by a slave who overheard the entire plan. He informed on them and they were all arrested and executed. The envoys were told to leave or they would be killed too.'

'Wait,' Lolly peered up into her son's face, 'are you saying Brutus raised no objection to his sons' execution?'

Titus laughed hollowly. 'Objection, Mother? It was Brutus who ordered their execution.'

Lolly covered her mouth with her hands, her eyes wide above the fingers. 'How could he kill his own sons?'

Titus looked at his father. 'I'm sorry, Father. We tried.'

'Lucius,' Lolly said in a calm voice, noting the grim expression on her husband's face, 'it wasn't Titus's fault. Rome is full of treachery, we know that.'

'Indeed,' Lucius nodded. 'So, what do you suggest we do? Do we buy a hut here in Tarquinii with the few aes we have, dear wife? Do we beg food and drink from our Tarquinii hosts for the rest of our lives?'

'No,' she said sternly, jerking her head at Titus to move out of Lucius's reach. 'We still fight. We will just have to do it without any help from inside Rome, that's all.'

'That's all?' Lucius roared, unable to contain his anger any longer.

'Yes,' Lolly shouted back. 'We've tried diplomacy and failed. Very well, but the Tarquinii have already pledged their support and we know the Veii will be with us too. Rome cannot summon up such an army. With such a force as we will have, Lucius, Rome will be ours again after the very first battle.'

Lucius took a deep breath, only a little mollified by her confidence. 'If you say so, Lolly.'

'I do,' she said, giving him a kiss. 'I promise, Rome's going to be very sorry she ever turned on us.'

Volumnia felt movement behind her in the bed and rolled over to see what Caecilius was doing. It was so unlike him to be restless; he normally got into bed and fell asleep straight away. She opened one bleary eye. 'Caius!' she cried in surprise. 'What are you doing in my bed?'

'Can't sleep,' Caius mumbled, trying to burrow closer.

She lifted her arm over her head and he shifted towards her. His small body crushed her breast but she didn't mind, didn't tell him to move. She vaguely wondered where Caecilius was. 'Did you have a nightmare?' she asked, stroking his hair.

'No. The banging woke me up.'

She felt him yawn. 'What banging?'

'In the room next to me.'

'The storeroom?'

Caius nodded.

She sat up, gently pushing him off. 'Which slave is it? I'll have them whipped for disturbing you.'

'It's Father,' Caius said, tugging at her elbow for her to lie down again.

'What in Hades is he doing?'

'I don't know,' Caius said impatiently, closing his eyes.

'Stay here,' she said, throwing off the sheet and getting out of the bed. She padded along the corridor, past Caius's cubiculum to the storeroom at the back of the domus. She could hear the banging now and pushed the door open. 'Caecilius, what are you doing?'

Caecilius looked up sharply, startled by her voice. 'Go back to bed,' he said crossly.

'You woke Caius with all...,' Volumnia waved her hand at the disordered room, 'this.' She looked behind him at the trunk whose lid was open and propped up against the wall. 'Why are you looking in there?'

'Because I'm going to war and I need my armour.'

'To war?'

'Oh, now you're interested.' He nodded behind her at the doorway. 'I see you've still got your shadow.'

Volumnia turned. Caius was peering around the doorway. 'You woke him up. What war?'

Caecilius looked down into the trunk. 'Where's my sword? I can't find it.'

'It's not in there,' Volumnia said impatiently. 'War with whom?'

Caecilius slammed the lid down on the trunk. 'The king. No, that's my mistake. I should say the former king of Rome. The Senate received a declaration of war from Lucius Tarquin this evening. The Tarquinii and the Veii are with him, maybe more of the tribes are too, it's not clear. But he has amassed quite a significant army, large enough to worry the Senate. So, all able-bodied men, and I daresay, even those that aren't, are to arm and present themselves by noon on the Field of Mars.' He straightened and put his hands on his hips. 'I suppose you're thinking how fortunate I am to be going to war.'

He was being sarcastic, Volumnia knew, but he was also right; she was thinking exactly that. She didn't give him the satisfaction of an answer.

'So, aren't I lucky?' Caecilius grinned mockingly at her. 'Off I go tomorrow to fight our king.'

'He's not our king any longer, Cae,' she said, refusing to rise to his bait.

He shook his head. 'Time was when you wouldn't hear a word said against the king. Now, you're happy to have me fight him.'

'Things change, husband.'

'They do indeed. So, tell me, where is my sword?'

'In the atrium, near the shrine. The gods protect it.'

'I haven't seen it there.'

'It's in the floor, beneath the largest tile. It's wrapped in leather, well protected. In every sense.'

'You think of everything.'

Volumnia had had enough of his sarcasm. She turned and guided Caius back to her cubiculum. She climbed into the bed and held the sheet up for him to do the same.

'Does Father not want to go to war?' Caius asked as he tucked himself in.

'He'd rather not, it seems,' Volumnia said, resting her head on the pillow and laying her arm across him.

'I wish I could go.'

'Of course you do,' she said, squeezing and pulling him closer, 'because you're a brave little man.'

'Isn't Father brave?'

Volumnia sighed. 'No, not any more.'

'Is the king a bad man, Mother?'

'I don't know, Caius.'

'If he isn't, why isn't he still the king here?'

'Such a lot of questions, my boy.'

'I just want to know.'

'Well, his son did something he shouldn't, and the people didn't like it. A man got up on the rostra in the forum and said we should throw the king and his family out of Rome and not let them back in. The people agreed and so now we don't have a king.'

'Is it better not to have a king, then?'

'I'm really not sure, my love. It's all so new. I expect you and I will hardly notice the difference. After all, your father had to go off to war before when the king ruled here. I suppose it doesn't really matter who in Rome tells you to fight, Caius. If Rome needs your sword, you provide it. You remember that when you're older.'

'I could go to war now,' Caius declared.

Volumnia's mouth puckered in a smile but she did not laugh. It would have suggested she was laughing at him and Caius would be hurt. 'But if you were to go to war with your father, and Uncle Menenius too, I suppose, I would have no one to keep me company, would I, Caius? You wouldn't want me to be all alone, would you?'

Caius sat up in bed and looked down at her, his expression serious. 'I'll never let you be alone, Mother. We'll always be together.'

Her throat tightened, and she sucked in her bottom lip, letting her teeth press into the soft flesh. 'I know you mean that now, Caius, but you will go off to fight some day and I wouldn't dream of stopping you.'

He frowned. 'I do want to fight, but...'. His face lit up with a sudden idea. 'You would have Grandmother and Uncle Menenius to look after you, wouldn't you?'

'Oh, you silly thing,' she said, taking his face between her hands and kissing his mouth, 'I was only teasing you. I don't need looking after, and I won't have you worrying about me when you're off fighting. I shall be perfectly well. I only meant that I don't want to lose you to war just yet. There'll be other wars for you to fight, there always are, but in a few years' time, Caius.'

Caius nodded and lay down, pressing his face into her breasts. Volumnia felt his breath moisten her skin and closed her eyes. They were both fast asleep when Caecilius returned to the cubiculum, having found his sword and gathered all his armour together. He took one look at the pair of them, then left to spend what remained of the night in Caius's bed.

11

Caecilius could hardly believe how his world had changed. Time was when he would have laughed at the idea of Lucius Iunius Brutus leading a rebellion against the king, let alone being in command of the equites. Now, Caecilius had to take orders from the pretended imbecile and charge into battle to fight against the father of his best friend. He supposed he really had chosen his side; there was no going back now. He had become a republican, despite all his better instincts and finer feelings. And he was sorry for it. Others would scoff, he knew, but he had genuinely liked Prince Titus and, he didn't think he flattered himself, Titus had liked him in return. Certainly, Caecilius had had hopes of gaining by the friendship when Titus became king, but that hadn't been all there was to the bond they shared. Titus had been a true friend.

Caecilius looked longingly at the forest to the right of the battle lines. He wished he could ride his mare into those trees and not stop until they came out the other side, far away from the battle, from the politics, from Rome herself. *Volumnia would despise me if I did that*, he thought, and Volumnia's disapproval was the last thing he needed. He knew his duty, knew what he had to do, what he had been trained to do from a boy. He had to plunge his sword into as many enemies as he could without dying himself, if he could manage it.

The order to charge came. Caecilius saw his fellow equites gallop away and kicked his mare's side to catch up. As soon as he felt the vibrations of hundreds of horses' hooves through his body, his mind focused and he held his sword out straight, ready to pierce the enemy.

When the clash came, everything became a blur. He stabbed and withdrew his sword, struggled to keep his seat, stabbed and stabbed again. The mare began to stumble as bodies littered the ground, not only those of his victims but those of his fellow soldiers too. She high-stepped and began to disregard his tugs on the reins. Too many bodies, too much screaming and slashing. She was frightened and he feared she would rear. He dismounted and slapped her rump to encourage her to leave the battlefield. She needed little persuasion and galloped away back to the camp.

His arm was aching, the muscles burning, and he knew his body was tiring. He fell, his feet slipping in the mud between bodies, and he stayed down, trying to catch his breath as sharp pains constricted his chest. He had had these pains before but not so harsh. His head felt like it would burst, blood pulsing up his neck and flooding his ears. He had to get away from the fighting. He was vulnerable here, down on his knees in the mud, trying to breathe. He crawled to the left, to a clump of bushes, and crouched behind them. After a minute or so, the pains eased away; he took tentative breaths, testing his lungs. He closed his eyes. He would stay here, behind the bushes, out of sight, out of the way, and to Hades with Volumnia's disdain.

But then Caecilius heard movement from the other side of the bush and he tightened his grip on his sword, cursing whoever it was for ruining his plan. He pushed himself up to a crouching position, his knees protesting, and waited. The bush shivered as someone pushed against it and Caecilius braced himself. He was about to raise his sword when he saw who it was.

It was Prince Titus.

They both stared stupidly at one another for a long moment.

'Titus, I—', Caecilius croaked, but got no further, for Titus lunged and his sword sliced through Caecilius's shoulder.

The skin split and Caecilius felt his own hot blood pour down his left arm. Astonished by Titus's attack, he froze, giving Titus the chance to lunge again. This time Titus got him in the side, above his left hip where his breastplate had risen up. Reacting instinctively, he thrust his sword arm upwards. He heard the cry of pain and felt the resistance of bone against the blade and knew he had wounded his friend.

It was enough. Titus was down; he had no desire to kill him. He got to his feet, wincing as his left side protested. He moved away from the bush and saw that the battle was almost over, the field nearly deserted save for bodies. Every step was painful. The edges of his vision began to darken; the way in front of him seemed to turn upside down. And then he was tumbling, and the ground, the muddy, bloody ground, hit him hard in the face.

Lucius opened his eyes, having to pull hard to break the crust sealing his lids. The light hurt and he closed them again, waiting for the pain to subside before risking opening them again. He bore the light this time and slowly, his vision focused. Fabric billowed above his head, and it took him a moment to realise he was in a tent. He drew on his senses to work out exactly where. He was lying on something hard and high off the ground. Not his campaign bed, then. A table, probably. He heard voices, lots of them: urgent words, groans, screams. Understanding washed over him; he was in the surgeon's tent. He had been found on the battlefield and brought here to be worked upon. He wondered how badly hurt he was. Everything hurt. His arms throbbed, skin tightened and tugged on his legs. He tried turning his head to the side, wincing as his neck muscles complained, urging him to stop. It was enough; he could see men laid out on tables just like him, bloody and battered.

If he was here, did that mean it was all over? Had he lost the battle? How was that even possible? His scouts had reported that the Roman army was far smaller than his, that his army had the best ground. They'd lied to him. Was there no one he could trust? Well, he was done. No more armies, no more fighting, no more hopeless dreams of being king of Rome once more. He would make his home in Tarquinii and live a quiet life, a private person, unambitious, content with his lot.

He heard a groan and there was something familiar in the sound. He turned his head again and focused on the man lying on the table a few feet away. The face was covered in dried blood but he recognised the profile. It was Titus. Lucius called to his son, reaching out an aching arm towards him but they were too far apart. He couldn't reach.

Someone grabbed his arm and forced it back to his side. 'Be still now, my king,' a voice said.

'That's my son,' Lucius gasped.

'Yes, I know. You must not exert yourself. You will open the stitches.'

'Is he dead?' Lucius cried, unheeding.

'No, the prince is not dead, but he is badly wounded.'

Lucius couldn't help himself; he began to cry. His tears were hot on his cheeks. He thought of Lolly, back in Tarquinii and safe. He suddenly longed to be with her, not here on this accursed battlefield, watching his son die. Lolly would never forgive him if Titus died. He would never forgive himself.

'Save him,' he implored through his tears. 'Save him and I will give you all my gold.'

'I'm doing what I can,' the surgeon said. 'You must pray to the gods to save your son.'

Lucius, a man who had always resented being told what to do, obeyed and mumbled prayers to Jove, to Bellona, to Mars, to Mercury, to all the gods he could think of, that they would show favour to this most unfortunate man who had lost his country, his fortune and his position, not to make him lose his son too.

She waved away the smoke stinging her eyes. The sword was heavy in her hand but she tightened her grip, anxious lest it should fall. She had rubbed grit into her palms, determined she wouldn't sweat and so risk her hold. She felt everything: the ground beneath her feet, the stones pressing into the soles of her sandals, the splatter of mud on her calves, the wind that blew her hair about her face. The enemy was there, on the other side of the smoke. She took a deep breath and began her roar, brewing it in the pit of her stomach, letting it build as it worked its way up her body, until it reached her throat and pressed against the sides. It had to come out, it had to be set free. She opened her mouth wide…

'Domina, domina!'

Volumnia started awake. ‘Wh… what is it?’

The slave shook her again. ‘The master has come home, domina.’

‘Now?’ Volumnia was incredulous. She knew it must still be night for the slave held an oil lamp and no light came in through the window. She threw off the bedsheet and held her arms out for her dressing gown.

‘The master is injured, domina,’ the slave said as he put it on her. ‘He was brought here on a cart.’

Volumnia didn’t wait to hear more. She rushed out of the cubiculum, her bare feet making slapping noises on the cold tiles, and ran through to the atrium. The front doors were closing as she arrived and she came to a stop as she stared down at Caecilius lying on a stretcher on the atrium’s floor. A blanket was pulled up to his chin and he was asleep, or unconscious, she couldn’t tell.

‘Volumnia!’

The voice startled her. She hadn’t noticed Menenius in the darkness. ‘Menenius, is he badly wounded?’

‘The doctor said so. He’s done all he can.’

‘Get him into bed,’ Volumnia instructed the slave she recognised as the man Caecilius had taken with him when he left for war.

The four household slaves had been roused and arrived en masse in the atrium. Each one took a corner of the stretcher and Caecilius was lifted into the air. As the stretcher passed Volumnia, she smelt a foul, decaying odour and shot a look at Menenius. ‘What is it?’

‘Gangrene,’ Menenius told her as they followed after the stretcher. ‘The doctor did consider amputation, but the wound is very near the shoulder and he thinks the infection has spread too far for amputation to be of any use.’

They had reached the door of the cubiculum and they

watched as Caecilius was lifted from the stretcher onto the bed. He stirred and mumbled but did not wake.

'He will die, then?' Volumnia whispered.

'Volumnia—'

'Speak truth, Menenius. You need not use soft words with me.'

'Yes, he will die.'

'Soon?'

'The doctor seemed to think so.'

'Does Caecilius know?'

'I couldn't say, my dear. He's been in and out of consciousness for days. We... we haven't really been able to talk.'

Volumnia felt his eyes on her. Was he expecting her to cry? Surely, he knew her better than that? She stepped to the bed and looked down on Caecilius. He looked so much older than when he had left her a month or so before. Her nose wrinkled as she pulled back the blanket and his injured arm was exposed to her view. Had the fool of a doctor waited too long to diagnose gangrene? If she insisted on the arm being amputated, would Caecilius live? But what if he did? she mused. The damaged arm was his left and so he would still be able to hold a sword but his balance would be off, and he would not be able to defend himself with a shield.

'And the war?' she asked. 'Is it over?'

'Yes. Tarquin was defeated and fled. But Brutus was killed in the battle.'

So, the man who had started all this and banished the king was dead himself. Perhaps that was for the best. Brutus's insistence on the execution of his sons had not gone down well among the plebs. No one could understand how a man could order his own sons to be killed, regardless of their crime, and it seemed to suggest he had a nature every bit as tyrannous as the Tarquins he had exiled. Better he was gone.

She turned back to Menenius but her eye caught something behind him in the doorway. She smiled, causing Menenius to frown and turn too. 'Caius, you're awake. Look, Menenius, hasn't he grown?'

'Indeed he has, Volumnia,' Menenius said, forcing a smile onto his face as he looked down at Caius. 'Caecilius will be proud of him.'

'Is Father sick, Mother?' Caius asked.

'Your father is very ill, Caius. See that wound there,' she pointed to Caecilius's shoulder. 'That has become infected and is poisoning your father's blood.'

Caius looked up at her. 'Is he going to die?'

'Yes, he is,' she said.

Caius returned his gaze to his father and studied him for a long moment. Then he looked back up at Volumnia and smiled. 'Then it will be just you and me, Mother.'

PART III

503 BC - 493 BC

12

Caius had lost sight of Menenius in the field below; he'd been distracted by the fighting. There was so much of it, and so many of the equites had been unseated that there was no telling who was who. Caius wanted to be there, in among it all, not in the camp, keeping an eye on the baggage carts.

When the news had come that the Volsci had declared war on Rome and his mother had told him he was going to war, Caius had thought he would be fighting. He hadn't expected to go to war as Uncle Menenius's servant. But that had been all his war had been: sharpening swords, repairing wooden saddles and ensuring his horse was fed its daily allowance of barley and keeping its wounds clean. Not that Caius minded looking after Menenius's horse. He liked horses and looked forward to the day when he had one of his own, but he did so want to fight.

And he was needed in the battle, Caius could see that. The Volsci were a fearsome enemy. The tales around the camp-fires, those that Menenius had allowed him to be present at, had been very candid about how well the Volsci fought. Caius had been shocked to hear the Roman soldiers talk of the

Volsci almost with awe. He had always believed the Romans to be the best fighters in all the world, that's what his mother had told him, but here were men who had actually been in battle against the Volsci saying how hard they fought and how they had been lucky to escape with their lives.

Caius heard hoof beats to his right and turned. Menenius's horse was galloping back to the camp. Its reins were hanging down and there was foam and blood at its mouth where the bit had dug into the flesh, but there was no rider. He ran towards the horse and grabbed the trailing reins. The horse pulled and jerked away but Caius held tight and spoke softly. The animal calmed and stopped its tugging, and began snorting and stamping the ground. Caius stroked its nose and looked out over the field. Where was Uncle Menenius?

He shouted to another of the camp boys to take the horse, knowing it was too frightened to take him into the battle. He would have to go on foot, though it was an indignity for someone of his patrician class, boy or no. He ran down the hill, his feet swift as if he flew, his footing sure. He reached the rear of where the battlelines had been and he started to run through fallen men. These were just the infantry, he saw, and besides, Menenius wouldn't be near the back where the cowards lingered. He'd be up at the front where the fighting was. Caius grabbed a sword from one of the fallen as he ran, a pitiful thing, battered and unbalanced, probably the sword of a farmer or a shepherd, but it would have to do. It had a sharp point, it could still kill, and that was all that mattered.

Caius headed for the fighting, having to jump over bodies now, for the piles had grown higher. His quick eyes searched for Menenius on the ground but did not find him there. He kept on, searching, searching. He was so near now to the fighting and he longed to jump into the middle of it, but he felt finding Menenius had to be his only duty. He skirted around the fighting, and drew up short when he spotted Menenius on the ground, one leg bent backwards, an arm flung out.

'Uncle Menenius,' he gasped, falling to his knees beside him.

'Caius,' Menenius croaked. One eye was bleeding, the flesh beneath pouchy and purple. Blood trickled from the corner of his mouth.

'Can you move, Uncle?' Caius asked.

'Get away,' Menenius panted. 'Get back to the camp.'

Keeping hold of the sword, Caius put his free arm around his back, clamping his hand beneath Menenius's armpit. 'You're coming with me,' he said, giving a great heave. But Menenius was too heavy, and he succeeded only in bringing Menenius up to a sitting position.

Menenius groaned with the effort, then cried, 'Look out.'

Instinctively, Caius gripped the sword tighter and shifted around on his knees. He saw a body hurtling towards him and he thrust his sword out, feeling it grow heavier as it entered flesh. The man crumpled and Caius withdrew the sword. A full six inches of blade was covered in blood. His heart beat faster. Another man rushed at him, and letting go of Menenius, he quickly got to his knees and charged, running the man through. Oh, the joy he felt as another body fell to the ground.

'Caius!' Menenius called feebly.

Reluctantly, Caius returned to Menenius's side. He moved behind him, and throwing down his sword, bent and put his arms around Menenius's chest. He heaved Menenius to his feet and staggered a little under his weight.

'Leave me,' Menenius gasped.

'I won't,' Caius said. 'I'll get you back to the camp.'

'Take care, then.'

'I will.' Caius saw that Menenius still gripped his sword. 'Give me your sword, Uncle.' He bent it free from Menenius's fingers.

Caius judged the quickest route back to the camp. They moved slowly. Caius hadn't been able to tell where Menenius had been wounded, but he could see that his left ankle was red and swollen and Menenius seemed unable to put any weight on it. It was hard going, dragging and lifting Menenius over the field littered with bodies, and it was a testament to his strength that Caius, a fourteen-year-old boy, could aid a full grown, injured man.

They reached the edge of the battlefield and Caius looked back over his shoulder. The battle seemed to be ending, the fighting lessening. Caius could not help but feel a little disappointed not to have been a part of it from the first.

'Nearly there?' Menenius asked hopefully.

'Nearly.'

'I thank the gods for you, my boy,' Menenius said. He turned his head towards Caius, the beginnings of a smile upon his lips, but then his eyes widened. 'Caius!'

Caius whirled around and his heart banged in his chest as he saw a young man running towards him. He let go of Menenius once more, not hearing Menenius's grunt as he fell to the ground, and prepared himself for the assault. When it came, it knocked the breath out of him. The young man was strong and determined, and Caius could only fend off his sword, growing frustrated at his inability to land a blow himself.

There were shouts from the Roman camp. He saw the young man look behind him and he turned to do the same. It was a foolish, unthinking action, for the next moment, Caius felt a sharp pain in the fleshy part of his forearm. He looked down and saw blood oozing from a small wound. Caius looked up, ready to respond in kind, but the young man had seen the danger he was putting himself in, alone and so near the Roman camp. He was retreating back to the Volscian lines, but not in fear, not in a hurry. He almost sauntered and when he got halfway across, he turned full square to the Romans, raised his arms high and wide and cried, 'Volsci.'

Caius watched the young man until he disappeared into the distance. He looked down at his wound. It was deep but not dangerous; the young man's sword had only pierced him. Why, when he could have run him through the guts? Caius wondered. As he bent to pick Menenius up, the answer came to him. It was his youth that had deterred the young man from killing him. There was no honour in killing a boy.

'Do you know who that was?' he asked as he bent to pick Menenius up again.

Menenius took a deep breath and allowed Caius to drag him forward. 'We should both be dead.'

'Why so, Uncle?'

'Because that, Caius, was Tullus Aufidius.'

Back in Rome

'I owe Caius Marcius my life, Gabinia.'

Menenius took a deep breath and braced himself for his wife's response. Part of him wished he had not broached the subject, but he could not in all honour ignore the service Caius had done him that awful day on the battlefield.

There had been other battles after that one — the Sabines had taken advantage of Rome's war with the Volsci to join in the attack — though none had been so fierce, and Menenius had fought bravely in all of them. His wounds had healed well and his recovery had been swift, and he had Caius to thank for that. Menenius had no doubt he would have died had Caius obeyed his orders that day and remained in the camp, looking after the horses.

'And I am grateful to the boy,' Gabinia said, 'but we mustn't take gratitude too far. The Senate have granted you a triumph. *You*, my dear, not Caius Marcius.'

'And I can have my triumph, Gabinia, I'm not arguing with you about that. I just think Caius and his mother should be with us, that's all.'

'I disagree,' Gabinia said, smiling even as she shook her head. 'This is your day. I daresay you could thank half a dozen men for their service to you during the war. Are you going to invite all of them to the feast?'

'No, of course not,' Menenius said irritably.

'Of course not. Just Caius and his mother,' Gabinia said, all pretence at indifference gone. 'Well, I won't have them there, Menenius. I will not share a platform with your whore.'

'Gabinia,' Menenius yelled, outraged. 'Volumnia is not my whore. She is the widow of a very dear friend to whom I owe a duty of care.'

'Fine words, husband,' Gabinia snapped. 'Call her what you will, I do not care. She can see your triumph from the streets with the plebs, and she can stuff her face with her own food afterwards.' She rose from the table and left the room without another word.

Relieved she had gone, Menenius finished his breakfast and then headed for his tablinum. He sat down at his desk and dipped his reed pen into the ink.

My dearest Volumnia,

I had hopes of having you and Caius with me on the day of my triumph but I fear it cannot be. My wife fails to appreciate the great service your son performed for me while we were away at war, but be assured, I do not. That a boy of fourteen could not only brave the battlefield, a truly fearsome place, but kill two men and see off a third in his rescue of me is remarkable. Volumnia, your son is truly favoured by the gods. I know it is due to your determination to see him a soldier that made him able to defend himself and me. You have much to be proud of, and I know Caecilius would be proud of you both.

He wasn't sure of that last, but felt obliged to mention Volumnia's dead husband. He wrote a final sentence assuring Volumnia he would see her and Caius as soon after the triumph as he could manage and then signed his name.

Menenius sent his slave to deliver the letter and then retired to his cubiculum to dress for his triumph. It was going to be a great day. It wasn't every soldier of Rome who was granted a triumph, and during the reign of the last king, no Roman soldier had ever been so honoured, for no man had been allowed to outshine the king.

Yes, Menenius decided, there was certainly something to be said in favour of a republic.

Someone was banging on the front doors. Volumnia pulled on her dressing gown and stepped out into the corridor, her eyes taking time to become accustomed to the darkness. She tutted, annoyed the slaves were taking so long to rouse themselves. Must she do everything herself?

A flickering light appeared in the atrium — so at least one of them had risen — and Volumnia headed towards it. 'Leave the bar down,' she called out to the slave who carried the oil lamp, 'and ask who it is.'

The slave nodded and moved gingerly to the door. He leant his body towards it. 'Who's there?'

'It's me. Open up,' a voice called.

Volumnia sighed. 'It's only Menenius Agrippa. You can let him in.'

The slave lifted the heavy wooden bar out of its brackets and opened the door. Menenius was leaning against the frame, grinning stupidly.

'Menenius Agrippa, what are you doing?' Volumnia said laughing, shaking her head in mock disapproval.

'I just came to say hello, and to say sorry.' Menenius stumbled over the threshold and the slave bent to catch him. He chuckled. 'I may be a little drunk.'

'More than a little, I'd say.' Volumnia took hold of his arm. She groaned as she pushed him upright.

Menenius leaned into her, his face a few inches from hers. 'How lovely you are,' he said, reaching up to run a finger down her cheek.

'Don't talk nonsense,' Volumnia scolded. She could smell the wine on his breath. 'It's too late to be paying a visit.'

'Did you see me today?' Menenius asked, putting his arm around Volumnia's shoulder and moving forward, forcing her to do the same, despite her attempt to head him back towards the door.

'Of course I did. You didn't think I would miss your triumph, did you? I saw you ride into the forum on your chariot, your face painted red like Jove himself. I saw the crowds cheering you—'

'Was I magnificent?'

'You were,' she nodded at him, noting that there were flecks of red paint around his hairline where he had not quite washed it all off.

Menenius tried to stand upright unaided, and without

thinking, Volumnia reached up to brush the paint away. He seized her hand and kissed it fervently. She was so surprised, she did nothing nor said a word. Her inaction encouraged him. Menenius grabbed her face and pulled her towards him, his wet lips sliding over her mouth.

'Uncle Menenius!'

They broke apart and stared at Caius standing in the atrium's doorway.

'Oh, Caius, are you up?' Volumnia said, her voice shaky with embarrassment. 'Shame on you, Menenius. You've woken the entire household with your foolishness.'

Caius stepped forward, the oil lamp the slave carried casting deep shadows over his face. But even in the semi-darkness, Volumnia could tell he was angry. He wasn't looking at her. He was looking past her at Menenius and she followed his gaze. Menenius had one arm outstretched against the wall, trying to stop himself from falling over.

'Menenius is a little intoxicated, Caius,' she explained with a little unsure laugh.

'I've been celebrating, Caius,' Menenius said cheerily.

Caius was unmoved. 'So I see, Uncle.'

'And as I didn't get to see you at my triumph, I thought I would come and see you now.'

'You should have waited until tomorrow.'

'Yes, yes,' Menenius agreed, nodding slowly, 'you're quite right. I should have come in the morning.' He stumbled towards the door, then turned and looked at Volumnia. 'I am sorry you weren't invited to the feast, at least. It wasn't my idea.' He was about to say more but then he glanced at Caius and something in that young man's expression changed his mind. 'I'll go now.'

The slave hurried to hold the door open and Menenius

walked unsteadily through it. He didn't look back as the slave closed the door and put the bar back in place.

'Why did you let him in, Mother?' Caius asked.

'He was banging on the door, Caius.'

'That was no reason.'

'Oh, and what should I have done?' she asked, her voice rising. 'Let him go on making such a noise? The neighbours would have been roused.'

'Better they be roused and see him making a disturbance than they see him being admitted to my domus in the early hours of the morning.'

Volumnia's breath caught in her throat. 'Why… what do you mean?'

Caius's eyes were hard. 'I won't have you his mistress.'

'How dare you say so!' Volumnia cried. 'As if I would—'

'He was kissing you,' Caius suddenly roared, his temper no longer kept in check. 'I saw you.'

Her breath was coming fast. Caius had never spoken to her like this before. 'He took a liberty,' she said as calmly as she could. 'I would have slapped his face had you given me a chance.'

They stared at one another for a long moment.

'I believe you, Mother,' Caius said at last. 'But I must insist that you never allow Uncle Menenius into this house when I am not here.'

He really is becoming a man, Volumnia thought, trying not to smile, *he's jealous of Menenius.* She drew a deep breath. 'Very well, Caius. I will not allow Menenius Agrippa to enter this domus if you are not in it.' Holding out her hand, she flicked her fingers at him. He hesitated a moment, long enough, she knew, just to show he followed his own inclination and not hers as he gripped her fingers. 'There, does that satisfy you?'

Caius squeezed her fingers a little too hard. 'It does, Mother.'

Menenius walked onto the Field of Mars and surveyed the scene before him. Caius and Volumnia were here, he knew, their slave had told him so when he called at the domus, but he couldn't see them. He took a deep breath and stepped into the crowd.

He was getting too old, he told himself for the umpteenth time that morning. He wasn't a young man who could drink five jugs of wine and feel no ill effects any longer. How much had he drunk? He couldn't remember. All he knew was that, here he was, two days later, still paying the price for his overindulgence.

He could have endured the physical discomfort if he could only forget his visit to Volumnia. He didn't recall every word he had uttered, every stumble he had made, but he knew he had made a fool of himself and the knowledge made his insides shrivel up in shame. And then there was the way Caius had spoken to him. He had deserved the rebuke, he knew, but still, to be told off by a boy...

He should have apologised straight away, the very next morning, but he hadn't woken until the early afternoon and then had barely been able to get out of bed. Now, it would look as if he didn't care what he had done, that he wasn't sorry. He could only hope both Volumnia and Caius would forgive him. Their friendship was not one he wanted to lose.

Menenius forced a smile onto his face as he wandered about the field, accepting congratulations on his triumph from those who recognised him. Several people tried to stop him and engage him in conversation, but he was determined not to be diverted from his task and sidestepped them quickly. He had a sudden flash of inspiration and made his way to where the wrestling took place. If Caius and Volumnia were on the field, that was where they would be.

Wrestling was a common sport among Rome's young men. It kept them fit when not training for war and gave them a chance to show off to the girls who would gather in groups to watch and make eyes at them. The wrestling often drew those wanting to win a few aes as bets were always placed on who would win. Caius often drew fewer gamblers than other wrestlers, simply because he was so difficult to beat; there were more riches to be made elsewhere on the field. But many people liked to watch him perform, all the same. Caius was so accomplished, it was a pleasure to watch him throw his opponent to the ground and lay across him, the dirt of the field mingling with the shining sweat on his long limbs and broad back.

Menenius had guessed right. Caius was there, in the middle of a circle marked out in the sand, his loincloth only a little stained by dust, for he had not yet been thrown. Young men were lining up on the opposite side of the circle to take their turn, all convinced they stood a chance of beating him. *Fools*, Menenius thought with a wry smile, *they will never beat Caius*. He scanned the ranks of onlookers and found Volumnia, feeling a lump form at the base of his throat. She was with Valeria, the wife of Publius Valerius, who was a terrible gossip. He could have done without her presence but there was no turning back now. Volumnia had seen him.

He edged through the crowd towards her. 'Salve, Volumnia.' He smiled a greeting at Valeria. 'I thought I would find you here.'

'Caius is wrestling,' Volumnia said, keeping her eyes on the match. 'Where else would I be?'

Valeria giggled. 'Never misses a chance to watch her son perform, do you, my dear?'

Volumnia ignored her. 'Nothing to do at the Senate today, Menenius?'

'Oh, yes, busy, busy,' he lied, for he had not been to the Senate house, 'but I wanted, that is, I needed to see you and Caius. Lady Valeria, would you mind if I spoke in private with Volumnia for a moment?'

Valeria, disappointed to be excluded from a conversation that sounded interesting, moved away.

Menenius took a deep breath. 'I apologise for my behaviour the other night. It was unforgivable.'

'And yet, here you are asking for forgiveness.'

'Yes, I suppose I am. Do I have your forgiveness?'

Volumnia turned to look at him. 'You have mine. I cannot answer for Caius. He was very cross.'

'I remember. And it grieves me that I angered him. I owe him so much.'

'You owe him your life, in fact.'

'I meant what I said. I did want you to be with me for my triumph. My wife would not allow it.'

'Are you a mouse that you do as your wife tells you?' she said scornfully. 'You, a celebrated soldier of Rome on his day of triumph being told by his wife that the young man who saved her husband's life cannot stand with him?'

'You are disappointed in me,' Menenius said, hanging his head.

'Very, I cannot deny it. For myself, it is of no matter, but Caius deserved the acclaim. He deserved to share a little of your glory. After all, you would not be alive to have had a triumph had it not been for him.'

'You're right,' Menenius agreed. 'I should have insisted. I owed him that.'

'You must do what you can to make it up to him.'

'I will. In whatever way I can,' he promised.

A cheer went up from the crowd. Caius had thrown his opponent and was holding out his hand to help him up. His expression showed only disdain for the applause from the onlookers and he glared at the girls who tried to attract his attention.

'Not that Caius has much to learn from me,' Menenius said, seeing Valeria out of the corner of his eye edging back towards them.

'Not in physical skills,' Volumnia agreed. 'But when he is old enough for the Senate, you will be of use.'

Menenius frowned. 'The Senate, Volumnia? Do you really think Caius has the right temperament for politics, my dear?'

Volumnia's eyes narrowed at him. 'It is his right as a patrician, Menenius. Caius deserves glory in every aspect of his life, and he will get it. He will prove himself in war, and then he will prove himself in politics. The gods have decreed it, Menenius. They have foretold that my son is going to be the greatest man in Rome.'

Antium

Gallio Aufidius wiped the sweat from Salonia's forehead with a cloth, folded it over, then wiped her throat and chest too. As he set the cloth to the side, he wondered why he was bothering. Salonia was asleep, she didn't notice his care of her. She had been like this for two days now. When would the fever break? He thought of taking her away when it did, back to the country, out of the city. She had never been ill when they had lived in their village. It was only since coming to Antium that Salonia had been coughing and complaining of aches and pains. But she wouldn't believe him when he told her so. She always said they were safer in the city, that living in the country in an isolated village made them vulnerable to attack. He couldn't argue with that. How many Roman raids had they endured when they lived in their village hut? Five, six? He'd lost count.

He wondered where Tullus had got to. Gallio resented his son's absence. Tullus should do his duty by his mother and spend some time tending to her, if for no other reason than to give his father a rest. He guessed where Tullus would be: with his friends, gambling and fighting, taking bets on who could land the first blow, who could keep his feet. Why did young men do it? Didn't they have enough of fighting in real wars that they had to play at it too? Tullus had nothing else to occupy him, that was the problem. His son should have a wife, he was too old to still be unmarried. With a wife to consider, Tullus wouldn't want to be always fighting. He would understand what duty truly meant.

Gallio heard footsteps in the corridor and turned towards the door.

'How is she?' Tullus asked quietly, tiptoeing into the room.

'Still the same,' Gallio said. 'Where have you been?'

Tullus shrugged in answer. He moved around to the other side of the bed and sat on the end, staring at Salonia.

Gallio studied Tullus. He looked excited. His leg jiggled and he kept tapping his fingers. 'What is it?'

'What?' Tullus looked up at him. 'Oh, nothing, it doesn't matter.'

'It obviously does matter. Tell me.'

Tullus looked down at his hands. 'There's news. The Romans are attacking again.'

'Attacking who?'

'The Romans have taken Fidenae and Crustumeria. They besieged Fidenae, so they had to surrender or starve or die from disease. As for Crustumeria,' Tullus shook his head, 'one battle, that was all it took for Rome to conquer them. And then I've heard only this morning that Praeneste have surrendered to Rome rather than fight. Do you hear, Father? Praeneste have sold themselves like a whore. And puffed up with their victories, Rome has now declared war on the Latin tribes. We'll be next, you see if we're not.'

'Tullus,' Gallio said, closing his eyes, knowing his son was working himself up into a fury.

'And you know what's been happening in Rome?' Tullus rose and began stalking the small cubiculum. 'They've had a triumph to celebrate. One of their commanders, Menenius Agrippa by name, was publicly lauded for his war service.'

'It is the Roman way, Tullus.'

'The bastards!'

'Tullus, hush. Think of your mother.'

'I do think of her. I think of how she nearly died giving birth to me because of Romans. I think of how you had to come and live in Antium to be safe from Romans. And it's because I think of her that I will be ready to fight Rome and destroy her utterly.'

Gallio looked at Salonia asleep in the bed and thought how proud she would be to hear their son talk so passionately about killing Romans.

13

Volumnia looked around the busy kitchen and wondered whether she had forgotten anything. She was not normally a woman to get easily flustered, but this day was so very important to Caius and she didn't want anything to go wrong. She checked over the food preparations, reminded the slaves of their duties, and headed towards the atrium where Aemilia, Kaeso and Menenius waited.

'There she is,' Menenius smiled at her as she entered. 'Is everything going to plan?'

'I think so,' she sighed. 'The slaves are getting the food ready for the feast and I had the domus decorated late last night. Does it look well?'

Menenius and Aemilia obligingly looked around the room at the decorations, the flowers and greenery that Volumnia had ordered cut from the garden.

'It looks lovely, my dear,' Aemilia said.

Kaeso fingered one of the roses. 'Don't do that,' Volumnia screeched almost hysterically.

'There's no need to shout,' Aemilia said, going to Kaeso

and gently taking hold of his hand. 'We mustn't touch, Kaeso.'

Volumnia sighed. She wished it wasn't the custom to have one's family present on this occasion. 'You will keep an eye on him, Mother. I won't have him embarrassing Caius.'

'He won't,' Aemilia said angrily, turning her back to her daughter.

'You must be calm, my dear,' Menenius said to Volumnia.

'It's such a responsibility,' Volumnia said. 'And I can't help feeling that we should have had this day years ago. I'm sure people have been gossiping about it.'

'What do you care?'

'What if they have been saying that I've put it off because I'm worried Caius is like Kaeso?'

Menenius laughed and shook his head. 'Don't be absurd, no one would ever think that. Everyone knows that Caius would have put on his manly gown when he was fourteen if he hadn't been so busy being on campaign with me. There simply hasn't been time to do this before.'

'Well, yes, you and I know that—'

'Stop worrying.' Menenius put his hand on Volumnia's arm. They both looked at it, knowing he shouldn't. He withdrew his hand as the door opened.

Cominius, Caius's closest friend, entered. 'Forgive me, lady,' he said to Volumnia, 'I fear I am a little late.'

'Not so, Cominius. Caius is still getting ready.' Volumnia nodded at the door. 'Are all his clients out there?'

Cominius nodded. 'All waiting. It will be quite a procession to the forum.'

'Well, that's the idea,' Volumnia said archly, and Menenius and Cominius shared an amused look.

The company talked quietly among themselves for a few

minutes until footsteps were heard coming from the corridor. They all turned expectantly as Caius entered.

Caius felt his cheeks reddening as his family and friends stared at him. How he wished he could perform this ceremony without anyone looking on, but there was no way around it. The putting on of a manly gown was a rite of passage and the world must see it. He forced a smile onto his face and went up to his mother, bending his head to accept her kiss.

'I am so proud of you,' she said, and he could tell she was fighting back tears.

'No need to cry, Mother,' he said, stepping away and holding out his hand to Cominius. 'Good to see you, Cominius.'

'And you, Caius. Thank you for inviting me to be a part of this. It's a great honour.'

Caius nodded. He greeted his grandmother with a kiss, and nodded stiffly to Kaeso, who tried to put his arms around him. Aemilia, knowing that neither Caius nor Volumnia would appreciate the embrace, took hold of her son's arms and shook her head. Kaeso, frowning, lowered his arms to his side.

'Uncle Menenius,' Caius said, holding out his hand.

'I think we can dispense with the 'uncle' from now on, don't you, Caius?' Menenius grinned.

'I would like that,' Caius nodded, 'though it may take some getting used to.'

'Caius,' Volumnia called, 'we should begin.'

'Yes, of course, Mother,' Caius nodded, and Volumnia gestured towards the shrine of the household gods.

Caius stepped up to the shrine. He lifted the leather thong that held the bulla, the charm Volumnia had given him when a baby to protect him against evil spirits, over his head and laid it on the ledge before the small idols. It felt odd not to have the weight of the carved stone on his breastbone. Then he took off his tunic with the crimson border, the symbol of the child. Standing only in his subligaculum, he laid the tunic at the base of the shrine.

He rose at the sound of squawking and turned to take the cockerel from the slave who had brought it in from the kitchen. Caius tucked the flapping bird beneath his left arm and took the knife that lay waiting on the shrine's ledge. He drew the blade smartly across the cockerel's neck and felt the animal's hot blood spurt over his arm and over the shrine. He stayed still as the animal died, feeling its body pulse as the blood drained out of it. When it was dead, he knelt and laid it beside his discarded tunic.

The slave returned with a bowl of hot, petal-scented water and Caius washed the blood from his arms and hands. Volumnia handed him a towel and they shared a brief smile. She turned and gestured to Kaeso, who as head of the Marcius clan since the death of Vibinius, had been given a pure white tunic to hold. Kaeso passed it to Caius, taking especial care to make sure Caius had hold of it before letting go. Caius knew Volumnia had made the tunic especially for this occasion and he fingered the soft wool appreciatively. He shook it out and lifted it over his head. It slid over his torso, coming to a stop halfway down his muscular thighs.

He was ready for the most important garment, the toga virilis with its two wide crimson stripes down the edge. Aemilia carried it to him and he took the yards of cloth with reverence. The length of cloth had to be folded around and across his body with precision. When he had finished, Caius looked to Volumnia for confirmation he had done it properly.

She made the slightest of adjustments, then stepped back and looked him up and down. Curling her bottom lip into her mouth and her chin dimpling, she nodded and said, 'Perfect.'

Aemilia pressed her hands together in front of her face, like Volumnia, feeling too much emotion. Caius hoped his grandmother wouldn't start crying; that would have been embarrassing.

'Is everybody ready?' he asked brusquely, keen to avoid such a sentimental scene.

Kaeso grinned. 'They're all out there,' he swung an arm at the front door. 'All your slaves and those you have freed — not too many of those, nephew,' he laughed. 'Your clients and your friends. And us, of course.' He clapped his hands as he looked round at Aemilia and Volumnia.

'Yes, that's enough, brother,' Volumnia said testily. 'Come now, Caius.'

They walked to the doors, and a slave opened them. As Caius stepped out into the street, a cheer went up that he was not allowed to silence. The street was cleaner than usual and Caius knew his mother had ordered it to be swept. He turned to her and extended his arm, palm outstretched, ready to take her hand so she could walk beside him. But Volumnia shook her head.

'You won't walk beside me?' he asked, confused and a little hurt.

'I cannot. You must do this alone. It is the custom.'

'Away with custom,' Caius snapped.

'Caius,' Menenius said warningly, 'it is not fitting for a boy about to become a man to have his mother walk him to the forum. You understand?'

Yes, Caius did understand, but it didn't mean he had to

like it. He nodded at Menenius, glanced at his mother, who was giving him an encouraging, if sorrowful smile, and set off to have his name inscribed on a stone that would proclaim him a citizen of Rome.

———

The sound of the water rippling as he moved in the bath was supremely soothing. It had been a very trying day for Caius, for he had been required to be sociable and amenable, to accept congratulations and give thanks, and to stuff himself with more food than he had ever allowed himself before. The feast that followed the sacrifice of a goat at the Temple of Liber had been sumptuous and had cost a great deal, Caius knew, his mind briefly wondering how much of a dent it had put in the family accounts, but he accepted it had not been a day on which to be mean.

Caius was glad his mother had noticed his patience growing thin and had encouraged their guests to take their leave. A few, eager to bask in his glory, had taken some persuading, but she had got rid of them all, even his grandmother and uncle, and they were finally alone. Volumnia had told him he should take a bath in case any of the blood from the sacrifice still lingered upon his skin and he obeyed, removing with relief the heavy white toga and tunic, and stepping naked into the hot water upon whose surface pink petals floated.

'You have made me so very proud, Caius,' Volumnia said, lying on her side by the bath, her head propped on one hand, the other trailing a sponge in the water.

'I'm glad, Mother,' Caius said.

She gestured for him to turn around and he moved so his back was pressed against the bath wall. Out of the corner of his eye, he saw Volumnia squeeze water from the sponge and then it disappeared as she drew it over his shoulders.

'You received many admiring glances,' she said as she stroked.

'From the senators?' Caius asked with interest.

'No, you goose, from the girls.'

'Indeed?'

Volumnia smacked the back of his head with the sponge. 'Don't say 'indeed' like that, as if you don't care.'

'I don't care,' Caius said with a shrug, grabbing a handful of petals from the surface of the water and crushing them.

'You should care, you know, now you're officially a man.'

'Why should I care?'

'Oh, Caius, my dear boy, you must realise you will marry soon.'

'I haven't given it any thought.' What time or use had he for girls? The only girls he knew were sisters of his friends and he barely gave them a second glance.

'Then it is time you should,' Volumnia sighed, pushing against his neck to make him lean forward, reaching down to trail the sponge along his spine. 'You never know, you may fall in love.'

He barked a laugh. 'No, I won't.'

'You sound very sure.'

'I am sure. I will never love another woman.'

The sponge stopped in the middle of his back. '*Another* woman?' Volumnia queried.

Caius turned to face her. 'The only woman I love or will ever love is you, Mother.'

'I'm talking of a different kind of love, Caius,' Volumnia smiled, mollified. 'I cannot be a wife to you.'

‘I know that,’ he said sulkily. ‘But I won’t be much of a husband, will I? I mean, a girl will expect me to love her.’

‘Only if she’s a complete fool. Only if her parents have allowed her to conceive some ridiculous notion of marrying for love.’

‘Besides, when do I have time to find such a wife, Mother? Now I’m a man, I will have the estate to manage, more clients than ever demanding my attention, and wars to win.’

‘Oh, hush, Caius. I will find a suitable wife for you if you wish.’

Caius considered for a moment. ‘Yes, you do that, Mother. If I must have a wife, she must be one you will like. Only make sure she won’t interfere with me.’

‘She won’t, I promise.’ Volumnia gave a loud, despondent sigh. ‘And then I must set about finding a domus of my own. I could move in with Mother and Kaeso, I suppose.’

Caius whirled around, splashing water and rose petals over the edge of the bath. ‘What are you talking about?’

‘Your wife will want to be mistress in her own home, Caius.’

‘I don’t care what she will want,’ he declared angrily. ‘You will not leave this domus, not for anyone. Any wife of mine will have to acknowledge you as the mistress of my home and she will have to answer to you in all matters.’

Volumnia placed her hand flat on his chest, and he knew she was feeling his heart beating hard beneath his warm flesh. ‘My dear boy,’ she purred.

Caius took her hand and kissed it. ‘My dear mother.’

Virgilia Paetina had walked up and down her garden she

didn't know how many times, unable to sit still for a moment. She was excited, certainly, but there was something else, something beneath the excitement. She thought it was nervousness, but she couldn't be sure. In truth, she didn't know how she felt; she'd never been told she was to be married before.

Caius Marcius. She was to marry Caius Marcius. She rubbed her hands over her arms, feeling the goosebumps that had risen as she said his name in her head. She had never met Caius, though she had seen him often enough on the Field of Mars. Her parents wouldn't have liked it if they'd known but she and her friends would often go to the Field just to watch the boys wrestle, and Caius Marcius was always the one they looked out for. They weren't the only ones. Caius Marcius was the young man every girl in Rome noticed.

Of all the young men Virgilia had watched, Caius Marcius was the one she had not been able to draw her eyes away from. Perhaps because he was different from the others. Most of the young men openly sought the attention of the girls, showing off their muscles and begging kisses as victors, even sometimes as losers. Caius Marcius seemed to find the onlookers an unwelcome distraction, and would stride away as soon as his match was over, not stopping to receive congratulations from anyone. Was it pride or shyness? She thought the latter and liked him all the more for it.

Had he noticed her on one of those occasions, she now had to ask herself? Why pick her from all the girls in Rome who would have jumped at the chance to be his wife if he hadn't noticed her? She thought she was pretty. Her parents had often lauded her beauty, but they were prone to exaggeration and she didn't entirely believe them. But her friends envied Virgilia her face, so there must be some truth, she reasoned, in her parents' assurances. She put her hand to her long brown hair, feeling the softness in the tresses, the slight curl. She did have lovely hair, she knew that. She pressed her fingers to her face, rubbed the pads over her cheeks. The skin was smooth, no blemishes there. Shyly, she let her hands fall to her breasts, smoothed them over the small mounds and down over her flat stomach, to the side, over her hips. Caius Marcius would not be displeased, she thought, with her body, and abruptly folded her arms over her chest at the thought of him seeing her naked. She shouldn't think such things, she told herself sharply.

Virgilia turned as someone called her name from inside the domus, and a moment later, her best friend emerged from the shadows into the brightness of the garden. 'Oh, Cordia, it's you.'

'Well, that's a pretty greeting,' Cordia Apellina said, putting on an affronted air. 'And here I was about to invite you to come shopping with me.'

'Cordia,' Virgilia said, trying not to smile, 'I have news.'

'Oh yes?' Cordia said, taking a seat on the stone bench and looking at Virgilia expectantly.

Virgilia perched beside her. 'I am going to be married.'

That took the haughtiness from Cordia's face. She gasped, her wide mouth opening a little and her dark eyes grew large. 'Who to?' she demanded.

'Caius Marcius.'

Cordia repeated the name reverently, then said, 'You!'

'Why not me?' Virgilia was indignant.

'I didn't mean that,' Cordia said hurriedly, taking the hands Virgilia was reluctant to surrender. 'I just... it's such a surprise. You haven't said anything about it before.'

'I only found out this morning. Father called me into his tablinum and said it was all arranged.'

'Well,' Cordia breathed, impressed, 'aren't you the lucky one?'

'Aren't you pleased for me, Cordia?'

Cordia looked away. 'I suppose so,' she said, shrugging her bony shoulders.

'I know you like him,' Virgilia said quietly.

'We all like him,' Cordia snapped. 'Octavia has been determined to marry him for as long as I can remember. If you think I'm not pleased, wait until you tell her. She will be furious.'

'But it's not my fault. I must do what Father tells me. And besides,' Virgilia said, drawing herself up, 'I want to marry him. I'll be a far better wife to him than Octavia ever would.'

'I daresay,' Cordia nodded, scrutinising her friend with a calculating eye. 'You are so placid that he will not be able to find fault with you.'

'I will be a good wife,' Virgilia asserted.

Cordia sniffed. 'And where will you live? Is your father buying you a domus?'

'No, Father offered, of course, but the Lady Volumnia said Caius wants to stay where he is.'

'On the Quirinal Hill? But I thought that was his mother's domus?'

'It's the family home, it belongs to Caius.'

'So, where's his mother going to go?'

Virgilia rose and tugged a leaf from a bay tree beside the bench. 'She's not going anywhere.'

'You don't mean she's going to keep living there when you're married? Oh, Virgilia, how awful for you. I've heard she's horrible.'

'I'm sure she's perfectly pleasant. And I think it will be fun to have her there. Father says I must realise that Caius will be away a good deal, what with his having to go to his farm and his estate, and, of course, going away on campaign, and I will be glad of his mother's company at such times.'

Cordia raised a heavy eyebrow. 'Well, I don't think even the most handsome, bravest man in the world would make me live in the same domus as my mother-in-law. After all, why do we marry if it's not to get away from parents and have our own home to run?'

'But that's not why I want to marry. I want to love my husband and... and I want children.'

'What a very dull idea you have of marriage, Virgilia,' Cordia said, shaking her head at her friend's naivete. 'I admit, I envy you getting Caius Marcius, but I certainly don't envy you getting his mother too.'

———

Cordia's words returned to Virgilia's mind a few weeks later as she shifted her backside on the cushioned couch. Would Cordia be feeling as anxious as she did now if she were married, she wondered? No, Virgilia thought, knowing Cordia, she would be busy working out how to edge her new mother-in-law out of the way, and out of the domus. *I wish I was more like Cordia*, Virgilia mused with a sigh.

She could hardly believe she was a married woman; the day had gone by in a blur. Her face ached, and she knew she must have been smiling for most of the day. She pressed her fingertips into her cheeks and pushed against the muscles, trying to ease the ache.

She glanced down at her plate; she had hardly touched any of the food she had picked from the serving platters. She should be hungry, but she was starting to feel nervous. So many people had come up to her to congratulate her and to talk to Caius. She could feel them looking at her from the other couches and she knew they were wondering why she had been chosen to be the wife of Caius Marcius. Who was she, after all? The daughter of a family that had been raised to the patrician class in only the last fifty years or so when King Servius had increased the patrician numbers. The Marcius family had been patricians since before the Tarquins, more than a hundred years ago, and were even said to be descended from King Ancus Marcius. Her own father, with a finger pressed to his lips and a twinkle in his eye, had said his daughter was marrying into royalty.

But she *had* been chosen, she had to remember that. Perhaps Caius had noticed her and had told his mother to arrange their marriage. He had certainly been kind to her once it was arranged. Her father had invited him to dinner and Caius had arrived, his mother on his arm, and she and he had been introduced, with smiles on both sides. True, they had not talked a great deal and she had discovered nothing of his likes and dislikes, but she was determined to find these out as soon as possible.

She turned towards Caius but he almost had his back towards her for he was deep in conversation with Menenius Agrippa. Virgilia liked Menenius. He was warm and funny, and he seemed genuinely interested in her, having tried to engage her in conversation ever since they had sat down to eat. But they hadn't had a chance to talk for Caius commanded his attention.

Volumnia leaned towards her. 'You did very well today, my dear.'

Virgilia started. 'Oh, did I? I'm glad.'

'You sound surprised. You needn't be. I told Caius I had chosen well.'

Virgilia blinked at her. '*You* chose well? I don't understand. Caius didn't ask for me?'

Volumnia laid her hand on Virgilia's arm. Virgilia shivered. 'My dear child, Caius had no idea you existed before I found you for him.' She laughed, as if she hadn't just spoken the most crushing sentence Virgilia had ever had said to her. 'But he is very pleased with you, I can tell.'

I sound like a dog his mother has brought home to look after, Virgilia thought, feeling suddenly sick. She took refuge in her cup of wine but the wine was sour in her mouth. After a while, as the laughter and the chatter around her continued, she tried to talk sense to herself. Of course Caius hadn't noticed her, she had been nothing to him. As far as she knew, he hadn't noticed any other girl either. But he was pleased with her, his mother had said so, and she told herself so over and over.

And then Caius looked over his shoulder at her, and smiled, and it suddenly didn't matter what anyone thought, what had gone on or hadn't gone on before. He had smiled at her and she pleased him. It was enough.

'It's time we went,' he said.

Her throat tightened, but she smiled and nodded. She was going to leave the home she had known all her life, and she was suddenly tearful. But she knew she must not give way to her emotions and cry; she knew, instinctively, that to cry would make her new husband, and her new mother-in-law, angry. She swallowed down her anxiety and watched as Volumnia signalled to Caius and they both began to say their farewells.

Virgilia saw the surprise in her father's face, but he covered it quickly. He led them to the door, kissed Virgilia on the cheek, and Caius took her arm and led her outside into the street.

'Are we not to be accompanied to your domus?' Virgilia

asked. 'I thought it is the custom for the wedding guests to follow us.' She saw Caius exchange a look with his mother.

'It is a custom we thought vulgar to observe,' Volumnia said. 'Caius doesn't like to have people staring at him.'

And so they walked through the dark streets, four slaves, two in front, two behind, carrying torches to light their way. At the door to the domus, Virgilia found herself being lifted effortlessly by Caius and carried over the threshold. He set her down just inside the door, said, 'Come,' and led her to his cubiculum, Volumnia following. Caius opened the cubiculum door and stood back for her to enter. She started through the doorway, then looked back to bid goodnight to Volumnia.

'I'm coming in,' Volumnia said.

Virgilia was confused. 'In here? But... why?'

In answer, Volumnia took hold of her shoulders and steered her into the room. Caius followed and shut the door behind him.

'I don't understand,' Virgilia said, aware her voice trembled.

'I'm not having you expressing any maidenly coyness,' Volumnia said, placing the room's only stool in the corner beneath the window and sitting down. 'This marriage will be consummated.'

'You're going to watch?'

'Certainly I am,' Volumnia said, folding her hands in her lap. 'Come now, Caius, get on with it. It's been a long day and I want my sleep.'

Virgilia was too astonished, too appalled to say or do anything as Caius moved towards her and began untying her belt. She felt her dress loosen. 'No, I won't,' she said, finding her voice. 'I won't do it. Not with you here.'

'Don't make such a fuss,' Volumnia tutted. 'It will be over in a few minutes and then I shall leave.'

'Caius, please.' Virgilia whispered, folding her arms over her breasts, each hand gripping the opposite shoulder.

'You must do as you're told,' he said, pulling her hands away, gently but forcefully. 'Mother knows best.'

She couldn't resist him. Her arms straightened to fall by her side and she stood immobile as Caius undressed her. She wondered if her parents had known of this, that her deflowering would be witnessed by her mother-in-law. Had they agreed? Why had they not told her? Why had they let her be surprised, shocked, in this way? Why had they not warned her?

It wouldn't have made any difference if they had, she told herself, as Caius pointed her towards the bed, and she padded, naked, meekly, towards it and lay down. She turned her face to the wall, listening as Caius shed his clothes. She heard Volumnia murmur, 'So fine,' and then felt the thin mattress move beneath her and knew Caius was by her side.

Her entire body was strung tight, she felt it, and knew it would not help her to be so. It would hurt all the more if she did not relax, and she wished she had drunk more, that she had drunk so much wine she didn't care about this indignity. She closed her eyes.

Virgilia almost cried as Caius lifted himself over her body. She kept her head turned away, not wanting to share this moment with him because she would be sharing it with Volumnia too. His knee pushed itself in between her legs and she obligingly shifted so he could settle there. His heat warmed her, and she felt a tremor of excitement run through her that was instantly quashed the moment his manhood pressed against her centre. *Relax, relax*, she kept repeating in her mind, but it made no difference. It hurt so much when he entered her and she could not help the cry that escaped her, nor the tears that cascaded hotly down her cheeks as Caius moved inside her. It seemed an age, but she knew the act lasted only a minute or so, and then she was free of him, left hurt and bleeding.

'Well done,' she heard Volumnia say, and then she heard the lifting of the latch, the creak of the door as it opened and shut, and knew her mother-in-law had left the room.

'I am glad to have such a wife as you,' Caius said, panting slightly. 'You have not complained, you have done your duty, as we all must. Clean yourself in the morning. I must sleep now.'

And then his breathing slowed and Virgilia knew he was asleep. She turned her head to look at him and saw his handsome face beside her on the pillow. Her tears were drying as the pain faded and she told herself it had not been so bad, though she wished she had been alone with Caius. She stared at her new husband for a long time until her own eyes, weary from crying and from the rigours of the day, closed.

14

Caius winced as his leaning over the desk to dip his pen in the ink sent a sharp stabbing through his body. The doctor had told him he had fractured at least two of his ribs on his left side and that there was nothing to be done but give his body time to heal. He supposed he should have been grateful that the fracturing had happened only at the end of the last war. Had he fractured his ribs in an earlier battle, chances are he would not have come home.

It had been a good war, he thought, plenty of battles, plenty of opportunities to prove himself. And he had done that, killing he didn't know how many enemies. All except one. He absently fingered the wound on his right shoulder. Like the one on the inside of his right thigh, it was healing well. The skin would be red and puckered when they had healed completely.

Touching the wounds made him angry for he knew the man who inflicted them still lived. They had fought fiercely when they met on the battlefield, fought so close their breaths intermingled, their eyes met, their flesh touched. But though they had wounded one another, they had neither of them been able to deliver a fatal blow. They were so evenly matched, it was incredible. *Tullus Aufidius,* Caius thought, *you are mine to kill when next we meet, and it will be the greatest honour of my life.*

This last war had taken him from Rome for almost nine months. When he was away, he was occupied and didn't miss home; now he was back, he realised how much he had missed his mother. She had missed him, too, and had held him tight for many minutes upon his return. But she never complained that he was gone so long. She knew it was his purpose to fight for Rome. Indeed, she had trained him for it.

It was different with Virgilia. He had left her only a week after their marriage and she had cried at his going. He had been touched that someone he barely knew and who barely knew him could feel pain at the prospect of his leaving, and he had been kind and kissed her and said his mother would look after her. He wondered why Virgilia's expression had altered when he said that last but then his mother had spoken to him and he had forgotten all about his tearful wife.

Caius had received a letter from his mother about two months later. Virgilia was pregnant, she told him. The news meant little to him and he did not bother to reply. Volumnia understood his silence and did not berate him in her next letter. She knew he was busy, she wrote, killing Rome's enemies and making her proud. He must not think of Virgilia or his child until that job was done. There would be time enough for all that when he came home.

And now, he was home, and he found a baby in his domus, an ugly, squawking thing that Virgilia showed him with tears in her eyes, wanting him to take it in his arms. He had done so and held it awkwardly so that it cried even more, and he had thrust it back at Virgilia, complaining he didn't want to come home to such noise. Volumnia had told Virgilia to take the baby away and she had done so, crying.

He hadn't cared. Volumnia had taken him through to the triclinium where food awaited him, a veritable feast after the rations he had eaten on campaign. He had told Volumnia all about his battles and she had listened, eager for details. He had seen the excitement in her face and had been pleased to gratify her interest. He had told her of the Volsci warrior he had fought, seven or eight times now, and whom he hadn't been able to beat. She had thought he was ashamed of himself and had sought to console him, but he had told her she need not, that he had been proud to fight such a man, a man as good as himself. She hadn't understood, he had seen that, and he hadn't tried to explain.

Aufidius was his to understand alone.

His toga was trailing in the dirt as he ran from his domus. Caius had received an urgent message from Menenius to come to the Senate house at once. Caius hadn't stopped to question Menenius's slave. He had thrown down his stylus, knocked over his chair and rushed out of the door, it closing upon the alarmed queries of his wife and mother.

Caius pushed people out of the way in his haste. He ignored their curses and shouts of outrage and hurried up the Senate house steps. He found Menenius and headed towards him.

'I'm here,' he said, catching his breath. 'What is it?'

Menenius's expression was grim. 'It's Lucius Tarquin.' He was about to say more but Mettius Trebonius clapped his hands for attention.

'The Senate has today received a dispatch from Lucius

Tarquin.' Mettius sighed. 'I shall be brief. Lucius Tarquin has declared war on Rome. He means to attack us wherever and whenever he can.'

The senators found their voices and expressed their outrage. Caius bent his head towards Menenius. 'He can't think he can win the throne back, can he? After all this time?'

'I think the man is quite mad,' Menenius said.

'Mad or not, if he has an army—'

'Yes, yes,' Menenius snapped, 'we will be at war.' He gave Caius a sideways look. 'How that does please you.'

Caius laughed and looked around at the senators, who had left their seats to talk with one another. 'I can't help it, Menenius, it does. I swear I am getting fat having nothing to do here in Rome.'

'Oh, Caius, don't exaggerate. Your wounds from the last war have not even healed yet. And you would have plenty to do if only you could set your mind to doing it.'

'Seeing clients, acting as arbitrator in disputes? That's not for me, Menenius, you know it's not.'

'I daresay your wife and mother are pleased you've been home for a while.'

Caius made a face. 'I'm made for war, Menenius. My mother understands that.'

'Your mother saw to it,' Menenius retorted. 'Anyway, you will get your wish. You will be sent off to fight for Rome.'

'And so will you.'

'Oh no,' Menenius shook his head, 'not this time. I am grown too old for battles. My body is no longer fit for service on the battlefield.'

Caius glanced down at the hand that was smoothing the toga over a rounded belly, the consequence of Menenius's love of food and wine. 'What will you do, then?'

'I've already had a word with Mettius,' Menenius said.

'Administration and organisation, that's where my talents lie these days.'

Caius frowned. 'But then, who will I serve under?'

'Don't worry about that. The commanders will be falling over themselves to have you in their ranks. They know how good a soldier you are. They will all want Caius Marcius. '

Caius could feel his mare growing tired beneath him. He looked back to her flank and saw a deep cut in the skin, her blood flowing freely down her legs. She wouldn't last much longer if the wound wasn't seen to. He waited for a break in the fighting, then rode her away a little so he could dismount. He smacked her uninjured rump, and she galloped away towards the Roman camp in the valley below. She would get the attention she needed when she arrived.

Caius didn't mind being on foot, even though, as a patrician, he should fight on horseback. He found it easier, more pleasurable, to fight with his feet on the ground. He could turn and manoeuvre more easily. On horseback, he often felt distanced from the fighting, just another man wielding a sword, but on the ground, he felt almost as if he himself was a sword, that the piece of metal in his hand was a part of his arm.

That arm of his had killed many men this day and would kill many more. Caius worked his way through the battlefield, stabbing, hacking, slicing, until his muscles burned and he was covered in blood and gore. He reached a hiatus — there was no one around him left to kill — and he took the moment to catch his breath. He looked around. There was no telling from this point which side was winning. All dead men looked the same.

He heard a shout and whirled around. He saw a tall man raising a spear a little way away. The next moment, the man jabbed downward and embedded the tip in the thigh of a Roman soldier writhing on the ground. It was a clumsy attack. Had Caius held the spear and had the Roman been his enemy, he would have pushed the point into the man's stomach or his heart. But even though the blow had been feeble, it was still damaging. The man with the spear pulled it out of the ripped flesh and raised it above his head to strike again.

Caius ran to the fallen soldier, and with his sword, knocked the spear away. The force of his blow sent the man falling backwards. He was an old man, Caius saw, his face heavily lined, though bodily, he still appeared robust. His clothing, muddied and bloodied though it was, suggested he was a man of some standing. Perhaps he had been unhorsed and forced to fight on foot and was unaccustomed to fighting so, hence the clumsy attack on the Roman soldier. The knowledge pleased Caius. This was no mere foot soldier, a ploughboy or tanner, he was about to kill. This was a man of substance and to kill him would be an honour.

But Caius didn't get the chance. His opponent regained his balance quickly and was tightening his grip on his spear to thrust it into Caius. Caius braced himself for the blow, but it came not from his opponent, but weakly from the side. He turned and saw that five men had joined them and were moving to stand between him and his opponent. Annoyed, Caius thrust with his sword and felt the satisfying feeling of metal passing through flesh. The man he had pierced fell and Caius turned back to the old man, but he was already being hurried away by the bodyguard. Who was he? Caius wondered as they retreated. He must have been someone very important to be worth saving in that way.

A trumpet blared and Caius turned towards the sound. It came from the Roman end of the field. He saw and heard men cheering, and realised Rome had been victorious, that they had won yet another battle. He was disappointed; he was not spent yet. But there was no one left to fight, and he began to make his way back to the camp.

'Caius!'

Caius, who had been looking down at his feet as he picked his way over the bodies that littered the ground, looked up at the shout. It took him a moment to locate the caller, but then he saw Cominius waving to him a little way off. He raised his hand in greeting and Cominius ran up to him.

'You're alive,' Cominius cried, the only points of brightness in his face his eyes. His face was streaked with mud and blood and when he grinned at Caius, there was blood staining his teeth. 'I saw your horse go back to the camp. I thought—'

'That I was dead? You know me better than that.'

Cominius nodded. 'Wounded, maybe. How many of these bodies are down to you?'

Caius looked about them. 'Ten or twelve.'

'More like twenty or thirty, I'd say. Come on, the commander sent me to find you.'

'Why?' Caius asked, a note of worry creeping into his voice.

Cominius didn't answer, just strode off towards the camp. Caius followed, hurrying so as not to be left behind. If the commander had sent Cominius to find him, Caius must be in trouble. Had he disobeyed an order?

He and Cominius reached the camp. The order of before the battle was gone. The tents were still set in rows, but men sprawled everywhere, some waiting to be tended to by the surgeons, others nursing injuries they could mend themselves, and so were washing with boiled water and bandaging one another with linen. Horses were being led from the field, their sides sweaty, some bloody, most foaming at the mouth.

The commander's tent was in the middle of the camp. There was no mistaking it for it was larger and far grander than any of the others. A small crowd had formed around the entrance and Caius's stomach lurched. Was his dressing-down to be made public? How could he bear the shame?

'Wait here,' Cominius said. He entered the tent and Caius heard him say, 'He's here, sir.'

Caius stood to attention, determined to take his reprimand or punishment like a man. He would not beg for mercy.

The commander, Aulus Postumius, emerged from his tent, his face grim, a deep cut on his temple causing blood to trickle down to his jaw. He was as dirty as the rest of his army and as weary, it seemed. He saw Caius and moved to stand before him. 'Caius Marcius, kneel.'

So, it is to be execution, Caius thought as he bent his legs and lowered himself to the ground, wondering what he had done to deserve it. The ground was hard and damp against his knees. He lowered his head and closed his eyes. And waited.

The moment seemed long, but it was probably only seconds, he realised later. He had expected to feel the point of the commander's sword pierce the top of his spine, but the pain didn't come. Instead, the commander touched Caius's head. When he removed his hands, Caius, confused, put one hand to his head and felt leaves tickle his fingers. He looked up in surprise.

'A victory wreath,' Aulus Postumius said with some solemnity, though his eyes were twinkling. 'Caius Marcius, I commend you,' and he gestured for Caius to stand.

Caius got to his feet to the sound of cheering. Astonished, he looked to Cominius for explanation.

'You fought well, Caius, put us all to shame,' Cominius said happily. 'And what's more, you fought the tyrant.'

'I did what?' Caius said, bewildered.

'Lucius Tarquin,' Cominius said, frowning at Caius's confusion. 'Didn't you know? You stopped him from killing the consul and we all know you would have killed him had he not been rescued by his bodyguard. It wouldn't be just a wreath for you if you had. You would have been welcomed back to Rome with a triumph. Better luck next time, eh?'

So, that had been Tarquin, Caius mused as he found his hand wrung by his fellow soldiers. *I should have gone after him and stabbed him in the heart*. He touched the oak wreath on his head and tried to stop himself from grinning like a fool. He didn't want the others to see how proud of himself he was.

Everyone wanted to celebrate the Roman victory. Cominius proposed they drink all the wine the camp held and get themselves a whore each. Caius declined the whore but agreed to the wine, saying he had something to do first.

Disentangling himself from his fellow soldiers, Caius walked out of the camp and to the edge of the battlefield where camp followers were looting the dead bodies of their goods. They edged away from him as he walked, and he found himself quite alone. He fell to his knees, and leaning forward, kissed the earth. He sank back onto his heels and closed his eyes to pray.

'Mars, I thank you for this victory.'

15

Volumnia winced as her grandson gave another of his ear-splitting screams. She touched her fingers to her forehead and pressed, as if pressing against skin and bone could lessen the pain inside her skull. It didn't, of course, and her arm fell back onto the bed with an exasperated thump. Why couldn't Virgilia do something with Little Caius and shut him up? All her daughter-in-law seemed to do was cuddle and coo with him. That was the problem; no discipline, always giving in. If the child was hungry, he should be fed and left alone. If tired, put in his cot and left alone. But no, Virgilia would insist on keeping him with her and thereby making him worse. The gods knew Volumnia had been attentive to Caius when he was the same age, but she had never mollycoddled him the way Virgilia did her son. There had been times when Caius had been fractious and demanding of attention but Volumnia had left him to wear himself out with crying. It hadn't made for pleasant hours in the domus, it was true, but eventually, Caius had learnt he couldn't get his own way all the time. Volumnia would have to tell Virgilia to do the same, and if she didn't... well, she would have a word with Caius when he came home and get him to deal with his wife.

Caius!

Oh, how she missed him. Now that Aemilia and Kaeso had gone to live on the Sidonius country estate, she had no one of her own around her. She had told her mother she would be fine when Aemilia had broached the idea of her and Kaeso leaving Rome. Aemilia had been concerned for her but Volumnia had waved those concerns away, confident she had no need of her mother and idiot brother. She had been wrong. She missed her mother, and yes, she even missed her brother, in a way. Whenever she had felt lonely, or just in need of a confidential conversation, she had been able to visit them and unburden herself. Now, there was no one. She could not speak with Virgilia without irritation. She and her daughter-in-law agreed on nothing; not on politics, not on people, not even on what they should have for dinner. Her friend Valeria popped round now and then to gossip, but she had a wide social circle of her own and Volumnia, especially when Caius was away, was low on her visiting list.

And what of Menenius? Volumnia had hardly seen him of late. She knew he was busy with war work, but she had expected him to visit more often now his wife was dead. She supposed he still thought Caius wouldn't approve of his visits, but Virgilia was always in the domus, and what better chaperon could Volumnia have than her son's wife?

There came an unfamiliar sound. Volumnia strained her ears to hear: murmuring, the front doors opening. Strange, they weren't expecting visitors. She pushed herself up onto her elbows. Yes, that was Virgilia's voice she could hear. And then she heard her daughter-in-law give a cry. Volumnia jumped off the bed, wincing as her brain rocked in her skull, and flung open her door. She rushed out into the corridor and hurried towards the atrium.

'Caius!' she cried.

Yes, it was him, standing in the atrium, trying to fend off the embraces of his wife. Virgilia was crying and kissing him all at once, while Caius's personal slave who had accompanied him to war, stood to one side, his arms full of his master's personal belongings.

Caius looked up at the sound of his name and grinned. 'Salve, Mother.' He pinned Virgilia's arms to her sides and steered her out of his way. He strode up to Volumnia and kissed her. 'Didn't expect me, did you?'

'No, I didn't.' Volumnia stood on tiptoe and put her arms around his neck. One quick embrace and she let him go. 'We thought you were still near Tusculum.' She took hold of his hand and drew him through the domus to the triclinium. She pushed him down onto one of the couches and ordered food and drink from a slave who had come running in from the kitchen at the sound of their voices. Volumnia looked around for Virgilia but she had disappeared. Caius's slave was standing awkwardly a few feet off.

'Set that down here and then get some food,' Caius said to him, and the slave set down the small wooden box he had been carrying and then hurried off to the kitchen.

'Well, what news?' Volumnia asked excitedly.

Caius grinned. 'The battle was won, and Lucius Tarquin has given up.'

'The war is over?'

'You sound disappointed, Mother.'

Volumnia shook her head. 'I had thought you would be away longer. Though, of course,' she reached across and touched her hand to his, 'I am pleased to see you.' She silently groaned as Virgilia hurried into the triclinium, Little Caius in her arms.

'Here he is,' Virgilia cooed, forcing the child onto Caius's lap.

Caius looked down at the squirming creature with apprehension. It wriggled and threatened to fall, and he grabbed at it clumsily. 'He's grown big.'

'He's almost two years old, Caius,' Virgilia said, sitting down next to Caius and laying her head on his shoulder. 'Isn't he lovely?'

'Here, take him.' Caius passed the boy back to Virgilia.

Volumnia saw her face fall at Caius's reaction to their son and felt a small thrill of pleasure. She had been worried that Caius would find his son of interest and have no time for her. Little Caius started crying and Virgilia pressed him against her breast, whispering that everything was well.

'Virgilia,' Volumnia said, seeing Caius glare at his son, 'take him away. Caius doesn't want to listen to that awful noise.'

'He can't help crying,' Virgilia protested, but rose and left to do as she was instructed.

'Has she been good?' Caius asked, watching her go.

Volumnia sighed. 'I can bear her well enough. But I don't want to talk about her. Tell me of the battles you've fought, Caius. I long to hear.'

'Better than that.' Caius moved to the small box and opened it. 'I have something for you, Mother.' He lifted back a hessian cloth.

'What is it?' Volumnia asked, trying to peer inside.

Caius held out the oak wreath.

Volumnia's mouth dropped open. 'Is that—?' she gasped and pressed her hand to her chest.

'A victory wreath, yes.' He passed it to her and she took it reverently.

'Yours?'

'Given to me by Aulus Postumius himself.' He sat down beside her. 'Do you like it, Mother?'

Volumnia looked at him with tears in her eyes. 'Oh, Caius,' she cried and leant towards him, kissing him full on the mouth. 'This is the most wonderful thing.'

'It's yours,' Caius said. 'I won it for you.'

'I knew you were destined for greatness, Caius.' She put the wreath on his head and stared at it through misty eyes. What better proof could she have that the Sibyl had prophesied truly?

16

495 BC

Lucius heard the rain tapping against the leather curtain at the window. It was a soothing sound, the perfect sound to die to. He moved his head slightly on the pillow but regretted the movement almost immediately as it wearied him immensely. *No strength left,* he told himself. *Don't move, don't do anything. Just lie here and wait until you drift away, never to wake again.*

Lolly would have said he was being maudlin and that he must buck up. He looked out of the corner of his eyes and saw his wife sitting in a chair by his bedside, her head upon her chest. She had been asleep for a while, he knew. He really should wake her up; her neck would ache terribly if she stayed in that position. But that would take effort too and he really didn't have the energy. Yes, he was being maudlin and feeling sorry for himself, but Lucius couldn't help feeling he had a right to be so. What had it all been for, in the end? The battle at Lake Regillus, almost three years ago now, had been his last attempt to restore his family's dignity and he had failed miserably. He had been dragged away from that young man who would have killed him and forced to flee back to Tarquinii. There had been no more battles for Lucius Tarquin, the king who had had his throne stolen by an idiot.

And all because of Sextus. He cursed his youngest son. He should have had him gelded when he was still a boy. The warnings had been there, if only he had paid attention. The Sibyl's scrolls had prophesied a child of Rome would bring shame on his father through the virtue of a woman and it had been Sextus's rape of Lucretia that had prompted the people of Rome to rebel.

To have lost Rome, after all he and Lolly had done to get the throne. Adultery, the murder of their siblings and parents... all for nothing in the end.

Lucius was worried for Lolly. When he was dead, how would she cope? She loved him, had always loved him, with a fierceness that had held him up and kept him strong, even in the worst of times. Now, they had little wealth, those bastards in Rome had seen to that. He hoped she would marry again. There was security for a woman in marriage. And he knew who would have her. Vopiscus Cantius was only waiting for Lucius to die to get his sweaty little paws on her. Shame, but Vopiscus Cantius was at least rich. Lolly would have a comfortable life as his wife. Yes, it would be best for her if she married Cantius.

He wished Lolly would wake up, just for a moment, so he could say goodbye, but she slept on. Lucius held on for as long as he could, but then he felt himself drifting and knew it was too late. He heard the gentle ripple of the river and saw the ferryman floating on his raft towards him. He stepped onto the wooden planks and felt them bob beneath his feet. He reached into his purse for the last of the gold aes he possessed and pushed the nugget into the outstretched palm, the tips of his fingers feeling the chill in the withered skin. He looked back but Lolly was gone. There was only the dark night and the sound of the water.

'To the Volsci!'

Some good news at last, Tullus thought as he emptied his cup of wine for the toast. Lucius Tarquin was dead. The Roman tyrant who had ground so many peoples beneath the heel of Rome was dead. He had died in his bed, which was not as Tullus would have wished it, but he was dead, all the same. The news made his day.

Of course, he told himself, that news shouldn't have made his day. The day should have been significant without the death of a tyrant to make it memorable, for it was his wedding day. But, try as he might, Tullus just couldn't summon up any enthusiasm for being a married man. There was nothing wrong with his new wife, he had to admit. In many ways, she was the perfect choice. Not young, though young enough; not clingy and demanding his attention all the time but still attentive to his needs; and quite content for him to carry on as he had before they were married. At least, that was what Junia had told him the day before. Time would tell as to whether she would keep all her promises.

Tullus looked around at the guests lying on the couches. *There's one person missing*, he thought miserably. His mother, Salonia, had died a few months before. She had suffered much at the end, and the memory of her pain tormented Tullus. She had been so brave, even then. As he picked at the bowl of olives before him, he recalled the last thing she had said to him: 'Make Rome pay!' She had never forgiven the Romans for the raid on her village on the night of his birth. Often had she told him the story of what had happened that dreadful night, how she and Gallio had had to run away to the forest to hide while the Romans burned their village and killed all they found. Of how she might have died giving birth to him, how he might have died, had it not been for her friend Atilia, whose own husband was murdered by the Romans. Tullus had heard his mother's prayers each night and morning beseeching the gods to punish the Romans for their deeds. Sometimes, the gods listened; sometimes, they didn't. Most often, it seemed to Tullus, they didn't. Why else were the Romans having so much success? Almost every month news reached Antium of how the Romans had conquered this or that part of Italy, how they had opened up lucrative new trade routes or agreed treaties that gave them the upper hand. Only the Volsci held out and refused to submit to Rome. Tullus could be proud of that, at least.

'I expect you'll be off soon,' Canus Elerius said, rousing Tullus out of his thoughts.

'Off?' Tullus frowned. 'Off where?'

'Wherever Rome is these days,' Canus shrugged. 'With Tarquin dead, they won't have him to fight any more. I'll daresay they'll be looking elsewhere for their battles.'

Tullus grunted agreement and shoved a handful of olives in his mouth. 'I hope they do.'

Canus grinned. 'Ever the warrior, eh? You should be proud of this son of yours, Gallio.'

'I am,' Gallio said. 'His mother was proud of him too.'

Had his father guessed his thoughts? Tullus wondered. *Was Gallio missing his mother too?*

'What of this Caius Marcius we keep hearing so much about?' Canus continued. 'Rumour has it he is so good at killing that he must be a son of Mars.'

'Oh, I think the gods have better things to do than go

around impregnating mortals these days,' Gallio said with a smile. 'He's no more a demigod than you, Canus.'

'He's a fierce warrior,' Tullus said, too loudly for the guests nearest quietened and stared at him. 'I've met him.'

'You've met him?' his new wife repeated, her eyes wide.

'On the battlefield,' Tullus said, wondering if that had been admiration he'd heard in his wife's voice. 'I've fought him many times.'

'Then why is he not dead? I just mean,' she said, quailing a little beneath his sudden glare, 'you're so good at killing, Tullus, everyone knows that. If you had fought him, surely you would have killed him?'

There was a titter of laughter, embarrassed, awkward.

'You've never been on a battlefield, Junia,' Gallio said quietly, his eyes flicking between her and Tullus. 'You have no idea what's it like.'

Junia opened her mouth to retort, took a quick glance at Tullus and thought better of it, biting down on a fig instead.

'But what is Caius Marcius like?' Canus's wife, Pinaria, asked eagerly. 'Is he handsome?'

Women, Tullus thought contemptuously, *is that all they think about?* 'It's rather difficult to tell, lady, when a man's face is covered in blood. And I am not the best man to judge as I don't know what makes for handsomeness. My face, I think, is very far from handsome.'

'I think you have a very striking face, husband,' Junia said dutifully, defiantly. 'I would not want a pretty husband.'

'I didn't say pretty, my dear,' Pinaria said with a sly look. 'I said handsome. I've heard tell Caius Marcius is.'

'If ever a Roman could be called handsome,' Junia shot back. 'Personally, I think every Roman must be as ugly as Vulcan and the gossip about Caius Marcius greatly exaggerated. Tullus has a much greater reputation than he.'

'Of course he does,' Pinaria said icily, her husband's warning hand sliding off hers.

Tullus had had enough. 'There is no exaggeration. Caius Marcius is a great warrior. We have met upwards of eight times, and each time we have come face to face, we have given one another wounds. But no more than wounds. We are so evenly matched that we cannot seem to kill the other. In truth, were he not a Roman, I would wish him my friend.'

'Oh, Tullus, really,' Junia laughed, glancing at their guests to see if they took her husband at his foolish word. 'You cannot love a Roman. It's impossible.'

'I know it, my love,' he said, the affectionate words coming more easily than he had thought possible. 'As he is not a Volsci but the enemy of my people, I hate Caius Marcius and will do my utmost to put my sword through him when next we meet.'

Gallio raised his cup. 'I'll drink to that, and to you putting your sword through many Romans. And you will, Tullus, one day. I know you will. It was your mother's dearest wish.'

17

The man came, limping into the forum. It had taken him five days to reach Rome. Ordinarily, the journey would have taken no more than three but his legs were not what they once were. Gone were the muscles that had enabled him to march for ten hours at a time. His muscles were shrunken now, the result of too little food and too much hard usage, but he had been determined to reach Rome and make his stand. In the past, he had been strong and clean, his clothing in food repair. Now, he was filthy and his clothes were little more than rags. He had let his beard grow, having no money to pay a barber to shave him and hands too tremulous to shave himself safely. His beard covered the bottom half of his face, so it came as a surprise when someone called his name in recognition.

It was an old army comrade, a fellow soldier who had fared better than he in the few times of peace Rome had enjoyed. The friend wanted to know how he had come to such a pass, and he explained how he had returned from the war against the Sabines to find his farm burned down, his goods looted, his sheep driven off. That was bad enough, he had said with a sad shake of his head, but then the Senate had levied a war tax to pay for the recent campaign, and he had not the funds to cover it. Rather than risk imprisonment for non-payment, he had taken out a loan, but now his creditors were calling in the loan and he simply had nothing with which to pay them. He had told them so, but they had not cared, had not shown any compassion. And here, he slid down the threadbare shoulder of his tunic to show where he had been whipped for his failure to pay.

The soldier was outraged and called over his friends to witness what had been done to this good citizen of Rome, a man who had obeyed his government's call to arms only to find himself betrayed by the very people he had fought to defend. All agreed it was a disgrace, and as the outrage swelled, so did the people's tempers. Soon, the cry of 'Death to creditors' was being shouted all around the forum and beyond into the streets. Creditors, fearing for their lives, hurried home and barred their doors.

A few senators were less fortunate. They had been in the Senate house when the cry had gone up and had found their way obstructed. They had tried to retreat into the Senate house only to find they were followed. It was demanded of them what they would do to correct this appalling situation this ragged man, and all the others like him, for there were many, had been brought to.

The current consuls, Publius Servilius and Appius Claudius, were of the party interrogated in the Senate house. They tried to calm the crowd, who were rapidly becoming a mob that threatened violence if they didn't receive the answer they wanted. Fortunately, there were some in the crowd who wanted reason to prevail and who were vocal enough to demand that the Senate be called to assemble so their complaints could be heard. But the summons the consuls sent to the senators were not answered and there were too few in the Senate for a quorum. No new laws could be passed without them and the crowd's fury intensified.

The consuls and the few senators enjoyed a moment's respite, however, when four horsemen burst into the forum and scattered the crowd as they pushed through to the steps of the Senate house.

'The Volsci are advancing on Rome,' they cried, flinging their arms towards the hills that flanked the city.

The consuls appealed to the plebs to stop their complaints so they could see off the troublesome Volsci together, but the plebs had a very different idea. They saw the Volsci as their allies. The gods had arranged for the Volsci to threaten Rome at this exact time so that the patricians could all be massacred, leaving the plebs to take over Rome. The plebs declared they would not fight for Rome again. Let the patricians take up arms and fight alone, the plebs cried.

Publius Servilius realised he must make a decision. The plebs would quickly pass beyond the Senate's control unless he acted. He decided to use language to control the plebs, not calling the crowd a mob but merely a public gathering as if it were a routine, everyday event. His words had a sobering effect on the plebs, and they listened as Publius agreed their grievances against the Senate and the creditors were entirely valid. He raised his arm for the plebs' complete attention, and into the silence, issued an edict stating no man could hold a Roman citizen prisoner to prevent him from enlisting in the Roman army and that no creditor could seize a debtor's goods while that man was serving as a soldier in the Roman army.

It was enough for the plebs. They cheered Publius Servilius, who breathed a deep-felt sigh of relief, hiding his shaking hands in the folds of his toga. He ordered the Senate house scribes to start taking down names as the plebs formed orderly queues to enlist in the Roman army.

After all, when all was said and done, the Volsci were marching on Rome.

The Volsci were close. Caius could almost smell them. The Senate had discovered that the Volsci had begun their march on Rome almost as soon as the news of Lucius Tarquin's death reached them, believing that without Tarquin continuing to threaten them, the Romans would retreat to their city and deal with the problems being created by their discontented populace. The plebs' discontent was well known outside of Rome and it was believed the Senate would never be able to muster an army. To the Volsci, Rome looked ripe for the plucking.

More fool them, Caius thought as he ran a cloth along the length of his sword. Even if the plebs had refused to enlist, there were plenty of patricians who were not cowards and who would fight the Volsci. If Caius could have his way, he wouldn't bother with the plebs at all. They were all mutinous dogs, ungrateful wretches fouling the air with their sour breath and bodies, complaining the Senate didn't care for them.

Caius wished he had been there in the Senate house when the plebs had made their complaints. He would have told them what they could go and do with themselves, and threatened to kill the lot of them if they protested. That was what was needed, not all this cowering and compromising. This war with the Volsci had come along at just the right time, in his opinion. It would be good for the plebs to die beneath Volsci swords. Rome needed a cull. If he were in charge, he would make sure the ringleaders of the forum incident were in the front line of the army where they would be sure to be killed.

It was good to be out of Rome, too; he had begun to feel stifled at home. Virgilia was always trying to get him to take an interest in Little Caius, putting the boy on his lap before dinner or whenever he took a moment to sit down. The boy would just stare and dribble, stick fingers in his mouth or cry for his mother, and Caius would thrust him back at Virgilia, telling her to take him away. Volumnia would remonstrate with Virgilia not to bother Caius with the boy, but Virgilia, obliging when it came to herself, was more insistent when it came to her son, and there had been many quarrels between the two women, arguments Caius simply didn't want to be a part of. That was the problem when a household contained too many women, he reflected, and looked around the camp, grateful for the male company it afforded.

He finished cleaning his sword and sheathed it. As he did so, there came shouts and cries, not just the usual clamour of men, but alarms. Caius got quickly to his feet. 'What is it?' he cried to one of his fellow patricians who hurried past.

'The Volsci are attacking,' the man said. 'Bring your sword, Marcius. We're going to need it.'

He didn't need to hear more. Caius buckled on his sword and dived into his tent to put on his breastplate and grab his spear. He hurried to where the horses were stabled. Taking the reins of his mare from his slave, he almost jumped onto her back, kicking her sides fiercely so that she galloped towards the fight.

Caius thrust with his spear, wrenching it from the chests of dying men to plunge it into others. One thrust was so deep, it lodged tight, and Caius could not tug it free. He relinquished the spear and drew his sword. His reach was not as great with the sword as with the spear and it meant that he must needs get closer to the men he killed. The right side of his body became covered in blood; the hot stench of it filled his nostrils and drove him on.

Was he here? he wondered with every sword thrust. Was Tullus Aufidius here? Caius longed to meet him again, to have the chance of killing the man who had matched him thrust for thrust on every occasion they had been in battle together. No one had ever before presented him with such a challenge and he was determined to prove he was up to it.

More death was caused by his hand and then suddenly, he knew, he just knew, that Aufidius was before him. Beneath the mud and the grime, there was a square jaw and striking eyes, and a scar across the neck Caius remembered, a scar he had put there.

'Marcius!' Aufidius cried and thrust at Caius.

Caius knocked the sword away, feeling the strength in the arm that held it. The sword swung at him before he could get in a thrust of his own and he was forced to knock it aside again. He shifted position, drew back a little, tilted and thrust. He got close to Aufidius's body, but Aufidius was alert to the danger, moving deftly to the side. Again and again this happened, neither man getting the upper hand, neither tiring, neither giving up. How long this went on, Caius had no idea; he just knew he had to stand his ground and fight.

And then there came a shout, clear and loud in the cold night air. 'Retreat.'

There was no knowing where it came from or which side had given the order. Aufidius and Caius fought on.

'Aufidius!' A cry came, nearer than the other voice. 'We must retreat.'

'Not now,' Aufidius shouted back, aiming another blow at Caius.

'You will retreat or I'll have you whipped for insubordination.'

Caius felt for Aufidius even as he sidestepped a blow. To be ordered to retreat when he felt sure, as Caius did, that he could win his fight, was disheartening to say the least. But to be threatened with a whipping like a low-born pleb! How would Aufidius bear such a disgrace?

The decision was taken out of Aufidius's control. The man, whoever he was, was at his side with two others, and Caius was having to fight four men instead of just one. He had to take the defensive and was forced backwards. He stumbled. He raised his arm to fend off the attack he knew was coming.

But it didn't come. Aufidius was being dragged away. Caius had no one to fight. A sudden and immense weariness came over him, the result of his long fight with Aufidius, and he sank into the mud. His breath coming heavily, he watched as what was left of the Roman infantry chased after the retreating Volsci.

Tullus was furious. How dare he be dragged away from Marcius, just when he felt sure he was going to defeat him?

'Let go of me,' he yelled, struggling so fiercely that he fell on his face when those holding him obeyed. He turned over onto his back and glared up at the men. 'I was winning.'

The commander spat. 'What if you were? I gave you an order.'

'I thought our orders were to kill the enemy,' Tullus said, scrambling to his feet and taking a few steps back towards the field. He stared down at the wide expanse.

'*You* were winning,' the commander said, '*we* were

losing. Look down there.' He pointed at the field. 'It's carnage.'

'How?' Tullus cried. 'The reports all said Rome was in chaos. They didn't have an army. This battle,' he waved at the field, 'was supposed to be easy.'

'Our information was wrong,' the commander said, shaking his head. 'The Romans are too strong.'

'Or we are too weak,' Tullus snarled.

'We will need you, Aufidius,' the commander said. 'For our next battle.'

'I wasn't going to be killed,' Tullus said, his jaw tight.

'You were fighting Marcius.'

'I know who I was fighting,' he yelled, then remembered who he was speaking to. 'I know who,' he said, more quietly.

The commander nodded, then turned back to the field. 'It's over.'

Tullus joined him. The field was clearing; both sides, those still alive, were returning to their camps. A thought suddenly occurred. 'Have you seen my father?'

The commander looked down at his feet. 'I saw him being helped off the field. He was injured. I don't know how badly.'

Tullus didn't stop to answer. He ran into the camp. If his father was injured, then he would be in the surgeon's tent. He headed for it, feeling sick.

The surgeons' tent was large, but in the aftermath of battle, it was crowded. Each trestle table had a man upon it, either groaning or screaming, the linen cloth beneath him soiled. There were only two surgeons and too many men. Some would bleed to death on the tables, despite the surgeons' efforts, while others would be ignored as not worth the saving.

Tullus hurried from table to table, moving on as soon as

he saw the man lying on each one was not his father. He had almost come to the last of the tables when he saw him.

'Father,' Tullus bent low over Gallio, his hand moving to cradle his father's head. The thinning grey hair was stiff with mud and it crumbled in his hand.

Gallio opened his eyes. They took a long moment to focus on Tullus. 'Thank the gods you are safe,' he whispered, his lips barely touching one another so the words came out in a hissed slur.

Tullus looked down the length of his father's body. There didn't seem to be one bit of it that wasn't covered in blood. 'Are you badly hurt?' he asked, hoping the blood was that of their enemies, not his father's.

'Don't worry about me,' Gallio said, closing his eyes.

Not worry? How could he not worry? Tullus sniffed and looked for a surgeon. He found one working on a man three tables away. Tullus hurried to him and grabbed his arm. 'Here,' he cried, pointing at his father.

'I already have a patient,' the surgeon snapped, trying to tug his arm free.

But Tullus's grip was tight. 'You will attend my father.'

'He'll have to wait his turn.'

Tullus grabbed the surgeon by his bloodied tunic and tore him away from his patient, dragging him over to his father's table. He pulled out his sword and held it to the surgeon's neck. 'Attend to my father,' he said, his voice hard, menacing.

The surgeon gulped and stared at the sword. 'Please,' he said, 'lower your sword, soldier. I will examine your father.'

Tullus waited a moment, unwilling to relinquish the power he had over the surgeon until he was sure he meant what he said. He read terror in the man's eyes and lowered his sword. The surgeon took a deep breath, and with trembling hands, began to examine Gallio.

'Will he live?' Tullus demanded.

'There are no wounds to the stomach or chest, only his limbs,' the surgeon replied. 'The wounds are deep and he has lost much blood. I cannot say if he will live or die.'

'If he dies, I swear you will follow him.'

The surgeon said nothing, but his face paled. Tullus jerked his head at his father, an instruction to the surgeon to begin his work. He took a step back, out of the way, watching as the surgeon threaded a needle to sew up his father's wounds. He had killed men in battle, had seen their insides spill out and never turned a hair, but to watch his father being sewn together made him sick to his very stomach.

The surgeon worked fast, no doubt spurred on by the memory of Tullus's sword at his throat. 'I've done all I can,' he said at last.

'Then you can go,' Tullus said, and the surgeon scurried away.

Tullus bent over his father once more, listening to Gallio's breathing. It was even, if shallow. His forehead touched his father's cheek, his hands grabbed hold of his shoulders and he began to sob. He couldn't help it. He had only recently lost his mother. He wasn't ready to lose his father just yet.

18

Volumnia stood in the doorway of Caius's cubiculum, staring at her son as he slept.

It had been more than seven months since she had seen him last, seven months of wishing she could have gone with him on campaign to watch him fight. So many battles, she mused, and she not able to partake in any of them because she had been born a woman. It wasn't fair. If only she had been born a man, she would have shown those Volsci what stuff the Romans were made of. But she had to content herself with knowing that Caius had done that for her, and done it extremely well. Throughout those seven months there had been reports coming back to Rome of his successes against the enemy and Volumnia had accepted with great pleasure the congratulations that had come her way: you must be so very proud; it's all your doing, my dear; Caius wouldn't be anything without you. True, all of it true. She had made him the man he was.

'You should leave him alone.'

Volumnia turned, her eyebrow already arching. 'Should I, indeed?' she said to Virgilia, who was standing a few feet away, her hand holding that of Little Caius, who stood staring at his grandmother as if he had never seen her before, mouth open, eyes wide. There were times when Volumnia wondered if he wasn't simple.

'You might wake him, that's all.' Virgilia said. 'He's very tired.'

Volumnia reached into the room and pulled the door shut quietly. 'I can see that, my dear,' she said icily.

Virgilia bit her lip. 'Menenius Agrippa is here. I... I came to tell you.'

Volumnia didn't answer, simply strode past her, making Virgilia pull Little Caius out of her way. She headed for the atrium. 'You're very early, Menenius.'

'Forgive me,' Menenius said, 'but I heard that Caius has returned.'

She nodded and began to lead him through the domus towards the garden, thinking she would like to have her breakfast in the sunlight. 'He arrived very late last night. We were already in bed.'

'How is he?'

'Exhausted. He's fast asleep.'

'Wounded?'

'Of course.'

'Oh dear. Seriously?'

Volumnia gave a little laugh. 'Oh Menenius, when has Caius ever been seriously hurt? No, just a few scratches, some bruises. There really is no one equal to him, you see.'

'Yes, I see,' Menenius nodded.

'I don't think you will see Caius this morning,' she said, clicking her fingers at the slave to bring her breakfast. 'And besides, I would have thought you would be busy at the Senate house with the army returning. Don't you have to add up figures or something?' She saw the look of irritation cross

Menenius's face and smiled to herself. Her opinion of Menenius had diminished slightly since he had decided not to go on campaign any longer but stay in Rome and concern himself only with provisioning and other such matters. His triumph, she reflected sadly, seemed like such a long time ago.

'No, nothing like that. The truth is I couldn't bear to sit in the Senate this morning.'

'Why not?' she asked, pouring him a cup of wine and adding water, knowing that he didn't particularly care for watered-down wine.

He took the cup, barely noticing, and gave a long, drawn-out sigh. 'I must confess to being ashamed of being a senator. Before the war, you may remember, that incident in the forum.'

'When the plebs stormed the Senate house and demanded to be heard? Yes, I remember. I remember too that not a single one of those men was punished.'

'Publius Servilius made promises to the plebs on that day. He promised there would be laws to protect them against their creditors. That is why they agreed to fight.'

'Agreed to fight,' Volumnia snarled, barely glancing at Virgilia as she came out into the garden and sat down at the table. 'I don't know what Publius was thinking, agreeing to such a thing. There was a time, Menenius, when the plebs knew their place. They wouldn't have dared act so when the Tarquins still ruled in Rome.'

'You cannot wish Rome to have kings again, Mother, surely?' Virgilia asked.

'Sometimes I do, daughter. Say what you want about King Lucius, he kept the plebs under control.'

'Until his wretched family pushed them too far,' Virgilia cried.

'Oh, what do you know of politics?' Volumnia scoffed.

'I know enough. More than you give me credit for.'

Volumnia opened her mouth to retort, but Menenius put out his hands. 'Ladies, please, I came here to avoid a fight, not start one.'

The women glared at one another but neither continued the argument.

'What do you mean by avoid a fight, Menenius?' Virgilia asked quietly.

Satisfied the women had ceased their quarrel, Menenius took the bread she offered and dipped it into the dish of olive oil. 'The army is returning and the plebs will expect the Senate to make good on their promises. They will discover that no new laws as promised have been made. Their creditors will be pursuing them as soon as they pass through Rome's gates.'

'But that's not right,' Virgilia said.

'It is right,' Volumnia asserted. 'Creditors must eat too. Are they to starve because the plebs overreach themselves?'

'But, my dear,' Menenius said, 'their methods are far too severe and should not be allowed. Creditors are permitted to whip their debtors, steal their goods from them. Romans against Romans. Such means of recovering debts should not be allowed to continue.'

'Then should you not say so in the Senate?' Virgilia asked.

Menenius sighed again. 'You're right, of course. I should speak for the plebs, but in truth, my dear Virgilia, I have not the stomach for it. At least, not today. Perhaps tomorrow. Or the day after.'

'Or perhaps not at all?' Virgilia suggested sourly.

'I daresay I shall get drawn into it,' Menenius said unhappily. 'The Senate likes to use me to speak with the plebs.'

'They think you understand them,' Volumnia said, her mouth turning up at the corner in amusement as she saw him bristle. 'It's a pity Caius isn't awake. He'd put some heart into you and tell you how to deal with the plebs.'

Menenius raised the wine cup to his lips. 'Yes, I expect he would.'

Virgilia's words, the implied criticism in them, had wounded Menenius a little. She was right, of course, he was being something of a coward. And he knew too that if he didn't speak up for the plebs, then no one would.

Menenius had gone to the Senate house intending to do just that, meaning to declare the promises made by Publius Servilius before the recent war should be honoured, but before he could open his mouth, Publius announced that the corn ambassadors were back in Rome. Corn was vital to Rome, as it was vital to any large city. Without corn, the citizens would starve, and so, Menenius was content to hold his tongue for the moment while this important matter was discussed.

Most of Rome's grain supply came from Sicily, and the ambassadors had been dispatched to negotiate a price, buy the corn and arrange delivery back to Rome. Publius announced that not only had they done this, but they had also accepted a free bounty of grain from Aristodemus. This was an extraordinary turn of events, for like Lucius Tarquin, Aristodemus was known to be a tyrant to his own people. So, why, Publius asked, this sudden generosity?

Some senators immediately said the ambassadors had been wrong to accept the free grain without orders from the Senate and that it ought now to be refused. To accept, they said, would put Rome under an obligation to Aristodemus. How could they be sure, these senators asked, that this known tyrant wouldn't make demands on Rome in a few months, or even weeks' time? And how could the Senate be sure this gift of grain really came from Aristodemus? Wasn't it to Aristodemus that Lucius Tarquin had once fled? Perhaps, before Lucius died, he and Aristodemus had plotted to somehow entrap Rome with this grain. Perhaps, one senator suggested excitedly, the grain had been poisoned.

This last idea was quickly dismissed. Poisoning would leave traces upon the individual grains, one senator, a farm owner, said with assurance, and besides, a small portion could always be fed to a dog to see if it died. Most senators, and Menenius found himself agreeing with them, thought it would be foolish to turn away a gift of free grain, whoever it came from and whatever their motives. Rome, they argued, could accept the gift in effectual ignorance. If the giver later demanded a favour in return, Rome could say they were beholden to no one.

Menenius stood up. 'I believe we should look on this gift of grain as most timely.'

'How so, Menenius?' Publius asked warily, knowing from past experience that Menenius often put forward ideas contrary to his own.

'The plebs are discontented. We all know this and have been wondering how to pacify them. Their discontent is real and valid.' This with a glare at Publius, who thrust out his bottom lip in defiance. 'As the new laws to protect the plebs from creditors have yet to be drafted, it would help to keep them happy if we were to distribute this free grain among them.'

'How much should we charge?' Menenius's neighbour asked.

Menenius laughed. 'Nothing at all. We should give it to the plebs free of charge.'

There was a moment's silence in the Senate house.

'Are you quite serious?' Publius sputtered.

'I am,' Menenius replied.

'Give the grain to the plebs? Why should we?'

'I have already said why, Publius. It will repair our relationship with them.'

'Why do you talk of repairing relationships? The plebs must learn that we rule Rome, not they.'

'To talk of giving it away is sheer nonsense,' another senator said. 'On the contrary, we should sell the grain at a high price. To do so will make the plebs entirely reliant on our good will. They will realise they have to obey the Senate or they will starve.'

The senator's words were roundly cheered. *By the gods*, Menenius thought, closing his eyes, *will the patricians never learn? They act as if Tarquin still sat on his throne. Rome has changed and the Senate hasn't changed with her.* He decided to make one last effort. 'Could we not distribute the majority of the grain to the plebs,' he pleaded, 'and then, because there is so much of it, sell the surplus at a low price? The Senate would still benefit and the plebs would be content.'

There was muttering among the senators, and for a brief moment, Menenius was hopeful. But then Publius spoke and his voice was full of jaunty mockery.

'Why are you so eager to please the plebs, Menenius? Is it because you have a special affinity with them?'

Menenius bristled. The taunt was an old one but it never failed to hit a nerve. 'There is not one patrician family in Rome that is not descended from the plebeian class, Publius, and you know it.'

'But some of us are more recently elevated,' another senator called, provoking laughter.

A voice, loud and stern, came from the open Senate house doorway. 'You dishonour yourself with such petty insults,' Caius declared loudly.

The laughing stopped abruptly.

'Caius Marcius,' Publius said, 'it is good to see you.'

You liar, Menenius thought, watching the bony lump in Publius's throat bob up and down. *Caius scares the life out of you.*

Caius strode into the Senate house and right up to Publius's chair. It was a liberty, but no one seemed ready to protest. Menenius watched with almost amused interest as Caius fixed Publius with a hard stare. 'Menenius Agrippa is one of our noblest patricians, a war hero and a beloved friend. You will make an enemy of me if you continue to defame him.'

'I meant no disrespect, Caius Marcius. My apologies, Menenius Agrippa.' Publius inclined his head towards Menenius, who, though he was tempted to prolong Publius's discomfort, decided to accept the apology. 'But surely, Caius Marcius, you do not think we should act to appease the plebs?'

Menenius groaned inwardly, knowing he had lost any advantage he may have had. Caius would never agree with him about the plebs.

'Indeed I do not,' Caius said. 'It is my opinion that the plebs should be shown their place and that the Senate gives them an ear too often. It's a pity we are not at war. A battlefield fight is an excellent way to cull a herd.' He laughed, enjoying his own joke, and out of fellow feeling, or just out of cowardice, Menenius didn't know, the senators laughed with him.

Menenius alone did not laugh. His focus was on the open Senate house door through which Caius had entered. For out there were the very plebs of which Caius spoke.

And they had heard every word he said.

Sicinius Vitellus watched the senators file out of the Senate house, his mind working hard. Often, did he watch the senators at work; often, did he listen to their debates; and often, did he think how greatly he would like to kill the lot of them.

He was a working man and he worked so very hard to feed his family. That was sometimes hard to do, especially when the Senate decided Rome should be at war again and conscripted him and others like him into the army. He didn't want to always be fighting. Day to day staying alive was difficult enough and the only fight he truly wanted.

And yet despite the duty he had shown Rome and had shown the bloody patricians all his life, they couldn't even bring themselves to give people like him an handout of free grain, grain that could make the difference between his family having enough to eat and starving. No, they wanted to charge for it, and charge an exorbitant rate they knew the plebs couldn't afford and which would undoubtedly put them in the hands of yet more creditors. And where were the laws Publius Servilius had promised? Why were creditors still allowed to imprison a man for non-payment of debts, to whip and flog them? They had lied to the plebs to get them to fight, and they didn't care.

Sicinius leant against the column as Caius and Menenius followed the last of the senators out of the Senate house. Caius Marcius was the worst of all the patricians. He loved war and no doubt urged his friends in the Senate to find enemies for him to fight. He had no love for the plebs. He had made that abundantly clear over the years, he didn't even bother to hide it. Even now, he was passing through the forum, pushing plebs out of his way with as little regard as if they were stray dogs.

How could Menenius Agrippa call that man friend, Sicinius wondered? It seemed to him an unlikely pairing. Of all the patricians, of all the senators, Sicinius thought Agrippa the only man to have any concern for the plebs. He had heard the gossip, of course, that Menenius was only a few generations away from being a pleb himself. To Sicinius, that was a good thing. It made Menenius Agrippa more approachable.

'You're deep in thought,' a voice at his elbow said.

'Did you hear them in there, Junius?' Sicinius asked, still watching Caius and Menenius.

'Some of it.'

Sicinius turned to his friend. 'And what did you think of it?'

Junius Brutus eyed him thoughtfully. 'That they're bastards, every one.'

Sicinius huffed and shook his head. 'Is that all you can say?' He continued before Junius could reply. 'They are planning to hoard grain that was given as a gift to Rome and sell it to us at a high price so they can fill their own money chests and keep us where they think we belong.'

'I know, I heard,' Junius said. 'But what can we do?'

Sicinius considered a moment. 'We're not without means,' he said, thumping the column with the side of his clenched fist. 'There are more of us than there are of them.'

'Oh, Sicinius,' Junius began shaking his head, 'haven't we fought enough?'

'I'm not talking about fighting, you fool. The gods know I

don't want to fight anymore, not unless I have to. I'm talking about standing up to the Senate.'

'How?'

'By going on strike,' Sicinius said excitedly, the idea growing within him even as he spoke. 'We, all of us, all the plebs, lay down our tools and refuse to do any more work for the patricians and senators until they give us the laws and protection they promised us before the last war.'

'We can't do that,' Junius said, aghast.

'Why can't we?' Sicinius demanded. 'What's to stop us?'

'They'll punish us.'

'How? They can't send an army against us. We're their army.' He laughed. 'It's so simple when you think about it, Junius. Without the plebs obeying the patricians' every word, they have no power. They have no army, they have no one to bake their bread, slaughter their cattle, make their clothes. Rome needs us, Junius, I promise you. This will work.'

'If you can get the rest of the plebs to agree,' Junius said.

'We will.'

'We?'

'Yes, we. I can't do this alone, Junius. We've stood together on the battlefield, we've saved each other's life. I'm asking you to stand by me again and save the lives of every pleb in Rome. Will you do it?'

Junius stared into Sicinius's eyes for a long moment. Then he took his friend's hand and held it. 'I'll do it,' he promised.

'They must be stopped,' Publius blustered, running back into the Senate house from the forum, where he had been watching the exodus of plebs from Rome. The plebs were making for the Sacred Mount, a few miles out of Rome, where a meeting was to be held to discuss how the patricians and Senate could be opposed. 'We must stop them.'

'And how do you propose we do that?' Menenius asked, caught between amusement and weariness. 'The people we would use to prevent this strike are the people doing the striking.'

'But... but...'

'Face facts, Publius, the plebs have got one up on us this time. A pre-emptive strike, if you will.'

Publius's face grew purple. He leered at Menenius. 'Did you have anything to do with this, Menenius Agrippa? Have you been instilling this rebellious spirit in the plebs?'

'How dare you!' Menenius snarled. 'If you're looking to lay blame for this, you need look no further than yourself, Publius. It was your desire to levy a high price on goods that were given to Rome as a gift that have caused this. Did you think what you said would not reach the ears of the plebs?'

'What is said in the Senate house is confidential—'

'They were listening at the door,' Menenius cried. 'If you want to have secret sessions of the Senate, you must needs close the doors first, you great fool.'

'I won't be spoken to like that, Menenius,' Publius declared, drawing himself up.

'I speak as I find. And you are a great fool.'

'Enough,' another senator said, moving to stand between Publius and Menenius. 'We are at fault,' he stared meaningfully at Publius, 'and we must remedy the situation. Menenius Agrippa, do you have any suggestions?'

Me again, Menenius thought irritably. *Doesn't anyone else have a brain in this place?* 'We must talk to them,' he cried, as if the solution were obvious. 'We must reach some accommodation. Begin by giving them the grain gratis, as I said we should do in the first place.'

'If we do that, they will be making demands all the time. Give us this, give us that, or we will walk out of Rome again,' Publius said. 'The Senate would have no authority whatsoever.'

'We have done them wrong, Publius, and we must acknowledge that and make amends. Else Rome is doomed. Do you want that?'

Publius fell silent, considering this dire eventuality.

'Talk to them, you say,' the other senator said musingly, one finger on his lips. He looked sideways at Menenius. 'Who should talk to them, do you think?'

'Why, Menenius should go,' Publius said, his eyes rolling dramatically. 'He understands the plebs so well, as he is always telling us.'

'I am not always telling you,' Menenius said through gritted teeth. Really, Publius was an infuriating little prick.

'But Publius is correct,' the other senator said eagerly. 'You do know — that is, you do understand the plebeian mind, Menenius, better than any of us.'

Menenius looked around at his fellow senators. They all looked back at him quite ingenuously, silently urging him to take up their cause on their behalf. He sighed loudly. 'Very well. I shall talk to the pleb leaders and see if I cannot resolve this appalling situation you have all got us in.'

He heard the murmuring as he left. He had annoyed the senators with that last little gibe.

Menenius knew who the ringleaders of this remarkable event were, a Sicinius Vitellus and Junius Brutus, the latter no relation to the man who had banished Lucius Tarquin. When he realised that Publius's words regarding the grain had been overheard by the plebs clustered around the Senate house doors, Menenius had instructed his personal slave to listen attentively to the gossip on the streets, and so had heard of this rebellion before it became a reality. He had mentally applauded the plebs for taking this stand even as he wished they had not done so.

As he came to the bank of the River Anio where the plebs had congregated to hear Sicinius and Junius speak, Menenius could not help but be staggered by just how many of them there were. He had decided to venture alone, thinking it would be less like a senatorial deputation, but now he was wishing he had brought someone with him. He saw Sicinius's eyes on him as he approached and readied himself.

'What do you want here, Menenius Agrippa?' Sicinius called.

All heads turned towards him. 'To talk,' Menenius replied, as casually as he could. 'Just to talk.'

'To tell us what to do, more like,' someone called.

'Not at all.'

'The Senate has sent you?' Sicinius asked.

'They have,' Menenius nodded, deciding honesty was the best strategy. 'They are eager to settle this matter.'

'I bet they are,' another voice called laughingly, setting off an appreciative ripple of chuckles.

'It will be in all our interests to do so,' Menenius said.

'We aren't doing anything the Senate tells us to anymore,' said a man standing a few feet away, a tanner by the look of him, his skin darkened from his trade.

'Indeed? And what happens when you want something from the Senate?' Menenius asked. 'They won't listen to you then, my friend.'

'So what? They're not listening now, are they?' the man countered.

'Ah, now there, my friend, you are wrong,' Menenius said. 'The Senate are prepared to listen to your complaints. Why else would I be here?'

Murmurings followed this last statement and Menenius felt emboldened that he had at least got their attention. 'Let me explain,' he continued, his mind working quickly to determine how best to state the Senate's position without angering the plebs further. A fable came into his mind, one he had been told long ago by his father. It would serve his purpose now. 'There was once a time when all the parts of the body rebelled against the stomach. The other parts claimed that the stomach did nothing all day but grow fat on their hard work. It gave nothing back, they claimed, while they laboured hard to keep it full. But instead of the stomach claiming indignantly that it was not true, the stomach merely laughed at their ignorance. For, it said, didn't the other parts understand what a vital service the stomach played in their wellbeing? The stomach digested all the fruits of their toil, it was true, but only so it could send out the benefits of that toil to all parts of the body. Without the stomach, the parts would starve, the stomach truthfully told them. So you see, fellow citizens, this is how we should see Rome. Rome is a whole body. You, the parts that feed her, the Senate the stomach that takes your noble toil and sends nourishment back to you.'

'What is this nonsense?' someone cried. 'We are not children to be told stories.'

Menenius raised his hands for silence. 'It is in the Senate that all the proposals and affairs of state are studied and transformed into action, and the decisions that the senators take bring usefulness to us all. Could you do this all on your own?'

'That may be true,' Junius said reluctantly, 'but they still don't listen to us. They've made us promises time and again and then go back on them once we've done what they wanted us to do.'

'I do not deny that you have valid grievances, but friends, this is no way to go about redressing it. We must work together, not against one another.'

'What's this now?' Sicinius suddenly cried and pointed over Menenius's shoulder.

Menenius turned and groaned. Caius and five or six of his friends were striding towards him, all of them carrying their swords. *And I had been doing so well,* Menenius thought ruefully. 'It's nothing, Sicinius,' Menenius assured him.

'Do you mean to frighten us with Caius Marcius?' Sicinius retorted.

Menenius asked him to wait a moment and hurried to Caius. 'What are you doing here?' he hissed.

'I thought you might need my help,' Caius said, looking over the crowd grimly. 'These mutinous dogs will fight dirty.'

'I have no need of you, Caius,' Menenius said, trying to keep his irritation in check. 'I thank you for your concern, but really, you may take yourself and your friends off.'

'Well, Menenius?' Sicinius called, looking askance at Caius. 'Has the Senate sent its butcher to slaughter us?'

'Caius Marcius merely comes to see what he can do for us all,' Menenius said.

'What, him?' Junius said scornfully. 'Caius Marcius has always been an enemy to the common people. He despises us.'

'And so I do,' Caius shouted back. 'Your problem is you don't know when you're well off. All this protesting and complaining. What have you to complain about? You're fed, aren't you?'

'Only just, Caius Marcius,' Junius spat back. 'Only enough to keep us beggars.'

'What would you have, then? A place in the Senate?'

'And why not?' Sicinius demanded, incensed by Caius's contempt. 'We can do no worse than those crusty old men.'

'By the gods, what arrogance! To think you could make laws and pass judgement on men like me.'

'What arrogance you have to think we are not worth considering,' Sicinius countered. 'We may not be patricians but we have power, never think we do not. We could bring you down if we all raised our arms against you.'

'Then raise them, and see how you fare, you dog.'

'No, no,' Menenius cried, stepping to stand in front of Caius and so block him from Sicinius. 'This is not the way. Caius, please, go home.'

'Yeah, go home back to mummy,' someone shouted from the crowd.

'Who said that?' Caius roared, pushing Menenius out of the way, his hand going to his sword. 'Come forward, you coward.'

'Quiet, all of you,' Menenius cried desperately. He grabbed hold of Caius's arm and tugged him around to force him back behind him. Caius resisted at first, but after a glare from Menenius, acquiesced. Menenius turned back to Sicinius to make an offer that had been brewing in his mind for some time but which he had hoped never to make, for he knew his fellow senators would despise it. 'You shall have representation in the Senate.'

'What did you say, Menenius?' Sicinius asked, patting the air, asking for quiet.

'I say you will have representation,' Menenius repeated. 'Men who will voice your complaints and desires directly to the Senate. They will be elected by you and ruled by you.

They will be tribunes of the people. And the Senate will have to listen to them.'

'Menenius, are you mad?' Caius hissed.

'Not mad, Caius, no, and not foolish either. I know what I am doing.'

'What you are doing is giving away power. The Senate will not like this.'

'The Senate will have to accept it. Times are changing, Caius. We have rid ourselves of one tyrant. We must not let the Senate become another. Now, please, do as I ask and go home.'

Caius turned his back on the plebs and lowered his voice. 'Do you think you can send me away, Menenius? I am not a boy to be told to go home.'

'You are endangering me and my mission here. You will stand to one side and say nothing more.' He didn't wait for Caius to comply. He turned his attention back to Sicinius.

'These tribunes,' Sicinius began. 'We can say who they will be?'

Menenius nodded. 'You must choose two among you to be tribunes.'

'One should be you, Sicinius,' a man cried. 'You have fought bravely for Rome and have our interests at heart. And you, Junius.' He turned to the crowd. 'I name Junius Brutus and Sicinius Vitellus to be our tribunes.'

I should have know they would be chosen, Menenius thought unhappily. *Two troublemakers to speak for the people. Oh well, it can't be helped now.*

'Do you agree to be elected tribunes of the people?' Menenius asked Sicinius and Junius.

The latter looked dazed and not at all sure he wanted the honour of being a tribune. His gaze kept sliding towards Caius and his armed friends as if he expected them to attack him for his impudence in being singled out in this way. Sicinius, on the other hand, was unable to hide his delight and answered for them both. ‘We do.’

‘Then come with me to the Senate,’ Menenius said, ‘and you shall be named so. The rest of you,’ he called to the crowd, ‘follow and witness this act and know you will have a voice in the Senate.’

The crowd began to move forward, back towards Rome.

‘I hope you know what you’re doing,’ Caius muttered as they watched them go.

‘So do I,’ Menenius muttered, wondering if he hadn’t just started something that would be all their undoing.

19

493 BC

The warm little thing was squirming in his hands. Tullus held it out from his body, unsure what to do with it.

This was his, he realised as he looked down upon his daughter. This small, pink bundle of flesh shared his blood, had part of him, and all his forebears, in her. Why then, did he feel so little? Surely, he should feel something, some tingle of emotion, some stirring of love? He shook his head, unable to locate any such feeling. 'What's wrong with me?' he chastised himself under his breath. Yet, despite the absence of feeling, he knew he would defend the small creature to his last breath. As a father, it was his duty to protect his offspring, but that was the only driving emotion and he knew it should not be so. He wondered if it was because his wife had given him a daughter. Would he have felt differently if he was holding a son?

He looked back over his shoulder at his wife asleep in their bed. It had been an exhausting labour, the midwife had told him, and she had fallen asleep long before he returned home. She had not even had the strength to stay awake and hold her child. *Best she doesn't know how I feel,* he thought. *I shall appear glad, overjoyed, when she wakes. I will not let her know this little thing means nothing to me.* Tullus replaced his daughter in her basket. She squealed a little, then fell asleep. He envied her the ease with which she did so.

Tullus looked up at a sudden noise coming through the small window. It was the sound of running feet, lots of them, accompanied by shouts of encouragement to follow. Something was afoot, Tullus realised, and he rushed out of the cubiculum, startling the nurse his wife had hired who was on her way in with clean cloths for the baby. Shouting an apology, he hurried out of the domus, stopping only one moment on the threshold to stare at the mass of people who were making their way along the street that led to the centre of town before joining them.

'What is it, what's happening?' he demanded of the man who became his neighbour in the procession.

'There's news about the Romans,' the man answered. 'An announcement is to be made.'

It was information enough for Tullus. He fell silent and said not another word until he and his fellows had reached the forum. The square was already full and Tullus found himself at the edge, too far away to hear for himself what the news was. If he stayed there, he would have to rely on it being relayed back to him and he knew from experience that often resulted in untruths and exaggerations. Tullus used his elbows to good effect and pushed his way closer. The speaker had begun by the time he was content with his position in the crowd. Tullus ignored the abuse hissed at him by those he had shoved out of the way, folded his arms and listened.

The speaker gestured for silence and the crowd fell silent.

'The Romans are laying siege to the town of Corioli,' he declared loudly.

Tullus could hardly believe it. Were the Volsci never to be free of Roman aggression? And Corioli, one of their largest and most valuable towns. For the Romans to seize it would mean disaster for the Volsci. He was more angry than he could say. But there was another part of him, he acknowledged, that was pleased. Here was another battle, another chance to face Caius Marcius and beat him. He hadn't gotten over being cheated of the chance to kill Marcius the last time they had faced one another in battle. Perhaps if their hero had been killed, the Romans would have thought twice about marching into Volsci territory.

And what glory there would be in that slaughter for me, Tullus thought. He strained to hear the speaker, who was trying to make himself heard above the din. There was a call to arms, he said. All able men should equip themselves with their finest weapons and meet on the field outside the city gates to march on Corioli and defend her against the Romans.

Tullus didn't need to hear any more. He turned and pushed his way out of the crowd. He hurried along the now empty street, back to his domus to grab his sword and spear. He forgot all about his wife and daughter asleep in their cubiculum. He got all his armour, called for his slave, and headed out the door to join the other Volsci assembling to go to war.

Virgilia pulled Little Caius towards her. He struggled, his small feet digging into the floor, but her pull was too great and his small body folded against her. He had been watching his father as he went down the street, but Caius had turned a corner and there was nothing to see other than street traders and stray dogs.

'Want to go with Father,' the boy said, turning his face first one way then the other to try and avoid the kisses his mother was planting on his cheeks.

'You can't go with him,' Virgilia told him. 'It's too dangerous. Come inside now.' She lifted him up and cradled him in her arms, her own eyes drawn inexorably to the spot where Caius had last been. She carried Little Caius through to the garden, taking him to her favourite spot, a stone bench shaded by a bay tree. Sitting, she arranged him on her lap.

She, like her son, was missing Caius already. She had grown used to having him at home, though she knew he had been restive and eager to return to soldiering. She had thought the incident with the plebs striking had put paid to Rome thinking of going to war again for some time but she realised she had underestimated the Senate's lust for territory.

'Why can't I go?' her son demanded.

'I've told you why,' she said. 'Your father is going to fight our enemies.'

'With his sword?'

'Yes, with his sword.'

Virgilia hated the sword, that pointed blade that had caused so much blood to spill, but her son had been fascinated by it when Caius had shown it to him. He had stared open-mouthed as Caius had turned the blade to catch the sunlight, and the boy's face had been illuminated by the reflection, so that he seemed to shine.

'Will Father come back?'

'Of course he will. He always comes back.'

Her son unclasped her hands from around his waist and wriggled off her lap to set his little legs on the paved floor. Reluctantly, she folded her arms across her chest, conscious of her desire to take him up again. She watched him waddle across the path to a lavender bush and bend over it. She thought he was smelling the purple flowers but then he gave a triumphant little shout and turned his face excitedly towards her.

'What have you got there?' she asked.

She saw that he had cupped one hand over the other and was holding something. He stepped carefully towards her, his mouth open, his little pink tongue probing the corner of his lips in his concentration. She bent over his hands and he opened them a little. There was a fluttering inside and she peered closer.

'You caught a butterfly, Little Caius.'

He nodded and drew his hands back, closing the gap and putting his nose to it.

'It's very lovely, isn't it?' she said. 'But let it go now.'

Little Caius frowned and shook his head.

'It will be frightened, my love. Come, open your hands.'

He took a few steps back as Virgilia reached for his hands to open them. He looked at her for a long moment, a look that made Virgilia catch her breath for it was so strange, so unlike her little boy. She watched as the little mouth pouted as she inclined her head and hardened her stare, an instruction to do as he was told. Little Caius clapped his hands together and ground them hard, all the while looking at her.

Virgilia's mouth opened, wanting to shriek at the savage thing she had just witnessed, but the deliberate cruelty was too horrible to vocalise. Little Caius scrunched his hands harder and she heard the crush of lighter-than-air wings and soft body. Then he opened his hands, palm downward, and the once beautiful butterfly became an ugly fragment of legs and wings on the ground. She heard a laugh and looked up.

'I remember his father doing the very same thing,' Volumnia said, smiling at her grandson.

He grinned at her. 'Look Grandmother, look what I did.'

'I saw, my little one,' Volumnia nodded. She looked at Virgilia. 'Isn't he a clever boy?'

Virgilia felt tears prick at the back of her eyes. She didn't want her son to be cruel, to take pleasure in killing anything. But she knew, with Volumnia encouraging him, her son stood no chance of being anything else.

———

Caius stared up at the walls of Corioli. The walls were impressive, but not, in his opinion, impregnable. If only Titus Lartius would listen to him; they would probably have been able to take the town by now. But no, the old man thought he knew best and had dismissed Caius's suggestion that they undermine the foundations of a small section of the wall with near contempt. And in front of the other commanders too. It had been almost too much to bear. 'Leave such matters to older, wiser heads,' Titus told him with a smile at the others. Caius had stormed out of the tent without a word. Oh yes, leave older, so-called wiser heads to work out how to bring Corioli to its knees, but Titus and the others didn't mind using Caius's strong arms when it came to the fighting, did they? Fools, all of them. Old men and fools. All he needed, Caius thought, was a few handpicked men, men he could trust and rely to follow wherever he led them, and Corioli would be theirs. He wished now he had gone with his friend Cominius on their scouting party. At least then he wouldn't have had to kick his heels waiting for an old man to make a decision.

Caius wiped the rain out of his eyes and rolled his shoulders to ease the ache in his muscles. He and the men had been standing in the rain for more than two hours waiting for an order to attack. His breastplate rubbed uncomfortably against his skin. If Titus didn't give an order soon, he would retire to his tent and take it off, and to Hades with any attack. His mutinous spirit was minded to leave at once, and Caius half-turned, a wistful eye on the camp, when something caught his attention. He turned back to the town. Narrowing his eyes, he craned his neck, trying to see beyond the descending darkness. Were they...? Yes, they were. The gates of Corioli were opening.

Caius drew his sword from its sheath. The rain had made the hilt slippery and he tried to dry it and his hand on his tunic. He flexed his fingers and gripped it tight.

Others had seen the gates opening and Caius could hear their murmurings and shuffling feet as they too grew expectant.

It was a strange sensation to see the huge wooden doors open slowly and to see the dark shapes, outlined by the braziers that burned inside the town's entrance, move forward. So, they were coming!

The usual thrill of excitement ran through Caius. He felt his heart hammering in his chest, the blood rushing in his ears. He could almost laugh too. Titus had been too slow to act even for the people of Corioli and so they had decided to come out to meet the Romans. No doubt they thought they stood a good chance of beating them. *Well*, Caius thought with grim satisfaction, *they haven't met me yet.*

He bent his knees slightly and angled his body forward, ready for the attack. The shapes were growing larger as they rushed the Roman lines, and still Caius, his training embedded in his very being, held his ground until the enemy was only a few feet away. Then he roared and surged forward, not caring, not knowing, if his good example was followed by his fellow soldiers. He crashed into the enemy, his sword arm moving fast, slicing, stabbing.

But there were more of them than he had realised, and though he fought hard, and suffered only the shallowest of cuts to his arms and legs, he felt himself being pushed backwards, he and the men who fought alongside him.

He gave himself a moment to look around, and saw that the Roman soldiers had turned their backs and were running towards the camp. The Roman soldiers were fleeing!

'Cowards!' Caius roared at them. Some of them stopped and turned around. A few even hesitantly took a few steps back towards him. Out of the corner of his eye, Caius saw a blade coming towards him and he swept it aside with his sword. He grabbed the bearer and rammed his hilt into his face. Blood spurted over him and he threw the man away.

The Corioli were running after the retreating Romans. Caius spied his opportunity and ran towards the open gates of the town.

Titus Lartius was not in a good mood.

The Corioli had taken him unawares. Who would have thought that the fools would come out of their safe stronghold and expose themselves to an attack? But, as his commanders pointed out, doing so had given them an advantage. See, they pointed, the Corioli were driving their soldiers back. As Titus watched, he was imagining the report he would have to send to Rome, and the Senate's disgusted reprimand for his failure to seize the town.

He was going to lose this battle, he could tell. Perhaps he could call it a skirmish in his report, play it down, so that it didn't seem all that much of a defeat after all, just a temporary setback. The Romans weren't used to defeats, it was true, but it wasn't unheard of. They couldn't win every time, could they?

'What is Marcius doing?' one of his commanders suddenly cried.

Titus followed his pointing finger. Caius Marcius was running towards the Corioli gates. The order for retreat had been given; he was disobeying orders.

'Get him back,' Titus said hurriedly. If Marcius entered the town he would be killed. By Hades, what would the Senate say then, if Titus, through incompetence, had lost them their greatest warrior?

'It's too late,' the commander said. 'Look, sir, the gates have closed upon him. He's trapped inside.'

———

He was in. He was through. He was not alone.

Caius sensed the Corioli about him, though he could not see them. They were there, crouching behind the carts and barrels that littered the town's entrance. They were there, in the rooms above, peering down through the windows at him.

He heard a loud thud and turned to see that the gates had been closed. There was no time to consider a strategy. Caius knew he would only survive by killing every man he could find inside Corioli.

But no one was coming out to fight. 'Are you all cowards?' he shouted. 'Come and fight me. I am Caius Marcius and I will kill you all.'

———

'Sir, should we not go to Marcius's aid?' The commander's

face was anguished, like so many of them who had seen the gates shut upon Caius.

'And send more men to their deaths?' Titus replied angrily.

The Corioli who had stormed the Roman lines had been dealt with, quickly becoming outnumbered as they foolishly ran deeper into the Roman camp, but with the gates shut, it seemed impossible for the Romans to gain access to help Caius. Titus suspected that if he ordered men to the city walls, they would be attacked from above, and what use would they be then?

'But to let Marcius fight alone—'

'Need I remind you that Marcius disobeyed my orders?'

'No, sir, you do not,' the commander said, stepping aside and falling silent.

He thinks I'm a coward, Titus thought unhappily*, and worse, a soldier who won't help his own men.* It didn't matter that almost his entire adult life had been spent in one battle or another, fighting for Rome, fighting for his fellow Romans, oh no. All that would be remembered of him now, once the gossip began and spread around the camp, was that Titus Lartius allowed Caius Marcius, the great Caius Marcius, to face the Corioli alone.

'We'll go forward,' he decided. 'If I feel that we can help Marcius, if he's still alive, then we'll attack. But you are to stay back until I give the order, is that clear?'

'Yes, sir,' the commander said, almost smiling and hurried off to line up his men.

That's made him happy, at least, Titus thought miserably. He waited until the men were ready, then he began to lead them over the field and towards the town walls. Titus kept his eyes firmly on the tops of the walls, expecting heads to appear any moment.

But nothing happened.

'It's very quiet, sir,' the commander whispered.

Titus nodded. He was right; it was quiet. No screams, no shouts came to them from the city. Surely, if Caius was dead, the Corioli would be celebrating. He called a halt and the lines stopped moving. Every man was watching, and waiting.

And then the gates were opening.

A tall, striding figure emerged and the men began cheering, 'Marcius, Marcius.'

It *was* Marcius, Titus realised, beneath all the blood that seemed to cover his entire body, it was Caius Marcius. How was it possible he was alive?

'By the gods,' he breathed as Caius drew near. 'Marcius, you are truly beloved of Mars.'

'I think I must be, sir,' Caius said with a laugh, his teeth bright in the blackness of his face. He was out of breath but otherwise seemed uninjured, despite the blood that covered him.

'Are they all dead?' Titus asked, looking back at the town.

Caius nodded. 'Alone, I did it.'

Caius, his legs almost buckling beneath him with every step, made his way back to his tent. As he passed through the camp, he felt hands touch him and mouths murmur thanks to him and to the god Mars for the victory he had given the Romans.

He had no true memory of the battle he had fought in Corioli, he realised. There had been darkness and there had been screams. There had been bodies falling beneath his sword, but of the details, he had no recollection. He knew, when he had rested and the new day had dawned, that he would be asked to recount the experience, and he wondered as he lifted the tent flap aside what he would say.

He staggered inside and fell onto his bed. It creaked beneath his weight and shuddered on its short rickety legs. He sat for several minutes, wanting to lie down and sleep but knowing that the tightening of his skin was the drying of blood and that he should wash. But he was exhausted. His arms felt incredibly heavy, his legs like lead.

His slave entered. 'Should I wash you, dominus?'

'Yes,' Caius sighed. 'I...I cannot rise just yet.'

The slave unbuckled his breastplate and set it aside. He tugged the soiled tunic over Caius's head, dragging it down his arms. He knelt and took off his greaves and unlaced his sandals. Naked now but for his loincloth, Caius closed his eyes as the slave drew a wet sponge over his body, the hot water a caress. The next thing he knew his body was tilting, his head sinking into the pillow.

Caius awoke to the sound of laughter. He opened his eyes and saw his slave sitting on the ground by the tent flap. 'How long have I been asleep?'

The slave got hurriedly to his feet. 'About two hours, dominus.'

Caius asked for water, and as the slave obeyed, he pushed himself up to a sitting position. He groaned as his muscles protested but he did at least feel rested. 'The men are happy, it seems,' he said as the slave handed him a cup.

'They say there are plenty of spoils to be had within the city.'

'Spoils?' Caius repeated, his mind still a little foggy. 'Do you mean to say the men have been looting?'

'And more, dominus. Women...'. The slave's voice trailed off.

'A clean tunic,' Caius demanded, getting to his feet. The slave had this prepared and he held it up for Caius to put on. Clean sandals came next, and so dressed, Caius hurried out. He made for Titus's tent, ignoring the men who called out to him in drunken voices.

'Is this true? Are the men being allowed to loot Corioli?' he demanded.

Titus looked up wearily from his desk and Caius noticed a look of impatience cross his face. 'Marcius, you are rested, I hope?'

'I am, sir. But are the men looting with your permission?'

Titus put down his stylus. 'Why this outrage, Marcius? You know as well as I that to loot is a soldier's privilege.'

'I know it is a custom, not a right,' Caius said, 'and one I do not in any way endorse. Did I take Corioli alone so that men who ran away can reap the rewards?'

'Need I remind you, Marcius,' Titus said, growing heated, 'that I am in command here and I do not have to answer to you. You may have performed an extraordinary act this night, but I will not tolerate insubordination.'

'We fight for the glory of Rome, do we not?'

'Perquisites, Marcius,' Titus retorted. 'Have you never helped yourself after a battle?'

'Never, sir.'

'Then you are a fool. The gods know the men have little enough from the Senate for their service to Rome. I will not begrudge them the opportunity to enrich themselves.'

'And while Corioli is being looted, what of Cominius? Have you heard from him?'

'Not yet. How does the looting here have anything to do with him. He is miles away.'

'Exactly, sir. He is miles away in enemy territory with only a handful of men. I am sure he could do with some help.'

'What would you have me do?'

'Send some of the men to meet him.'

'The men are tired, they are not fit for marching, let alone fighting.'

'They are not fit because they are all drunk or debauching, sir,' Caius's voice was rising in his indignation.

'That's enough, Marcius,' Titus ordered. 'I will send no men after Cominius. If however, you feel compelled to go after him yourself, I will not hinder you.'

'I will go, sir, as you say I can,' Caius said defiantly. 'And I will take my men with me.'

Titus raised an eyebrow. 'Your men are just as likely to have looted as all the others. If you can find any of them sober, and willing, you can take them. And may the gods go with you, Marcius.'

His men were writing their wills by the aid of the moonlight. It was a ritual Cominius loathed. For soldiers to write their wills before an expected battle, to Cominius's mind, was almost as if they expected to die. He didn't believe that a good expectation for a soldier, as if the expectation made the dying more likely. He had a will, of course, but his was kept safe in the Temple of Vesta and had been written years before when he had first become a father. He had not had sight of it since.

Cominius rose from the large flat stone he had been using for a chair, feeling his legs beginning to stiffen and his backside grown numb. He needed to stretch his legs but he dare not go far. He and his men were inside Volsci territory and he had no idea how near the enemy was. The nearest town was Antium. It was likely the news of the latest Roman campaign had reached Antium, and also likely that the Volsci had dispatched their army to meet them. At this moment, the Volsci might be ten miles away or ten feet. In the darkness, surrounded by trees, there was no way of knowing.

Cominius heard a wolf howl in the distance and wondered if they dare light a fire to keep the pack away. But a fire would give away their position, so he decided it would be better to be cold and alive than warm and dead.

He heard a noise and halted. The night was full of noises, of course, the calls of small animals in the trees, the rustle of leaves, the blowing of the wind, but this was something different. The noise was stealthy, in its way, as if the maker was trying not to be heard. Cominius's hand was on his sword hilt and he slowly pulled it out a few inches. He peered into the darkness ahead. Was that movement or was his mind playing a trick on him? He waited and watched.

The strange, stealthy noise grew closer and Cominius held his breath. If he called out to warn his men, the Volsci would rush him and he would be a dead man in seconds. If he did not call out, then the Volsci could kill him silently and then do the same to his men. What to do, what to do? He began to edge backwards, small half-steps that made no noise. He would rejoin his men. They would see him coming and understand they were to take hold of their swords and be ready for the attack.

The noise was catching up with him; he wasn't able to move fast enough. He had just decided to call out to his men and then run back to them, when he saw who was making the noise.

'Caius,' he called with relief, 'thank the gods it's you.' He laughed at his own nervousness and held out his hand. Caius's hand was reassuringly strong in his.

'I thought you might need my help,' Caius said, gesturing for his men to move forward and join the others. He looked up at the trees that surrounded them. 'Have you seen the enemy?'

'Not yet. But tell me, I see fresh wounds on you. Has there been a battle?'

Caius grinned. 'A fierce one. Corioli, my friend, is taken.'

Cominius was astonished. 'But how? We thought the town impregnable.'

'They opened the gates and in I went.'

Cominius frowned. 'In you went? What do you mean?'

'I took the town, Cominius. I alone. I killed every man I could find in that miserable place.'

'And yet you live?' Cominius shook his head. 'I would not have thought it possible.'

'Lartius said I am beloved by the gods, Cominius, and in truth, I think it true. There is none that can stand against me.'

'Save for that Volsci,' Cominius said, a little irked by Caius's boasting. 'What's his name?'

Caius stared down at the ground and Cominius saw him gnaw his bottom lip in irritation. 'Tullus Aufidius. But I shall kill him yet.'

'Well, he lives in Antium, I think, and that is where we are heading.'

They had reached the soldiers and Cominius noticed that his men were looking at Caius with awe. So, Caius's men had told their tale of Corioli. How his fame grew!

'Is it true, sir?' one of them asked Caius. 'Did you take Corioli all by yourself?'

Caius had the good grace to blush, Cominius noticed. He might boast of his own prowess but he would become embarrassed were others to do so. 'Corioli is ours,' Caius said dismissively. 'The gods were on our side, that's all.'

'That's a great deal, sir, if you don't mind me saying so. Will you be taking command now?'

Cominius started at the impudent question. His own men asking Caius to take over his command. How dare they? He felt Caius's eyes upon him and waited to hear what he would say.

'You are under Cominius's command,' Caius said, 'and you should want no better commander. I am sure I do not.'

'But if you are beloved of the gods, sir,' the man continued, oblivious to the discomfort he was causing between the two friends, 'then it is best we are commanded by you. Sir,' he appealed to Cominius, 'is it not so?'

What can I do but agree? Cominius thought resentfully. 'I insist, Caius,' he said, forcing a smile onto his face. 'Any man who can take a town alone should be given command as a right. My men are yours, as am I.'

Caius clamped a hand on his shoulder. 'I thank you, Cominius, and I accept.'

'You are not too weary?' Cominius asked hopefully.

'Not a bit of it. I feel ready to fight the whole of Antium. Corioli has only whetted my appetite for Volsci blood. So much so, I say we should not wait for the Volsci to find us. Let us march towards Antium and get to them first. What say you, men? Are you ready for a walk?'

They all cheered, entirely heedless of the danger they might put themselves in. *And why should they?* Cominius thought miserably as he and the others gathered their things. *After all, we march with Caius Marcius, and as Lartius said, he is beloved of the gods.*

20

Another battle, another victory, though this one not as sweet as Corioli. Before they could reach Antium, the Volsci had come out to meet Caius and Cominius, and the fighting had been fierce.

As much as he relished his victory at Corioli, Caius was not such a fool to believe he could fight like that again so soon after. The truth was he was tired, his body exhausted from the battle inside Corioli. He had fought well when they had encountered the Volsci a few miles out of Antium, but he could not deny that Cominius had fought just as bravely as he, and certainly more effectively, for men had fallen easily beneath Cominius's sword while Caius had, once again, met and failed to kill Tullus Aufidius.

It was strange, he reflected, but it was almost as if he and Aufidius had been drawn to one another. The other soldiers had seemed to distance themselves from the two men, as if they knew Aufidius and Marcius were destined to fight each other and no one else. Caius had tried to kill Aufidius but he could not do it. He had wounded him, Caius had felt his blade pierce Tullus's skin and seen him bleed, but they were as pinpricks to the Volscian, it seemed, for he kept coming on and Caius was forced back, though never allowing himself to lower his sword. If he could not kill Aufidius, then Aufidius would not have the pleasure of killing him, he promised himself. He hardly noticed that the Romans were winning that battle. It was only when Aufidius was dragged away by his own men that Caius knew the battle was over. Had he been stronger, he would have hurried after Aufidius. As it was, he was content to accept the victory for what it was, a Roman victory rather than his alone.

He had fallen asleep as soon as his head hit the pillow, and he slept deeply. He awoke to sunlight bleeding through the tent and the sounds of a camp outside. He tried to lift his head and felt the pull of muscles either side of his spine. He tested his body, flexing his legs and his arms, and hissed as the muscles protested. He lifted the sheet from his body and saw his wounds had been cleaned and dressed. It must have been done while he was asleep because he didn't remember the surgeon attending him. His throat was parched and his bladder full. He forced his body up, working through the pain, and relieved himself before pouring himself some wine and downing the lot.

He moved to the flap. He untied it and flipped it backwards, blinking as the sunlight hit his eyes and blinded him. And then there was cheering and clapping and men chanting his name. What was going on?

'Awake at last, Caius,' Cominius greeted him. 'I was beginning to think you would sleep forever.'

'Where are we, Cominius?' Caius asked, his mind still foggy.

Cominius frowned at him. 'Back in camp. Don't you remember?'

'I...', Caius put his hand to his forehead, 'I'm a little confused.'

'You don't have a head wound, do you?' Cominius asked worriedly.

'No, no,' Caius laughed. 'I'm just a little tired still. The camp, yes, of course. We beat the Volsci on the way to Antium and returned here.'

'To the scene of your victory,' Cominius nodded, still frowning, evidently not entirely convinced Caius had not taken a blow to the head. 'I hope you're awake enough for the surprise we have for you. Come.'

Cominius gestured for Caius to emerge from his tent. The cheering, which hadn't ceased while he and Cominius were talking, grew louder as more men gathered. It hurt Caius's head and he wished it would stop so he could get something to eat and go back to his bed.

But Cominius was patting the air for quiet. 'My fellow Romans,' Cominius called and the crowd fell silent, 'we have won two great victories. Both of these victories we owe to one man. Caius Marcius.'

The crowd cheered and clapped and Cominius grinned at Caius. Caius felt his cheeks reddening and he dropped his gaze to stare at his feet. Cominius knew he hated this kind of thing, so why was he putting him through it?

'For the great service Caius Marcius has done Rome,' Cominius continued, 'and for his extraordinary defeat of Corioli, it is right that he be permitted the greatest spoils the town has to offer. Marcius shall have one-tenth of the gold and the best horse.'

Cominius clicked his fingers and from behind Caius's tent a slave led a fine black horse with a white stripe down its nose to stand before Caius. He felt its hot breath on his face and reached up to stroke its nose.

'I thank you,' Caius called to the clapping crowd, 'but I did no more than my duty. And I shall not be rewarded for doing my duty. I will not take any spoils, no, not the gold. It was my honour to serve.'

'But, Caius, you cannot refuse—'

'I can and I do, Cominius,' Caius said with a smile, patting him on the arm. 'But,' he said, holding up a bandaged hand to the crowd, 'I will take this horse. He is too beautiful a creature to be denied.'

Cominius, looking a little offended, Caius thought, relented with a nod. He turned and raised his chin towards the crowd. Caius followed the gesture and saw the crowd parting to allow Titus Lartius through. Titus's face bore an odd expression, happiness mingled with resignation.

'I trust you will not refuse this next reward, Marcius,' Cominius said quietly and turned to the crowd. 'For his service, I declare that from this moment onwards, Caius Marcius will be known as Caius Marcius Coriolanus.'

The cheering grew even louder and the name Coriolanus was chanted throughout the camp.

Caius did not blush nor hide his face. He was proud of his new name. It gave him far more pleasure than the prospect of wealth could ever do. And as he accepted the cool, congratulatory embrace of Titus Lartius, his only thought was of how proud his mother would be too.

Volumnia ran her forearm over the curling papyrus to smooth it flat and reread the words. Caius had written at last; it had been almost two months since his last letter, when he had written of his triumph at Corioli, and Volumnia had felt starved of news of him. She had even taken to visiting Menenius uninvited, just to see if he had heard from Caius, but all Menenius had heard was the official dispatches. He sympathised with Volumnia but would say that Caius was too busy killing Volsci to be able to write.

It was true, by all the accounts that were relayed by the preach in the forum. Everywhere the Roman army went, enemies fell beneath their feet.

Volumnia did not take as much pleasure in this as she thought she should. She was proud of Caius, of course, but she was beginning to wish him home, out of danger. There was none so brave or so skilful at war as Caius; the proof of this was in his being still alive after so many battles. The wounds he had received were merely testament to his success. That was the point. He had done more than his duty to Rome. It was time for others to do theirs.

She wondered what was wrong with her to be thinking this way. It was so unlike her. *Perhaps I'm getting old*, she mused as she picked up the letter for the third time. The gods loved Caius, to be sure, but they could be fickle and decide a wound could become fatal on a whim. She didn't think she would be able to bear that.

Stop thinking of such things, she told herself angrily, and bent her head to the letter. Caius had written after a battle near Antium, another great victory for him and all Romans, he wrote. He and Cominius, who had fought alongside him, had surveyed the city after the battle and found a huge supply of grain. Cominius had suggested they bring it back to Rome and distribute it among the plebs but Caius had scoffed at such an idea. He reminded Volumnia of how many of the plebs had refused to fight in this last campaign, how he had had to go to war with a reduced following, and he was not going to reward those cowards with free grain. Those men who had followed him would be the only ones to benefit from the grain and the rest could stamp their feet as much as they liked, he wouldn't turn a hair.

Volumnia smiled. That was just like Caius, to care nothing for public opinion. So unlike all the other men she knew, men like Menenius who seemed to weigh every word before he opened his mouth. He only said what the plebs wanted to hear and Volumnia was certain they could see through the platitudes and downright lies. They must be desperate for someone to tell them the simple, direct truth. Someone like Caius.

'Someone like Caius,' she mused, putting the letter down and staring at the wall. Now, there was an idea. Hadn't she once said to Menenius that when Caius was done with fighting he could turn politician? Why wait any longer? He had made his name as a soldier. It was time he made his name as a politician.

21

The crowd was cheering as Caius entered Rome. His horse wore a rich harness and saddle, and it set its hooves down proudly. Junius Brutus, standing next to his fellow tribune Sicinius Vitellus, shouted in his ear that Caius Marcius looked almost like a king.

'Caius Marcius falls short,' Sicinius shouted back to Junius. 'Look at him, staring straight ahead, grim expression. Would a king act like that? A king would be smiling upon the people, encouraging their cheers. Marcius courts none of these fools' good opinions.'

'And yet they cheer,' Junius said.

'Of course they cheer,' Sicinius said sourly. 'The people enjoy a good spectacle. But they wouldn't if they knew all.'

'*I* don't know all,' Junius said irritably. 'What are you talking about, Sicinius?'

Sicinius pointed. 'You see all those carts that follow Marcius? They are filled with grain, all of them. How many would you say there are? Twenty or more? Those were won in a battle in which Marcius played but one part, unlike his escapade at Corioli. And yet, none of that grain is intended for the people of Rome. All of that is either going to Marcius's own followers or into his own grain stores. Do you think the people would cheer Marcius if they knew that?'

'How do you know?'

Sicinius tapped his nose and smiled. 'I have my sources, my friend.'

Junius looked around at the happy, smiling crowd. 'It's outrageous that Marcius should be allowed to keep possession of the grain.'

'You and I think so,' Sicinius nodded. 'The Senate are more than happy to let him keep it.'

'But the people must be told of this.'

'They shall be told of it, never fear,' Sicinius said determinedly. 'You and I shall make sure of it.'

'You will engender a great deal of ill feeling if you go ahead with this idea of yours,' Menenius said, refusing the plate of plums that Virgilia was trying to distract him with.

Menenius knew why Virgilia wanted him to desist. He understood why. Caius had just come home and she didn't want there to be any quarrels or disagreements. She wanted a happy home for her husband. He wasn't surprised by Virgilia's desire but he was surprised when he realised Volumnia seemed to want it too.

He had noticed a change in Volumnia over the last year. She seemed to crave company where before she had been content to be mostly alone. She called round at his domus uninvited where before she would always send her slave to ask if it would be convenient to do so. Menenius didn't mind the change but it worried him a little. He was sure Caius was at the root of it.

'It's not an idea, Menenius,' Caius said. 'I have ordered it.'

'None of the grain is to go to the plebs? Why not, Caius, when you have no need of it all?'

'I've explained why,' Caius said testily. 'The plebs did not answer my call for their strong arms. Why should I answer their call for full stomachs?'

Menenius shook his head. 'Your mother will tell you why.'

Caius looked expectantly at Volumnia. 'What does he mean, Mother?'

Volumnia put down her cup and took a deep breath. 'I've been talking with Menenius about you taking up a political role in Rome, Caius. I think it is time you put your sword away.'

'I do what?' Caius cried.

Volumnia held up her hands. 'Hear me, my boy, please. You have done enough for Rome on the battlefield. You have been remarkably successful, Caius. There is nothing greater for you to achieve as a soldier. But you could do more, much more, if you became a politician.'

Caius shook his head. 'I cannot believe you are saying this, Mother. After everything you have told me, taught me, from my earliest days. Be a soldier. That is what you have drummed into me.'

'I know, I know,' she said helplessly.

'I think your mother is right,' Virgilia said. All three looked at her in surprise at her interjection. She swallowed, determined to explain her thinking. 'Your son hardly knows you, Caius. I hardly see you. And I am scared there will come a day when you will not return home from war.'

'Oh, for Jove's sake,' Caius said, turning his head away. 'Would you have me play the woman and spin wool all day?'

'Do not be foolish, Caius,' Volumnia said sharply. 'That is not what Virgilia is saying at all. I shall be blunt. You are growing older. You will be growing slower in your reflexes. You know yourself you have received more wounds in this last year than in the previous ten. There will come a day when you will not be able to fight like a god. You have already met an enemy you cannot beat.'

'Have not yet beaten,' Caius corrected through gritted teeth. 'One man, Mother. I have beaten a thousand others.'

'I will not risk you again,' Volumnia suddenly screeched, unable to control herself any longer. She covered her mouth as if in shame of her outburst.

Menenius reached out his arm and touched her hand. 'Caius,' he said quietly, 'you see how your mother worries about you. It is not kind on your part to put her through such torment again if it can be avoided. Now, your mother has suggested another path you might take. Will you at least consider it?'

'To be a politician?' Caius raised a sceptical eyebrow at Menenius.

Menenius inclined his head. 'I must admit, it is not a career I think you are eminently suited for, but you can learn.'

'You will help him, won't you, Menenius?' Volumnia said eagerly, clutching his hand to her breast. 'When the time comes?'

He felt her warmth and something of his old passion stirred. 'I will,' he promised.

'There, Caius, you see?' Volumnia smiled uncertainly at her son. 'Say you will try, for my sake.'

Caius looked from his mother to his wife and back to his mother, his expression sulky. 'I will try. But if I cannot get on with it, I will be a soldier, Mother. You cannot deny me.'

'I won't,' Volumnia said happily. 'But you will succeed, Caius. I know you will.'

Menenius returned the grateful smile she bestowed upon him with less enthusiasm. He had meant what he said; Caius was not a natural politician, indeed, far from it. This latest affair of the grain proved how little he cared for public opinion and if there was one thing a successful politician needed, it was the support of the people. He had said he would help and he would be true to his word, but he doubted it would be a task he would find easy.

PART IV

491 BC - 488 BC

22

It was to be another two years before Caius succumbed to his mother's entreaties and finally agreed to leave off war to try his hand at politics.

A vacancy in the consulship arose, and it was decided by Menenius and Volumnia that Caius would stand for the nomination. If Menenius were honest with himself, and with Volumnia and Caius too, he would say that, in his opinion, Caius had very little chance of winning the election for the consulship but those were words he knew they did not want to hear. He had been right about the people disliking Caius's decision not to share the grain he had won from the Volsci. The cheering that had accompanied his entrance into Rome had soon turned into mutterings of discontent in the taverns that Caius Marcius was an enemy to the people, however many victories he won for Rome. The Comitia Centuriata might nominate Caius for the consulship because they were impressed by his martial record and his noble background, but it was the people whose votes he would have to solicit to win the election. Perhaps, Cominius had said, Caius can convince them that he has the plebs' best interests at heart, despite all appearances, and Menenius had shaken his head and replied that Caius didn't have a deceitful bone in his body. Cominius had nodded, saying that was an unfortunate trait for a politician.

But despite everything, and perhaps because of Menenius's advice and coaching, Caius won the nomination for the consulship. That obstacle overcome, now all he had to do was win the people to his cause.

Sicinius pushed his bowl of olive oil aside. 'This is a black day for us, Junius.'

They had just heard the news about Caius's nomination and neither of them found they had much of an appetite as a consequence.

'It's remarkable that the Comitia Centuriata agreed to his nomination,' Junius said, tossing aside his small chunk of bread. 'I never thought they would.'

'They were dazzled by his reputation,' Sicinius said, his lip curling. 'The victor of Corioli and a dozen more conquests.'

'But Caius Marcius the consul!' Junius said doubtfully. 'How can they think that a good idea?'

'Maybe we are worrying unduly,' Sicinius said more hopefully than he felt. 'Just because he has been nominated doesn't mean he will be elected. The people will not be swept away by his successes as the Comitia were.'

'You say that, but you don't believe it. The plebs are fickle. You've said so time and again.'

'I know and they are. I hate to admit it, there is a..,' he searched for the right word, 'a purity about Marcius that is very attractive. He is steadfast in his endeavour to fight for

Rome, unchanging in his opinions of the plebs. In that respect, you can trust him. There will be no soft words from Marcius, no false promises. If he says no to a thing, then no it will stay. He won't say yes to win the plebs' love and then do nothing.'

'What a feeble politician he will make,' Junius laughed hollowly.

'But don't you see? The plebs may not think of it that way. The plebs might, may the gods help us, see that kind of attitude as having integrity. A rare commodity among politicians, I'm sure you'll agree.'

Junius frowned and leant forward. 'Sicinius, you don't think Marcius has a chance of being elected, do you?'

Sicinius sighed heavily. 'Unfortunately, Junius, I rather think he does.'

Caius stood in the hall, arms outstretched while Volumnia fussed around him. 'Why must I undergo this indignity? Have I not done enough for Rome that I must walk naked before the plebs?'

Volumnia sank to her knees and tugged at the toga to make the folds fall straight. 'Menenius, will you tell him to behave?'

'Caius, stop complaining,' Menenius said. 'You won the nomination from the Comitia Centuriata and now you have to win the plebs' vote. Parading yourself before them to show your wounds is how you do this. And you will not be naked.'

'I wear nothing but this ridiculous toga,' Caius protested. 'Not even my tunic.'

'How else will the people see your wounds?' Volumnia said despairingly as she got to her feet. Her knee bones cracked loudly. 'And you should be proud to show them off. Shouldn't he, Menenius?'

'He should, but we all know Caius too well. Don't glare at me like that, you two. Caius hates to show off, we all know it. But I'm afraid there's no getting out of it.'

'It's so undignified. You agree, don't you, Virgilia?' Caius asked as she came into the atrium with Little Caius holding her hand.

'I think you look very handsome,' she said.

Caius rolled his eyes. 'Are you finished, Mother?'

'Yes, all done.' She looked him up and down. The toga was immaculate upon his impressive frame, the absence of his tunic showing off to startling effect all Caius's scars.

'Ready?' Menenius asked.

Caius nodded and headed for the door. Volumnia followed close behind.

'Hold a moment.' Menenius held out his hand to her. 'Where do you think you are going?'

'With Caius, of course,' she said in an affronted tone.

'You mean to walk with him? Forgive me, Volumnia, but it is just not acceptable. Caius cannot have a woman following him.'

Volumnia glared at Menenius then shot a look at Caius. Menenius knew she was expecting Caius to tell him to be quiet, that of course his mother could go with him. Menenius was surprised by Caius's response.

'Menenius is right, Mother,' Caius said. 'You should stay here.'

'But Caius—'

'I must not look weak, Mother,' Caius said fiercely.

She opened her mouth to protest further but then seemed to think better of it. She drew herself up. 'Very well,' she said tight-lipped. 'The last thing I want to do is make you look weak.'

Satisfied, and not a little relieved. Menenius gestured Caius towards the door. As they stepped outside, he cast a look back at Volumnia. She was in shadow now and he could not see her face. He smiled apologetically at her, hoping she could see he was genuinely sorry he had had to refuse her.

Cominius was waiting outside. He looked Caius up and down and nodded appreciatively. 'Ready?'

Caius nodded and the three of them began their slow walk towards the forum. As they went, the people stopped their business and stared at Caius. Some even came up close, bid him stop, and then peered at his scars. Caius endured their stares, turning his head to one side so he would not have to see their faces. Menenius could well imagine how much this parade was hurting him and felt a twinge of sympathy.

They eventually reached the forum where a large crowd had gathered to see him. Caius walked through the people, face down, never once looking up. The crowd grew denser and Menenius found himself being elbowed and pushed away from Caius until he couldn't see him any longer. He cursed, knowing that he would not be able to help Caius should he need it. He hoped Caius would continue to behave and not say anything he shouldn't. After about fifteen minutes, Menenius breathed a sigh of relief as he saw Caius making his way back towards him. He raised his eyebrows in enquiry and Caius returned the slightest of nods. It had gone well.

Volumnia and Virgilia were waiting for him. Caius doubted they had moved from the atrium since he and Menenius had left. Both their expressions asked silently how it had gone and he had provided them with a short answer. They had had the sense not to press their enquiries and he had taken himself off to his cubiculum to change, leaving Menenius to give them a full report. Caius knew Menenius would not say that he had found it a torment, that the stinking breaths of the people had seeped into his skin, that their dirty fingers had poked and prodded at his wounds as if testing them for soundness, and it had taken all his self-control not to push them out of his way and run home to the domus. Menenius would merely say that he had won the approval of the plebs.

Caius consoled himself with the knowledge that he would get his reward for the morning's humiliation. A second procession to the forum was now required, but this time he would go with all his clients and friends accompanying him, a show of strength and power. Properly dressed now in his toga, Caius returned to the atrium.

'Ready to go back to the forum?' Menenius asked.

'Yes,' he said with a sigh.

'Ah, but this time you will return home as consul,' Volumnia said smiling. 'Menenius tells us the people were pleased with you, Caius.'

'I hope they saw enough to satisfy them.'

'They did. Menenius, didn't they?' Virgilia appealed.

'They certainly seemed satisfied,' Menenius nodded.

'Seemed so, Menenius?' Virgilia asked, perturbed by his doubtful tone.

He shrugged. 'The people can say one thing and do another. I have seen it often.'

'Not this time,' Volumnia said decisively. 'They have seen Caius's scars and he is worthy of their voices.' She put her hand on Caius's arm. 'All will be well.'

'I have no doubt. And this time, dear mother,' he said,

taking her hand and putting his lips to it, 'you are coming with me. Let Menenius shake his head at us all he wants.'

Menenius held up his hands. 'No, no, this time, I agree,' he protested. 'It is fitting that she does, and you too, Virgilia, though I suggest Little Caius remains here.'

His suggestion was agreed upon, and with Volumnia and Virgilia immediately behind him, Caius once more left the domus to process to the forum. His clients and followers, Cominius among them, cheered him on, and it was with a sense of assurance that Caius climbed the steps to the rostra and held his hands up for the people's attention.

'People of Rome,' he began, deliberately ignoring Menenius's suggestion that he call them good, 'I come to receive your voices for election to the consulship. As tradition demands, I have shown you my wounds obtained in service to Rome and you have been satisfied. So I ask, do I have your voices?'

There were a few murmurs in response to this question, but, oddly, not one man raised his voice in support of Caius.

Caius frowned, perplexed. 'Why do you not speak?' he demanded.

Menenius recognised irritation in Caius's voice and hurriedly moved to stand by him. 'Good people,' he said, holding out his arms to quieten the disgruntled murmurs. 'Caius Marcius Coriolanus asks for your voices and you greet him with silence. Speak now, I beg of you.'

'Do not beg, Menenius,' Caius ordered. 'I forbid it.'

'We'll not elect him,' someone shouted.

'Why will you not?' Menenius asked.

A smiling Sicinius stepped out of the crowd and joined Menenius on the steps. The crowd hushed. 'Because, Menenius Agrippa, the people are not fools. They see what Caius Marcius is.'

‘What?’ Caius sneered at him. ‘What am I?’

‘A proud man,’ Sicinius replied, raising his chin defiantly at Caius. ‘You come with all these,’ he indicated Caius’s followers, ‘as if you were a very king. But we have had enough of kings in Rome. This is no place for proud men who think they can do without the will of the people.’

‘I spit on the people,’ Caius scoffed, turning his back on Sicinius.

‘Ah,’ Sicinius crowed, ‘now we see what the great Coriolanus thinks of the people of Rome. Nothing, that’s what he thinks. He would see all of you slaughtered in his unnecessary wars.’

‘Lies,’ Menenius cried. ‘Marcius is a man who has given his very lifeblood for the people of Rome. He has been ready to lay down his life to protect you all and you would call him a... a…’. He fumbled for the word he wanted.

‘A traitor!’ Sicinius shouted. ‘That is what we would call him, for that is what a man is who puts his own honour before that of his country.’

‘You dare to call me traitor, you dog,’ Caius roared and made a grab for Sicinius.

Menenius moved to stand between them and felt the full force of Caius’s might. He called to Cominius for help and Cominius hurried up the steps to the struggling pair. Together, they managed to restrain Caius and force him down from the rostra, pushing their way through the crowd that was growing ever more belligerent.

‘Stop this, Caius,’ Menenius yelled in Caius’s ear as they reached the edge of the forum.

‘I’ll kill that bastard,’ Caius shouted.

‘Think of your mother, your wife,’ he begged and felt the struggle leave Caius’s body.

‘Where are they?’ Caius asked.

'In the crowd somewhere,' Cominius replied, apprehensively letting go of Caius and waiting to see if he would stay.

'I must go to them,' Caius said and started back towards the forum. Menenius and Cominius grabbed hold of him again.

`No,' Menenius ordered. 'Cominius will go. It'll be safer for all of us, Caius.'

'I won't leave them,' Caius protested.

'Cominius, go,' Menenius roared, and Cominius disappeared into the crowd. Menenius gave Caius a shove in the other direction. 'You will do as I tell you, Caius. Come.' He gave him another push and Caius moved, his feet moving forward but his eyes cast backwards over his shoulder.

'I'll murder anyone who puts a hand on my mother,' Caius swore.

Menenius didn't answer, just kept pushing him forward until they reached the domus. It was an extremely uncomfortable and anxious half hour before Cominius arrived with Volumnia and Virgilia. Both were unharmed but very shaken.

Caius took his mother to his breast and held out an arm to Virgilia. 'You're safe now,' he said, kissing first one woman's temple, then the other's.

'My poor boy,' Volumnia said crying. 'How those dogs treated you.'

'I know,' he said. 'But they'll pay. You'll see.'

'You won't be elected consul, Marcius,' Cominius said, standing by the door, holding it open an inch and peering out to make sure they had not been followed. Satisfied they had not, he closed the door.

'To Hades with the consulship,' Caius snarled. 'I never wanted it.'

Volumnia broke away from him. 'I made you do it,' she sniffed. 'I'm so sorry.'

'You're not to blame,' he assured her.

'It was the tribunes,' Cominius told them grimly. 'They stirred up the people against you as soon as you left the forum after showing your scars.'

'Why did you not stop them?' Volumnia yelled at Menenius.

'Me?' Menenius said, astonished.

'You made the tribunes,' she cried. 'You should be able to control your creatures.'

'Volumnia, my dear—'

'No more of that, you wretch,' she said, slapping him away from her. 'You saw what those beasts did to my boy. And it's all your fault. Go, get out. I won't have you near me.'

No one defended him. Caius stared at Menenius and there was contempt in his eyes. Virgilia was weeping and Cominius opened the door for Menenius to leave.

'I will go,' Menenius said quietly. 'But I am not to blame for this, Volumnia, and I hope you will come to realise that. I am, and always have been, a friend to you and Caius.' He strode out without another word.

'Well,' Cominius said as he closed the door. 'I think we all need a cup or three of wine, don't you?'

23

It had been an unpleasant month, Menenius reflected as he took his seat in the Senate house. His dismissal from the Marcius domus had been extremely hurtful — had he not done all he could to support and protect Caius and his family? — and a resentment at his treatment had developed that quickly overwhelmed his sorrow. He made no entreaties to be forgiven during the week that followed, all the time wondering if Caius or Volumnia would regret their actions and make an approach to him. But no, he should have known better. Neither Volumnia nor Caius were in the habit of apologising and he shouldn't expect them to make an exception for him.

Menenius was not a man to bear a grudge for long, and missing their company, had sent his slave with four amphorae of his finest wine from his country estate as a gift to the Marcius domus. He had waited anxiously while the slave went on his mission, half expecting to have his present refused. But the slave returned empty-handed and Menenius was content. The next day he sent a haunch of boar, and the day after, a letter asking if he could call.

Volumnia replied she and Caius would be happy to receive Menenius. It was a cool response but Menenius had expected nothing more. He dressed carefully and made the visit. It was awkward at first. Caius was unbending, Volumnia civil and aloof. Only Virgilia seemed warm and he was grateful to her. He paid a visit each day after that and gradually, the ice had thawed until now there was almost no memory of that dreadful day in the forum when Caius had been refused the consulship.

And yet, Menenius could see that the humiliation had wounded Caius deeply. It was nothing Caius said, but behind his eyes, Menenius saw that the incident had left its mark. When Menenius dared to talk politics, Caius's jaw would tighten and he would lean back on the couch as if wanting to take no part in the conversation. Menenius was not displeased. In his opinion, Caius was not suited to politics and it was better he not pursue a political career, for everybody's sake.

But he should have know the calm wouldn't last, that Caius was brooding over his humiliation and was just waiting for the right moment to have his revenge. The right moment came soon enough.

Yet another shipment of free grain arrived at the port, this time a gift from Gelo of Syracuse. Gelo's envoys told the Senate the grain was offered as homage. If accepted, the Romans would agree that they would not attempt to conquer Gelo and leave Syracuse alone. It was a good idea, Menenius supposed, to try and prevent war in this way, or at least, it would be, if free grain didn't always seem to cause problems between the plebs and the patricians. As before, the patricians wanted to keep the grain for themselves. The plebs wanted it shared out among the populace. Another row was brewing and Caius intended to take full advantage.

Menenius had wondered why Caius said he would accompany him to the Senate house that morning. It was unusual, for Caius had been intent on staying away from the forum ever since his nomination had been refused. But as he made himself ready, Virgilia had whispered to Menenius that Caius intended to make a speech about the grain. Menenius had cringed but said nothing. He didn't want to risk their friendship again, but it wasn't without apprehension that Menenius watched Caius get to his feet in the Senate house.

'It is my opinion,' Caius began in a loud, clear voice, 'that the tribunes have been granted too many rights and allowed too great a freedom to speak against the patricians and this house. Now, they are demanding the grain from Syracuse be given over entirely to the plebs. Who do these men think they are that they can dictate to us? This grain was gifted to the Senate, not the people, as part of a political understanding between the patricians and Gelo. The plebs have nothing to do with this gift and indeed, bear no entitlement to any such future gifts. The plebs, roused by the tribunes, are continually challenging the Senate's authority, yet they demonstrate no obedience or duty towards Rome. They have refused to fight when called upon to defend our country against our enemies. It has been left to us, the patricians, to defend Rome and increase our territories, risking our lives at each step. The plebs have done nothing and still they complain. The Senate heeds their complaints and threats out of fear, but I tell you, we need not fear these dogs. I tell you too that if the Senate gives in to their demands, as I know some of you think we should do,' Caius paused to glare at a few men, who coloured and looked away, 'then we are in great danger of making the plebs even more discontented and filling them with the belief that they need only threaten to get what they want. If you grant them the right to this grain, they will not regard this as generosity on your part. They will conclude you gave them the grain because you are afraid not to give it to them. They will become ever more disobedient and ready to challenge us at every step. To be brief with you, I say that to give into the tribunes' demand and hand over this grain to the plebs will be sheer madness. I will go further and say the office of tribune should be abolished with immediate effect. The tribunes are causing this discontent, setting plebs against patricians and dividing Rome. I tell you, and you would do well to listen to me, that Rome will never be whole while the tribunes are allowed to hold office.'

Despite his misgivings, Menenius was impressed. He had not expected Caius to make such a long speech nor one so eloquent. True, his speech had been devoid of Senate etiquette, but it had been powerful and had certainly made an impression on his listeners. Perhaps Caius was more suited to politics than he had believed.

But would they heed Caius, Menenius wondered, and abolish the tribunes? It was a dangerous step to take but Menenius had to admit the tribunes had made life very difficult for the Senate. The speaker of the house rose and declared the matter should be discussed after a short recess. The Senate broke up.

Menenius made his way to Caius. 'Well done,' he said.

'Thank you,' Caius replied tightly. 'It needed saying. I only hope the Senate heeds me and does away with these wretched tribunes. I daresay you disagree.'

'No,' Menenius shook his head. 'I cannot disagree with you. The tribunes have caused a great deal of trouble.'

'You made them,' Caius said.

'Thank you for reminding me,' Menenius sniffed, watching the senators file out of the doors. There was a sudden noise. 'What's that?'

He and Caius hurried outside. The senators had been prevented from leaving; Sicinius and Junius were standing on the Senate house steps, surrounded by more than twenty men.

'What do you mean by this?' Menenius demanded.

'We know what Marcius has said,' Sicinius returned loudly. 'We know he wants the Senate to abolish the office of tribune.'

How did they know? Menenius wondered. The doors had been closed. Someone inside must have told them of Caius's speech.

'I don't deny it,' Caius yelled back before Menenius could restrain him. 'I say Rome would be a deal better off if the tribunes were put in a sack and thrown in the Tiber.'

Sicinius turned to the people. 'You see?' he called, smiling and nodding in vindication. 'This is what Caius Marcius thinks of you. Nothing. He wants you to have no say in Rome. I stand here and I say now that Caius Marcius is an enemy to the people of Rome.' He turned back to the senators. 'We, the tribunes, demand Caius Marcius be made to answer this charge. We, the tribunes, the voice of the people, demand Caius Marcius give answer as to whether he has actively incited the Senate to set aside the constitution of Rome and thereby abolish all the powers of the people.'

This couldn't be happening, Menenius thought as he watched Sicinius accept the cheers and applause of the plebs. He glanced at the senators, who each seemed to have one wary eye on the crowd and one on each other. They were talking urgently and gesturing for the Senate speaker to calm the crowd.

The speaker stepped forward nervously. 'We will retire into the Senate house and discuss this,' he declared.

'In our presence,' Sicinius insisted.

The speaker hesitated, but then nodded. The senators

turned back towards the Senate house doors.

'Come,' Menenius hissed, grabbing hold of Caius's elbow.

'Come where?' Caius asked.

'Home.'

'I'm not going home. This charge is nonsense and I'll tell them they're all fools to countenance it.' He made a move towards the doors.

'It's bad enough without you making it worse, Caius,' Menenius said, refusing to relinquish his hold.

'Who do you think you are to tell me to come away?' Caius snarled. 'I'm not a child, old man.'

This was too much. Menenius glared at Caius. 'I really don't know how much more of your insolence I can stomach, Caius.'

'Then do not stomach it. Be gone.'

'I will ask you one last time, Caius. For your mother's sake, leave this place and go home. This crowd can easily become a mob and I will not have Rome turn against itself. The matter will be discussed without you and better it be so. Your mother would wish you home.'

Menenius knew the invocation of his mother's desire would be the greatest spur to Caius's intent. He watched as Caius glanced at the Senate house, then towards the crowd.

'I will go home,' he said after a long moment, 'because it is what I wish, not because you tell me I must.'

'To tell truth, Caius,' Menenius growled, 'I really don't care why you come as long as you do. Now, move.'

———

Volumnia stood behind Caius, rubbing his shoulders with enthusiasm. 'How dare the tribunes make this charge!'

Menenius and Caius had reached the domus with difficulty. The crowd were reluctant to allow Caius to leave and there had been several scuffles, mostly pushing and shoving, before he and Menenius were able to reach the street off the forum that would lead them home. The women had been waiting anxiously and Volumnia demanded their news as soon as they had crossed the threshold.

'They thought they had good reason to accuse him when they heard what Caius had said,' Menenius said.

'I made that speech today, Menenius,' Caius said proudly, 'because the Senate needs to realise what fools they have been in allowing the tribunes to flourish. You said you agreed with me.'

'I do. I just wish it had not come to this.'

Volumnia took a seat and gestured for Menenius to take another. 'Tell us what this charge against Caius means.'

Menenius sat and took a deep breath. 'If successful, I suppose there may be a fine levied by the Senate.'

'Is that all?' Virgilia asked, relief evident in her voice.

Menenius smiled at her. 'Caius has been too useful to the Senate for anything more dire. They will not want to upset him, though they will, I think, need to make a token gesture towards the tribunes' accusation.'

'Those blasted tribunes,' Volumnia spat. 'They are all your fault, Menenius.'

'Now, Mother, let's not start blaming Menenius again,' Caius said. 'He knows he made a mistake there.'

Menenius resisted the urge to slap Caius's face at these words. It was infuriating to be spoken of in such a way by the boy he had helped raise, but he knew to show anger now would not help the situation. So, he said nothing, though inwardly he seethed.

Volumnia called for some food and wine to be brought

from the kitchen and they occupied a rather tense half hour in eating and drinking, mostly in silence. Then a message arrived from the Senate. The slave handed the papyrus to Caius and left.

'What does it say?' Volumnia asked.

Caius snorted and threw it across to Menenius, who read it quickly.

Menenius forced a smile. 'Just a formality, I expect. Nothing to worry about.'

'What? What is it?' Volumnia said impatiently.

'The Senate orders me to present myself tomorrow morning to answer the tribunes' charges,' Caius said through gritted teeth.

'How is this possible, Menenius?' Volumnia demanded. 'You said the Senate would not act against Caius.'

'They have only told him to answer the charges,' Menenius said, in truth a little shaken by the summons. 'A sop to the people, nothing more.'

'You should have stayed in the Senate and spoken up for Caius.'

'Yes, I should,' he acknowledged stiffly. 'Yet another mistake I've made.'

'What are the charges?' Virgilia asked.

'That I have spoken unjustly against the people,' Caius said contemptuously.

'But you've merely expressed an opinion, surely?'

'Quite right, Virgilia,' Volumnia said decisively. 'They cannot act against you for expressing an opinion. Can they, Menenius?'

Menenius scratched his head. 'They might, if by doing so, Caius encourages discontent in the people. The Senate are very wary of upsetting the plebs.'

'The cowards!' Volumnia spat.

'The Senate have every right to be cautious, Volumnia,' Menenius said. 'The mob roused can be a fearsome thing.'

'Not so fearsome as my boy,' Volumnia declared proudly. 'Really, Rome these days. We never had this kind of thing when Tarquin was king.'

'Would you have Rome ruled by a king again?'

'Indeed, I would,' Volumnia eyed him fiercely, 'and I know who I would have king too.' She looked at Caius meaningfully. Caius smiled and took hold of her hand.

'Volumnia, please,' Menenius pleaded, 'no more talk of kings. You will forget yourself and say it in the street one day, and then there will be trouble indeed.'

'I'd say it to the tribunes' very faces if they had the courage to stand before me.'

'And you, Caius?' Menenius raised an eyebrow at him. 'Will you accept the Senate's summons and face your accusers tomorrow?'

'Oh, I'll face them, Menenius,' Caius nodded, his eyes narrowed. 'I'll face them and then I'll run them through with my sword.'

Menenius jumped to his feet. 'You will not, Caius, not unless you are intent on destroying your family.'

'How would that destroy us?' Volumnia demanded. 'It would put an end to all this nonsense. I say Caius should kill those cursed tribunes and rid Rome of their pernicious influence.'

'If Caius were to do so, Volumnia, I do not doubt the Senate would be compelled to punish him, and in the harshest possible way. He would be executed,' he said as Volumnia continued to look at him with defiance. 'And perhaps you, too, Volumnia, perhaps Virgilia, perhaps Little Caius.' He turned to Caius. 'Would you condemn them all?'

'No one will touch my family,' Caius said menacingly.

Menenius sighed. 'Then answer the charges the tribunes will bring against you calmly. No violence, no roughness. State your opinion and stand by it, if you must, but do not threaten.'

Caius looked at Virgilia and Volumnia, who both stared at him, waiting for his response. 'I will answer the charges,' he said.

———

Caius was more upset than he could say. The shame of being called to account for his words had wounded him deeply and he had had to work hard to hide it from his family and Menenius. He knew he would be the centre of attention in the forum; no doubt all of Rome would turn out to see the tribunes try to bring him down. What a grand spectacle for them all!

Volumnia had insisted he wear his finest toga to the Senate house, saying he would show them what a true Roman looked like. He had allowed Virgilia to help him with the toga in the privacy of their cubiculum, then had emerged to be examined by Volumnia and Menenius, who had arrived early and intended to accompany him. They had looked him up and down and agreed he looked well.

Virgilia came out of the cubiculum crying, declaring through her tears that she was sure Caius would be attacked by the mob and begging him to stay at home. Volumnia had snapped at her and told her to stop making such a terrible noise, that of course Caius would go. She was not going to give the tribunes the opportunity to call her son a coward. It was decided that Virgilia would stay in the domus. Volumnia was adamant she would go with Caius, despite Menenius's entreaties.

No one appeared to be waiting outside the domus to abuse them as they emerged and Volumnia slipped her arm through Caius's. She held on to him tightly. Was she frightened? he wondered, glancing down at her. There was a strain upon her face he had never seen before and he realised she was very worried. The realisation both pained and angered him.

They walked in silence, having nothing to say that would make any of them feel better. The sound of a multitude grew louder as they approached the forum and Caius felt his heart beat faster. He told himself not to be absurd. He had fought entire armies and won; a garrulous mob need hold no fear for him. The mob was his enemy, he told himself, and would be treated the same as any of his enemies: no mercy given or asked for.

Faces turned towards him as they entered the forum. He met none of their eyes. As he moved forward, he felt Volumnia hang back a little, and he clamped her hand to his side. It unsettled him, this fear of his mother's. Had she been threatened by some of these plebs? Had these creatures dared to hurt her?

The crowd parted before them. Caius almost wished they wouldn't. It would have pleased him greatly to have a reason to push and hit them out of his way. To think that he had to answer to these plebs! It was outrageous. These filthy creatures were like ants crawling over his skin. Well, as soon as he got the chance, he would stamp on their anthill and kill them all.

They reached the steps of the Senate house and Caius looked up at the platform. The entire Senate house were there waiting for him. Caius released Volumnia, who gave him a defiant smile which didn't reach her eyes, and he ascended the steps. At the far end of the platform he saw Cominius and gave him a nod of acknowledgement. On the other side stood the tribunes. Sicinius had the most infuriatingly smug expression upon his face and Caius glared at him with contempt.

Sicinius wasted no time. He stepped forward and addressed the crowd to state the charges Caius had come to answer. Caius Marcius, he said, had spoken against the people in the Senate house, claiming they should have no representation in Rome, contrary to Roman law. Caius Marcius had deliberately and maliciously retained the grain won at Antium, saving it for himself and his followers and thereby denying the people their right to the grain as legitimate spoils of war. By these acts, and others too numerous to name, Sicinius said, Caius Marcius had tried to provoke a civil war in Rome, in which he would emerge as victor thanks to his prowess and the soldiers he commanded, and so had proved himself to be an enemy of the people. When he finished speaking, the crowd cheered loudly.

Sicinius turned to Caius. 'How do you plead?'

Caius glanced down at his mother. Menenius had left her at the front of the crowd to take his place with the other senators. Volumnia looked small and vulnerable among the people, and the sight of her, along with Sicinius's accusations, made Caius;s blood boil.

'I see now I have made a mistake,' he said with deceptive calm. 'I have done you the honour of coming here to answer these charges when you deserve no such consideration.' He looked up and met Sicinius's eye. 'I will answer none of these charges, nor will I stand here and make excuses to peasants.'

'If you will not answer the charges,' Sicinius said archly, 'then you will be found guilty by default.'

Caius snorted, a sign of his contempt for the tribune, and turned his back on Sicinius.

'Punishment!' Sicinius screeched, enraged by the insult. 'Caius Marcius must be punished.'

The crowd cheered again.

'Death!' Sicinius declared. 'He must be thrown from the Tarpeian rock.'

There was no cheering, but there was a scream, loud and close, and Caius looked down into the crowd. A few feet away from Volumnia was Virgilia in great distress. She had come after all. *Curse her*, Caius thought, looking for his mother. Volumnia was staring up at him, her eyes wide, her mouth open. She hadn't seemed to notice Virgilia or her scream at all. 'Mother,' he called and gestured towards Virgilia.

Volumnia came out of her trance and blinked at Virgilia, who was waving her arms, trying to fend off the people trying to calm her down. She pushed through the crowd and slapped Virgilia about the face. The assault worked. Virgilia froze and stared at her mother-in-law, tears tumbling down her red cheeks. Then she bolted up the steps and hurled herself at Caius. Unprepared, he stumbled backwards, his arms instinctively curving around her waist.

'You see what you've done,' Menenius yelled at Sicinius. 'You talk of the rights of the people but ignore the rights of all men, that of the right to trial. You condemn Marcius to death for such paltry charges and fright the women so.'

'They are not paltry,' Sicinius insisted. 'Only a patrician would claim so. And so what if his women are frightened?'

'You are too harsh,' Menenius said.

Caius despised the pleading tone in his voice. He pushed Virgilia away against Volumnia, who had joined them on the platform. 'If Rome needs my death to make her feel better, then so be it,' he called, making his voice heard throughout the forum.

Junius grabbed Sicinius's arm. 'We cannot do this, we

will be called butchers. Look how the people are reacting, Sicinius. They didn't ask for Marcius's death.'

Sicinius looked at the crowd. He had expected support for the death sentence but it seemed as if no one wanted it for the hero of Corioli. What fools the people were! Didn't they realise this was their chance to be rid of Marcius for good? 'What do you suggest then?' he muttered angrily.

'Let me speak,' Junius said, and stepped forward before Sicinius could reply. 'Hear me, all of you, please. Sicinius Vitellus spoke too hastily. We, the tribunes, would not have Caius Marcius executed for his faults. We acknowledge that he has done much for Rome and has been favoured by the gods. We would do him and them insult if we were to execute him.'

'What punishment then?' one of the senators asked.

Junius considered for a brief moment before replying. 'Banishment.'

Menenius cast a quick look at Caius, then moved to the senators who had huddled together to discuss this proposal from the tribune. Dismayed, but also relieved, he listened while the senators agreed to the banishment. It was the best he could hope for, better than death, and he did not argue. One of the senators said Menenius should make the announcement, and with great reluctance, he moved forward to stand by Junius.

'Caius Marcius is hereby banished, never to return to Rome,' he said in a voice heavy with emotion.

'You banish me?' Caius said incredulously and Menenius wished he could explain why this was for the best. 'Oh no, oh no, you don't banish me. I banish you. You fools, all of you. What will you do when you need a champion to defend you? Will you take up arms?' he demanded of Sicinius. 'Will you?' he asked of Junius who backed away.

'Go,' Sicinius spluttered, unnerved by Caius's anger. 'Go now before the people come to their senses and let me do what I long to do. We would all be better off with you dead, Caius Marcius.'

Before Caius could speak again, the senatorial guards had surrounded him and told him to move. It was happening now, he realised, taken aback. He was to be escorted to the city gates this very minute, not even allowed to return to his domus to collect some things to take with him.

Caius decided he would not argue. He would not give the tribunes or the plebs the satisfaction of seeing that he needed anything. In the middle of the escort he walked, head erect, back straight, to the city gates, followed by Volumnia, Virgilia, Menenius and Cominius.

'Can we not do something, Menenius?' Volumnia pleaded as they reached the gates and came to a stop. 'How can they do this to my son? Why did you agree?'

'To bide us time,' Menenius explained. 'We must let the ill feeling against Caius die down. In a few weeks I will be able to petition the Senate for Caius's return. Banishment is better than death, Volumnia.'

'I would have gone to my death gladly if I meant I never had to see Rome again,' Caius snarled.

'I would not have been glad, nor Cominius, nor any of your friends,' Menenius chastised. 'And think of your mother and your wife, Caius.'

'You will keep them safe, Menenius,' Caius said.

'No harm will come to them,' Menenius promised. 'You just look after yourself. Where will you go?'

'I don't know,' Caius said. A chill came over him and he wanted to be gone before he embarrassed himself. 'Be strong, Mother,' he called over his shoulder.'

He stepped through the city gates and didn't look back.

24

It seemed to have been raining ever since he left Rome. He'd been in bad weather before, of course, when on campaign, but for some reason, he had never seemed to mind it much then. Now, it felt like he would never be dry or warm again.

Maybe it had been foolish to leave his country farm but Caius had not been able to settle there. He had no idea of how to farm and his farm manager had resented his inept interference, so he had taken to haunting the villa. It had been dull without company and he soon began to imagine the slaves and workers were talking about him and his exile from Rome, for he knew the news had spread to the country. He had walked out one day about three weeks after his banishment and met his neighbour. The man said he thought Caius might turn up, having heard he was no longer welcome in Rome, and had proceeded to invite him to dinner. Caius knew he had been rude when he refused the invitation but he hadn't cared. It had kept the neighbour away, at any rate and there had been no further invitations, from his neighbour or anyone else, for that matter. They had probably been told to keep away from the man Rome had banished.

And so, he had left his country estate, eager to be free of the gossip and rumour. He had set out with little idea of where he would go. He had considered going to the Latin tribes, but they were friends to Rome and he did not not want to ally himself with any who were. The problem was that left only a very few places he could go, and in those places, he was known to be an enemy. Where did that leave? Was he destined to roam the earth forever, never finding a home? He remembered often Menenius's assurance that his banishment would be revoked soon, but he had been weeks at the farm and heard nothing from his old friend save hopeful words and empty promises. He doubted whether Menenius was working for him at all. In his darkest moments, he believed Menenius had engineered his exile, for with Caius out of Rome, Menenius was free to court his mother. Caius had never forgotten that disgusting scene when he had walked in on Menenius kissing Volumnia, even if he had forgiven it. And so, believing himself unfriended, Caius had not written to anyone in Rome that he was leaving the farm. He was determined to be on his own.

But the rain was wearing that determination away. Caius took refuge beneath a large tree, the rain thinned by the leaf cover, and sank to his knees. He held his hands out, palms upwards and closed his eyes.

'My protector Mars, I ask for your advice. I am shunned by my fellow Romans who resent the success you have bestowed upon me. They took their revenge upon your favoured servant and shut their gates against me. Wherever I go, I am followed by rumour and suspicion. And yet, I must needs have a place to rest. Tell me where I can go where I would be welcomed as your beloved servant.'

He kept his eyes closed and felt the droplets patter upon

his cheeks. He waited. Mars would answer him; he always had in the past. Mars would know what he should do.

The rain stopped. The birds began to sing.

Caius dropped his hands to the dirt and pushed himself up onto his feet. Mars had not failed him. Mars had told him where he could go. He could go to Rome's constant enemy. He could go to the Volsci.

Tullus drank his fourth cup of wine that evening and wondered how much longer he had to sit and listen to these interminable stories told by old men and their snobby wives.

He really would have to stop Junia from giving these dinners. This was the sixth dinner this month he had had to endure and he was getting mightily sick of them. Always the same people, those whom Junia thought were worth cultivating, claiming that when he was too old to go to war, he would need friends such as her guests who could put him in the way of good opportunities. So, it was only for his benefit, he would say, raising a sceptical eyebrow, that she played hostess so often? She would smile, tweak his nose and say he should be grateful he had such an enterprising wife who never interfered with him. It was true, he supposed. Junia never said he couldn't leave Antium to visit a friend miles off, never told him he must be home at a certain time or not get drunk with his friends. She was a good wife in that respect. But if he wanted to keep her as a good wife, the implication was clear, he must not object to her dinner parties. But six in one month!

Cordius was talking to him again, of what Tullus didn't know or care. He smiled an answer and was amused to see Cordius's expression change from enquiry to confusion,

Tullus's smile not being the answer he had anticipated. Tullus grinned more broadly and Cordius evidently decided his question wasn't worth pursuing, turned away. *Well, that had worked,* Tullus thought with pleasure. *Now, I just have to do that for the rest of the evening.*

He reached for the wine jug, looking up to summon the slave to bring more, when he noticed another of his slaves, one of those gifted by the Antium people in gratitude for his efforts against the Romans, enter the room and head for him. The slave bent down to murmur in his ear.

'Dominus, there is a man demanding to see you.'

'What man?'

'He would not give his name, but he looks like a beggar.'

'Oh,' Tullus groaned, 'don't bother me with it. Feed him and send him on his way.'

'He doesn't want food, dominus. We've offered and he's refused. He insists on seeing you.'

Tullus frowned. He was not used to having demands made upon him by beggars but this man gave him a good reason for excusing himself from his wife's guests. He told the slave he would come and made a slurred apology to the diners. He followed the slave to the atrium, wondering what kind of beggar had the effrontery to go to the front door rather than the back.

The slave held back as Tullus entered the atrium. The beggar was crouched before the shrine as if he was praying, but he had no right to pray to Tullus's household gods and Tullus grew angry. 'What do you mean by demanding to see me?' he asked loudly.

The beggar turned to face him, lifted his arm and threw back the hood of his cloak.

Tullus's stared, open-mouthed. His hand flew instinctively to his hip, reaching for the sword that was not there.

'Will you hear me?' Caius asked quietly, spreading his hands to show he carried no weapon.

'Hear you?' Tullus cried. 'You come here, into my home—'

'You should strike me dead,' Caius nodded. 'I know. All I ask is that you hear me first. If my words do not satisfy you, then you must kill me.'

'Fetch the men,' Tullus ordered the slave, who was looking from his master to the stranger in utter perplexity. He hurried away, leaving Tullus and Caius alone.

'I mean you no harm,' Caius said.

'You expect me to believe that,' Tullus scoffed. 'You have done me much harm over the years.'

'I know. But the Fates have altered my life.'

Tullus's eyes narrowed. 'I heard you had been exiled from Rome.'

'And delighted in the news, I daresay,' Caius managed a wry smile.

'No,' Tullus admitted, surprising himself.

Before he could say more, the slave returned with three burly men close behind. Tullus ordered them to take hold of his unexpected visitor. They obeyed and Caius, offering no resistance, was forced to his knees. The slave had had the sense to snatch up a long knife from the kitchen on his journey to fetch the men and he handed it now to his master.

Tullus walked slowly towards Caius and held the blade to his throat. 'I will hear you, Caius Marcius, and then I will kill you.'

Caius did not flinch from the blade but raised his eyes to Tullus. 'I am an enemy to Rome. I have been an enemy to you, but no more. If you will have me, I would join with you in attacking Rome in any way I can and so have my revenge.'

Tullus pressed the blade into the skin of Caius's throat. A

thin line of blood crept onto the metal. 'What kind of fool do you think I am?'

'No kind of fool. You are the only man I could trust to understand.'

Tullus withdrew the knife a little. 'Understand what?'

'What it means to be a soldier. To live for killing and have the honour to kill for your country. And what it means when that country, for whom you have spilt your own blood, turns against you.'

'I could not believe the news when I heard of your banishment,' Tullius admitted. 'I wondered what the people of Rome could be thinking of to treat you so impiously.'

'The people don't think,' Caius spat, his anger renewed. He struggled to control himself. 'That doesn't matter. All that matters is what happens now to Rome.'

'And for that you need me?'

'The only man I can trust.'

Tullus laughed. 'What makes you think you can trust me?'

'Because we are both sons of Mars. We are so alike, I feel you inside me, as if we are one.'

Tullus stared at him. 'Do you truly mean what you say? You want to have your revenge on Rome?'

'It's all I want. The desire consumes me.'

Tullus's arm dropped to his side. He turned on his heel and walked around the atrium, rubbing his chin, thinking. Caius remained on his knees, watching him, saying nothing.

Tullus didn't know what to think. If this was a trick of Rome's, he couldn't see the point of it. His mind was fuzzy; he wished he hadn't drunk so much. Was he being made a fool of? Was he being a fool to even listen to this man, the Volsci's worst enemy, the man he had tried to kill on at least twelve separate occasions? He looked at Caius and tried to find the truth in the handsome face. He knew this man, he *knew* him. To deceive in an underhand manner would be impossible for him. Tullus knew it as well as he knew his own self. And how often had he dreamed about standing side by side with Caius rather than against him, dreams he had been ashamed to admit to himself in the morning? He looked closer at Caius. Were those tears he saw in those tired eyes?

Tullus sank to his knees before Caius and stared into his face. The scrutiny seemed too much for Caius for he turned his head away in embarrassment, but Tullus grabbed his face and kissed him full on the mouth, feeling Caius's cracked lips press against his.

'You will help me have my revenge on Rome?' Caius asked, needing confirmation.

Tullus nodded. 'I will.'

25

Menenius had barely stepped through the doorway when Volumnia came towards him in a rush. ‘Have you heard anything yet?’

She looks ill, Menenius thought as he took her hands. ‘Nothing,’ he said, apologetically. ‘Caius left the farm more than four weeks ago. I’ve written to everyone I can think of. No one has seen him. The last bit of news I have managed to glean is that he was heading towards Antium.’

Volumnia tugged her hands away with a cry. ‘Why would he go there?’

‘I couldn’t say,’ Menenius lied. He didn’t want to say what he feared, that Caius had become so unhappy that he had decided to put himself in harm’s way. Once in Volscian territory, his life would not be worth a fig.

Menenius followed Volumnia through to the triclinium. Virgilia was already there, Little Caius on her lap, her arms clutched tight around him. She looked up at Menenius and asked the same question as Volumnia. He gave her the same answer.

‘Do you know why he would go there?’ Volumnia asked

her accusingly. 'Did he ever say anything to you about Antium?'

Virgilia shook her head. 'No, never.'

'Then, why?' Volumnia cried desperately.

'You must not torment yourself with such questions,' Menenius said, taking a seat. 'We cannot know the answers.'

Volumnia curled her bottom lip over her teeth. 'I think I should go and find him.'

Menenius was astonished. 'You, leave Rome? Alone? You're mad.'

Volumnia laughed. 'Yes, I am mad without Caius. I cannot bear it.' She started crying, her head in her hands. Virgilia put an arm around her shoulder carefully, fighting back her own tears.

'This is not like you, Volumnia,' Menenius said, genuinely worried by what he was witnessing. 'You have always been so strong.'

'Not without him,' Volumnia sniffed.

'Caius would not want you to be like this, I am sure.'

'I cannot help it. I have lost my boy.'

Menenius patted her hand, hoping to comfort her. But in truth, there was little comfort he could offer. 'I am addressing the Senate house tomorrow,' he said, in a tone he hoped conveyed hopefulness. 'I will speak again for Caius's banishment to be ended.'

'What makes you think they will listen this time?' Virgilia asked.

Menenius was surprised by the coldness in her voice. It was so unlike her. 'I can but hope, my dear.'

'And meantime, my husband goes we know not where. He may even be dead, for all we know.'

'I am sure Caius is alive,' he said, hoping he sounded surer than he felt. 'If there is one thing Caius is good at it is staying alive, we know that. Take heart, Volumnia. You will see your boy again, I am sure of it.'

'You promise?' Volumnia asked, looking up at him with puffy, bloodshot eyes.

May the gods protect me from my lies, he thought as he repeated his assurance.

Steam rose lazily in the bathhouse and Caius leant back against the edge of the pool, feeling warmed through for the first time in many weeks. He had never been one for soft living back in Rome, but after his deprivation, and in Tullus's company, he was discovering a new liking for comfort and luxury.

'I disgusted your wife that first night,' he said, remembering his arrival at Tullus's domus. 'She called me filthy and lice-ridden. Am I clean enough for her now, do you think?'

Tullus grinned from the other side of the pool. 'Don't you mind about her.'

'But she was right, I was foul. I must have smelt like a pleb.'

'May the gods forbid such a thing. You're looking better too. Your bones aren't sticking out as much as they were.'

'I hadn't realised how little I'd been eating. You have been very generous with your food and wine.'

Tullus crossed to Caius's side of the pool, the water rippling around him. He pointed to the diagonal scar on Caius's left breast. 'Was that one of mine?'

Caius glanced down to where Tullus was pointing. 'Possibly,' he said. 'I forget.'

Tullus ran his finger slowly over the raised, red skin.

Caius watched him through half-closed eyes, enjoying the feeling.

But Tullus suddenly drew back. ‘I’ve had to keep your presence here a secret, you know,’ he said, a little too loudly. ‘If the elders had known you were here, you would have been arrested. But now I’m sure of you, I think it’s time I presented you to them. I can’t guarantee they’ll accept you as I have done. They may kill you.’

‘I’ll take that risk. I have good hope, though, with you at my side.’

Tullus shook his head in wonderment. ‘I never thought this would happen.’

‘Nor I.’

‘But I am glad of it. The elders have been reluctant to move against Rome, what with so many cities giving in without a fight, and the beating you gave us last time. But with you here and the proposition you have made me, they will think again. With you beside me, our success is inevitable.’

‘If the gods are with us,’ Caius said.

Tullus grinned. ‘What need we of gods, Marcius? But,’ he added, when he saw consternation cross Caius’s face, ‘if you prefer, we will bind ourselves to the gods and to one another.’

He reached over the edge of the pool and grabbed a small knife from off a plate of figs. Caius watched him with curiosity. Tullus drew the blade across his palm. His blood seeped out slowly, too slowly, and he curled his fingers to force out more. Blood dripped from his palm to spread in the water below and he held the knife out to Caius. Caius took the knife and cut his own palm, waiting until the wound bled profusely. Tullus wrapped his fingers around Caius’s and they pressed their palms together, their blood mingling, each warming the other.

'I swear before the gods to stand by your side and lay waste to Rome and all her dominions,' Tullus said.

'And I swear to fight by your side,' Caius said, 'to be your brother in arms, your lover in warfare, your other self and to bring Rome to her knees. As a son of Mars, I make this oath.'

They kept their hands together until the blood dried and crusted, until the water cooled and their skin wrinkled. They would have stayed that way all night had not Junia entered and bid them get dressed for dinner was on the table.

His heart was fluttering in his chest. Caius couldn't remember being this nervous before, not even when he first went into battle all those years ago. Excited, yes, apprehensive, but not nervous. He had no idea if he would be accepted by the elders of Antium. If not, then these minutes could very well be his last, and he without a sword in his hand to defend himself. It was not a situation he welcomed. He didn't mind dying but he needed to have his revenge on Rome first.

Tullus had told him to wait in the adjoining room where he couldn't be seen from the atrium, and not to come out until he called for him. Tullus had summoned the elders to his domus, not telling them why, just insisting they attend. One by one, the elders had come, and Caius had heard each demand to know what Tullus meant by summoning them to his home. Caius got the distinct impression they thought Tullus impudent, and that made him smile; he and Tullus were so alike. He heard Tullus say that what he was about to show them would surprise them but that they were not to be alarmed. And then Tullus called, 'Come out.' Taking a deep breath, Caius entered the atrium.

'This is Caius Marcius,' Tullus declared proudly, grinning at Caius.

Caius could not return the smile. His attention was entirely focused on the gasps and cries of outrage. Some of the elders even stepped forward as if to grab him, but his expression had become fierce and defensive and they stayed where they were.

'I know what you're thinking,' Tullus said, moving to stand by Caius's side. 'I thought the same when Marcius walked into my home and demanded to see me. That night, I put a blade to his throat and threatened to cut. But he bid me listen, and I did. And after I had listened, I withdrew my blade and sheathed it. For know this, Caius Marcius has become my brother and my friend. And if you will but listen to him as I did, you will find him a friend to all the Volsci.'

'Are you mad?' one of the elders demanded.

'Not mad, no,' Tullus assured him with a smile, 'I just have a better understanding than you. But let me explain. We have heard of how Marcius was banished from Rome and wondered how she could do such a thing. But we should have known better. Rome is a cruel mother. Did she not turn against her king not long ago? We in Antium are not so cruel. We would not turn away anyone who professes to be our friend, which is what Marcius has sworn to me he now is. And he has sworn more. Caius Marcius has sworn to attack Rome and, when she is won, to give her to the Volsci.'

'Why should he do so?' another man scoffed.

'I'll let him speak for himself,' Tullus said, gesturing for Caius to address the elders.

Caius licked his lips for they had become dry. 'I do so because I no longer have any allegiance to Rome. She forsook me, so I have disowned her.'

'But you have family in Rome, do you not?' the man asked.

Caius nodded. 'A mother, a wife, a son.'

'And yet you want to attack her? Are you not afraid for your family's safety?'

'I ask for my family to be spared, if possible. If not...', he shrugged. 'Every war has casualties. They will understand.'

The elders looked at him unbelievingly. Caius glanced at Tullus, curious to see if he too did not believe he would sacrifice his family for his revenge. But Tullus knew him, understood him. He saw belief in Tullus's eyes.

'Why should we believe this Roman?' an elder asked.

'He is no longer a Roman,' Tullus said, 'he is a Volsci. And because this man does not lie.'

'Aufidius, he has bewitched you,' another man said.

'There has been no sorcery. Marcius has opened my eyes to what is possible for the Volsci. Are we to miss this opportunity the gods have given us because we are too stupid to see beyond past grievances? We hold Rome's fate in our hands. Accept Marcius and put me in charge of the army. With Marcius at my side, we will beat Rome into the very earth from which she rose and raise a Volsci city over her.'

Aufidius makes a good speech, Caius thought as he watched the elders discuss the matter. *He could be a politician if he put his mind to it*. He had had enough of this spectacle. He wanted to disappear back into the other room, away from their searching, sceptical eyes. He could do it too, but knew it would not look good for Tullus if he did. He reluctantly stayed where he was, and waited for the verdict.

It came a few minutes later. The chief elder stepped forward. 'We agree,' he said.

26

Menenius blew his nose on his handkerchief and examined the contents before tucking it into the sleeve of his tunic. He wasn't feeling well; he had had a cold for more than two weeks now, seemed to have a perpetual headache, a continually running nose and worst of all, had lost his sense of taste so that he was not even enjoying his food these days.

The news from the Senate did nothing to lift his mood. He had neglected his duties in the Senate since falling ill. Up until that point, he had been assiduous, not only in routine matters but in speaking for Caius and asking for his banishment to be lifted. His pleas had continued to fall on deaf ears, so much so that he had become wary of irritating his fellow senators and had made an appeal only once a week. Having no good news to report, he had called less frequently at the Marcius domus, for it upset him to see Volumnia so anxious and Virgilia become so hard. How would the women take this latest news from the Senate, he wondered?

Menenius had refused to believe the rumours when the first reports of attacks on Rome's colonies began to filter through to the Senate. Survivors of these attacks arrived in

Rome seeking sanctuary and they spoke of two fearsome Volscian commanders. They described them in detail and it became clear that one was Tullus Aufidius. But the other? From the descriptions given, the other sounded like Caius. But how was that possible? Caius become a commander in the Volscian army? It was nonsense. Wasn't it?

But the Senate had received confirmation. It was Caius Marcius.

The more Menenius thought about it, the more he realised he should have seen this coming. Caius had been moulded by his mother to be a fighter. Once he'd pulled himself together and got over the shock of exile, he would rally and refuse to accept banishment without a fight. He would need help, Caius would know that, and to whom would he apply for help but to the man who so closely resembled him in ability and determination? That Tullus Aufidius was Rome's avowed enemy would make Caius's revenge all the sweeter.

Caius and the Volsci were working their way through Roman territory towards Rome herself. The dispatch from the Senate said the army had reached Lavinium, not twenty miles away, no distance at all. They could be attacking Rome within the next few days and the Senate were panicking.

Menenius's thoughts turned to Volumnia once again. She loved Rome, though her affection had been sorely tested since Caius left, and Menenius felt sure she wouldn't want to see the city invaded by Volsci, whoever was at their head. And what of her and Virgilia, and Little Caius? If the Volsci attacked, how safe would they be? A chill went through him as he wondered whether Caius blamed his family for what had happened to him. Did he truly not care if they were killed by Volsci swords?

No, he couldn't believe that. Caius would not see his own mother killed, Menenius was sure. But then, why had he not sent word for her to leave Rome? Why had he not warned them the Volsci and he were coming? Menenius closed his eyes. The feeble light from the oil lamp was wearying his eyes and he decided to go to bed. His dreams were full of Caius. Caius was always covered in blood, and somehow, Menenius knew it wasn't his own.

———

Tullus strode into the tent, two cups held in one hand, a jug slopping wine in the other. 'I won't have you skulking in here alone, Marcius,' he cried. 'Come outside. We must celebrate.'

Caius grinned half-heartedly. 'You go. I'd rather stay here.'

'What's wrong?' Tullus asked, setting down the cups and jug. 'You're not wounded, are you?'

'No,' Caius shook his head. 'I just... I am not in the mood for celebrations.'

'But we've won a great victory.'

'We've won many great victories.'

'And you've always joined the men before,' Tullus pointed out, raising an eyebrow. 'It's expected, Marcius. At least, it is with the Volsci.'

Caius heard the criticism in Tullus's voice.

'I know what it is,' Tullus continued, waggling his finger at Caius. 'It's Rome. You're having second thoughts. I'm right, aren't I?'

'We *will* attack Rome next,' Caius said. 'That hasn't changed.'

'Your family?'

Caius sighed. In some ways, it was a pleasure to be so easily understood; in others, irritating. 'They are on my mind,' he confessed.

'Of course they are,' Tullus nodded. 'They'd be on my mind too. But,' he held up his finger, 'I wouldn't change my plans.'

'I've told you, we will attack Rome,' Caius said irritably. 'Rome has this coming. Nothing will stop me.'

'Good. You realise I can't guarantee your family will be safe? I'll give the order your domus is not to be touched, but if your family are in the streets, then…', Tullus gestured helplessly.

'I know,' Caius nodded and reached out his hand to touch Tullus. 'I'm grateful.' They both turned as the tent flap was opened and Tullus's friend, Virius, entered.

'Marcius,' Virius said, 'come out. Five more amphorae have arrived and you haven't had a cup yet.'

Tullus shook his head at his friend. 'Marcius has no thirst for wine, Virius.'

'But we can't have a celebration without you, Marcius,' Virius persisted. 'We might not have had a victory at all if it wasn't for you.'

It was gratifying to hear a Volsci speak so, but Caius glanced at Tullus as Virius finished and noted the tightening of his friend's thin lips. As much as he would like Virius's words to be true, Caius had to admit Tullus deserved equal credit for their success. 'Both Tullus and the god Mars fight by my side, Virius.'

'I'm thankful for it,' Virius laughed. 'I wouldn't fancy attacking Rome if they didn't.'

'We could take Rome without Marcius,' Tullus declared irritably.

Virius glanced at Tullus, surprised by his tone. 'Aye, Tullus, but let us speak truth. We wouldn't be trying if it wasn't for Marcius.'

Tullus turned on Virius, ready for an argument, and Caius,

eager to avoid one, rose to intercede. He stepped up to Virius and touched his shoulder. 'We'll be out in a moment.'

Virius nodded, shot a resentful glance at Tullus, and departed.

Caius turned to Tullus, who was grinding his teeth and staring at the tent flap where Virius had exited. 'We've done this together, my friend.'

Tullus turned his furious glare on him. 'I bloody know we have,' he growled, and stormed out of the tent.

Menenius had never seen so many frightened men in one room before. *The senators have reason to be scared*, he thought ruefully. *I'm scared too. We all know Caius is coming.*

The Volsci had conquered Lavinium the month before and the Senate had received reports that they had set up their camp at Fossae Cluiliae, the huge trench dug two hundred years before by the Alba Longa tribe, only five miles from Rome. The gossip going round the city was that if you climbed to the top of one of Rome's seven hills, you'd be able to see the Volsci camp.

'We have to stop talking about this and do something,' Decius Buccio declared earnestly. 'The Volsci are going to attack any day now. The plebs are refusing to fight and we have no way of defending ourselves.'

'What do you suggest we do?' Mettius asked.

'Treat with them. There is nothing else we can do. We must go to Marcius and ask him to see reason.'

'Reason? From Marcius?' Mettius said, his eyebrows rising to his hairline.

'Even Marcius must be able to see reason,' Decius said.

'He wants to return to Rome, yes? So, we offer to lift his banishment.'

It was no good, Menenius said to himself, *I shall have to speak up. They still think there is hope this affair can be easily settled by our magnanimity.* 'I think we're beyond the question of Marcius's banishment,' he said. All the senators turned to look at him. 'I have been like a father to Marcius since Caecilius died. I know him probably better than he knows himself and I can say with some certainty that Marcius does not just want to return to Rome. He wants to punish Rome.'

'You should go to him,' Decius said, a tremble in his voice. 'You said it yourself, you were as a father to him. He will listen to you. Tell him the banishment is lifted.'

Menenius opened his mouth to protest, but no words came. The thought was horrifying. He didn't want to face Caius and plead with him for his life and the life of everyone in Rome. 'He may not listen to me,' he managed to say at last.

'You must try,' Decius insisted. 'Cominius,' he said, catching sight of him standing near the entrance, 'you too. You have fought together. You're his friend.'

'I was, once,' Cominius said doubtfully.

'It's enough,' Decius said, nodding eagerly. He looked around at his fellow senators for their agreement and they nodded back, just as eager.

Menenius looked at Cominius, who shrugged one shoulder as if to say they had nothing to lose by trying.

'Very well,' Menenius said, 'Cominius and I will go to the Volsci camp. But we're not promising anything.'

———

Caius had known they would come. As much as Rome liked to fight, she also liked to preserve what she believed she owned, and he knew the Senate would always try diplomacy before resorting to force.

He had prepared well for the deputation from Rome. He had dressed with care, shaved and had chosen his seat to be set on a slight mound so that he would be higher than the Roman envoys standing before him. He had also ordered some of the Volsci to stand with him so the Romans would see the kind of authority he had over them.

But where was the pleasure? Caius wondered as the envoys approached. He should be feeling joy at their reversals of fortune, not this nagging sense of unease.

His anxiety increased as the envoys drew nearer and Caius could see their faces. Why, he cursed himself, had he not foreseen that the Senate would send Menenius and Cominius to treat with him? He should have known the Senate would try this trick, trying to use sentiment to force him into turning the Volscian army around. They were fools if they thought that would work. Menenius and Cominius were nothing to him now. Neither of them had spoken for him when he was banished. They had let him leave Rome alone. They could have offered to go with him, to share that burden, and so demonstrate to whom they were most loyal, but no. Both had shown they cared more for themselves than he. And so, the Senate had achieved nothing by sending them to treat with him. Nothing was going to sway him from the course he had set himself upon. He had sworn to the gods, and to Tullus, he would destroy Rome and destroy Rome he would.

'Do you know them?' Tullus murmured in his ear.

Caius nodded. 'I know them.'

Menenius looks older, he thought as they came to a halt before him. His eyes seemed sunken and the lines around his mouth had deepened. Cominius wasn't much altered, save for the anxious expression on his face.

'It's good to see you, Caius,' Menenius said uncertainly, his eyes lingering on Tullus standing by Caius's side. 'It's been a while.'

'It has,' Caius said, not wanting to waste time on pleasantries. 'Why have you come?'

'We are here, Caius, to invite you back to Rome.'

'There's no need for an invitation. I will be coming to Rome very soon.'

'We mean,' Cominius said hurriedly, 'you can come home. The Senate have lifted the banishment.'

'Of course they have,' Tullus laughed. He waved his hand at Cominius and Menenius. 'Caius, tell these fools to go back to Rome.'

Caius acknowledged his words with the slightest inclination of his head, keeping his eyes on Menenius. 'Is that all?' he asked. 'The banishment is lifted?'

'What more do you want?' Cominius asked.

'For the Senate to acknowledge their mistreatment of me, for one thing.'

'Well, I am sure they would be willing to make a public statement to that effect,' Menenius said.

'And what else?'

'What more do you want, Caius?'

Caius raised his chin. 'Something the Senate cannot give me.'

'What is that?'

'Revenge. You know me, Menenius. Would you say I am a forgiving kind of man?'

Menenius sighed. 'No, Caius, I would not say that.'

'So, why do you think you can persuade me to do the Senate's bidding?'

'I didn't want to. To tell the truth, it was the last thing I wanted, to come here and plead with you, Caius. I knew it would be pointless but the Senate would have it so.' He shrugged and held his hands open. 'Is there nothing I can say that will move you to think kindly on us?'

His honesty and sad expression made Caius pause. Tullus glanced down at him, wondering why he was silent. He decided to speak.

'Rome can be saved,' he said.

Menenius's gaze shifted to Tullus. 'How?'

'If Rome were to restore all the Volscian territories she has taken and to give the Volsci the same rights she has granted the other Latin tribes, then we will not attack.'

'The same rights as the other tribes?' Menenius blurted. 'But the Volsci have been considerably more trouble to Rome than they have been. The other tribes have made treaties with us.'

'You mean they've capitulated,' Tullus scoffed. 'The Volsci have been ready to defend and protect what is ours.'

'The Volsci have not been willing to talk with Rome,' Menenius began heatedly, then held up his hands as Tullus opened his mouth to retort. 'But I agree that these are terms I can take back to the Senate.'

'Then go back,' Tullus said, folding his arms, 'and speak to your Senate. Tell them our terms. Then return and provide us with proof Rome has agreed to them.'

'*If* they agree,' Cominius said defiantly.

'They'll agree if they want to survive,' Tullus said. 'And quickly too. You tell them we're not willing to wait forever for their answer. It won't take you long to return to Rome. You meet with the Senate and you tell them that if you're not back here before sundown with their answer, then we will attack tomorrow.'

'Tomorrow!' Menenius burst out in horror. 'But we have to discuss this—'

'Tomorrow,' Tullus repeated with a grin.

'Thirty days,' Caius said suddenly.

Tullus rounded on him. 'What?'

Caius waved him silent. 'Tell the Senate you have thirty days to consider our terms. Tell the Senate they would be wise to agree to them because be assured, I will spare no one.' He glared at Menenius. 'No one.'

He rose and strode away to his tent, leaving Tullus and the other Volsci staring after him.

The Roman envoys had gone and Tullus could not hold in his anger any longer. He brushed aside the enquiries of his fellow soldiers and strode into Caius's tent. 'Why give them thirty days?' he demanded.

Caius was pouring himself a cup of wine. He didn't look up. 'Why not?'

'Because a lot can be done in thirty days, that's why not,' Tullus said, snatching the cup from Caius's hands and throwing it to the ground. 'The Romans can gather an army, build defences, appeal to the Latin tribes for help.'

'Tullus, calm yourself. They won't be able to gather an army,' Caius said confidently. 'The people are not with the Senate. They refuse to fight, they always refuse to fight. The defences are the walls of Rome; they're already in place but we know their weak spots, thanks to me, and we know we can break through them. As for the tribes, they will not come to Rome's aid. They are waiting to see what will happen, hedging their bets. We are a formidable enemy, Tullus.'

'You say this with such certainty,' Tullus said, shaking his head. 'But you can't know all this to be true.'

'I can and do. Now, no more arguing, my friend. I've given Rome thirty days. It is done.'

'And what are we to do in all that time?' Tullus asked. 'Just sit here and wait?'

'No, we'll seek out the allies of Rome and take their towns. Rome will have no one to appeal to. And then we will return to hear Rome's answer. They will have no choice but to agree to our terms.'

'I don't like it.'

'You don't have to like it,' Caius said carelessly, 'you just have to do as I tell you.'

Tullus stared at him. 'Do as you tell me?' he repeated incredulously.

'I phrased that badly,' Caius admitted. He held out his hand to Tullus. Tullus stared at it. 'I should have said you will have to trust me about this. I told you I would restore the Volscian territories and I mean to make good on that promise.'

'*We* will make good on that promise,' Tullus said, taking his hand.

'Yes,' Caius said after a moment, 'of course. We.'

27

Thirty days had passed and the Volscian army had returned to the countryside around Rome. As Caius had promised Tullus, Rome's allies had quickly fallen beneath the Volscian onslaught, and it truly seemed that Rome had nowhere left to turn.

Yet, despite this, the Senate refused to agree to Caius's terms. They had simply too much to lose, they had claimed when Menenius and Cominius had returned from the Volscian camp and relayed the details of their meeting. Rome had been too successful in making treaties and conquering others, it seemed, for to undo all those trade treaties and give land back to the Volsci would ruin them as certainly as an enemy horde.

Menenius could not blame them. He even admired them for deciding to take a stand against Caius and his newfound friends. But he doubted whether many of these senators, puffed up with pride for Rome, would be alive beyond the morrow. The Volsci would come and Caius would be at their head, and Menenius had no doubt that Caius would show no mercy.

He wanted to be the one to tell Volumnia and Virgilia the

news and so made his way to their domus. It was a longer than usual journey, for people kept stopping him to ask what the Senate had decided. They were scared. They could see the Volscian army, they cried, flinging their arms in the camp's direction to illustrate their point, and begged Menenius to change the senators' minds when he told them their answer. He had to shake his head and tell them he could do no more.

Menenius reached the Marcius domus and stared up at it in dismay. The front of the building was covered in graffiti. From the colour and smell, the graffiti was written in dung and blood. Curses, threats, insults — they were all there. He should not have been surprised, he supposed, as he stepped forward and banged on the door. The people couldn't abuse Caius himself so they took their anger out on his women. He just hoped that none of the inmates had been subjected to any physical abuse.

The shutter of the small window in the door opened a crack and Menenius saw two eyes staring out at him. 'Who is it?' the slave called.

'Menenius Agrippa,' he said, putting his mouth to the iron grate.

The shutter closed and Menenius waited. He heard the bar being lifted on the other side of the door and it inched open. Sensing it was not going to be opened wide, Menenius twisted his body around the door and stepped inside.

The slave quickly closed the door again, dropping the bar neatly in place. He jerked his head at Menenius and led him through the atrium to the room beyond. Volumnia was standing there, looking anxious.

'I'm glad you're here,' she said, although to Menenius's eyes, she didn't look anything but afraid.

He strode to her and grabbed hold of her hands. 'You've had some trouble.'

'Oh, the graffiti, yes. I haven't seen it myself but the slaves tell me so. Should I have them clean it off?'

He shook his head. 'Best leave it for the moment.'

'What's been decided?' she asked, leading him into the triclinium. 'Oh, it's bad news, isn't it?' Her hands went to her mouth as she searched his face.

'The Senate have refused to concede to Caius's terms. He and the Volsci are setting up their camp. They will attack soon.'

'I don't understand how Caius can do this,' she cried. 'Doesn't he know how much this hurts me? Doesn't he care?'

Menenius wanted to say that no, he didn't think Caius did care. It was a hard and bewildering thing to acknowledge after how close he and Volumnia had been, yet all the evidence seemed to point to the fact that Caius had turned his back on Rome and everything and everyone living in her. He looked up as he heard a long wailing cry.

Volumnia sniffed and wiped her nose. 'That's Virgilia. All she does is cry these days. I've told her to stay in her room. I can't bear to listen to her.'

'How's Little Caius?'

'Wondering what is going on,' she said. 'He keeps asking for his father. I don't know what to tell him.'

'Volumnia, my dear,' Menenius said, taking her hands again, 'I think you should leave Rome.'

She looked up at him in astonishment. 'Leave Rome?'

'Immediately. Caius will be coming and he means to kill anyone who stands in his way. And the Volsci will be merciless. It's not safe for you.'

'Caius will not allow them to kill us,' Volumnia said, shaking her head. 'Will he?' she asked, suddenly doubtful.

'It's not a question of allowing them,' Menenius said. 'He

will not be able to stop them. I think he is so consumed by hatred that he will risk everything he once loved.'

'Even us?'

Menenius couldn't answer truthfully. He had said Caius wouldn't be able to stop the Volsci, but would he even try? Was every Roman, his mother included, his enemy now? 'You need to leave Rome tonight. Use the darkness and get out of the city. Go to your farm. Take the slaves and shut up the domus. I should have seen to it weeks ago, not let you stay here to be abused by the plebs.'

Volumnia whirled away from him, too upset by his words to look him in the face. 'I cannot believe it,' she said after a long moment. 'Caius would never—'

'Caius has changed, Volumnia, you would hardly recognise your boy. The Volsci revere him. He was the one in command, not the Volsci leaders. And he enjoyed being in command, I could see that. He was so proud.' He laughed ruefully. 'You remember once how you said Caius was fit to be a king? Well, he almost is, in all but name.'

'Of course they revere him,' Volumnia said, sniffing through tears. 'The Volsci have no one to match him. Not even that Aufidius.'

'Oh, he was there with Caius,' Menenius said.

Volumnia turned to him. 'With him?' she whimpered.

'By his side,' Menenius nodded. 'All enmity seemingly forgotten. Maybe we should not be surprised. They must be very alike.'

'They are friends, then?'

Was that jealousy he heard in her voice? Menenius wondered. 'Allies more than friends,' he said, wanting to be kind.

Volumnia gave a little nod, understanding. 'Will Caius kill me, do you think?' she asked quietly. 'When he comes?'

'How can you ask that?' Menenius cried, horrified that she had been thinking it too.

'I have betrayed him,' she shrugged. 'I should have gone with him when he was banished. I didn't. I didn't think of doing so, nor did Virgilia.'

'You were too shocked to think of such things,' Menenius said soothingly. 'It all happened so quickly. And how could you just leave? What of the domus and your slaves? You couldn't have just left them.'

'Oh, you fool, what does the domus or the slaves matter when I have lost my son? He must hate me,' Volumnia said quietly. 'He must hate all of us.'

'Indeed,' Menenius nodded. 'I do not think I will be spared.' A thought suddenly occurred and he murmured to himself, 'Why not? We have nothing to lose.'

'What was that?' Volumnia asked.

'I said,' Menenius said with sudden energy, 'we have nothing to lose.'

'What do you mean?'

'You, Volumnia, I mean you. You must go to him, you must go to the Volsci camp,' he urged. 'He will see you, I am sure, and perhaps you can persuade him to desist.'

Volumnia's eyes lit up. 'Do you think he would see me?'

Menenius nodded. 'If nothing else, it will be a chance to see him again before the killing starts. Won't it?'

'I long to see him again, Menenius,' she said, her eyes filling with tears.

'Then you will go?'

She nodded. 'Oh, yes, I will go.'

Caius hadn't really expected the Senate to agree to their

terms. It was no surprise to receive the Senate's envoy — not Menenius or Cominius this time — and hear him relate the Senate's refusal, fear making his voice quiver. The envoy looked around at the gleeful Volscian faces and asked hurriedly for Caius's response. Caius gave it and the man scurried away.

As soon as he had gone, Caius wished he had asked about his family. He hoped they had taken the thirty days he had given Rome to get out of the city, to go to the farm in the country. But what if they hadn't? What if his mother, wife and child were still in Rome? He would give orders that they were not to be touched but he knew what soldiers were. There was no guarantee they would be safe.

He heard Tullus talking with his commanders as they examined a map of Rome. He knew they were working out a route through the city based on information he had provided. He had no sympathy for his former citizens, they deserved what was coming, but he could not rid himself of this anxiety about his family.

Tullus finished examining the map and straightened. His gaze drifted from Caius to over his shoulder. 'Who's this now?'

Caius turned and his stomach lurched as he saw who it was. No, they couldn't be coming here, not here. He yelled at them, 'What are you doing here? You shouldn't have been let through.'

'Caius,' Volumnia cried and rushed towards him, but Caius took a step away. She halted, her feet digging into the earth, spilling soil over her sandals to pierce her soles.

Caius's throat tightened. What had happened to his mother? She looked so thin and old, so ill. Virgilia was coming up behind, her hand holding onto Little Caius, who stared around at the soldiers with childish curiosity.

'Who are they, Caius?' Tullus asked.

Volumnia heard Tullus's question. 'I'm his mother,' she said.

'And I am his wife,' Virgilia said, surprising Caius with her defiant tone. 'This is his son.'

'They shouldn't be here,' Tullus said, turning his back and standing between them and Caius. 'Send them away.'

'Please, Caius,' Virgilia begged.

'Send them away,' Tullus growled.

Caius wanted to do as Tullus said. He wanted to send his family away, but he could not. Just the sight of them had wounded him, knowing he was the cause of their distress, and he could not simply dismiss them.

'Get away from me,' he snarled at Tullus. They stared into each other's eyes until Tullus stepped to one side.

Virgilia bent down to Little Caius. 'Go to your father.'

The boy walked over to Caius and held up his arms. Caius's breath caught in his throat. He tried not to look at the little boy, but it was no good. The boy had his blood in him, he was part of him, and Caius bent and picked up his son. The boy put his arms around Caius's neck and pressed his face against his father's throat.

'I've missed you so, Caius,' Virgilia said, her voice breaking as she watched her son and husband embrace.

Caius didn't trust himself to speak and merely nodded at her.

'Caius,' Volumnia said, 'we must talk.'

'In private,' Virgilia added.

'No,' Tullus answered, stepping between Caius and the women. 'You talk here, in my presence.'

'Who are you?' Volumnia demanded. Tullus told her and her look hardened. 'I've heard of you,' she said dismissively.

'All Rome has heard of me,' he retorted.

‘As all Italy has heard of my son,’ she hit back. ‘Fortunate for you, fortunate for all the Volsci, that my son turned to you in his distress.’

‘Mother,’ Caius chided, setting down his son and pushing him back towards Virgilia. ‘Tullus Aufidius is my friend. You will not speak to him so.’

‘Does your friend tell you what to do, who you can talk to?’

‘He does not.’

‘Then we can speak in private?’

Caius hesitated, but then nodded. ‘Stand a little way off, Tullus.’

Tullus’s lips tightened. ‘Concede nothing,’ he warned and retreated, but to no more than twelve feet away.

‘It’s strange company you’ve been keeping, Caius,’ Volumnia said, trying to smile.

‘Company I have been forced to keep,’ Caius said.

Volumnia nodded. ‘Yes. Rome has treated you very badly. But does Rome deserve this?’ She gestured at the camp and soldiers.

‘How can you ask that? After what she has done to me, she deserves to be beaten.’

‘But do *we* deserve it too?’ Volumnia gestured at Virgilia and her grandson. ‘I know we disappointed you and have let you down.’

‘Do not say so, Mother.’

‘I will say so,’ Volumnia said determinedly. ‘We should have been with you in your banishment.’

‘I would not have asked you to suffer with me.’

‘We suffered anyway,’ Virgilia said. ‘To be without you was to suffer.’

He stared at her, feeling tears suddenly prick at the back

of his eyes. 'You can say that when I have never been much of a husband to you?'

'You were all I wanted, Caius,' Virgilia said with a sad smile and shrug.

He looked away from her, unable to bear her adoration. 'I would have given orders you were to be spared.'

'We both know those orders would be impossible to keep,' Volumnia said, reaching up to touch his hair. 'We would be killed, you know that.'

'You should have left Rome,' he burst out angrily. 'I gave you time, I gave you thirty days.'

'It never occurred to us to leave Rome,' Volumnia said. 'Rome is our home, it is your home. We kept hoping the Senate would see how wrong they were to banish you and let you come home. But they didn't and now the wolves are howling at the gates.'

'Am I a wolf now? Is that how you see me?'

She straightened and looked him in the eye. 'I saw you as a great man, Caius. That is what the Sibyl prophesied you would be before you were born, but I should have paid more attention. She warned me that misery may ensue. And here we are.' She gestured about them. 'I have made you who you are, Caius, I must bear some responsibility for where we find ourselves now.'

'You are not to blame for this.'

'Then who is?'

'Rome,' he said despairingly. 'She is to blame. Rome disowned me, after all I had done for her, and so I have disowned her.'

'And so I will be blamed for bringing forth a son who has brought woe to Rome,' she shrugged. 'Even if we are not killed by your new friends, Caius, we will be killed by your enemies if you attack Rome.'

‘It cannot be undone. I have sworn to attack Rome, Mother.’

‘To whom have you sworn?’

’To the gods. And to Aufidius.’

‘You are bound then,’ she said with finality. ‘You cannot break your oath to the gods. You could to him.’ She looked with disgust at Tullus hovering nearby. ‘You must attack Rome.’

‘Yes, I must. But you will be safe. You will stay here.’

Volumnia shook her head. ‘And watch as you destroy Rome? No, Caius, I cannot.’

‘Go to the farm, then. Or go to Grandmother.’

‘I will return to Rome.’

‘I will not allow it,’ he said, gripping her arm tightly.

She looked down at his hand. ‘You will not stop me, Caius. Virgilia and Little Caius can stay if they want.’ She tugged her arm away and made to go.

‘Stop!’ Caius cried and put his hands to his head as if in pain. ‘I cannot bear this.’

He could not bear it; he was in torment. When it had been only him and Tullus and the other Volsci, his path had been clear. Rome had wronged him and she deserved her punishment. But then Menenius and Cominius had come, and though he had believed himself impervious to their pleas and assured Tullus he had no mercy in him, they had managed to get in under his rage and pierce his heart. And so, he had given them thirty days to get the Senate to change its mind, a final chance for Rome to save herself, for his old friends to save themselves. It was not his fault they had failed.

But this, this coming of his family was too much, it was not fair. How was he expected to hold firm to his purpose when his mother appealed to him with tears in her eyes? The woman who had raised him, loved him above all others, who blamed herself for his desperate need for revenge, and who was prepared to die for her part in Rome's impending downfall. And die she would, he had no doubt, and that would be his fault.

Neither Volumnia nor Virgilia had spoken. He felt they must be holding their breaths, waiting to see what he would say or do next. He let his hands drop away, his arms fall to his side. He raised his face to the sky, closed his eyes and drew in a huge breath. He released it slowly, feeling his whole body shudder. It felt better to have come to a decision, but even now, he could not speak without resentment. 'Ye gods, Mother, what have you done?'

'What, what have I done?' Volumnia asked sadly.

He turned to face her, tears running down his cheeks. 'You have saved Rome. ' He smiled ruefully. 'And destroyed me.'

'Do not say so, Caius.'

'It is so,' he said. 'It must be so. The gods will demand it.'

Volumnia clapped her hands to her mouth to stifle her cry. Caius held out his arms and she went to him, pressing her face into his neck, breathing deeply the smell of his skin, the warmth of his flesh, so long denied her. He held her for a long moment, then pushed her gently away.

'Go now,' he said, wiping his eyes angrily. 'Go back to the Senate and say the Volsci will be leaving.'

Virgilia gathered her son into her arms and crushed him to her chest. 'And then you can come home, Caius,' she said, smiling through her tears.

Caius looked at Volumnia. 'Wouldn't that be lovely?'

Volumnia's face screwed up as she nodded.

'Pity,' he said. 'I would have liked to come home.'

'But,' Virgilia said frowning, looking between him and

Volumnia, 'you *can* come home. The Senate have already said so.'

'Virgilia,' Caius said, holding out his hand but not looking at her, 'you will tell the Senate that my mother and you have done great service to Rome. Between you, you have saved her, and that accomplishment must be honoured.'

'I don't care about the Senate or honours. I just want you home, Caius,' Virgilia whined.

She didn't understand, he realised. She didn't understand that he wasn't coming home. His eyes met Volumnia's. His mother understood.

'Take my wife and son home, Mother,' Caius said, glad his voice was sounding stronger.

Volumnia gave a sob, as if her heart was being torn from her body. She turned from him, wiping her face with the hem of her dress.

Caius kissed Virgilia and his son and then took a step back. Volumnia groped for Virgilia's wrist and tugged her away. They had gone only a few feet when Volumnia halted and turned back to Caius.

'I will see you soon, Caius,' she called, her tone decided, defiant. 'If you get there before me, wait for me.'

He felt a lump form in his throat at her words. 'I will,' he promised.

'But Mother,' Virgilia said as they stumbled along the track out of the Volsci camp, 'we'll be in Rome long before Caius.'

She really doesn't understand, Caius thought as he watched his family walk away.

Volumnia had hurried back to Rome, forcing Virgilia and Little Caius to run to keep up with her.

When they arrived through the gates, Volumnia dispatched one of the guards to the Senate with the message that the Volsci would not attack and that Rome was safe. As the doors of their domus closed, Virgilia and Volumnia heard the beginnings of celebrations in the streets outside.

Menenius was waiting for them. 'Success?' he asked hopefully.

Volumnia nodded, not looking at him.

'May the gods be praised,' Menenius breathed. 'You have worked wonders, my dear.'

'Isn't it wonderful, Menenius? Caius is coming home,' Virgilia beamed and told him of their encounter, leaving out not one detail and repeating most of them.

'When?' he asked, when she finally paused for breath. 'When is he coming?'

'Soon, I hope. And we must have a great feast to celebrate. All Caius's favourite dishes. You should have seen him, Menenius. He was so thin. I don't think he's been eating properly.'

'We must fatten him up, mustn't we, Volumnia?' Menenius looked around. 'Where has she gone?'

'I thought she was here,' Virgilia said, perplexed. 'Mother? Mother? Where are you?'

A slave appeared in the atrium and told them. 'Domina retired to her cubiculum.'

Menenius nodded. 'Yes, she looked very tired. I will leave you to rest, Virgilia, and go to the Senate. I will have them announce a public holiday to celebrate Rome's salvation and Caius's return. They owe him that.'

'Oh yes, Menenius,' Virgilia clapped her hands together and bent down to cuddle Little Caius in her joy.

'I must just say goodbye to Volumnia,' Menenius said and knocked on Volumnia's cubiculum door. There was no answer. He knocked again. A strange foreboding came over him. He lifted the latch and thrust the door open. A cry escaped his lips.

Volumnia lay on the bed, one arm dangling over the edge. Blood ran down in a thick stream from the crook of her elbow. A dagger, its tip smeared with blood, lay on the floor where it had fallen after opening its mistress's vein.

Caius had given the order to pack up the camp and retreat. The commanders had looked at him in surprise and confusion. Why, they asked, were they not attacking Rome? The thirty-day amnesty had passed and Rome had not conceded. They were supposed to attack, weren't they?

There would be no attack, Caius told them, but offered no explanation. He had walked away, head bowed, eyes on the ground, and returned to his tent. He knew Tullus would be waiting for him.

'Reverse the order,' Tullus said as soon as he entered.

'I will not,' Caius said quietly.

'Then I will,' Tullus declared, and strode past him towards the entrance.

Caius grabbed his arm. 'They won't obey you. I am their commander.'

'Joint commander,' Tullus snarled.

Caius laughed humourlessly. 'Oh Tullus, we both know that isn't true.' He was glad Tullus was so angry. He wouldn't have been able to bear an understanding Tullus, nor would it suit his purpose.

'You've betrayed me,' Tullus said.

'Yes, I know, and I am sorry for it. But it can't be helped. I cannot let you attack Rome.'

'Let me! You wouldn't be letting me do anything. I don't need your permission.'

'You need me to fight with you, though,' Caius said. 'You don't stand a chance without me.'

Tullus laughed contemptuously. 'Why? Because you are the great Caius Marcius?'

Caius didn't answer but gave him a sly, calculated smile instead. He heard the short snorts of breath from Tullus and recognised the rise of his friend's notorious temper.

'And why are we not attacking Rome?' Tullus continued. 'Because some women asked you not to?'

'Not some women, Tullus. My mother, my wife. Would you defy your wife and mother if they asked you to desist?'

'By the gods, I would,' he declared vehemently, 'and curse them for trying to talk me out of it.'

Caius shrugged. 'We are different, after all, then.'

'You're right about that. I'm no mummy's boy.'

The insult struck home and they were both angry now. Caius grabbed Tullus by the throat. They wrestled, each trying to force the other to the ground, but as always, they were too evenly matched. They broke apart, their breaths coming fast and heavily.

'You dare call me boy,' Caius panted.

'I'll call you boy,' Tullus growled. 'I'll also call you traitor.' He spied Caius's sword poking out from his trunk. He grabbed it and pointed its tip at Caius's breast. 'I will kill you for this treachery.'

'I know,' Caius said.

'You should have gone with your women, then.'

Caius shook his head. 'I have broken my oath to you and

to the gods but I still have my honour, Tullus. Betrayal cannot be forgiven. I deserve to die at your hands.'

Tullus hesitated. 'You don't have to die, Caius. We can go back to the way things were. Just give the order to advance.'

'I will not.'

'Don't make me do it,' Tullus cried, his face screwing up, not in anger but in pain.

'You can't allow me to live, Tullus. The Volsci will not be so merciful and they will kill you too. You have to kill me to save yourself.'

'Shut up!'

'You are the only man worthy to kill me, Tullus.'

'I said shut up!'

'Are you a man, Tullus?' Caius demanded. 'Or are you a coward, after all?'

'I'm no coward.'

'Then do it,' Caius yelled furiously and held his arms wide to Tullus.

Tullus screamed and forced his arm forward.

So, this is what it feels like to die, Caius thought as the blade entered his body.

It had been a strange day. First, there had been the certainty among the men that Rome would be captured. Then had come the reversal of orders and the news that they were to return to Antium, leaving Rome untouched. A few were glad at this turn of events, for the truth was they had had enough of fighting. There had been so many battles. True, they had won all of them, but those successes had not come without a great deal of suffering and death. But most of the men were angry to have their prize snatched away from them. Had not

Marcius always claimed that Rome would be their final battle? And now, it seemed, Marcius had simply changed his mind and all their efforts had been for nothing.

Tullus Aufidius would not allow this to lie, many of the men said, men who had served with Aufidius for years and knew how greatly he hated Rome. Ah, but Aufidius has changed, others said, waving their fingers. Marcius has won him over completely and he will do anything Marcius says.

And then the yelling had drawn them to Marcius's tent.

The crowd swelled as the yelling increased, straining their ears to listen. That Marcius and Aufidius were arguing was clear. The older warriors nodded knowingly; Aufidius would not let them down. There would be a march on Rome.

But then the argument stopped and there were strange noises coming from within the tent. What was going on? they mouthed to one another.

Minutes passed until one man, braver, perhaps, or just more curious than the rest, pinched the tent flap between finger and thumb and quietly drew it back. He gasped and his fellows crowded around him. An astonishing sight met their eyes.

Tullus Aufidius was crouched on the ground, his arms wrapped around the fallen Caius Marcius, whose stomach had been split open. Blood was gushing from the wound to stain the earth. But what astonished the watchers most of all was Aufidius.

He was crying. Tears were pouring down his face, some sliding into the mouth that yawned in an anguished groan. Then their brave commander, hater of all the Romans, bent his head and put his lips to the chill lips of Caius Marcius Coriolanus.

AUTHOR'S NOTE

Caius Marcius is best known as the hero, or antihero, of William Shakespeare's *Coriolanus*. The play begins with the corn crisis in Rome when Caius Marcius is an adult and has already proved himself a great soldier. As I watched the play, I became fascinated with the idea of Caius's life before this event.

The play was my starting point for the story but, of course, I needed to consult other material to gain a fuller picture of the lives and times I was to examine in the novel. The main source material for *Coriolanus* is acknowledged to be Plutarch's *Great Lives (Makers of Rome)* and I have also used this, along with Livy's *The Rise of Rome* Book 2 and Dionysus of Halicarnassus's *Roman Antiquities*. While there are some minor differences between these source materials, the main 'facts' about Caius Marcius are the same.

In writing *The Eagle in the Dovecote*, I have played with some of these facts. For example, in these ancient texts, Menenius Agrippa dies long before Caius Marcius is exiled, but Menenius was too important a character to be lost so early and so survives beyond the story. There is also no mention of

Volumnia committing suicide, but I thought her death entirely plausible and in keeping with the loss of her son. Also, Lucius Tarquin made several attempts to regain his throne, but I felt that to cover every war he waged against Rome would become repetitive and so have only included the decisive ones.

Lastly, as I did in *The Last King of Rome*, I have altered one of the names of the conspirators to avoid confusion with other characters sharing the same name.

PLEASE LEAVE A REVIEW

If you have enjoyed this book, it would be wonderful if you could spare the time to post an honest review on whichever book platforms you use.

Reviews are incredibly important to authors. Your review will help bring my books to the attention of other readers who may enjoy them.

Thank you so much.

JOIN MY MAILING LIST

Join my mailing list to stay up-to-date with my writing news, new releases and more.

It is completely free to join and I promise I won't bombard you with emails. You can easily unsubscribe at any time.

Join here:
www.lauradowers.com

CONTACT

I'd love to hear from you. If would like to comment or ask a question about one of my books, then get in touch. You can find me at:

www.lauradowers.com

Printed in Great Britain
by Amazon

59619039R00206